# THE MOTHER OF ALL COMEBACKS

Also by Kathleen Whyman

*Wife Support System*
*Would You Ask My Husband That?*
*Has Anyone Seen My Husband?*

# THE MOTHER OF ALL COMEBACKS

Kathleen Whyman

embla books

First published in the UK in 2026 by

embla books

An imprint of Bonnier Books UK
5th Floor, HYLO, 105 Bunhill Row,
London, EC1Y 8LZ



A CIP catalogue record for this book is available from the British Library.

ISBN: 9781471419133

*Also available as an ebook and an audiobook*

1

Typeset by IDSUK (Data Connection) Ltd
Printed and bound by CPI Group (UK) Ltd, Croydon, CR0 4YY

FSC www.fsc.org MIX Paper | Supporting responsible forestry FSC® C013604

The authorised representative in the EEA is Bonnier Books UK (Ireland) Limited.
Registered office address: Block B, The Crescent Building, Northwood, Santry, Dublin 9, D09 C6X8 Ireland
compliance@bonnierbooks.ie
www.bonnierbooks.co.uk

*For my much bigger, little brother Adam*

GFY

# Chapter 1

'Hi, Sophie.' I tried not to sound too eager or too grateful that my daughter, whom I'd given the gift of life to, had accepted my FaceTime call.

'Hi, Mum.'

Her words were muffled by her duvet, but the sound of her voice still had me welling up. It was a wonder I had any tears left. Dropping her off at Manchester University and driving back to Norwich in September had been the second most heart-wrenching moment of my life. I'd cried so much in the car on the way home, the East Anglia water shortage would have been resolved if they'd been able to collect my tears. And I'd barely stopped since.

'How are you?' I asked, blinking hard.

'Fine.'

'Still enjoying your course and getting on with your housemates?'

Sophie blew her pink fringe out of her eyes. 'Yes.'

I waited, in case any more information was forthcoming. It was not.

She yawned and I smiled fondly, drinking in her rosebud lips, smattering of freckles and perfect white teeth. How on earth had I managed to create such a beautiful being? In fairness, some of it was down to the local orthodontist. And of course Steve had played a small part in her conception. I flushed guiltily. That was a bit harsh. Average-sized part was fairer. From what I could remember.

'Stop staring,' Sophie said. 'You're being weird.'

'Sorry.' I leant back, so my nose wasn't pressed up to the screen.

Sophie frowned as my backdrop came into view. 'Are you in my room?'

My cheeks grew even hotter. I'd taken to spending much of my free time lolling about on her bed, stroking her pillow and talking to her Peppa Pig toy. The sheets were stained with fake tan and the pillow with pink hair dye, and even a forensics team would recoil at the stains on Peppa, built up over the years, but being there made me feel close to Sophie.

'Er, yes. I just opened the window to air the room.' I nibbled on a nail. 'What did you have for lunch?'

'Nothing yet. I've just woken up.'

It was two o'clock in the afternoon, but that could be viewed as daybreak, depending on what time she'd gone to bed.

'Late night?' I asked.

'Yeah. It ended up being a big one, 'cause everyone came back yesterday.'

'Came back from where?' My stomach tightened at the thought of her all alone. 'Are you all right?'

Sophie rolled her eyes with a smile. 'Chill, bruh. I'm fine. They just went home for reading week.'

'Doesn't your course have reading week?'

'Yes,' Sophie said matter-of-factly.

'Why didn't you come home, then?' I asked, trying not to sound too needy.

Sophie shrugged. 'Felt a bit soon. I've only been here six weeks.'

So had everyone else, and they clearly didn't feel it was too soon. I swallowed hard. Of course I wanted Sophie to be happy and settled, but not quite so happy and settled that being in a strange city on her own was preferable to being with me.

'It was a bit quiet, but nice having the kitchen to myself,' she added. 'No one moaning about puddles and crumbs and washing-up left in the sink.'

Her flatmates had my sympathy. Being the one who cleared up after Sophie at home, I knew it was no fun leaving a perfectly clean kitchen only to return two minutes later to a scene fresh from a frat party.

'It's bound to take a while to get used to sharing a space,' I said diplomatically. 'You'll get into a rhythm soon.'

'I was talking about you,' Sophie said. 'No one here cares about that stuff.'

A whimper escaped me. *I* was the reason she hadn't wanted to come home. I'd driven her away by prioritising basic hygiene over her happiness.

'Don't deep it, Mum,' Sophie said gently. 'I'll be back in seven weeks for Christmas.'

My heart pinched. That was a lot of sleeps to get through.

'Are you seeing G this afternoon?' Sophie asked.

I nodded glumly and hoped that Sophie didn't dread our weekly call in the same way that I did my weekly visit to my mother, Josephine. Well, it should be weekly. It was currently daily because she'd fractured her wrist after 'losing her footing'. The phrase 'had a fall' was banned, on account of the fact it made her sound elderly. She must be anticipating living a very long life, as she was under the illusion that seventy was middle-aged.

'She FaceTimed me yesterday,' Sophie said. 'That place she's staying at gives me the creeps. So many old people.'

'It's a respite centre for the elderly and infirm,' I pointed out. 'What did you expect?'

'Yes, but the other people were *really* old G isn't like them.'

In fairness, my mother was in very good shape for seventy, thanks to a combination of exercise, healthy eating, rigorous skincare and sheer bloody-mindedness. I wasn't sure why she was in a respite home when all she'd done was fracture her wrist, but her health insurance was covering it and it meant that she got to boss other people around, rather than me, so I wasn't questioning the arrangement.

Sophie yawned again. 'I'd better go.'

'Wait,' I said, desperate to prolong the conversation. 'I painted your room to freshen it up.' I flipped the camera phone and did a 360 of the room.

'It looks the same as before.'

She was right; but when I was doing something for Sophie, I could almost delude myself she was still here and needed me.

'Wait, stop,' Sophie said, as I did another turn of the room. I paused in front of her full-length mirror. 'What are you wearing?'

'My new mum jeans.' I smiled. 'Like them?'

'No.' Sophie grimaced. 'You look boxy.'

My face fell. I hadn't a clue what to wear when skinny jeans suddenly lost favour after being a staple of my wardrobe for fifteen years. When I stumbled upon mum jeans, I thought my denim dilemma had been solved. Surely, they were the obvious thing for mums to wear. The clue was in the name.

I nibbled on a hangnail. 'Boxy?'

'You're not IRL,' she added charitably. 'It's those jeans. The waistband's too high. You've got no body left.'

I tugged the hem of my long-sleeved tee down to try and create some length in my torso. 'Shall I go back to my skinnies?'

'Ew, no. Get some wide-legged jeans.'

'OK,' I said, knowing I wouldn't. It had taken me months to garner the courage to try the mum jeans. The thought of trying on another style, and probably getting that wrong too, filled me with more dread than cleaning the bath after Sophie had re-dyed her pink hair.

'Say hi to Dad for me,' Sophie said.

'Do you want to speak to him?' I asked. 'He's downstairs.'

'Better not,' Sophie said. 'I've got an assignment due in a few days.'

We both giggled. It was very possible she'd miss her deadline if Steve started one of his monologues now.

'I'd better go and get on with it,' Sophie said.

I didn't know if this was true or an excuse to get off the phone so she could do something much more important, such as check her Snapchat streaks or go back to sleep, but I reluctantly accepted that I had to say goodbye.

'Make sure you eat properly,' I said. 'And don't leave your drink unattended in a pub. Or walk home alone.'

'I know.' Sophie sighed. 'You don't need to mother me.'

'But I'm your mother. It's my job.' I tried to sound light-hearted, but my voice cracked mid-sentence. If Sophie no longer wanted me to mother her, then what purpose did I have?

'Don't cry,' Sophie said gently. 'You'll be seeing me again in less than two months.'

'I know, sorry,' I sniffed. 'It's a mum thing. You'll understand one day.'

'G's not sentimental, like you. She even gets you to call her Josephine, rather than Mum.' Sophie blew her pink fringe out of her eyes. 'It must be you – you're not getting the emotive satisfaction you need, so are desperately seeking it elsewhere. Many artists express their desperation through their work. Try that instead.'

'I'm not desperate,' I said, desperately eking out the conversation and wondering, not for the first time, if her History of Art degree wasn't turning her into a mine of bullshit.

'I'm going now,' she said. 'Love you, bye.'

'OK, speak soon. Love you. Bye.' I blew kisses into the phone.

Sophie ended the call. I stared miserably at the blank screen where her face had been a moment ago. A tear plopped onto the phone, then another. She didn't want me to mother her. She didn't want to come home and see me. She didn't even want me to wear mum jeans.

I'd known it'd be hard when she left. Empty nest syndrome was a recognised emotional experience. Even Michelle Obama had had therapy to deal with it. And if a strong, self-assured woman like her was affected, then there was definitely no shame in it. And it's not as if it had come out of the blue. All summer I'd been gearing myself up for Sophie's departure and trying not to be jealous of women I saw with a young child, who still had all those years ahead together. When the child wiped snot on their mum's dress or exclaimed loudly that they'd just done a poo – while clearly not wearing a nappy – it helped lessen my envy, but only momentarily.

Even though I'd anticipated being upset, nothing had prepared me for how empty and lost I'd feel without her at home. It was as though when I'd driven away in September, barely able to see the road through my tears, not only had I left my child in Manchester – I'd left my identity behind too.

Wiping my cheeks, I separated my ponytail in two and tugged each half sharply to tighten it, then went downstairs. Steve was stretched out in his imitation La-Z-Boy armchair, his feet up, completing a Sudoku.

'Apparently, last week was reading week at uni,' I told him. 'All of Sophie's friends went home for it, but Sophie chose to stay up there by herself.'

'Good job, too,' he said. 'Train fare here and back would have cost a fortune.'

I'd have happily paid her train fare or driven four hours each way to collect her if it meant spending time with her, but Steve always went for the most frugal option. He had no idea that I'd secretly squirrelled money away for years and now paid Sophie's rent, as her maintenance loan wasn't enough to cover it. He already thought uni was a waste of money, and that was without knowing some of the money being 'wasted' was ours. I wouldn't actively call him mean. But only because I couldn't handle the following three-hour monologue on how imperative it was to be economical. Or the prison sentence that was enforced after murdering your spouse.

'Term's only just started,' he added. 'Ridiculous to come back so soon when she can read up there as well as she can here.'

I bit into a nail and wondered, as I had with increasing frequency over the past six weeks, if, as well as leaving Sophie, I'd also left any closeness I felt to Steve in Manchester. I'd been vaguely aware for some time that we didn't have much in common, but without Sophie at home to occupy my time and give me a focus, it had become much more apparent. Like when the optician first prescribed me reading glasses and I realised how blurred everything had been till that point. Or how sharp photos were after I cleaned the camera on my phone. Or how attractive a fairly average TV presenter became after performing a sizzling salsa on *Strictly*. Except that with Steve, things had been better before the eye test or phone clean. And, as for a sizzling salsa, I couldn't imagine anything less appealing than him gyrating around me in a flammable outfit.

'Did you know,' Steve started, 'that a typical university term time in the UK is twenty-eight to thirty weeks, and of that . . .' And he was off, citing what an outrage it was to charge so much for tuition fees and accommodation when students were barely there, before moving on to details of how the length of terms originated in Medieval times and they were built around the Christian calendar.

Talking was Steve's hobby. No topic was too mundane to warrant commentary, from the range of sandwiches on offer at lunchtime, to the deterioration of the pothole in the work carpark. Before marrying, I'd felt sorry for those couples who sat in silence in restaurants. I prayed that I wouldn't end up in a relationship where we had nothing of interest to say to one another. Now when I saw couples barely utter a word during their meal, it took all my self-control not to go over and ask what their secret was.

At least I no longer had to listen to his monologues at night-time. Since he'd developed sleep apnoea, he'd moved into the spare room, so his snoring wouldn't disturb me. The fact that the operation he'd had three years ago completely cured it, but he'd stayed in the spare room anyway, was never discussed.

I went into the kitchen to marinade some chicken for that night's dinner. Steve followed to ensure I didn't miss his commentary on how the long summer breaks had been scheduled for students to come home and help with the harvest.

'Harvest,' he scoffed. 'Sophie doesn't even load the dishwasher when she's here.' I looked pointedly at the mug he'd just left by the sink. He picked it up and placed it in the dishwasher, lying on its side. I considered showing him yet again how to correctly stack it, but knew it'd take less effort to just put it right later.

My phone beeped. I whipped it out in case it was a message from Sophie, but it was a voice note from Josephine. I braced myself for whatever her latest request was and gestured to Steve that I was listening to a message. He was too busy rambling about migration patterns to notice.

'Becca, it's your mother,' Josephine said, although I'd explained many times that her name came up on the screen, so even if the voice I'd been hearing for the past forty-nine years eluded me, I'd know it was her. 'Pop to my house on the way here, would you, and get my portfolio. Once the staff see my photos, they'll understand why this injury is so devastating. One of the nurses got quite shirty this morning when I asked for help with my heat mitt. But it's my career, isn't it? That's more important than helping someone change their surgical socks. They don't need their feet in the same way I need my hands.' She sighed heavily. 'I'm sure they'll appreciate the magnitude of the situation when they see my body of work. So get it here as quickly as you can, please. This is urgent.'

The voice note ended, immediately followed by another.

'And bring more hand cream. And my ball. I need to build up my left hand, as my right will be out of action for a few weeks.' Her voice wavered as the message ended and I felt a flash of sympathy. Her modelling work had dried up years ago, but, always hopeful of a comeback, she was determined her hands wouldn't. Consequently, they were constantly submerged in solutions, like laboratory specimens. The door handles in her house were so coated in cream, they were impossible to turn. She also did daily hand workouts, flexing and pointing and squeezing a little foam ball between each digit. All in the hope she'd receive a call from her agent, Audrey, with the news that an advertiser had just realised that people over retirement age still had hands. The call never came. Not that Audrey would hear it if it did. She was now so old, she was practically a laboratory specimen in her own right.

My phone beeped with a third voice note. 'Put some mascara on before you come. Without it, you look more washed out than some of the residents here.'

My earlier sympathy evaporated.

'I'm going to visit Josephine,' I said to Steve. 'Fancy coming?'

'No. Going to the Glasgow office tomorrow, so I need to get ready for that.'

We both knew this was an excuse. My mother also liked the sound of her voice, and on the rare occasions they got together, it was a battle of who could talk longest and loudest. Christmas and birthday meals were as relaxing as being on the front line.

'Would you mind getting my case out of the loft, please?' Steve asked.

I nodded.

'Super. Thank you.' He picked up his Sudoku book and wandered back to his armchair in the living room.

Steve had had an attack of vertigo a few years ago and now avoided heights, in case it triggered a repeat episode. We both knew this wasn't how it worked, but questioning the vertigo might lead to questioning the sleep apnoea. And if I had to shinny up and down something, I'd take the mute loft ladder over Steve any day.

# Chapter 2

I pulled up at Josephine's house and walked across the gravel drive with the same resignation I experienced every time I went to her house. She'd never asked me to stop calling her Mum, as Sophie assumed; I didn't want to after what had happened. Ironic, as she was the actual biological parent.

I let myself in and picked up some leaflets from the doormat. They were very well targeted. An invitation to visit the local retirement village, a will-reading service, and cheap flights to Switzerland. One-way, presumably. I'd take them to the respite centre. Josephine always claimed to be up for trying new things.

I went through to the living room to get her portfolio. It was on a stand, past her mustard, velvet, statement armchair and the many framed photos on the walls of her hands in various poses – holding an apple; a diamond necklace laced through her fingers; water cascading over her outstretched palms. My dad had taken that one.

My heart squeezed, as it always did when I thought of how cruelly he'd been taken away thirty years ago by SCAD, Spontaneous Coronary Artery Dissection, which had lain dormant and undetected in his body. He'd been perfectly healthy, till the moment his artery wall tore, far too young. And, at nineteen, so was I. He hadn't seen me grow up and he hadn't met his granddaughter. My throat tightened. In many ways that was the hardest thing. He'd have loved Sophie so much. These walls would be covered in photos of her. Would he have ever wondered why she, like me, looked nothing like him? Although as we'd both inherited Josephine's red hair, pale skin and freckles, there'd have been no reason to question it. I wouldn't have known myself if Josephine hadn't decided that the best way to allay my fears of inheriting SCAD was to tell me that my lovely dad wasn't actually my biological father.

I gripped the portfolio, trying not to relive the shock and betrayal of that afternoon. Turning, I knocked my knee against the sofa. It wasn't the same sofa I'd been sitting on when she'd told me, but it was in the same place. I could almost see a montage of my younger self playing out. Initially dazed from the sadness of scattering my dad's ashes, then petrified as it occurred to me that I could have inherited SCAD. The realisation that what had happened to my dad could happen to me. I remembered vividly struggling to breathe, convinced it was just a matter of time till I went the same way. Josephine had been dismissive, telling me that the likelihood was so slim, it wasn't worth worrying about. Funnily enough, this hadn't been much comfort to a panicked nineteen-year-old. Eventually, when I was on my knees, gasping for air and clawing at my throat, she'd gripped my arms and shaken me.

'That's not going to happen to you,' she'd said.

'You don't know that.' My words had come out in short, sharp bursts.

My mum had stared at me long and hard. 'That's not going to happen to you,' she'd said again.

'You can't guarantee that,' I'd sobbed.

She'd pressed her lips together so tightly that they'd disappeared and stared at me. Really stared. Her green eyes had burnt into mine, while I writhed and hyperventilated.

'Yes, I can,' she'd said. 'I *can* guarantee that you're not at risk of inheriting SCAD.'

And then she'd dropped the bombshell that she and my dad had been having some time apart and she'd become close to a male friend. Apparently, it had been a one off, which reinforced how much she cared about my dad, and they'd got back together. When she found out she was pregnant, she let my dad think I was his.

'He might not have provided the sperm, but he was your father in every way,' she'd told me, her usually translucent face so flushed, her freckles had disappeared. 'I didn't want to tell you, didn't think I'd ever have to, but I don't want you to live in fear that you've inherited his condition. That's why I can guarantee you haven't. You don't have his genes. You're not his biological daughter.'

It turned out my actual biological father was an agent who'd briefly covered for Audrey when she was off work. Josephine had never worked with him again and he had no idea I existed. No one knew. I wish I didn't.

I stopped calling her Mum after that. Addressing her by her first name started out as a defiant two fingers up to her disloyalty to my dad, and it stuck. It wasn't just how I addressed her that changed that day. The foundation of our relationship changed. She'd betrayed my dad and lied to us both. Then pulled the rug out from under me when I was in turmoil, trying to understand and accept that my beloved dad had died. Shocked, hurt and disgusted by her actions, I'd emotionally stepped back. The previously unquestioned security and certainty about her was gone. When I had Sophie, this feeling was amplified. I knew without doubt that I'd never do anything to hurt her, which made it even harder to understand why Josephine had chosen to tell me something so unbelievably hurtful.

'You were distraught,' she'd say if ever I asked her why she'd done it. 'I truly wish I hadn't said anything, but it was the only way I could calm you down.'

It was a pathetic reason, but I gave up trying to make sense of it. Instead, I focused on making sure Sophie knew that she was loved and adored, and nothing would ever rock her little world. My life had revolved around her ever since she'd arrived, which was possibly why her absence was hitting me so hard. But I needed to put this into perspective. I hadn't lost Sophie the way I'd lost my dad. Or the way I'd lost my mum that day too – not physically, but emotionally.

I visited Josephine regularly, not out of a burning desire to see her – or even a lukewarm one – but because it was the right thing to do. It was my duty. Like paying taxes or military service, but less enjoyable.

Dismissing the memories, I walked out of the living room and back into the hall. There was another leaflet on the doormat, this one promoting a budget-price handyman. I placed it with the others and slipped them inside the portfolio to deliver to Josephine. Then I locked up the house and walked to my car, readying myself for my visit. Duty called.

# Chapter 3

There was a park next to the respite centre, similar to the one I used to take Sophie to. I stood and watched the families playing for a few minutes, my throat tightening at the memory of Sophie's gleeful laughs, as I pushed her on the swings, and her squeals of delight as she descended the slide.

I wanted to yell: 'Make the most of it,' to all the mums who had years ahead of being needed and wanted. In the blink of an eye, they too would be surplus to requirements. I didn't shout, though. The last thing you wanted to hear when you'd been awake since five in the morning and were navigating potty training, nits or times tables was some busybody telling you to savour every moment. Instead, I released a heavy sigh. It came out with such force that a man leaning against the car next to me turned around.

'Are you all right?' he asked, holding his phone away from his ear.

My cheeks grew hot. As did the rest of me, when I clocked how handsome he was. I opened my mouth to say yes, thank you, but my throat was so dry from holding in tears that the words came out as a raspy grunt.

His eyes widened behind his glasses and he visibly gulped. Oh no. He didn't think that my primal groan was some sort of a come-on, did he? As if I'd proposition a stranger in a carpark – even one who looked like an older version of Nikesh Patel.

The man was looking wary now and I realised I'd been staring. To ensure he knew I wasn't trying to seduce him, in case the mum jeans weren't enough of a clue, I pulled my khaki waterproof jacket tightly around me, turned and marched across the carpark to the respite centre.

* * *

'Visitor for you, Josephine,' the nurse said, knocking lightly on Josephine's door before opening it. 'Goodness,' she exclaimed. 'I've not seen that before.' She glanced at me, a look of bafflement on her face, before leaving. I braced myself for what I was about to see. Knowing my mother, it could be anything from a one-armed plank to cell regeneration.

Josephine was in an armchair by the window, her fractured wrist supported by a sling across her chest. Her friend Pervinder stood over her, squashed in the narrow space between the bed and the chair, expertly threading Josephine's eyebrows.

'What are you doing?' I spluttered. 'This isn't a beauty salon.'

Josephine waved her good hand theatrically, never missing an opportunity to demonstrate the emotion and expression she could create with a finger flourish. 'Just because I'm injured doesn't mean I should let myself go,' she said. 'Pervinder was more than happy to come here when I explained the situation.'

Pervinder nodded. 'It's nice to visit somewhere new.'

I admired Pervinder's positive outlook. Visiting a respite centre for the elderly wasn't usually on a par with a National Trust property.

I put the portfolio and hand supplies on the tray over the bed. 'How are you both?'

'Can't complain,' Pervinder said.

By contrast, Josephine had a long list of complaints, from the state of the food – 'I'm sure that avocado was out of a tin rather than fresh.' – to the flimsiness of the curtains – 'Nowhere near substantial enough to shield my skin from the UV rays.' – and the lack of personal care – 'I had to do my own hair and makeup, one-handed!'

While she talked, I perched on the edge of the bed and watched Pervinder's fingers flying through the air, as she deftly shaped Josephine's brows with fine thread.

Eventually, Josephine exhausted her litany of grievances and turned her attention to me. 'What are you wearing?' she asked.

'Mum jeans,' I said, nibbling on a nail.

'They're not very flattering.' She pursed her lips, then remembered that could cause lines and forced her face to relax.

Pervinder tactfully changed the subject. 'Sophie's enjoying uni, I hear. My grandson, Saif, is in his first year too. Here at UEA, but he isn't having a good time at all. My son, Reyansh, has come up from Brighton to support him.'

'Poor man's sleeping on Pervinder's sofa,' Josephine said. 'It was that or on a toddler bed in their spare room. Can't do that long term.' She snapped the fingers of her good hand silently in my direction. They didn't make any noise because she didn't want to risk damaging her digits by creating friction. 'He could lodge with you. You've got a spare room.'

'No, I haven't.' My cheeks grew warm. 'Steve's in there because of his sleep apnoea.'

'Is that so?' Josephine said, sarcasm dripping from every word. 'What about Sophie's room, then? That's empty at the moment.'

I inhaled sharply. 'No! She hasn't moved out. She could visit any time.' This might be wishful thinking, but I refused to give up hope. Plus, her room wasn't empty – I was in there half the time. 'Why are you asking me anyway?' I said. 'You're the one with the Airbnb.' Josephine's property had a detached coach house above the garage. It had once been my dad's photography studio and was now a self-contained apartment, which Josephine sometimes let out.

Josephine couldn't respond, because Pervinder had moved on to threading her upper lid, rendering her speechless. I'd give Pervinder good money to eke that task out for the remainder of my visit.

'No hot water,' Pervinder explained on her behalf. 'Your mother can't get a plumber to come and fix it for six weeks.' She sighed heavily. 'Poor Reyansh's back is playing up from sleeping on the sofa. But Saif is in halls and Avani doesn't have room for him.'

Avani was Pervinder's daughter. She and her husband were both doctors, and Pervinder had moved from Brighton to Norwich ten years earlier to help look after their children. They clearly had a very different relationship to the one Josephine and I had. If I moved to another city, it'd be to get away from her. The last thing I'd want was her following me there.

'There are lots of Airbnbs in Norwich,' I said. 'He'll find something.'

'I hope so.' Pervinder finished Josephine's hair removal and sat next to me on the bed.

'Thank you, darling Pervinder,' Josephine said. With her working hand, she gently eased off a hairband to release her pale-copper waves and checked her reflection in a hand mirror. Her makeup was pristine, despite having applied it with one hand. She certainly wasn't your average septuagenarian care-home resident.

She caught me watching and snapped her fingers silently at me, before I could pretend I wasn't. 'You must get yours done.' She turned to Pervinder. 'You wouldn't think she works in media, would you? Not a scrap of makeup, apart from that inch-thick foundation. And look at the state of those nails. I'm sure she bites them to spite me.'

'It doesn't matter what I look like,' I said, picking at a hangnail. 'It's not like I'm the face of BBC *Breakfast*.'

'Don't I know it,' Josephine sighed. She spread her free arm wide and rotated her hand. 'She used to be so adventurous, Pervinder. Was going to be editor of a glossy magazine, after travelling for a year. No idea what happened to those plans.'

I tugged hard at the hangnail and winced as it tore down too far. She knew exactly what had happened to those plans. I couldn't concentrate on my media course after she'd revealed that my whole life had been a lie. I'd left uni and taken a job that was as closely linked to journalism as I could get – as a receptionist for *Norwich Now*, the city's monthly lifestyle magazine. The salary just about enabled me to rent a room in a house, but there was no money for going out, let alone travelling.

Josephine sighed dramatically. 'She dropped everything to settle down with Steady Steve.'

'Nothing wrong with being steady,' Pervinder said, studying my face.

'Thank you, Pervinder,' I said. It was true. Being steady and reliable was, when I met Steve, his most appealing trait. Admittedly, there were now plenty of traits that weren't so appealing, but steadiness wasn't one of them. 'And I might not be an editor,' I added, 'but I am a writer.'

'For *Norwich Now*,' Josephine said with disdain. 'It's not exactly *Vogue*, is it?'

I gritted my teeth. *Norwich Now* was a perfectly good local magazine. I was extremely lucky to have worked my way up from the reception desk to the marketing and events management department, and then to the editorial team where I was taught on the job by the senior journalist, Nikki, who was now my closest friend. I'd never have become a journalist without a recognised qualification anywhere else.

'Would you still like to travel?' Pervinder asked.

Josephine snorted before I could respond. 'Hardly, Pervinder. They go to the same villa in Spain every year. Steve rents it cheaply from a colleague.'

'We always go to the same place on holiday too,' Pervinder said. This was a beautiful town in Pakistan, where she caught up with family and returned with exquisite saris, jewelled shoes and exotic spices. Our self-catering villa in Spain, from which we returned with mild sunburn and a suitcase of sand, wasn't quite in the same league. Pervinder patted my shoulder. 'Stick with what you know and you can't go wrong.'

I gave a weak smile, but there was a gnawing feeling in my stomach. Sophie had already announced that she wouldn't be coming next summer. She was going to Ibiza with friends instead. The prospect of it just being me and Steve on holiday was not an appealing one. How would I survive an entire week without Sophie there to dilute his verbal stream of consciousness?

The gnawing grew. Never mind the holiday, how would I survive the next however many years? Since Sophie started uni, I'd felt lost. Home didn't feel like home without her there. It was just a house. I'd never been keen on it, but Steve got a great deal, as the owners were in a hurry to sell and we had a cash deposit – mainly his cash – so I went with it. I hadn't expected to have my own house at the age of twenty-five, and that security had been everything I longed for. Never mind that the furniture, bought from car boot sales or rescued from the skip at work, wasn't what I'd have chosen. Not sure anyone other than Steve would have chosen a dented filing cabinet with a spider plant permanently attached as a chest of drawers, but, as he rightly pointed out, the house was the investment, not the contents.

I'd met Steve Monaghan when I was helping to organise the Best Local Business Awards run by *Norwich Now*. The insurance company he worked for was one of the finalists and he'd volunteered to coordinate the event. Steve was ten years older than me, very organised and focused, and liked everything planned out. It was refreshing to meet someone like that rather than the men my age, who had no plans beyond which pub they'd start in that night. It was comforting that he liked certain meals on certain evenings and always parked in the same spot and set his clothes out for the next day before he went to sleep. Even his job was perfect – as an insurance risk assessor, he was primed to identify and remove potential hazards.

He actually had a surprisingly buff physique beneath his starched shirts, as he'd played badminton for the county. It had been exciting going to matches with him. I'd felt a rush of adrenalin when he'd leapt across the court and scored a winning point, and I was proud to be the one going home with him. He'd taught me to play and while I'd never be anywhere near his league, I'd loved it when he wrapped his strong arms around me to help improve my serve. He'd retired from playing at the age of thirty-eight, twenty-one years ago, and the broad shoulders and toned biceps had retired with him. Not that that mattered, I told myself sternly. I hadn't married him for his muscles. No, it was because he made me feel safe, secure and stable. Nothing dangerous or unpredictable or unexpected could happen with Steve. He'd never spring a shock, life-changing announcement on me, such as, for example, that my dad wasn't actually my dad.

Sophie had arrived a year after we married and was the best thing that had ever happened to me. I hadn't known it was possible to feel love that intensely. Providing a secure home and stable upbringing was all that mattered after that. Steve was so busy with work that I solo parented most of the time, but I didn't mind. As long as Sophie was happy, I was happy. I didn't need anything more. And it kept me busy. My stomach tightened. But now Sophie wasn't around to keep me busy and without the badminton matches to occupy us, it was clear that Steve and I had no shared interests. So what happened now?

Pervinder took advantage of my distracted state. Before I could say monobrow, she'd lunged across, pinned me to the bed with one knee and begun threading my eyebrows.

'Ouch!' I squealed.

'Don't be so dramatic,' Josephine said. 'I've fractured my wrist and I'm not moaning.'

'Do you listen to what comes out of your mouth?' I spluttered. 'You never stop moaning.'

Josephine's nostrils flared.

'Your brows are quite wavy,' Pervinder huffed, the task seeming much more arduous than it had been when tending to Josephine. 'Strange, when your hair is straight.'

'She has the most beautiful curly hair,' Josephine said. 'But she straightens it every day and pulls it back into that ponytail. Breaks my heart.'

I straightened my hair, and slathered foundation over my freckles, in an attempt not to look exactly like Josephine. We were the same height and build, but I wasn't prepared to do daily pie-eating contests or develop a hunch to change those physical similarities. My stubbornness had some limits.

'You don't have to do this,' I said to Pervinder, as a bead of sweat trickled down her face. She was in her seventies and I wasn't sure this level of physical exertion was good for her. Plus, it bloody well hurt.

There was a light tap on the door. 'A gentleman to see you, Josephine,' said the nurse who'd shown me in earlier. 'You're popular today.'

A gentleman? My back was to the door and I couldn't turn to see who it was.

'Hello there.' Josephine waved flamboyantly to whoever it was. 'As you can see, she's occupied at the moment, but hopefully it won't take too long. Although, Pervinder's got her work cut out there.' She released a high-pitched girlish giggle. Who was it? Only Steve knew I was here, and his appearance would not warrant a girlish giggle. 'I'll get the nurse to bring you a chair.' Josephine pressed a buzzer. She hadn't deemed it necessary to summon a chair for me, I noticed.

'Don't worry. I don't mind standing.' Her visitor walked around the bed and I froze. It was the handsome man from the carpark I'd grunted at, then ran away from. What was he doing in Josephine's room?

'Reyansh,' Pervinder said warmly.

Of course. It would have to be her son, wouldn't it?

# Chapter 4

'Are you all right, Ammi?' Reyansh asked his mother. 'You look exhausted.'

Pervinder gestured to me. 'Tough follicles, this one.'

My cheeks burst into flames and when Reyansh's eyes flitted to me, I wished the rest of me would too.

'Almost done,' Pervinder said, before lunging at me again with her thread.

'Have we met before?' Reyansh asked.

'No, never,' I said quickly.

'This is my daughter, Becca,' Josephine said. 'Your mother very kindly offered to do her brows after mine, but they're proving to be a bit of a challenge.'

Reyansh's eyes narrowed behind his glasses. He was clearly trying to place me. I prayed he wouldn't be able to. 'Ah, from the carpark,' he said. That'd teach me for being an atheist.

Josephine unfurled her good hand in the direction of the window. 'What happened in the carpark?'

'Nothing,' I said quickly.

'Are you all right?' Reyansh asked. 'You seemed a bit unsettled.'

'I am, thank you for asking,' Josephine said in a delicate voice, assuming he was talking to her. 'I have to wear a splint for at least a month. My main fear is how it'll affect my career. I'm a hand model.'

'Yes, I remember,' Reyansh said.

'You can look at my portfolio if you like.' She gestured to the table and Reyansh picked it up and let her talk him through each photo. He was very handsome, but if he was genuinely as interested in her photos as he seemed to be, then he really needed to get a life. Admittedly, so did I, but I was here under duress.

Pervinder released me at last and slumped down on the bed next to me.

'Thank you,' I said, for my unauthorised and unwanted treatment.

'Get it done regularly to weaken the hairs and make them come out easier,' she said. 'There are many salons in the city that can do this.' She wasn't offering to do them herself again, then. Presumably, for respiratory reasons.

'How much do I owe you?' I asked.

'My treat,' she wheezed.

If this was what Pervinder classed as a treat, I pitied any children who called round at Halloween. 'Thank you. Really kind of you,' I lied.

Pervinder took a tissue from a box on the table and blotted her face and neck. 'How's Saif?' she asked Reyansh shakily.

'So-so,' Reyansh said. 'Just been on the phone to him. He says he almost wishes he hadn't gone home for reading week, because it's made it harder coming back.'

My heart pinched. Was Sophie the only person in the country who'd chosen not to go home for reading week?

'Your mother told me he's having a tough time settling in,' Josephine said. 'At least he's still going. Becca dropped out in her second year.'

I bristled. She was the reason I'd dropped out of university, but I couldn't say anything to defend my actions without my lovely dad's role being tarnished.

'If he didn't want to go anymore, that wouldn't be a problem,' Reyansh said. 'But he wants to get a degree. I thought if I got a place in Norwich for the rest of this term, he'd have somewhere to come to if he wanted a break or needed some support. My parents and sister are great, but it's not fair to put that responsibility on them. Luckily, I work from home, so it doesn't matter where I'm based.'

'He has his own company, designing websites,' Pervinder said proudly.

'My photos would look wonderful on a website.' Josephine tapped the page Reyansh had open. 'That one was taken to promote a new perfume. The photographer said I had the most expressive wrists he'd ever seen.'

I zoned her out, a skill I'd honed to perfection thanks to living with an Olympic-standard waffler, only registering the odd word. Something about her agent Audrey and stroke of genius. Audrey – a genius? That was a laugh. She'd coasted on Josephine's success in the early days and hadn't got her any work for years. The nurse who'd shown me in had mentioned that Josephine's agent had visited earlier. Given that Audrey was in her nineties, it was a wonder they'd let her leave again.

'Becca,' Josephine snapped. 'Reyansh is talking to you.'

Reyansh nudged his glasses up. 'I understand your daughter's just started uni too and is settled already. Any advice on how I can help with the transition?'

What transition? Sophie had clicked instantly with her flatmates, fallen in love with Manchester and fully embraced the student lifestyle, striding into her new life without a backward glance. It was *me* who needed help with the transition. A huge lump formed in my throat. I tried to answer Reyansh's question, but the words wouldn't form. I gave a feeble shrug instead, aware I was coming across as rude, but unable to speak.

Reyansh studied me for a moment then gave a curt nod. 'Well, I'm glad your daughter's enjoying her time away.' He didn't add that he could understand why, but the implication was clear in his tone. I squirmed, but there was too high a risk I'd dissolve into tears if I tried to speak and I'd already made enough of a fool of myself. The only comfort was that I'd never see him again.

He turned to Pervinder, who was slumped on the bed, still breathing heavily. 'Ready to go, Ammi?' She nodded and he helped her to her feet.

'Good luck with the flat hunting,' Josephine said. 'Such a shame about the hot water in the coach house. If I find a plumber who doesn't have a six-week waiting list, you'll be the first to know.'

'Thank you, Josephine.' He smiled at her, but any warmth in his deep brown eyes was gone by the time his gaze reached mine.

'Lovely to see you again, Reyansh,' Josephine cooed.

'Please, call me Rey. I hope you're better soon.'

'Thank you, Rey.' Josephine waved elaborately with her good hand. 'He's rather easy on the eye, isn't he?' she stage-whispered once he'd closed the door.

I grimaced. 'Urgh. He's your friend's son.'

Josephine's nostrils flared. 'I'm just stating a fact. You don't see many handsome divorcés with their own businesses.' She picked up a tube of hand cream. Like rats in London, you were never further than two metres away from moisturiser in Josephine's company. 'Massage this into my good hand, would you,' she said, passing it to me.

'OK, but I can't stay long. Steve's going away with work tomorrow.'

'Needs you to pack his case for him, does he?'

'No, he packs his own case,' I said defensively. She didn't need to know I got it out of the loft for him first.

'You do too much for that man,' Josephine tutted. 'Plump my cushion up, would you. And really get into those cuticles. I can feel the skin shrivelling up inside this splint.' She glanced sorrowfully at her right hand resting on her chest in its sling. 'I need to be in prime condition in case a job comes up.'

'Mmm,' I said, rubbing hand cream into her digits as quickly and efficiently as I could.

'I know I haven't had any work for a while,' she continued. I didn't point out that it had been ten years. 'But I'm keen to get back out there.'

I wished I was as keen about my own job. I found it hard to get back out there after a lunch break. Work hadn't been the same since Nikki had left earlier that year. The replacement editor, Declan, a thirty-something Millennial, viewed me in the same way he would a fax machine. I'd possibly provided a relevant service at some point, but was now needlessly taking up space. The interviews and profile features that I'd loved writing had been reassigned to a much younger member of the team, and I was lumbered with the pieces no one else wanted.

Nikki thought I should get a new job, but the thought petrified me. I wasn't good with change. As my new jeans had proved. Plus, I was almost fifty and didn't have any formal qualifications. No one would employ me. Much better I sit tight for the next ten years, till I could retire.

Once I'd massaged the hand cream in to Josephine's satisfaction, I replenished her water and lemon, plumped up her cushions again, and made sure her mirror, TV remote and hand exercise ball were all within reach.

'Anything else?' I asked, edging towards the door.

'Yes. Open my portfolio out on the bed, so the staff here can see my work. No, not that page – find a photo where my wrists are fully exposed, so they appreciate how important they are in my profession.' I flicked through a few pages until I reached one that she was happy with, then zipped up my khaki waterproof jacket and told her I'd see her the next day after work.

'Could I have a quick word?' the nurse, Susannah, said, as I was leaving. 'We were wondering what your plans are for your mother.'

I decided not to mention the leaflet advertising flights to Switzerland that I'd just left in Josephine's room. 'What do you mean?' I asked.

'All being well, the doctor will sign her off on Wednesday. She's well in herself and the doctor's pleased with how her wrist is recovering. Her physio will start in three weeks, when the cast comes off, and she can do that at home.'

I nodded. 'I'll book Wednesday morning off work to collect her.'

'She mustn't use her right hand at all for the next few weeks,' Susannah said. 'Just one small knock and she'd be back to square one. She's very fragile.'

Josephine fragile? Fragile people didn't have their brows threaded, apply a full face of makeup with one hand and plan their career comebacks from their hospital beds. She made the family in *Succession* look delicate.

'OK. I'll go round in my lunch break each day to check on her.' As if my working day wasn't monotonous enough already.

Susannah shook her head. 'She'll need more than that. Ideally, four visits a day while the fracture is so fresh.'

My eyebrows shot up. Four visits a day? Steve and I didn't interact that often, and we lived together.

'Don't let her fool you,' Susannah said. 'She's in amazing shape for seventy, but that doesn't change the fact that she *is* seventy.' She glanced over her shoulder, as though checking Josephine wasn't within earshot. Wise move. If Josephine heard her referencing her actual age, she'd sue for defamation of character. 'If four visits is too much for you to manage, you could employ carers. I'll give you the details of a company we use but, be warned, it'll be costly.'

Thanks to her modelling work and my dad's fairly successful photography career, Josephine was comfortably off, especially when she rented out the coach house. That was out of action at the moment, but she should have enough in her savings to cover the costs. I pushed away a stab of guilt that she'd have to pay someone to look after her. I worked full-time and it wasn't my fault I didn't have any siblings to share the burden.

'Another option is moving in,' Susannah said. 'I always think it'd be quite nice to have an excuse to get away from the husband and kids for a few weeks.' She laughed, but I couldn't join in. Not when I'd give anything to *not* be away from my lovely Sophie. As for moving in with Josephine, I'd be the one in need of respite care if we tried that.

# Chapter 5

The house was quiet and cold when I got in. Sophie's absence shouldn't have made much of a difference, as she was out or in her room most of the time – the only sign she lived here being empty cartons and packets in the fridge and cupboards, and missing glasses and plates that never made their way back down – but somehow it did. I took my coat off but kept my scarf on. Steve wouldn't allow the heating on till temperatures dropped so low that we could see our breath. Sometimes I went so numb with cold that seeing my breath was the only indicator I was still alive. I stood in the hallway, straining to hear any sign of life, hoping Steve was out.

'In here,' he called from the living room. I felt a rush of irritation, immediately followed by a stab of guilt. How could I begrudge my husband being in his own home? He had as much right to be here as me. And where else would he be? Sunday was research day for the work Christmas quiz he put together every year – a role he took very seriously. It seemed like a bit of an excuse to sit on his backside all day, doing crosswords and watching quiz shows – but every now and then he'd gasp with delight and jot down one of the questions to justify sitting on his backside all day. And it kept him occupied, without the need for me to entertain him in any way. Nikki and her husband Chiwetel often spent Sunday afternoons in bed. I'd only voluntarily go near a bed with Steve in the daytime if one of us was having our last rites read.

I went into the living room. 'Found a super word for the quiz,' Steve said, his slippered feet tapped together on his footrest. 'Absquatulate. It means to leave abruptly and originated in America in the early nineteenth century.' He smiled at me as I sat down on the sofa across from him. 'Hornswoggle's from the same etymological dictionary,' he added. 'And discombobulated.'

Discombobulated. That was how I felt and I had no idea where it had come from or why Steve was irritating me – and by irritating, I meant pissing me right off – more than usual. He wasn't doing anything different than he had for the last twenty-four years we'd been together.

'What time were you thinking of for dinner?' Steve asked, pausing from analysing the English language with such intensity that Gyles Brandreth would tell him to give it a rest.

Frustration welled up within me. I wished he'd bloody well absquatulate. 'Is that your way of asking me to make dinner?' I yanked my ponytail tightly. 'How about you make it for a change?'

Steve looked bewildered. 'But you always make dinner.'

I felt a jolt of anger, as much at myself as at him, because he was right. I did always make dinner. Just as I always did everything, not just the obvious jobs – cooking, cleaning and laundry – but all the invisible ones too. Life admin, defrosting the freezer, scraping out the remnants of lunchboxes, disinfecting the food caddy, refilling soap dispensers, unclogging hair from the plughole and vacuum cleaner, and unmatting the furballs that Sophie's bedroom carpet seemed to breed.

I gnawed on a nail. It hadn't been like that when we'd first married, but when I was on maternity leave, I'd taken on all the household chores. We'd never had a discussion about it, I'd just automatically done them, as I was the one at home – even though looking after a newborn didn't exactly leave time for sitting around. Then I'd carried on doing everything when I went back to work. How had I allowed this to happen, to the point where it was expected, rather than appreciated? And why had I?

While waiting for my response, Steve took his glasses off, inserted one lens in his mouth and breathed on it, before polishing it with a handkerchief he'd pulled from his pocket. I watched him squint at it to make sure it was spotless, before putting the other one in his mouth and repeating the process. It wasn't an aesthetically appealing cleaning method and certainly didn't have me wishing he'd move back into the marital bed.

He caught me watching him. 'Have I done something to upset you?' he asked quietly.

My default setting of guilt returned. No, he hadn't done anything wrong. He was behaving in exactly the same way he always did. It was me who was being out of character. Why was I making such a fuss about cooking dinner?

I was in a hugely privileged position. Thanks to his hard work and rise within the ranks to the dizzy heights of chief risk assessor, we never had to worry if we could afford to go on an annual holiday, or put food on the table, or buy unflattering mum jeans. Admittedly, Steve preferred it if the food had a yellow 'discount' label, but that was no reason to complain.

'I'm sorry,' I said. 'It's not you. I feel lost without Sophie here.'

He nodded. 'I miss her too.'

I felt a surge of affection towards him. We were in this together. All we needed was to find something we enjoyed doing together and everything would be OK.

'I was thinking we should try and find a hobby,' I said. 'It'd be nice to have a shared interest, wouldn't it? Maybe badminton? It was fun when we used to play.' There was an ulterior motive for that suggestion. Perhaps bringing Steve's biceps back would help my surge of affection expand from solely matters of the heart to matters below the waist.

'Badders? I wish.' Steve snorted and was then forced to reclean his glasses. 'The old plantar fasciitis has put paid to that, unfortunately.'

That was a shame, but I wasn't giving up there. 'How about a cookery class, then?' The prospect of being cooked for was even more arousing than ripped forearms.

'I've another idea.' Steve's eyes gleamed as he slid his glasses back on. 'They're putting together a pub quiz team at work. Partners are welcome to join. It'll be every Thursday.' He smiled hopefully.

My heart sank. His colleagues were unbelievably dull. Spending time with them once a year at the Christmas party was bad enough, especially when they played 'Pin the endowment on the donkey'. Seeing them every week was more likely to drive a wedge between me and Steve, rather than bring us closer.

'Maybe,' I said carefully, not wanting to dismiss his first suggestion immediately. There was plenty of time to dismiss it later. 'Why don't we put together a list of ideas and see what we both like the look of?'

Steve smiled. 'Okey-dokey.' Like me, he loved a list. So, we *did* have something in common. What was I worrying about?

My phone rang in the kitchen. 'I'll just get that, and then I'll put dinner on,' I said. The call was from an unknown number. 'Becca Monaghan,' I said.

'Hi, Becca, it's Susannah, from Grosvenor Respite Centre. I'm sorry to say that your mother's had another fall.'

My stomach tightened. 'Is she OK?'

'Yes. Fortunately, she tumbled onto the bed, so no more broken bones.'

I breathed a sigh of relief.

'But it is concerning that she's had two falls in ten days. She claims she tripped over her foot spa, but her blood pressure is a little low, which explains the dizziness she experienced last time.'

'Is that serious?'

'No. The doctor has prescribed medication and she should see results in a few weeks.'

'OK. Well, thanks for letting me know.'

Susannah was silent. Was she expecting more of a reaction? It didn't sound that big a deal. Low blood pressure was surely better than high blood pressure, and she was getting it sorted.

'I'll come and visit tomorrow after work. Thanks again.' I was about to say goodbye, when Susannah spoke again.

'Until her blood pressure gets back to where it needs to be, she's at risk of more dizzy spells and falls.'

'Does that mean she'll be staying with you for longer?' I asked.

'No, she doesn't need medical care,' Susannah explained. 'But she could do with someone around, in case it happens again, especially while the fracture is so fresh.'

Guilt gnawed at me. Should I be stepping up and doing the four visits a day? In theory, I could go in before and after work, in my lunch break and at bedtime. Is that what most daughters would do? But most daughters didn't have the relationship that Josephine and I had. As in a polite, but distant one. I couldn't sustain that several times a day. No, a visit from me once a day and a rotation of carers was the best arrangement. More people for Josephine to show off her portfolio to. She'd be in her element.

'I'll call the care company you told me about first thing tomorrow,' I said. 'Get them to go in three times a day, and I'll make it up to four.'

'The night is when they're most vulnerable,' Susannah said. 'Just one small knock when she gets up to go to the loo in the night and she'll be back to square one. Is there anyone she could stay with, or who could stay with her for a while?'

I swallowed hard. Josephine couldn't move in with us. She and Steve ended up in a monologue-off on the rare occasions they had to see each other. If they shared a living space, it would lead to more broken bones. All of them Steve's. And I couldn't move in with her. I was struggling to adjust to life without Sophie. I didn't have the mental strength to deal with that *and* Josephine.

'Are you sure she can't stay with you until she's completely healed?' I asked. There was more than a note of desperation in my voice. Enough notes to fill an entire symphony, in fact.

'No. We're a medical resource, not a guest house.' Susannah's earlier friendly tone had been replaced with a colder one. She probably thought I was a complete cow for not automatically taking my mother in and lovingly caring for her. But she didn't understand. We didn't have that kind of relationship.

I racked my brain. Was there someone else? Audrey was too old, and Josephine couldn't bunk up with Reyansh on Pervinder's sofa, much as she'd probably like to. I inhaled sharply. Reyansh! He needed somewhere to live. Could he move in and keep an eye on Josephine while he was there?

'How much help will she need?' I asked.

'A fair amount initially,' Susannah said. 'She can't use her right hand, so will need assistance getting changed, washing, and so on.'

I almost choked on the sliver of nail I'd just chewed off. Reyansh couldn't dress and bathe Josephine. Not even in exchange for free bed and board and trauma counselling.

My right eye began to twitch, which it only did in extremely stressful situations. And this definitely qualified as one of those situations. Because there was only one person, other than a medical professional, who could be expected to perform such duties.

And that person was me.

# Chapter 6

'You're leaving Steve?' Nikki's expression was a mixture of incredulous and ecstatic. Not dissimilar to the one she'd had when spotting Hollywood superstar Hugh Jackman at The Waffle House in Norwich.

My mouth dropped open. 'No! Where have you got that from?'

Disappointment spread across Nikki's face. Again, not dissimilar to her reaction when Hugh Jackman politely refused to autograph her breast. 'Why else would you move in with Josephine?'

We paused to order our lunches, then took a seat by the window.

'I'm not moving in,' I said firmly, taking off my jacket and hanging it on the back of my chair. 'I'm staying in her coach house for a few weeks to help out while her wrist heals.'

The idea of staying in the coach house rather than in Josephine's house had come to me at 3 a.m., after hours of tossing restlessly and wondering how on earth I was going to survive this ordeal. She couldn't rent it out currently because there wasn't any hot water. That wasn't ideal, especially as it was November, but I could shower at Josephine's after my early-morning check-in. If she felt dizzy or had another fall, she could ring me and I'd be there in seconds. I didn't need to be in the actual house. I felt much more comfortable with this arrangement. It'd just about be manageable, particularly with some boundaries in place. Heavy-duty boundaries made of reinforced steel with barbed wire trim.

Nikki coiled a curl around her finger. 'Are you OK with this?'

She was the only person I'd ever told about mine and Josephine's history. Steve and I weren't the type of couple that lay in bed confiding our deepest secrets, dreams and fears. Which was fine by me. Steve talked enough in the day; I'd have lost the will to live if he'd continued long into the night too. But the absence of soul-searching in our relationship wasn't really why I hadn't told him. I didn't want the memory of my dad tainted in other people's eyes, or for my sadness on his birthday and Father's Day to be viewed as superficial because he wasn't my biological dad.

'I'm dreading it, but I don't have a choice.' I sighed. 'At least we won't be living in the same house. I'll keep my visits to a minimum and pray for a speedy recovery.' I picked at a hangnail. 'When I said I no longer had a purpose now that Sophie's at uni, I didn't mean for Josephine to become my purpose.' I sipped my water, wishing it was something stronger. 'There would never be a good time, but I'm already depressed about Sophie. This might finish me off.'

Nikki smiled sympathetically. 'Perhaps it'll help distract from missing Sophie. Josephine's as demanding as your average teenager.'

'Yes, but I want *my* demanding teenager.' I blinked hard to avoid breaking down in tears in the middle of the café in the middle of the day. I might be having a midlife crisis, but I didn't need to advertise it.

'Hey.' Nikki reached over and squeezed my hand. 'Try and focus on the fact that Sophie's happy and settled, and a big part of that is down to you. You've given her the tools she needs to adjust to a new environment and make friends.'

I swallowed hard. 'Thank you.'

'What you need is a new baby,' Nikki said.

I almost spat out my water. Not only was I too old, but that'd mean having sex with Steve.

'Not an actual baby,' she clarified. 'A project. Something that you can get excited about.'

Definitely not sex with Steve, then.

'You'll be turning fifty in a few months,' Nikki continued. 'You're coming into an exciting next act, when you can focus on yourself. Think of it as your comeback era.'

As Nikki was sixty – although you'd never know it to look at her – I couldn't complain about turning fifty, but it filled me with dread. According to all the cards, candles and novelty merch, I should be feeling fabulous. There were certainly enough kick-ass role models out there proving you could be – Emma Thompson, Michelle Yeoh, Kylie (Minogue, not Jenner), *The Golden Girls*. But they had something to show for the fifty-plus years they'd been around. What had I achieved? OK, I'd brought a person into the world, kept her alive, encouraged her independence, and supported her education to the extent that she was now at university, but that was hardly a remarkable achievement. People didn't stop me in the street to ask how on earth I'd managed it. Nor did anyone ever compliment me on how up to date I was with the laundry or how I never missed bin day. Reporters didn't camp outside my house to discover the elusive secret to maintaining a tidy home, keeping the house plants alive and always having milk in the fridge.

'What was Steve's reaction to you moving out for a few weeks?' Nikki asked.

I recalled his manic blinking. 'Disbelief, initially. Not dissimilar to when Peacocks stopped stocking his favourite jumper.' Nikki raised her eyes to the ceiling, clearly remembering the hours I'd spent finding a suitable replacement. 'His main concern is what he's going to eat,' I continued. 'I said I'd do some batch cooking and fill the freezer, so he doesn't have to think too much about food.' Nikki levelled her gaze at me. 'I know, I know. I do too much for him.' I nibbled on my thumbnail. 'I almost refused to make dinner last night.'

'Sweet Jesus. He must have *almost* been worried.' Nikki winked at me and we both giggled.

'How are things at home?' she asked. 'Is he still annoying you more than usual?'

'It's not that bad,' I said, guilt gnawing away at me. 'We just need to find something fun to do together. Got any ideas?'

Nikki thought for a moment. 'How about singing? That could be mutually fulfilling.'

I shook my head. 'I've got a terrible voice.'

Nikki giggled. 'No, swinging.' She emphasised the 'w'.

I shuddered. 'No, thanks.' Aside from the fact I didn't want to sleep with my own husband, let alone anyone else's, it was unlikely I'd be allowed to switch the lights off and lightly doze throughout, which had become the norm in the twilight years of mine and Steve's sex life.

Our salads arrived and I put the thought of swinging out of my mind so that it didn't put me off my food. 'How's retirement?' I asked. 'It seems to suit you.'

Nikki nodded. Happiness radiated out of her as she chatted about the fun things she and Chiwetel were doing and their future plans. I was genuinely delighted for her, but a little envious. Nikki embraced life and made the most of every opportunity. I was just going through the motions. Mundanely doing the boring tasks at home and work and counting down the days till Sophie was back. It wasn't healthy. Nikki was right – I needed something for myself, and to try and get my career back on track. I pulled myself up tall.

Nikki raised her eyebrows. 'Are you rethinking the swinging?'

'Definitely not.' I laughed. 'Maybe I should speak to Declan about going back to doing face-to-face interviews and reviews and in-depth pieces? That was the part of the job I enjoyed, but he's taken it all away and gives me the crappy jobs no one else wants.'

Nikki clapped her hands together. 'Yes! It's time you pushed back. You've been at *Norwich Now* for thirty years. You should be running that place, not being treated like an intern.'

My stomach tightened at the prospect of confronting him. 'How can I do it without getting his back up? The only thing I've asked for before is decaf pods for the coffee machine, and he said a flat no to that.'

'Don't let him talk down to you,' Nikki said. 'Declan is a mere child. Imagine you're talking to Sophie. Show that you're capable and aren't going to take any back-chat or bullshit.'

My optimism plummeted. If I recreated a conversation with Sophie, instead of a promotion, I'd leave the meeting having agreed to pay off his car loan, clean his flat and bring a packed lunch into work for him every day.

Nikki must have registered the doubt on my face. 'Remind him what a valuable asset you are and how much more you could give to the magazine than you currently are,' she said. 'You've got years of experience. He's a dick not to take advantage of it.'

I raised my water glass. 'You're right. I'll arrange a meeting when I get back to the office. Although I might not call him a dick. Not out loud, anyway.'

'Good for you.' Nikki chinked her glass against mine. 'Threaten to leave if he says no. That'll make him realise how important you are.'

'Are you mad?' My right eye twitched. 'I'm nearly fifty. I'd never get another job.'

Nikki waggled her fork at me. 'Reframe that midlife BS attitude right now. Your age is an advantage. It means you have life experience to share.' She looked me up and down. 'Can we go shopping first so I can transform you into the sexy, sassy, almost-fifty-and-fabulous journo you should be? I'd love to see you in something new.' She wouldn't if she saw the mum jeans. I really should take her up on her styling offer sometime. She was wearing a white T-shirt emblazoned with 'Girls Just Want to Have Fundamental Human Rights' and wide-legged fern-green trousers. Her dark, coiled hair was immaculate and her makeup was subtle, but perfect. She looked incredible. 'Bonus points for still being able to fit into the same clothes you bought a decade ago,' she continued, 'but if you're staging a comeback you need an update. You've got a great figure. You should show it off.'

'My lunch break's only an hour,' I reminded her. 'And my figure's not great. Yes, I'm slim, but I've no boobs, bum or waist. There's nothing to show off.'

'Nothing to sag either.' Nikki grabbed her own ample bosom and hoisted it up. 'I have to wear two heavy-duty sports bras when I go to Zumba. Two! And the blasted things still get in the way.'

I glanced down at my own meagre chest. No fear of them getting in the way of anything. I'd hated how I looked when I was younger, but it didn't seem important anymore. When had that happened and why?

My phone beeped with a message from Josephine. I sighed as I read her request for factor 50 sunscreen to protect her from the damaging effects of the overhead strip lighting.

I showed Nikki the message. 'How am I going to get through the next few weeks?'

Nikki smirked. 'You might not think this now,' she said, 'but this temporary move could be a blessing in disguise.'

I frowned. 'It's a bloody good disguise.'

'A break from Steve could be exactly what you both need, to work out what you need and want from each other, and it might give you the opportunity to work out what you want for yourself. I know it'll be a challenge looking after Josephine, but looking after Sophie and Steve has been a full-time job for the past eighteen years. Now you're going to have some time to yourself. Try and enjoy it.'

Enjoy was a tad optimistic. But, a change of scene might do me good. Our home just felt so empty without Sophie there. While staying in the coach house, I wouldn't walk into a room half-expecting to see her, only to be hit repeatedly with disappointment when, of course, she wasn't. Perhaps this was what I needed to get back to normal and stop feeling so lost.

'Shame I can't move in with you,' Nikki said. 'Chiwetel's cousins arrive from Nigeria tonight and will be taking over the house. For a whole month!' She rolled her eyes theatrically, but we both knew it was a front. She loved entertaining. 'It'll do Steve good to realise how much you do for him,' Nikki added. 'He'll have to do it all himself if you're not there.'

That was a good point. I'd better write down which bins went out when, and how to use the washing machine.

We said goodbye and I walked back to the office feeling slightly more positive. A short break would help Steve and I appreciate what we had. I'd stop being annoyed with him and, as Nikki had said, he'd realise how much there was to do around the house and help out more. If we were getting on better, then I wouldn't feel Sophie's loss as keenly, especially if I was more fulfilled at work. I resolved to see if Declan was free that afternoon. There was no point delaying asking, and I had nothing to be afraid of. After all, the worst he could do was say no.

* * *

It turned out that the worst thing Declan could say wasn't 'no'. It was: 'You're fired.'

Well, 'You're being made redundant,' actually, but he said it with the gusto of Alan Sugar gleefully dismissing a tiresome candidate.

So much for a comeback. Rather than almost-fifty being fabulous, my thirty years of experience went against me, as Declan wanted to take the magazine in a fresh direction. The implication being: younger. It didn't help that my eye started twitching frantically when pointing out that *Norwich Now*'s demographic was middle-aged people – like me. He'd visibly recoiled, as though my age could be catching, then told me that HR would be in touch about my redundancy package and to clear my desk on my way out.

I walked home in a daze. What was I going to do now? Print media was a dying art form and I'd just been let go from Norwich's main publishing house. I was too old to start another career. Not that I wanted to. I loved writing, but who would offer me a job when I wasn't technically qualified?

At home, I resumed my default position of lying on Sophie's bed. Tears ran down my cheeks as I buried my face in her pink dye-tinted pillow. I was redundant as a mum, an employee and, thanks to Josephine's fracture, as a wife – temporarily. I had reached peak insignificance.

# Chapter 7

I didn't mention my redundancy to Josephine that evening when I visited her. The last thing I wanted was for her to think that I was now available to provide round-the-clock care. As far as she was concerned, I'd be out all day at work, apart from a quick visit in my lunch hour. The coach house had its own front door, which wasn't visible from Josephine's house. I should be able to come and go undetected. She'd never know if I was in or not.

I didn't tell Steve either. We rarely spoke when he was away and some small, very foolish, part of me hoped it was a mistake. Maybe HR would ring to tell me that Declan was actually a bot that had malfunctioned and could I please come back to work immediately, with a massive pay rise to compensate, a placement in a new Manchester office and the use of a full-time carer for family members.

Sadly, the call didn't come so, on Wednesday morning, I had to accept that I was officially unemployed. And that I was officially moving into Josephine's coach house, albeit on a temporary basis. My only consolation was that things couldn't get any worse. And as consolations went, that was a crap one.

At the respite centre, Josephine was pushed to my car in a wheelchair by one of the orderlies. Standard behaviour, apparently, despite the fact it was her wrist, not her ankle, that was injured. Josephine also displayed her standard behaviour by waving flamboyantly with her good hand to everyone we passed, as though she were a royal dignitary ending a state visit. She seemed genuinely surprised that the entire staff didn't line up to wave her off as we drove away.

When we reached her house, I pulled up by her front door rather than in the space round the back of the coach house, so she didn't have far to walk. She clung to my arm as we walked across the gravel and I realised that her fear of falling again must be greater than she let on.

'Don't worry,' I said softly, unlocking the front door and helping her up the step. 'I've got you.'

'That's what I'm worried about,' Josephine tutted. 'You're always falling over.'

My earlier sympathy evaporated. 'Only because you make me wear stupid shoe covers in the house. It's like walking on ice.'

'No, it's because you're clumsy.' She gripped the banister and pointed to a dent in the wall where I'd had an indoor sledging accident hurtling down the stairs when I was seventeen. 'Can't blame that on shoe covers,' she said shaking her head.

'Your jowls wobble when you do that,' I lied.

Josephine inhaled sharply and checked her reflection in the hall mirror. 'I do not have jowls,' she said, managing to squirt moisturiser onto her neck and massage it in with rapid upward strokes with her good hand. 'I have the neck of a thirty-year-old.'

'A thirty-year-old what?' I asked, wondering which of the less fortunate-looking creatures in the animal kingdom to list.

'You're not allowed to upset me,' Josephine said. 'It could affect my blood pressure.'

That shut me up. The last thing I needed was a prolonged recovery period.

'I'll put the kettle on,' I said, taking some bright blue plastic covers from a basket by the front door and tugging them over my ballet flats.

It took me a few attempts to open the kitchen door because the handle was coated in hand cream. There was no risk of any of Josephine's door handles ageing.

'Make sure you wipe the sink out after you've emptied the water,' Josephine said, following me. 'Mrs C gets a lovely shine on it and I don't want it dulled.'

Mrs C was the cleaner who came three times a week to ensure Josephine didn't sully her hands with anything more arduous than loading and unloading her tiny dishwasher or flushing the toilet. Mrs C also did Josephine's ironing, as a burn could be catastrophic for her career. At least this meant I wouldn't have to do all the housework, on top of being nursemaid and general slave.

'Hot water with fresh lemon for me. Combats liver spots,' Josephine said. 'You need to start being careful of those now. Wear factor 50 at all times.'

'All times?' I asked. 'Even at night?'

Josephine nodded. 'The glow from lightbulbs is terribly damaging to the skin.'

'Says who?' I scoffed. 'The sunscreen manufacturers, by any chance?'

She didn't answer, but her nostrils flared. I hoped they weren't linked to her blood pressure. They were rarely in a state of rest. The less time we spent together, the better.

'Help me through to the living room, would you,' she said. 'I'm not supposed to stand for too long.'

I escorted her to her statement armchair, then went back to the kitchen and poured boiling water into the cups and lobbed half a lemon into each one. I'd planned to adopt Steve's stance of doing a job so badly that I wouldn't be asked again. Back in the living room, I placed Josephine's cup on her side table and sat opposite her, wondering how long till I could escape to the coach house. Josephine picked up her cup and did a double take at the half lemon. 'Are you sucking on the other half?' she asked. 'That'd explain your uptight expression.'

'I'm only uptight around you,' I said. 'Why could that be?' I pretended to ponder the question. 'Oh yes.' I glared at her over my cup. 'Maybe it's something to do with the fact my whole childhood was a lie.'

Josephine's knuckles whitened as she gripped the armrest. 'It wasn't a lie. Geoff *was* your father. Whose sperm it was is irrelevant.' She shook her head. 'You have no idea how much I regret saying anything. I only told you, so you'd stop worrying.'

'Well, you did tell me, so . . .' I didn't know how that sentence finished. I'd been asking myself for the past thirty years and the answer was no clearer. I took an angry gulp of my drink and almost gagged. The lemon was so sharp, it actually brought tears to my eyes. Although they were never far from the surface these days.

'I do appreciate you helping me,' Josephine said quietly. 'Thank you.'

I gave a curt nod. It wasn't as if I'd had a choice. I took the information pack Susannah had given me from my bag. 'When's your next lot of medication due?' I asked, wondering if she had any going spare.

'Not till bedtime.' She gestured to the compression stockings on her feet. 'Take these off would you, please. It was bad enough wearing them in hospital. I refuse to dress like an invalid in my own home.'

I shrugged. 'OK, if you don't mind getting varicose veins.'

Josephine sighed. 'Leave the blasted things on, then.'

I read from the information sheet. 'Keep hydrated, eat small meals frequently, exercise regularly, have nine hours' sleep a night.' It actually said seven-to-nine hours, but the more time Josephine spent asleep, the less I had to interact with her. 'Think you can manage all of that?'

Josephine sighed, looking at her stockinged feet with disdain. 'Yes. It's no different to what I do already.'

It was true. She was remarkably fit, active and healthy. Her fall had come as quite a shock. Unless someone had pushed her, which I could totally empathise with.

I turned back to the sheet. 'You need to gently move your fingers to prevent stiffening and promote circulation.'

Josephine scoffed. 'I can do better than that.' She flicked each finger in a fluid motion, replicating a fan opening and closing. In fairness, it was an impressive display of grace and dexterity. She clearly thought so too, as she repeated the movement several times before giving me a triumphant smile.

I made sure she was completely finished before speaking. 'They mean the hand with the broken wrist.'

Her nostrils flared.

I stood up. 'I'm going to unpack and settle myself in. Is the key in the usual place?'

Josephine frowned. 'What key?'

The fall seemed to have affected her mentally as well as physically. 'The key to the coach house,' I said slowly.

'What do you want that for?'

This was getting worrying now.

'So I can move my things in.' I crouched down to better study her reactions. 'I'm staying for a few weeks while you recover, remember?'

'Of course I remember,' Josephine said sharply. 'I haven't lost my marbles. What I don't understand is why you want to get into the coach house when Reyansh is in there.'

My right eye spasmed. 'What?'

'Pervinder's son. You met him at the hospital. He needed somewhere to stay, remember?' Josephine spoke slowly, imitating me. 'As soon as the hot water was fixed, I said he could have it.'

I swallowed hard. 'I thought you couldn't get a plumber in for ages.'

'I rang the number on a leaflet for a handyman that you brought into the hospital on Sunday. He did it the following day.'

'But I was going to stay in the coach house,' I wailed. 'What am I going to do now?'

'You'll stay here in your old bedroom, of course,' Josephine said. 'I assumed that was what you were doing anyway.'

My right eye twitched frantically. Living next door to my mum had been a scary enough prospect. How the hell was I going to handle living in the same house?

# Chapter 8

This was my fault. I'd picked the leaflet up off the mat and taken it to the hospital. If I'd thrown it away, the coach house still wouldn't have hot water and Reyansh wouldn't have been able to move in. But I hadn't. And now he was in there. I pulled my ponytail so tight, the hairband creaked in protest.

'That's not a problem, is it?' Josephine asked. 'You'll be at work all day.'

No, I wouldn't. I hadn't told her that I'd been made redundant.

'I'll have a bath first thing before you go,' Josephine continued. 'Rey has said he'll pop in at lunchtime, to save you having to come back, but obviously I don't want to risk having a dizzy turn in the bath while he's here.' I suspected that this wasn't strictly true, as her cheeks turned pink.

'About work . . .' I picked at a nail. 'I've been made redundant. The new editor, who's not much older than Sophie, doesn't think I'm the right fit for the magazine.'

Josephine shot up in her chair. Ageism was rife in her industry and she was hyper-sensitive to it. 'Did he say you're too old? That's illegal.'

I shook my head. 'Not in so many words. They're having a makeover and editorial reshuffle.'

Josephine tapped the fingers of her good hand on the armrest. 'Your days will be free, then?'

'No,' I said quickly. 'I'll be *extremely* busy job-hunting and having interviews. It'll be like I'm out at work.' I hadn't been with a risk assessor for twenty-five years without knowing the importance of identifying an escape route.

'Is that so.' Josephine smoothed her cream cashmere sweater. 'I'm sorry about your job, but it's quite well timed.'

'In what way?' It couldn't be worse timing, as far as I could see.

'Mrs C's off for six weeks having a hysterectomy. I was wondering how I was going to manage. With you around all day, you can do the cleaning and ironing.'

My eye twitched. Josephine's standards were so high that I suspected Mrs C was recruited from an elite finishing school. This situation was getting worse by the minute. The one saving grace of moving here was to have a break from the monotony of housework and doing everything at home. This had now been replaced by the monotony of doing everything for Josephine, as well as looking after her and finding a job. The solitary time I'd intended on using to find a new purpose to fill the gaping chasm of despair Sophie's departure had left, as well as conjuring up an exciting hobby to reignite my marriage and the odd Netflix binge, was vanishing before my twitchy eyes.

I decided to take my leave before Josephine bestowed more tidings of joy, such as news that an asteroid was headed for Earth. 'I'll get my case from the car and take it upstairs, unless you need anything?'

Josephine looked around. 'Put the cups in the dishwasher, would you?'

I picked them up, fighting the urge to say, 'Yes, ma'am,' and curtsey. Numbly, I fetched my case and went upstairs, past the framed photos of Josephine's hands that adorned the walls and along the narrow corridor to my old bedroom, where I pushed open the door. The bed was stripped and all surfaces were bare, but the peach walls, dado rail and Laura Ashley curtains were the same. Time had not been kind to 1980s décor. On the plus side, my poster of Harrison Ford as Indiana Jones was still up and time had been very kind to him.

'Oh, Indy,' I sighed. 'What am I going to do?'

I gazed up at him, even though I knew that hoping for a response was as futile as my existence felt right now. Until very recently, I'd had Sophie at home, a job, a stable – if uneventful – marriage and my own home. Now I provided nothing of worth and, to top it all, I was living with my mother in my childhood bedroom.

I slumped against the full-length mirror screwed to the wall. Something fell out from behind it and I looked down to see a photo on the floor. As a teenager, I'd wedged pictures all around the mirror and this one must have slipped behind. I was about fifteen in the photo, my glowing young face grinning, my brace glinting against the sunlight. My curls were wild and free, my smile so full of joy. I was wearing a *Choose Life* T-shirt. I tucked the photo into the corner of my mirror and stared at it for a long time, then at my reflection – at the person I was now, unrecognisable to the person I'd been back then.

I definitely wasn't choosing life at the moment. But it was about bloody time I did – starting with finding a job. I sat at my childhood desk and nibbled on a nail. I needed a CV, but as I'd been at *Norwich Now* since I was nineteen, I had no idea how to put one together. Sophie did, though. The one she'd produced to apply for weekend and holiday jobs had been so creatively crafted that she looked overqualified for a position at NASA.

Well aware I could google how to write a CV, but glad of an excuse to call, I FaceTimed Sophie.

'Hi.' She was sitting in front of a bright wall and I could hear the chink of crockery in the background.

'Where are you?' I asked, surprised to see her up and out of bed.

'At my local café.' She held up a slice of buttered toast. 'They do amazing sourdough here.'

Paying for toast sounded a lot more expensive than buying a loaf and having it at her halls, but I didn't want to waste our precious time with a moan or, worse, sound like Steve.

'Nice,' I said. 'You'll have to take me next time I come up.'

Was it my imagination or did Sophie's eyes widen with alarm? 'You don't need to come up. I'll be back in a few weeks.'

The subtext was clear. She didn't want me to visit. My heart pinched, but I forced a smile. She'd stop answering the phone if I cried every time.

'Why are you pulling that weird face?' Sophie asked. 'Your eye's gone funny too.'

'Just a bit of dust.' I pressed my fingertips into my right socket to try and stop the twitching. 'I was calling to ask how to put together a CV.'

'Why do you need a CV?' Sophie asked.

I opened my mouth and closed it again. I hadn't told Steve yet that I'd been made redundant. I couldn't tell Sophie before him. 'It's for G,' I lied.

'G?' Sophie sounded doubtful. Unsurprisingly, given that very few seventy-year olds were actively seeking employment.

'She's trying to revive her hand-modelling career.'

'Why doesn't she show them her portfolio?'

Good question. She showed everyone else.

'Are you at G's now?' Sophie leant closer to the phone. I resisted the urge to stroke the screen.

'Yes. In my old bedroom. I'm staying for a few weeks to help while her wrist heals and her blood pressure gets back to normal.'

'I told her that many artists went through injuries. She liked that.' Sophie wound a pink tendril round her finger. 'Frida Kahlo had multiple surgeries, was in constant pain and was bedridden for much of her life. She used her turmoil to create a powerful portfolio of magic realism artwork.' She blew her fringe out of her eyes. 'Van Gogh suffered from depression. Monet had cataracts. Gentileschi was sexually assaulted. Goya survived war and political upheaval. Da Vinci had what would now be identified as ADHD. Michelangelo had a penis inferiority complex.'

It was good to know that what she was being taught on her History of Art course was sinking in, although the Michelangelo theory might need fact-checking before she included it in her dissertation. I decided not to spoil her enthusiasm by raising such a small point, especially as that seemed to be the root of the problem.

'G will be pleased to know she's in good company, then,' I said. 'Suffering for her art.' She was certainly making me suffer.

'She didn't say anything about a CV,' Sophie said.

I nibbled on a nail. Lying to Sophie wasn't setting a good example. And she and Steve never spoke unless it was through me, so there wasn't really a risk of him finding out from her.

'It's for me, actually.' My face grew hot. 'I've been made redundant.'

'No.' Sophie's face fell. 'That sucks.'

I nodded. 'It certainly does.'

'You'll get another job easily.' Sophie's confidence in me was comforting. 'You've been a journalist for about forty years, haven't you?' Sophie's perception of how old I was wasn't so comforting.

'I didn't start work at the age of nine,' I spluttered.

'Oh yeah. Sorry.' Sophie grinned. She could tell me I looked a hundred and get away with it, with that smile.

'Go on Canva,' she said. 'For your CV. They've got loads of templates you can use.'

'Thanks. Any you recommend?'

'Don't deep it. Just pick one.' Sophie held up her toast. 'I need to go. My breakfast's getting cold.'

'OK. Thanks for your help. Love you.'

'Love you.' Sophie waved and hung up.

I opened my laptop, determined to stay positive. This was going to be OK. I was being proactive and taking control. I'd do my CV, take it to some recruitment firms and hopefully have a job in no time. I lowered my fingertips to the keyboard, then leapt up, as a screeching, siren-like noise pierced the air. It was coming from downstairs – where Josephine was. I hurtled down the stairs. My shoe covers slipped on the carpet and my feet shot out from under me. Shrieking, I bumped down the final few steps and landed heavily on my bottom.

'What on earth are you doing?' Josephine called from her armchair. She had to shout to make herself heard above the shrill ringing.

'Are you OK?' I yelled, hauling myself up and dashing into the living room.

The noise stopped mid-shout and my words boomed around the room.

'I'm perfectly fine,' Josephine said. 'It's you I'm worried about. Throwing yourself down the stairs and screeching at the top of your voice. Why are you being so dramatic?'

'I thought you'd had another fall.' I rubbed a tender spot at the base of my spine and winced. 'It sounded like an alarm had gone off.'

'It had.' Josephine held up a small object. It was a personal alarm that Sophie had gifted her. They'd given them out at sixth form, so we all got one last Christmas, including Steve.

'You set it off on purpose?'

'Of course,' Josephine said, looking at me as though I were an imbecile. 'To get your attention. Would you prefer I ring a bell?'

I'd prefer it if she'd wring her own neck, but she'd need two hands to do it effectively, so that wasn't an option right now.

I yanked my ponytail tightly. 'I've only been upstairs for ten minutes. What do you need?'

'Lunch,' Josephine said. 'I have to eat small meals regularly, remember? Help me up, would you.' The doorbell rang before I had a chance to and she nodded towards it. 'Get that first.'

Gritting my teeth, I walked to the front door. So much for choosing life. A lab rat had more options.

Rey was on the doorstep. He was breathing heavily, his chest heaving against his form-fitting shirt. An unfamiliar sensation swirled around my stomach and I gripped the door frame.

'Is everything all right?' he panted.

'Yes.' My voice was raspy and I cleared my throat. 'Why wouldn't it be?'

'I heard an alarm. Thought Josephine might have fallen again.' He pushed his hair away from his face, his deep brown eyes sincere behind his glasses.

The swirling intensified. 'No,' I said, backing away. 'No fall – she's just hungry.'

Rey frowned. 'Hungry?'

'Take no notice of her.' Josephine appeared at my shoulder and giggled girlishly. 'I had a mishap with a personal alarm my granddaughter gave me. It's important to keep yourself protected, isn't it?'

'Yes, it is. Very important,' Rey said more earnestly than was required or appreciated. It'd only encourage her.

'I thought you needed help getting out of your chair,' I said.

'Don't be silly, I'm not an invalid.' Josephine gazed up at Rey. 'Becca has a tendency to be dramatic. She's staying here till my wrist is healed.'

Rey smiled. 'That's nice.'

'It really isn't,' I said without thinking, then registered the shock on his face. 'I mean, it really isn't necessary for you to come round and check on Josephine. I'm capable of looking after her, thank you.' Even without Josephine's nostrils flaring in my peripheral vision, I knew I was speaking sharply, bordering on rude. But it was so unfair. Sophie didn't even want me to visit her, whereas Rey's son was happy for his dad to live on his doorstep. The last thing I needed was to have Rey on Josephine's actual doorstep rubbing this fact in.

Rey looked past me. 'Glad you're OK, Josephine,' he said. 'If you do need anything—'

'That's what I'm here for,' I said quickly. Josephine would be setting that alarm off every two minutes if she thought Rey would come running, all tousled and breathy. 'No need for you to trouble yourself.'

Rey crossed his arms. 'What if you're out?'

My eye twitched. Chance would be a fine thing. 'If I'm out, then by all means, feel free to come in and save the day.' I spun round and strode into the kitchen, ignoring the rustle of my shoe covers against the carpet.

'Thank you, Rey,' Josephine simpered. 'Such a comfort knowing you're next door.'

I pulled the kitchen door shut. If he was that much of a comfort, what did she need me for? Oh yes, to be her personal slave, starting with making her lunch.

As I prepared a salad, it struck me that while I was staying here, I could buy food I actually wanted to eat, rather than being restricted to end-of-date sale items. For the first time since I'd had to leave my home, I felt a glimmer of positivity.

# Chapter 9

After lunch, I settled Josephine back in her armchair and ensured all her essentials were within reach – water, phone, TV remote control and hand cream. Luckily, her favourite brand came in a pump bottle, so she could access the lotion with one hand.

'Do you need anything else?' I asked. 'I'm going up the city to register with some recruitment consultants.'

'Isn't that dress a bit mumsy for job-hunting?' Josephine waved a glistening hand at my floral, calf-length, shirt dress. 'Just because you are a mum doesn't mean you have to dress like one. Being a mother does not define you – it's a small part of your persona.'

Sadness washed over me. It was too small a part now that Sophie was at uni.

I ignored her comment and left, walking briskly down the drive. Rey jogged around the side of the house, wearing a T-shirt and shorts. The earlier swirling sensation returned. The last thing I needed was to hear him banging on about his amazing relationship with his son. Staring ahead, I pretended I hadn't seen him.

'Becca,' Rey called, easily catching up with me.

'I'm in a rush,' I said without stopping. 'Sorry. Haven't got time to chat.'

'Neither have I,' he said flatly.

'Then why—'

'Thought you'd like to know you've got plastic covers over your shoes.' He shrugged, as he jogged by. 'Each to their own.'

I stopped in my tracks and stared down. Why hadn't Josephine mentioned these when commenting on the rest of my outfit? Bloody cow. I tugged them off and stuffed them into my bag. That'd have made a great impression on the recruitment consultants. I wanted to come across as a confident, capable, experienced asset. Hard to achieve that with bright blue, plastic feet that rustled every time I crossed my legs.

Rey was already a fair distance away by the time I'd sorted my footwear out and continued my walk up towards Norwich city centre. He must be pretty fit to run that fast. The London Marathon T-shirt he'd been wearing suggested he took exercise seriously. His toned calves and muscular arms did nothing to contradict this theory. Not that I'd noticed.

Rey's bobbing form turned a corner. Relieved we were headed in different directions, I planned what I'd say to the recruitment consultant, as I walked the mile to Queen Street, where at least two offices were. My nerves increased with each step. Would they judge me for having been made redundant? Would it go against me, like the equivalent of an employee's criminal record? What if they said I was no longer eligible for work? What would I do then? My strides grew slower and slower as my earlier optimism waned. Then I remembered Sophie's encouraging words. She had faith in me. I would do this. I *would* find something.

* * *

I did not find something. Apparently, everything was done online now. When I told the very young woman at the recruitment agency that I was there to register, she couldn't have looked more bewildered if I'd said I was hoping for a date with Harry Styles.

After feigning an understanding as to why they had a High Street office, with a consultant in it, if they were unable to actually consult, I went to The Book Hive – as I did every time I went up the city – and stared wistfully at the wall of beautiful books in the travel section. I knew I'd never get to visit any of these exotic countries – not so long as Steve could get the bargain-basement villa in Spain, and especially now I didn't have a salary. That dream belonged to a very distant version of me, but it was nice to look. After politely turning down a second offer of help, I left without buying anything – again, as I did every time. Thoroughly dejected, I headed to the nearest café and ordered myself a coffee and an enormous slice of chocolate cake. It might not be possible to eat your feelings, but I was going to give it a bloody good go.

While I waited for my order, I did a Google search for how to find a job in midlife. An article came up, advising that fifty per cent of recruiters believed applicants aged fifty-seven and over were too old to be looking for a job. A chill ran down my spine. I was only eight years off that. I scrolled through the article, chewing on my thumbnail, as I read the advice to omit your date of birth and early jobs in your career on your CV, as these would indicate your age.

In other words, if I wanted to prove I was a confident, capable, experienced asset, as opposed to a petrified middle-aged woman, I was going to have to fib.

My phone beeped with a voice note from Josephine. 'When will you be back?' she asked.

My coffee and cake arrived and I shovelled an enormous forkful into my mouth. 'On my way,' I typed back. Might as well start getting some practice in now.

# Chapter 10

My rucksack was heavy on my back as I headed back to Josephine's, laden down with shopping. As well as a variety of fresh food that didn't have to be eaten within the hour to avoid food poisoning, I'd bought some fresh coffee to go in my little cafetière. Josephine didn't keep coffee in the house as she worried that the diuretics would dry out her skin through the cupboard door. If she dared complain then I'd suggest she slept in an oxygen chamber. I was going to need a serious amount of caffeine in my system to handle living with her.

I'd also got Josephine two pairs of wide-legged, elasticated-waist trousers. She'd visibly flinched when I'd asked earlier if she had any, but getting me to undo her flies every time she went to the toilet was surely less dignified than pull-on pants.

I approached Josephine's house with the trepidation usually reserved for approaching Sophie's laundry when she returned home from a five-day festival without washing facilities. Actually, scrap that. I'd give anything to rewind to the summer, when Sophie had been home and Nikki and I still worked together. With my friend making me laugh every day in the office and Sophie keeping me occupied at home with numerous demands, I'd been content to bob along. It hadn't occurred to me to question what came next and if there was enough in my life to sustain me. Perhaps I'd been born in the wrong era. My grandmother's generation hadn't expected fulfilment. Stimulating relationships with their offspring, rewarding careers and husbands who gave a shit didn't come into it. If they reached fifty with their teeth intact and enough housekeeping to treat themselves to a blue rinse once a week, they were winning at life.

When I eventually arrived at Josephine's, I used my key to go in rather than ringing the doorbell. I was living there after all, much as I wanted to deny it. A delicious smell of bhajis and samosas came from the kitchen, along with Josephine's delicate tones. Pervinder must be round, which was good news. As well as being a threading expert, she was a phenomenal cook. I appreciated one of her talents much more than the other. Also, safety in numbers. Pervinder's gentle presence would dilute Josephine's all-consuming one.

Slipping my ballerina flats off – I'd had enough of shoe covers – I went into the kitchen. Josephine leant against the kitchen counter, one hand in a sling, the other twirling a pair of tongs as though they were a majorette's baton, smiling up at her guest. Pervinder would not have warranted such fawning. Her son, it seemed, did. Why was Rey here? Shouldn't he be with his own son if that was his reason for moving to Norwich?

'Ah, Becca, you're home.' Josephine extended the tongs in my direction, as though she'd conjured me up.

'You're not supposed to be standing.' I pulled out a chair from the table. 'Your blood pressure will never recover at this rate.' And I'd never get out of there.

'I'm not an invalid,' Josephine tutted, but she let me lower her into a seat. 'Say hello to Rey,' she instructed, as though I were a sulky child.

'Hello, Rey,' I said doing a pitch-perfect impression of a sulky child.

'Hi.' The sleeves of his forest-green, long-sleeved tee tightened across his biceps as he crossed his arms. I busied myself putting my shopping away in the fridge, thankful of the cool air on my inexplicably warm cheeks.

When I turned back round, Rey was taking a tray of samosas out of the oven.

'Did Pervinder make those?' I asked, my stomach rumbling.

'No, Rey did,' Josephine said. 'Isn't that wonderful?'

'Mmm.' I yanked my ponytail tight. Why was it wonderful when a man cooked? No one told me, or any of the other women who provided three meals a day for their families, that we were wonderful. Our catering was a given. We didn't even get Christmas Day off. Quite the reverse. While everyone else celebrated the birth of Christ by drinking from noon onwards and mainlining their favourite Quality Streets before anyone else got to them, we were expected to provide five times as much food as usual, a dessert containing an authentic sixpence, and enough surplus buffet for each guest to take home and live on for the next week.

Rey arranged the food on Josephine's Royal Doulton platter and we all sat at the table. To be cooked for was a very rare treat and the food was so incredible that a moan of pleasure escaped me when I bit into a samosa. The alien sound startled me and I felt my cheeks redden. Josephine smirked.

To divert attention from the fact I'd almost climaxed at the table, I went on the defensive. 'You could have told me I still had shoe covers on when I went out.'

Josephine let out a tinkly peal of laughter. 'I assumed you'd take them off before you went out. Most people do.'

I tutted. 'Most people don't have to remember to take them off, because most people aren't forced to wear them in situations other than a crime scene.'

'So dramatic,' Josephine whispered theatrically to Rey. The possibility of her home becoming a crime scene was looking increasingly likely. 'How did you get on with the recruitment agency?' she asked. 'She's just been made redundant,' she added, leaning in close to Rey.

I glared at her. Steve didn't know yet and while it was unlikely he'd hear it from Rey, I thought it best not to make it public knowledge yet. Plus, it was none of Rey's business.

He pushed his glasses up. 'Sorry to hear that. It happened to me a few years ago, so I know how horrible it is.'

'Mmm.' Would having four samosas be a bit greedy? I decided I didn't care if it was and bit into another.

'LinkedIn's a great place to connect with people and find jobs,' he said.

'Is it? I'll have to get on there,' Josephine said. 'As soon as my wrist's healed, I'm going to revive my career. Don't know if I told you, but I'm a hand model.'

I rolled my eyes. Everyone she'd ever met had been told she was a hand model.

'Primarily photography,' Josephine continued. 'But I was in a television advert once for double glazing.' She mimed opening a window and waving at a fictional passer-by. 'I improvised the waving and they liked it so much, they kept it in. So important to express personality in each role.'

Rey nodded. 'Impressive, but I'm not sure LinkedIn is the right platform for that industry. For you though, Becca—'

'Pervinder told me you're divorced,' Josephine interrupted. I flinched at her directness. 'And your ex-wife has remarried. Such a shame.'

Rey looked momentarily taken aback, but quickly recovered. 'It's been a few years now and it's all amicable. We had joint custody of Saif, so I've always been able to see him a lot. Maintaining our relationship was the most important thing to me.'

There he went again, banging on about how close they were.

'It's great that your daughter's settled into uni so well,' Rey said to me, unwittingly rubbing salt into the wound. 'Saif hasn't gelled with his flatmates at all.' My eyes flitted to Josephine. I knew how Saif felt.

Josephine's mobile phone rang from the living room. 'I'll get that,' she said, scurrying out of the kitchen and closing the door behind her. Good of her to answer her own phone rather than expecting me to bring it through on a silver platter.

Rey and I eyed each other across the table. My stomach swirled. Four samosas was clearly too many.

He cleared his throat. 'Sorry about your job. It's never a good time, but particularly not with Sophie at uni. Financially, I mean,' he added.

'Thanks for pointing that out,' I said sharply.

'It wasn't a criticism.' He pushed his glasses up. 'I was saying to Saif earlier—'

'I need to get on,' I said, gathering the plates. I didn't need to hear about his cosy get-togethers with his son, who wanted to spend time with him.

Rey reached for the platter, but I whipped it away. Ironic, as it was the first time in twenty years it wasn't automatically expected that I'd do it all, but I wanted him to leave as quickly as possible.

He stood and pushed his chair in. 'Have I done something to upset you?'

Other than being a permanent reminder of how pitiful my relationship with my child was in comparison to his? 'No,' I said tightly.

Rey crossed his arms, clearly not convinced. It looked as though he was going to say something else, so I threw everything in the dishwasher, including the oven glove.

He shrugged. 'Suit yourself.'

'I will.' I turned my back on him, so he couldn't see my eye twitching, and ran a cloth under the tap. 'Bye.'

When the front door closed, I exhaled loudly. It wasn't in my nature to be rude, but he made me feel like such a failure as a parent. And I was quite capable of doing that without his input.

When Josephine had finished her call, it was time for her to get ready for bed. I helped her in and out of her clothes, while looking the other way, then squirted cleanser on cotton wool and squeezed moisturiser onto the end of her forefinger, which she dotted all over her face before rubbing in.

After I'd eased her into bed and made sure she didn't need anything else, I went to my own room to begin an online job search, as my in-person search had been futile. My bed hadn't done the decent thing in my absence and made itself, so I went to the airing cupboard. The only single duvet cover was the tired old peach floral one I'd had back when I lived here. Sighing, I took it from the shelf and closed the door. A figure stood on the landing, framed in the window. Screaming, I dropped the bedding and clutched my heart.

'No need to be so dramatic,' Josephine tutted. 'It's only me.' Screaming seemed a perfectly reasonable reaction to this news. 'Who did you think it was?'

Quite frankly, anyone was preferable.

'Why are you up?' I asked, trying to calm the tremor in my voice. 'I've just put you to bed.'

'I'm not tired.' Josephine gestured to the bathroom door. 'Get my wicker hamper, would you. You can give my left hand a deep heat treatment while we watch something.'

I shook my head. 'I'm going to bed.'

'It's only eight o'clock.'

Seriously? It felt like midnight. How was I going to get through the next few weeks if each day lasted this long?

'I'm tired.' I faked a yawn, which then turned into an actual yawn. Perhaps that was the way forward. Living with Josephine wouldn't be so bad if I slept through most of it.

'Youth is wasted on the young,' Josephine tutted.

'I'll give your hand a massage if you get into bed.' I used to have to bribe Sophie to get into bed some nights, when she was little, I remembered wistfully. Now I had to bribe her to get out of it.

'Was that Audrey on the phone earlier?' I asked once I'd got her into bed again.

Josephine looked taken aback, as though this was a ludicrous suggestion. Again, I worried if her mind was starting to go. I wouldn't blame it. I'd have left decades ago if I'd inhabited her body.

I eased her hand into a rubber glove full of cell-regeneration moisturiser. 'Was it Audrey?' I said gently.

'Er, yes. Yes, it was. Not that it's any of your concern,' she added tightly. 'If we're going to live together, you have to respect my privacy.' I opened my mouth to point out that I was doing *her* a favour, not the other way around, but she cut in. 'What did you and Rey talk about?'

'Nothing. He left straight away.' My stomach tightened at the memory of his 'suit yourself', as he'd left.

'Don't like to think of him on his own in the coach house,' Josephine said.

I didn't like to think of him in the coach house at all, be it on his own or with enough friends to fill Wembley Stadium.

She silently clicked her gloved fingers at me. 'You could show him around Norwich.'

'Why me? His family live in Norwich.'

'They're too busy.' Josephine leant forward, so I could puff her pillows. 'It'll give you something to do.'

I gritted my teeth. 'Looking after you and job-hunting is more than enough to be getting on with.'

'Nonsense. You won't be job-hunting all the time and I'm very low-maintenance. Pop my eye mask on for me, would you.'

So low-maintenance.

'See you in the *morning*,' I said, emphasising 'morning', as I switched the light out.

I went back to my room, sat down at my laptop and googled jobs in journalism. Never mind the salary, fulfilment, sense of value and self-worth. I needed a job so that I could get out of this bloody house!

# Chapter 11

'No, no, no,' Josephine tutted. 'You're doing it all wrong.'

I gritted my teeth, as I tried to coax her pale copper curls into what she deemed to be the correct position. Our first morning together wasn't going well. She'd applied her makeup with her left hand – with a lot more skill than I could do with two working hands – but couldn't manage her hair. My offer to tie it back was treated with such derision, you'd think I'd suggested placing a bowl on her head and cutting around it. Pointing out that I wore my own hair in a ponytail only seemed to cement her argument. It wasn't even eight o'clock and I was exhausted. And that was before I started on the list of jobs she'd dictated to me, including ironing fresh sheets onto her bed.

The doorbell rang downstairs.

'Get that, would you,' Josephine said.

'I'm not dressed,' I said. I hadn't even had a chance to make a coffee, let alone have a shower, as Josephine kept finding jobs for me to do.

'I can't go, can I?' Josephine indicated her sling. 'Hurry. I'm expecting a delivery and don't want them to throw it behind the bins.'

I huffed downstairs. There must be a way to speed up her healing process. I'd have to explore alternative medicines, such as reflexology and reiki. Or, failing that, witchcraft and voodoo.

My cheeks grew hot when I opened the front door and saw who it was.

Rey gave me a curt nod. 'Sorry to call so early.'

I pulled my dressing gown tightly around me, suddenly aware of how old and worn it was.

'Come on in, Rey,' Josephine called from halfway down the stairs, her earlier invalid status miraculously improved. 'Becca will make you a cup of tea.'

'I'm OK, thank you,' Rey said, stepping into the hallway. 'Just needed to make you aware of something.'

I seized the opportunity to have two minutes to myself. 'I'll leave you two to it,' I said, darting into the kitchen. As soon as the kettle had boiled, I filled my little cafetière and placed it on a tray with a mug and crept out of the kitchen, towards the stairs.

'Becca,' Josephine called, as I was halfway across the hall. 'Come here for a moment, would you.'

Sighing, I turned and went into the living room. Josephine was in her armchair and Rey on the sofa opposite.

'Would you prefer coffee to tea, Rey?' Josephine said, gesturing to the tray I was holding. I gripped it protectively and prepared to run if he accepted. Mercifully, he didn't. 'I'll have it, then.' Josephine nodded at me to put the tray on her side table.

I frowned. 'You don't drink coffee. The diuretics are ageing, remember?'

'I'm doing you a favour, then, aren't I?' Josephine gave a high-pitched, girlish giggle.

My right eye twitched.

'Don't just stand there,' Josephine tutted. 'Sit yourself down.'

'I'm going to have a shower.' I turned towards the door.

'That's why Rey's here,' Josephine said.

I stopped in my tracks. He wasn't joining me, was he? My cleaning service did not extend to his personal hygiene. My stomach tied itself up in knots at the thought.

Rey cleared his throat. 'Unfortunately, the hot water's stopped working at the coach house.'

Josephine sighed. 'Turns out the plumber I called was cheap and available for a reason.'

It took every ounce of self-control I had to refrain from cartwheeling around the room with joy. Well, self-control, and a lack of appropriate clothing and ability. Rey couldn't possibly stay in the coach house now. He'd have to move out – which meant I could move in.

'What a shame,' I said brightly. 'I'm sure you'll find another Airbnb soon.'

'No need for that.' Josephine twirled her hand and pointed to the ceiling. 'Rey can use the family bathroom here until the plumbing issue's resolved. Get the spare key, would you, Becca.' She smiled at Rey. 'Feel free to let yourself in and out any time. My *casa* is your *casa*.'

'Thank you,' he said. 'It's very kind of you.'

Josephine beamed while I silently fumed. She wasn't the one cleaning the bloody *casa*, was she? I eyed Rey's thick head of hair, which no doubt shed follicles aplenty in the shower tray, and his cropped beard, which, presumably, he trimmed over the sink in the bathroom that we'd be sharing.

'The cleaning products are in the cupboard under the sink in the bathroom,' I said tightly. 'Please make sure you clear up after yourself.'

'Of course. I am house-trained.' His smile didn't reach his eyes.

'Good.' I tightened my dressing-gown cord, marched out of the room and stomped up the stairs to the bathroom, before Rey got in there.

Once I was showered and dressed, I sat down at my little desk. I hadn't heard from *Norwich Now* about my redundancy package, so fired off an email to the HR manager, asking for details. Having been there for thirty years, I should get a fairly decent pay-off. An out of office reply came back immediately, advising that she was on medical leave. I sighed heavily and, for the umpteenth time, wondered if I should have gone for the editor's role when Nikki left, rather than sitting back and letting egotistical Declan take it. I'd have loved the opportunity to expand the magazine content to cater for all demographics, but I'd been too scared to apply. Scared that people would think I was arrogant to go for it, or that I'd make a fool of myself in the interview. Most of all, I'd been scared that I'd get the job. As editor, I'd have to make decisions and delegate and take charge. Sometimes I'd have to challenge people, question their work ethic or actions. I'd once stood on a train for two hours rather than ask someone to move their bag, which was occupying a seat. If I couldn't even do that, how could I possibly orchestrate an editorial team?

I'd used Sophie's A levels as an excuse not to apply, convincing myself that I needed to be around for her. In reality, the only thing she'd needed was for me to wake her up and make her packed lunch. Both of which she was more than capable of doing herself. I'd let fear of failure dictate most of the decisions I'd made over the past thirty years. And now I didn't have a job at all. My fear of failure had resulted in the biggest failure of all.

I shook myself. Dwelling on the past was pointless. I needed to focus on the future and not repeat the same mistakes.

The article advising there was more probability of Elvis rising from the dead than a fifty-year-old woman getting a job was still open in my search engine. I was about to close the window, when an advert in the sidebar caught my eye – 'Middle-Aged and Magnificent'. This was the first positive perspective I'd come across since starting my investigation, and I clicked on it eagerly. Middle-Aged and Magnificent – MAAM, for short – was an online community that championed women in midlife. I signed up to their weekly Substack newsletter and scanned the relatable features and topics under discussion. One, about changing careers midlife, was welcoming feedback from members. I eagerly read the comments, feeling understood for the first time in a while.

Fired up, I opened a new window and found a local job search site. Before I'd even had a chance to register my details, the screeching of Josephine's alarm rang out and I stomped downstairs. If she was summoning me to clear away my cafetière, after she'd drunk the contents, I'd stop looking for a job and start googling spells for finger warts.

'What is it?' I sighed, striding into the living room. She wasn't there, or in the kitchen. 'Josephine?' I called out, my annoyance replaced with concern. 'Where are you?'

'In here,' she called from the toilet off the hall.

'Are you OK?' I asked, tapping on the door before opening it. Josephine sat on the loo, tears streaming down her face. My stomach clenched and I sank to my knees. 'What's happened?'

'Oh, Becca,' she sobbed. 'It's going from bad to worse.'

'Did you have another dizzy spell? Have you knocked your wrist?'

She shook her head. 'I was trying to get some toilet roll, by pulling it against the holder to tear and I . . .' She released a long, juddering sob. 'I caught my nail on the holder and it bent back . . . and broke.'

'That's it? A broken nail?' I suppressed a wail of frustration.

Josephine glowered at me. 'It's not just a broken nail. It's a symbol of my shattering career.'

I patted her shoulder. It'd be cruel to point out that she hadn't had a modelling job in more than a decade and that it was unlikely any future work hinged on this one nail, particularly given that her wrist was fractured.

'Would it help if I separated the toilet roll sheets, so you don't have to tear them yourself?' I asked.

Josephine nodded miserably. 'What about this nail, though?' She held her middle finger up. I chose to believe she didn't know what she was doing.

'I'll file it down for you.' I tore a few sheets of toilet paper off and handed them to her before retreating and closing the door. It looked as though my job-hunting would have to wait a little longer.

Half an hour later, after I'd filed her broken nail while she gave precise instructions on technique, pressure and shape – and still managed to get it wrong – I worked my way through a nine-pack of toilet rolls, tearing off each individual sheet. I placed a giant stack in her en suite and another in the downstairs toilet. I put the kettle on to make myself a long-overdue coffee and went into the living room to ask Josephine if she wanted a hot water and lemon.

'Thank you for your call,' Josephine said, putting her mobile down.

'Who was that?' I asked.

'No one,' she said, her cheeks flushed.

I eyed her warily. A recent Age Concern report had stated that a fifth of older people were targeted by fraudsters every week. Technologically inexperienced and vulnerable, they were a scammer's wet dream. The report hadn't actually used the term wet dream, but that was the underlying message.

I crossed my arms. 'Never give out any passwords or bank details, or allow anyone access to your computer.'

Josephine huffed. 'I know. I'm not stupid.'

'I'm not saying you are.' There were far more interesting insults to hurl if I chose to go down that route. 'These con artists are very manipulative. Intelligent people get scammed all the time because they're convinced the person they're talking to is genuine. And don't agree to pay for a Visa or airfare, no matter how good he looks in a uniform.'

Josephine smoothed her curls away from her face with her good hand. 'If you're worrying about your inheritance, then don't.'

'I'm not.' I was under no illusion there'd be one. Josephine was so health conscious, she'd live till a hundred and would have spent every penny on hand masks, moisturisers and manicures by then – with perhaps a small amount set aside for a funeral and final hypodermic embalming treatment to prepare her hands for the afterlife. Given the choice between a priest or a manicurist on her deathbed, there'd be no contest.

Josephine stood up. 'I'm going for a drive.'

I pointed to her sling. 'One-handed?'

Josephine tutted. 'Of course I'm not driving myself. Do you think I'm a fool?'

I politely didn't answer.

Josephine handed me a tube of factor 50 sunscreen. 'Put this on my face, would you.'

'Who's taking you for a drive?' I asked, squirting sun cream into my palm and dabbing it onto her skin. 'It's not Audrey, is it? She can't possibly still have a licence.'

Josephine pursed her lips, caught sight of herself in the mirror and relaxed her face. 'No, she doesn't drive anymore,' she said sharply. 'Her son Anthony is taking me to see her, if you must know.'

'I didn't know she had a son.'

'Well, she has. And he's collecting me in a few minutes.' Josephine slipped some sunglasses on. They were so large, they practically covered her whole face. Was she aware it was November and that we lived in the UK?

'Do you need the bathroom before you go?' I asked.

'I can manage by myself with the elasticated-waist trousers and the toilet roll in individual sheets.' She gave a small nod. 'Thank you for doing that.'

There was a crunch of car tyres on gravel outside.

'I'll be back in a couple of hours,' Josephine said, pushing past me and wrenching the door open with such force that she almost fell backwards.

'Careful,' I said, steadying her. She accidentally trod on my foot and I gasped with pain, as her heel dug in. Then I gasped again at the realisation she was wearing heels. I looked down. 'You shouldn't be wearing boots.' I pulled the hem of her trousers up, revealing sheer knee-highs. I inhaled sharply. 'Where are your compression stockings?'

'On the coffee table,' Josephine said in a small voice.

'Wait here,' I instructed, before going into the living room to get them. A movement outside the window caught my eye and I watched in disbelief as she hot-footed it across the gravel to the waiting Audi. Funny how her wrist rendered her helpless every time I tried to do something for myself, but miraculously held up when she wanted it to.

A tall man, Audrey's son presumably, held a car door open for her. He was very distinctive. His silver hair had more shine than a glitter ball. I watched as he helped her into the car, did up her seatbelt, then walked round to his side and got in. I snatched up Josephine's compression stockings and raced out to the hall, but my hand was coated in sun cream and by the time I got it open, the car was already edging out of the drive into the road.

I closed the door and leant against it, feeling Sophie's absence more than ever. Even creepy Audrey's son voluntarily visited her. Tears threatened to engulf me again, but then I spotted the dent in the wall from my sledging attempt back when I was seventeen. I'd been spirited once. I'd believed in my worth and valued myself as an individual – and I would again.

But first, I really needed to put Josephine's compression socks down.

# Chapter 12

I made a coffee, while muttering about the injustice of having to wash out my cafetière when I hadn't got to enjoy its contents, and then I opened my laptop at the breakfast bar and searched for jobs in the area.

Ten minutes later, I reached the conclusion there weren't any. Not for me anyway. If I were a lorry driver, I'd be laughing. Well, no . . . I'd be crying, actually. Parallel parking in anything longer than a hatchback was non-negotiable. I'd once had to pick Sophie up from nursery in Steve's ridiculously long company saloon car. Getting in and out of the minute nursery carpark, with sensors beeping and other drivers giving me death stares, as though I were intentionally trying to run over their children, was one of the most distressing things I'd ever had to do in my life. And that included giving birth and securing a home delivery slot for the Tesco Christmas order.

The front door banged and I jumped.

'Hello?' a male voice called out.

My shoulders relaxed from where they'd shot up over my ears. It was only Rey. No, wait – it was Rey? What was he doing here again? I thought he'd moved to

Norwich to be near his son, not me. Sighing, I swivelled round on my bar stool. Rey stood in the doorway, sweat glistening on his skin, a sleeveless Brighton Marathon T-shirt sticking to his chest.

'Is it OK if I have a shower?' He held up a towel and sports bag, and the muscles on his arms tensed. My stomach, inexplicably, did the same. 'Don't worry, I'll clean the bathroom afterwards,' Rey added coolly when I didn't respond.

'Sure,' I said briskly.

His eyes darted to my screen. 'Don't forget about LinkedIn,' he said.

I pulled my ponytail tight. 'Thanks, but I'm getting on fine with the local recruitment consultants.'

'Good.' Rey hooked his sports bag behind his shoulder. 'Hope your HGV licence is up to date.' His mouth twitching, he turned and jogged up the stairs.

I swivelled back and minimised the screen, even though it was too late. Why did that have to be on the screen, rather than an opening for editor-in-chief at *Vogue*? Although, that would be even further beyond my capability than an artic lorry driver. I waited till I could hear the shower running upstairs, then opened up LinkedIn and searched for editorial jobs in Norwich. A reassuring number came up, but I quickly realised with dismay that they were in specialised fields – scientific, medical, data-driven. Not only was I woefully unqualified, but I was also woefully uninterested. I couldn't imagine anything duller than writing about these topics. And that came from someone married to an insurance risk assessor.

I put my head in my hands and released a slow, shaky breath, my earlier resolve gone. There were no jobs for washed-up middle-aged women. Which meant no distraction from Sophie's absence, no excuse to get away from Josephine, no purpose and no income.

'Becca?'

I shrieked. Bloody Rey again.

'Sorry.' He nudged his glasses up. 'Didn't mean to make you jump.'

I knew I should apologise for being short with him earlier. Shouldn't be hard for someone who said 'sorry' automatically for everything, from the weather conditions to the kettle taking too long to boil. But for some reason the word failed to come now. Instead, all I could think was how nice Rey smelt.

Rey frowned at my lack of response. 'Are you all right?'

'I'm fine,' I said.

Rey rubbed his cropped beard. 'It's OK not to be. Being made redundant, worrying about Josephine, having a child at uni, being away from your husband . . . That's a lot to deal with.'

My cheeks grew hot. Steve didn't know about my redundancy yet. If I was going to discuss the logistics, it should be with him, not this random, musk-scented stranger.

'I'd rather not talk about it, thank you,' I said tightly.

Rey shrugged. 'Suit yourself.' He turned to go, then spun back. 'I only asked because I thought you might like to talk to someone who can empathise.'

'It's hardly the same situation, is it?' I crossed my arms. 'You went straight into running your own business. I can't do that.'

His deep brown eyes narrowed. 'It wasn't handed to me, you know. It took a lot of work to build up, and now to sustain it. I didn't get that by doomscrolling online.'

My mouth fell open. 'You told me to go on LinkedIn.'

'Yes, but you need to do more than just look at the ads.' He thrust a hand in the direction of my laptop. 'Reach out to your network, build up connections through communication.'

I didn't have a network or connections. I wasn't even confident in my communication skills anymore, as all I seemed able to do was stare at him blankly.

Rey frowned, probably misinterpreting my lack of response as a lack of interest. Better that than the truth – a lack of intelligence. 'Look,' he sighed. 'If you want to achieve something, you've got to put the effort in. Up to you if that's worth doing or if you'd rather scroll aimlessly and have a pity party at the end of each day.'

'I am *not* having a pity party.' I glared at him. He glared back. This was so awkward. And would continue to be, as the water wasn't going to be fixed any time soon. The cheap-as-chips plumber had gone AWOL and Josephine was now back at the bottom of the queue with the reputable plumbers in the area. Which meant Rey would be using the bathroom facilities for the foreseeable future. I'd have to make sure I wasn't around when he came over.

'What time do you shower each day?' I asked. He looked at me with surprise at the change in topic.

Unfortunately, my right eye chose that precise moment to launch into a twitching frenzy. Rey's own eyes widened behind his glasses. Oh crap, he didn't think I was winking and suggesting we shower together, did he?

'So I can make sure the bathroom's always free for you,' I added quickly, pressing my fingertips into my right eye to steady it.

Rey cleared his throat. 'It varies. I fit in my runs in between client calls or seeing Saif.'

There he went again, rubbing it in about their amazing relationship.

'But it's always in the day?' I asked.

'Yes.' He glanced down. 'I don't like running in the dark.'

At least I didn't need to worry about bumping into him on the landing in my fleece Snoopy pyjamas.

'OK, well I'll probably be busy when you come round. No need to feel you have to say hello or anything.' I swivelled back to face my laptop.

'Suit yourself,' Rey said once again.

A few moments later, the front door closed and I glowered at my screen. Pity party? I'd show him. Rather than scroll aimlessly through unsuitable adverts, as he'd so eloquently put it, I went to the MAAM magazine and reread the feature on changing careers in midlife. Instead of just reading everyone else's comments, I posted my own, saying that I'd recently been made redundant. I'd show Rey that I could put the effort in, I thought, hammering hard on the keyboard as I added that I was available for any writing jobs anyone had or knew of. I then went back to the home page. There weren't that many features, but they were clearly targeted at women like me. One was about reigniting the spark in your marriage. I decided to look at that later, when the scent of Rey's shower gel wasn't still in the air. Instead, I read a piece about dealing with men who were on transmit. As in, men who talked *at* you, rather than *to* you. As in, I realised with a sinking feeling, men like Steve. I chewed on a nail, as I read the advice – change the topic or excuse yourself from the conversation, then leave the room if that doesn't work. Steve and I would never spend any time together if I tried that tactic.

A message pinged on my screen, saving me from the dilemma of what to do with this new-found knowledge. It was a comment on my post.

*Your experience is your superpower. Don't let anyone tell you your age is a barrier to getting another job.*

I felt a rush of adrenalin. A response from someone who wasn't viewing my age as a 'past its best' date. I gasped with excitement when I realised that the message was from MAAM's co-founder Nina Jasniak. Another one popped up.

*We're actively looking for writers for our site.*

My stomach somersaulted. This was fantastic. To write for a community that I admired and understood was a dream.

*What's your current situation? Do you have any feature ideas?*

My excitement ebbed away. No, I didn't have any ideas. It'd take time to pull some together that would prove my worth. I gnawed on my thumbnail. But I didn't have time. I needed to respond now, at least to show I was interested, while Nina was online. This was too good an opportunity to miss.

*Great to hear from you*, I typed, my heart pounding. *I've just discovered MAAM and love the site. It'd be fantastic to write for the community. Thank you for inviting me to submit ideas.* I paused, wondering whether to embellish my current situation. It didn't exactly paint the picture of a successful, sought-after newshound. But honesty was the best policy. Unless it was about Steve's sleep apnoea, of course. *At the moment I'm an empty nester, looking after my mother. I'm having to start again in midlife after a shock redundancy from the magazine I'd worked on for thirty years.* I cringed, as I typed. *Not sure anyone wants to read about that, so I'll get some feature ideas to you by the end of the day, if that's OK. Thank you again.*

I pressed send, then reread it and winced as I thought of all the wittier and more intelligent ways I could have worded it. Just as I was wondering if it was possible to delete it, another message came through.

*This is exactly what our community wants to read about! Your circumstances will be very relatable to our members. Please DM me your ideas. I look forward to reading them and will be in touch. Nina x*

The shriek of joy that exploded out of me would have rivalled Josephine's personal alarm. They weren't put off by my embarrassing fiasco of a life. On the contrary, they wanted to hear more. Going back to MAAM's magazine section, I read through the online features, jotting down thoughts of follow-up and complementary pieces. The longer my list grew, the more my excitement grew with it. I'd found my tribe. Perhaps a career comeback was a possibility.

It wasn't until the front door opened that I realised two hours had gone by. If I hadn't been so absorbed with what I'd been doing, I'd probably have started to worry for Josephine's safety. Not that I needed to. If Audrey's son had taken her hostage, he'd be swift to return her. Her list of demands would far outweigh any kidnapper's.

'Why didn't you invite him in?' I asked, going out into the hall. I should meet this man, in case he was dodgy. He was Audrey's son, after all, and I'd always had my suspicions about her. No one lived as long as she did without having made some sort of pact with the devil.

'Because you'd interrogate him,' Josephine sniffed.

'No, I wouldn't.' I paused. 'Has he tried selling you something, though? Or asked you to invest in a pyramid scheme?'

'Of course not,' Josephine snapped.

I narrowed my eyes at her. 'How do you know he's Audrey's son and not someone masquerading to earn your trust?'

Josephine's nostrils flared. 'Because we met years ago.' She went through to the living room. 'Now stop being so dramatic and get my foot file, would you. I've got a stubborn callus I need you to tend to.'

The prospect of being a lorry driver suddenly became very appealing.

# Chapter 13

A week later I blinked nervously into the screen while I waited for the host to start our Zoom meeting. The host being MAAM's founders Cath Underwood and Nina Jasniak. Following my online conversation with Nina the week before, I'd emailed them my feature suggestions, and they'd replied a few days later asking if we could talk in more depth.

Adrenalin had coursed through me as I'd replied eagerly, confirming the time and date. Now, though, I was plagued by imposter syndrome. Making up article ideas was the easy bit. To give each feature substance, relevance and credibility, I'd need to find suitable women to interview and persuade them to give up their time to speak to me. Me – a nobody. Not that I should assume Cath and Nina would want me to write for them. They might want me to invest in the company. I kept warning Josephine about scammers. How ironic if I ended up getting scammed myself. With shaky hands, I smoothed the collar of my floral shirt dress and pulled my ponytail tight.

A WhatsApp message popped up in the corner of my screen.

*The food caddy smells. Any idea why?*

Seriously, Steve? He wasn't to know I was about to have such an important meeting, but even so. His day job involved him identifying potential hazards and implementing measures to avert disasters. Surely, he could figure out that the best way to stop a bin smelling was to empty it?

I minimised Steve's message as Cath appeared on the screen. She had a mass of blonde curls piled high on her head and sparkling blue eyes, and she wore a black roll-neck. Before either of us could speak, another box opened and Nina joined us on the call. She had a sleek, dark bob, red lipstick and also wore a black jumper. They were about my age, very different, but both attractive. They both seemed very comfortable with who they were. I shrank into my seat, feeling decidedly mumsy in my floral dress. My imposter syndrome reared up. How could I bring anything of worth to the conversation with these two confident, sophisticated women?

'Hi, Becca.' Cath grinned and waved.

'Nice to meet you,' Nina said in a Polish accent, making her even more glamorous.

Nina clapped a hand to her chest. 'Cath – not again.' She giggled, shaking her head. 'Becca, apologies. You must think we have no imagination. We keep dressing the same. It's so embarrassing.'

'Oh no.' Cath burst out laughing too. 'This wasn't planned, honest, Becca. We don't have a uniform.'

They were clearly close friends. It was tempting to just smile and nod and keep quiet, but Rey's words from the previous week came back to me: *you have got to put the effort in.*

'I can put a black jumper on too if that'd help?' I asked, exaggerating my laugh to make it clear I was joking.

'Ha! No, your flowery dress is gorgeous,' Cath said. 'Don't wear boring black like us.'

'Although with your amazing red hair, you'd liven it up,' Nina added.

I blinked, taken aback by how lovely they were. Women who supported other women. Nikki was like that too, but my experience of working for Declan had left me so dejected, I'd forgotten what it was like to have a positive business interaction.

'Thank you,' I said. 'And thank you for meeting me today. I really appreciate it.'

'The pleasure's ours,' Nina said. 'We love your feature ideas. They're very much in line with MAAM's ethos of being relatable, as well as entertaining and informative. We appreciate the detail you've gone into. You're clearly experienced at getting to the heart of a subject.'

My cheeks flushed, but with pride rather than the usual embarrassment.

'Would you write one of them up for us?' Cath said. 'We can only afford to pay £150, I'm afraid. We launched six months ago and are establishing ourselves. Until we increase our advertising revenue, we haven't got much of an editorial budget.'

I hesitated. Did I dare mention my experience in that field? Yes, I decided. Put the effort in. 'I might have some ideas that'd help with that,' I said. 'I worked on a few of the marketing campaigns for the magazine I used to be at.'

Cath and Nina exchanged a glance, although it was hard to tell, since they were in separate boxes on my screen and another WhatsApp from Steve had popped up. This time asking where the spare lightbulbs were. Irritation coursed through me, as I closed it. He might be on a tea break currently, but he shouldn't assume I could drop everything to answer these mundane questions just because he couldn't be bothered to work out the answers.

Before I could minimise his message, another popped up. This time from Sophie.

*pls can i have ur amazon Prime password x*

What was going on? I rarely heard from either of them and now, when I was trying to focus on something for myself, they were both clamouring for my attention.

'We'd be very interested in hearing your ideas,' Cath said. 'How easy would it be for you to get to London?'

I felt a flush of excitement. I could be in London in less than two hours on the train.

Nina nodded. 'Could we take you for lunch? It'd be nice to meet you in person.'

A proper grown-up business lunch, with two amazing women who ran their own business. That'd show Rey and his pity-party theory.

'Lunch would be great.' I smiled, discreetly typing my passcode to Sophie. 'I can come any time.'

A rush of excitement coursed through me at the freedom I had to go into London now that I didn't have to make sure I was around to chauffeur Sophie somewhere.

'Great. How about we email some dates over?' Cath said. 'Let us know which is best for you, when you've checked your diary.'

A shrill alarm rang out, punching a hole in my dream of making a bid for freedom. What had I been thinking? I couldn't just jump on a train. I had to look after Josephine.

'What's that noise?' Cath asked, screwing up her face.

'My mother.' I smiled good-humouredly to hide my burning disappointment. 'I'm looking after her while she recovers from a fractured wrist. She uses a personal alarm to get my attention.'

Cath's and Nina's mouths formed an 'O' in unison. My cheeks grew hot as I realised how ridiculous this situation was. Why on earth did I allow myself to be summoned, like a dog? She even had me fetching her exercise ball for her. Cath and Nina wouldn't want to work with me, now they knew how pathetic I was.

'Sandwich generation,' Nina said grimly. 'That was one of your feature suggestions. So many women our age are going through this – looking after both children and parents.' She winked. 'Not sure which is more demanding.'

Wait, they weren't dismissing me? If anything, they were sympathetic.

'So relatable.' Cath nodded. 'Seems like the perfect feature to start with, as you're in the thick of it.'

'That'd be great.' I smiled back. 'I could—' My sentence was interrupted by Josephine's piercing alarm again.

Nina grimaced. 'Sounds as though she's determined to get your attention.'

'We'd better let you go,' Cath said. 'It's been great talking to you.'

A determination not to let this opportunity go override my self-doubt. I needed to end this meeting on a positive note. 'I'll get started on the feature straight away,' I said. 'Looking after my mother is good material for the piece and won't get in the way of my work.' I smiled broadly, hoping my desperation didn't come across. 'What's the word count and deadline?'

'I'll email you our feature specifications,' Cath said. 'And a few date options for lunch.'

'Oh, almost forgot to say, we're starting an online monthly meet-up,' Nina said, speaking quickly. 'We'll be leading it, and giving our members the space to talk about whatever they want and go deeper than they can in the group chat. Cath will include the details in her email. It'd be great if you could join in.'

I nodded and cringed as the bloody alarm went off again.

Nina winked. 'Good luck with your mum. Speak soon.'

We waved our goodbyes. As soon as the screen went blank, I released a squeal of excitement. Then a squeal of frustration, as the alarm went off for a fourth time. This had better be good.

'What took you so long?' Josephine called from her armchair as I stomped down the stairs. 'I should have taken my blood pressure tablet ten minutes ago.'

'Why do you need me for that?' I huffed. 'You're perfectly capable of opening your own mouth.' Getting her to shut it was the tricky part.

'I can't undo the safety clasp on the bottle.' Josephine gently cupped the fingers that protruded from her cast. The very fingers that she'd used to self-administer a paraffin wax treatment the night before.

I snapped the bottle open, popped a pill into her hand, then passed her a glass of water. She swallowed it, then looked me up and down. 'Why are you dressed for church?'

I bristled. Cath and Nina had complimented my dress. I wouldn't let Josephine put me off it. 'I've just had a sort of online interview. Well, I was trying to, anyway. We had to end it because of your alarm.'

'An interview?' Josephine threw her good hand theatrically into the air. 'Why didn't you tell me?'

I nibbled on a nail. 'Didn't want to jinx it, I suppose. It's potentially to do some feature writing. It's not a permanent position and doesn't pay much, but I really like the women who run the organisation and I think I could do a good job.'

Josephine nodded. 'I've done shoots in the past because I wanted to support the brand or the photographer, rather than for monetary value. Tell me next time you have an interview, so I don't disturb you.' I smiled my thanks. The smile she gave was appreciative in a different sense. 'If I need anything while you're unavailable, I'll ask Rey to help.'

'You don't need to get him round,' I said. 'Just show a little patience. If I don't come running immediately, there's a reason, and I'll come as soon as I can.'

'I am patient,' Josephine said indignantly. Her foot spa beeped and she silently clicked her fingers at me. 'Help me get my feet out, would you.'

Before I could, my phone pinged. Probably Steve wondering why I hadn't yet replied to his urgent enquiry about the food caddy. But the message wasn't from Steve. It was from Sophie. I expected it to be about my password, but instead it read:

*Coming home tomorrow.*

My heart soared. She *did* want to see me! Rey wasn't the only one whose child craved their company. My smile wavered. But why was she coming home? Was something wrong?

# Chapter 14

I went into the kitchen and dialled Sophie's number. After several rings, it went to voicemail. My throat tightened. Had something happened to her?

*Can't talk*, she immediately messaged.

*Are you OK?* I replied.

*Yes. You know I don't like talking on the phone.*

Of course. I'd temporarily forgotten about Gen Z's aversion to speaking on the phone, even though a two-minute conversation was a much quicker and easier way to arrange something than a back-and-forth text exchange where sentences were subject to interpretation, and abbreviations had to be deciphered with the skill of a Bletchley Park intelligence officer.

*So excited you're coming back!* I typed.

*Me too.*

My heart soared. I hadn't expected to see her for weeks and now, all of a sudden, she was coming home! Except, I realised, my excitement skidding to a halt, I wasn't at home. I had to convince her to come here. I'd cry if she was back in Norwich and I was stuck at Josephine's, unable to make the most of her visit.

*I'm staying at G's because of her fractured wrist,* I wrote. *Are you OK to come here?*

*Where will I sleep?*

Good question. She could hardly squeeze into my single bed with me, and Josephine's spare room was full of boxes. There was always the sofa, though. I'd sleep on it, if need be.

*We'll figure it out*, I wrote.

*K. I'll msg train time when booked so u can pick me up. Love you x.*

I went back into the living room, a huge smile on my face.

'You look happy,' Josephine said.

'Sophie's coming tomorrow for a visit. Is it OK if she stays here?'

Josephine's face lit up. 'Of course. It'll be lovely to see her.'

'Thank you.' I knelt down, my happiness at the thought of seeing Sophie almost making me not mind tending to Josephine's feet. Provided she didn't shake them and scatter exfoliating crystals over the carpet again for me to gouge out with a pair of tweezers.

'How long will she be here?' Josephine asked.

'She didn't say. Not long, I suppose, or she'll miss her lectures.' The scent of tea tree oil filled the room as I rubbed gel into her feet. 'One of us will have to sleep on the sofa.'

'No, you won't.' Josephine twirled her hand in the direction of the ceiling. 'There's a camp bed in the loft. You can get that down tomorrow and set it up in the spare room.'

'But it's full of boxes. Where are they going to go?'

'In the loft. Plenty of room up there.'

I opened my mouth to ask who was going to put all the boxes in the loft, but the answer was obvious. Fair enough, this was for Sophie.

'You could always go home for a night while Sophie's staying.' Josephine picked up a fresh towel and wiped her oily hands on it. 'She can look after me and you can have some time with Steve. You must be missing him.'

'Stop using clean towels,' I snapped. 'Reuse the one I've just dried your feet on.'

Josephine looked taken aback. 'What's got into you?'

'Nothing.' I put my head down to hide my twitching right eye, panic rising within me. Josephine was right. I should be missing Steve after two weeks apart. But I wasn't. Not one bit.

# Chapter 15

Josephine watched as I hoisted a box onto my shoulder and side-shuffled up to the loft on a foldable stepladder that looked older than me. Each time I passed her to collect the next box, she swept her good arm from the direction of the spare room to the foot of the ladder. Not being blessed with magical powers, this didn't result in the boxes merrily making their own way to me.

I'd woken on a high, elated to be reunited with Sophie today, but Josephine's micromanagement was starting to wear me down. 'This would be a lot quicker if you passed the small boxes to me,' I huffed, shuffling up another step. 'You've got one working hand.'

Josephine clutched her fractured wrist through its sling. 'They're my livelihood. I can't risk damaging them. Yours are merely attachments to your arms.'

I extended my mere attachments to push the box through the hatch and manoeuvred it onto the hardboard floor without it falling onto my head. She certainly found plenty to occupy my hands, in the name of saving her own. I needed something to divert her attention, otherwise I wouldn't have any time on my own with Sophie.

If only Josephine was still modelling. That'd keep her busy. I gripped the ladder. That was the answer.

'You haven't had a modelling job for ten years,' I said, climbing down. Maybe it's time to—'

Josephine recoiled as though I'd slapped her. 'I will never retire. As someone who's facing ageism in the workplace, I'm horrified that you think I'm too old to work.'

'I don't.' I yanked my ponytail tight, fired up with enthusiasm for my idea. 'But the industry does. The models they use to advertise senior products, such as stairlifts and bath doors, are far too young. It's time to fight back. You've invested time and money in your hands and they deserve to be showcased.'

Josephine nodded. 'People stop me in the street to comment on how young and elegant they are.' It was more likely that Josephine shoved them under passers-by's noses and blocked their passage till they repeated the compliments she fed them, but I let it go. 'All the advertising agencies have my details,' Josephine continued. 'But they must take one look at my age and assume I'll have coarse, weathered hands like yours.'

I clenched my coarse weathered hands and forced a rousing smile. 'The system is wrong. Almost twenty per cent of the population is over sixty-five. That demographic deserves to be represented with age-appropriate models in adverts and features. You can be the one to lead the way in correcting this injustice.'

'But what about my fractured wrist? There'll be a . . .' She closed her eyes. 'A scar,' she said, her voice trembling.

'That's your USP,' I said. 'You can advertise medical products authentically. Or any product, really. The industry's much more inclusive now, at long bloody last.'

Josephine opened her eyes. 'Really?'

I nodded. 'While you recuperate, you can channel your energy into researching the market.'

Josephine looked at me expectantly. 'How do I do that?'

'Isn't that what your agent's for?' I gestured to the stairs. 'Call Audrey and do some in-depth brainstorming.'

Josephine gave me a sharp look. 'Audrey?'

'Yes, Audrey,' I said impatiently. 'Your agent.' God, she really was losing it. 'Maybe her son could take you to see her again. No need to rush back. It's important to get your strategy right.' I nodded encouragingly. 'Really get the message out there that silver supermodels deserve to be in the spotlight.'

'Spotlight on silver supermodels. I like that.' Josephine ruffled her pale copper curls. 'Of course I'm not grey yet, but—'

'Audrey,' I interrupted, steering her back on track. 'Call Audrey now and get the plan in motion.'

Josephine gave me a quizzical look. No doubt blown away by my genius.

'I, er . . .' She smoothed down her cashmere jumper. 'I'll call now.' She hurried down the stairs. Funny how selective her fear of falling was. That morning she'd clung to me as though on a ski slope, yet here she was, descending the stairs with the agility of a mountain goat.

A few minutes later, she called up the stairs. 'Anthony said he'll pick me up. Might get some lunch, so I'll be gone a while.'

'Great idea,' I called back, trying not to sound too elated. 'I'll come down and help you with your shoes.'

'No need,' Josephine said. 'I can manage. Don't want to disturb you.'

That was a first. Usually her main mission was to disturb me.

I went back to moving boxes. Ten minutes later, Josephine shouted goodbye and the front door closed. I dropped my head back and enjoyed the sound of silence. Sophie wasn't arriving till late afternoon. Plenty of time to get the spare room nice for her, then do some more work on my feature for MAAM, so I could focus on her fully during her stay.

I got the last few boxes up in the loft, located the folded-up camp bed behind a mound of suitcases and hauled it to the loft hatch. The bed seemed wider than the opening, but as it had managed to get up there, logic dictated that it must be able to go down again. After a few aborted dummy runs, I realised the only way this would work was by holding the bed frame above my head as I descended the ladder. I lowered my feet onto the top rung and lined the frame up, before stepping down to the next rung and then the next. My arms trembled under the weight and precision with which I had to hold it. My hands were moist with sweat, making it hard to grip. I paused to rest the bed just inside the hatch, my body below the loft opening, my head and shoulders still above. I hooked the cuffs of my loose jersey top over my hands to get a better purchase on the frame and took another step down. The frame caught on the sides of the hatch and I extended my arms to dislodge it, my top riding up as I did so. Taking a deep breath, I lowered myself to the next rung, my arms burning with the exertion of supporting the weight of the camp bed.

My phone vibrated in the back pocket of my jeans, making me jump. My foot slipped off the rung, knocking the ladder, which swung from side to side before falling to the floor with an almighty crash. My legs plunged after it and I screamed as I plummeted towards the floor. There was a toe-curling screeching noise as the bed frame wedged in the loft hatch. My body jerked back, leaving me hanging, suspended in mid-air. I clung to the frame for dear life, unable to see anything, as my top had travelled upwards and was now covering my face. There was a draught around my midriff, in stark contrast to my arms, which felt as though they were on fire.

The situation was far from ideal, but I wasn't dead, which was the most positive piece of news I'd received for some time. Now, to get down, all I had to do was release my grip on the bed frame. A bead of ice-cold sweat trickled down my back. With my top covering my face, I couldn't see where the ladder had fallen. I was probably only a metre from the floor, but I could still injure myself. Landing crotch first on a rung might not kill me, but it wasn't exactly going to tickle.

The front door opened and closed.

'Hello?' Rey called out.

I whimpered. No, no, no, no. He would choose this moment to come round for a bloody shower, wouldn't he? Well, that decided it. I was letting go. I'd rather impale myself on the ladder than let Rey see me dangling from the ceiling with my top over my head, as though embroiled in a depraved sex act. Taking a deep breath, I let go of the bed frame. But instead of dropping to the floor, I didn't move. What the hell? The step at the foot of the stairs squeaked. I wiggled my hands. Why wasn't I falling? Rey's footsteps grew closer. A ripping sound came from the cuff of my sleeves and I dropped a centimetre. The fabric must have got caught on the frame. I wriggled with all my might, twisting my wrists so that the cuffs would rip completely. But they didn't. Instead, my hands worked their way out from within the cuffs, hooked over the bed frame, and I dropped to the floor. Fortunately, I landed on my feet, nowhere near the ladder, my safety intact. *Un*fortunately, my top stayed where it was.

Rey's eyes ballooned as he reached the top of the stairs and clocked me standing in my jeans and bra. Great. Last time I saw him, I'd been winking and asking about his showering habits. Now I was practically topless, outside the bathroom door, as though waiting for him.

Rey spun to face the wall so fast, his glasses flew off.

'I'm not propositioning you,' I shrieked, whipping my hands up and crossing them over my chest. 'I was trying to get a camp bed out of the loft.'

The back of Rey's head didn't look convinced.

'Give me a sec,' I spluttered, then darted into my room, threw on a sweatshirt and came back out onto the landing.

Rey had retrieved his glasses and was surveying the scene – the fallen ladder, the camp bed wedged in the loft hatch, and my top dangling from the frame.

Rey pointed to the ladder. 'You didn't fall off that, did you?'

'Not exactly. The ladder fell, but I didn't.' I glanced up at my top, which was hanging as innocently as though on a washing line.

Rey's mouth twitched and he ran a hand over his cropped beard. 'Are you OK?'

'Yes, thank you,' I said in a small voice.

'I'm glad I've seen you,' he said. His eyes widened as he realised what he'd said. 'I mean I'm glad I've seen you to talk to, not that I'm glad I've seen you in your, er . . .' he trailed off.

My face turned so red, I could probably be seen from space.

Rey cleared his throat. 'I wanted to apologise for my "pity party" comment the other day. It was harsh and I shouldn't have said it. I'm sorry.'

'That's OK.' His words had stung at the time, but they'd spurred me on to contact MAAM. 'Probably what I needed to hear,' I added.

Rey glanced up. 'Do you still need to get that camp bed down?'

I nodded. 'Sophie's coming to stay for a few days.'

'Would you like me to help?'

What I'd have actually liked was for him to leave and forget this mortifying incident had ever happened. But I'd be a fool to say no when it was clear I couldn't do it by myself. 'Yes, please,' I said reluctantly.

Rey put his sports bag down, picked up the ladder and placed it under the loft hatch. He frowned as it wobbled. 'You shouldn't go up this without someone holding on to secure it.'

'I know,' I mumbled, my cheeks reddening. Being married to a risk assessor, and in possession of some intelligence, I was aware of this, but my eagerness to make the spare room nice for Sophie had overridden common sense.

Rey climbed up and I gripped the ladder to stop it swaying, lowering my gaze so that I wasn't staring directly at his groin. Was staring at his taut thighs any better? Or his toned calves? I settled on his knees. Hopefully, that wasn't too voyeuristic, although they were very nice knees.

'Who got this up here?' Rey asked. 'Houdini?'

I looked up to see his biceps bulging, as he hoisted the camp bed into a variety of positions. His breathing became laboured as he tussled with the bed. My own breathing seemed to be coming out more heavily too. Must have been in sympathy. Eventually, Rey managed to get the bed through the hatch opening. Flakes of paint sprinkled down on me and I winced at the scraping noise of metal against wood, as he eased it down the ladder.

Panting, he let it fall to the floor and rolled his shoulders. Beads of perspiration covered his face, causing his glasses to slip down his nose. I'd never have got the bed down on my own. Although, now that it was down, I wasn't sure that was a good thing. It looked as though it had come out of a disused World War II bunker.

My top was still attached, so I disentangled that, then cranked the metal frame open, wincing at the screeching sound it made. I stood up and the bed immediately snapped shut, like a crocodile clamping its jaws together. Rey and I leapt back.

'Your daughter can't sleep on that,' Rey said, clutching his heart.

'No. I'll have to go and buy another one.'

'No need.' Rey nudged his glasses up. 'I feel bad about being in the coach house. As Sophie's staying, the least I can do is . . .'

I held my breath. Was he offering to move out so that I could move in?

'Lend you an airbed,' Rey finished.

Oh. Not quite such a great offer, but I mustn't be ungrateful.

'Thank you,' I said, possibly with slightly less enthusiasm than I'd have shown for the coach house. 'That's very kind.'

He smiled. 'I'll be back in five minutes.'

As the front door closed, my phone rang in my back pocket and I remembered the text that had come through earlier. Somehow it had slipped my mind as I'd dangled precariously from the ceiling, fearful for my life. The call was from Sophie. My heart leapt into my mouth. Something serious must have happened for her to ring rather than text.

'Are you OK?' I asked.

'Yes. I'm at the station. Where are you?'

I checked my watch. 'Your train's not due in for hours.'

'I changed it. Didn't you read my message?'

'No.' I glanced up at the loft hatch. 'I was in the middle of something.'

'Can you come and get me now, please? I'm freezing.'

'Of course. I'll be there in ten minutes.'

I went into my room and grabbed my car keys and bag. My darling daughter was back!

# Chapter 16

After I'd picked Sophie up, we had a lovely lunch at The Waffle House (sadly, no Hugh Jackman there), chatting about the Halloween parties she'd been to, what films she'd watched and our highlights from *Celebrity Traitors*. As she chatted, I gazed adoringly at her, all bright pink hair and glowing youth, as though she'd just emerged from a chrysalis rather than a four-hour train journey.

'It's so nice to see you.' I beamed. 'What made you decide to come back?'

'My lecturer's off sick.' She smiled over a spoonful of ice cream. 'And I wanted to see you.'

The equivalent of a confetti cannon went off in my heart. I *was* still an important part of her life.

* * *

Josephine wasn't home when we got to hers. Sophie opened and closed cupboard doors in the kitchen, as I filled the freezer with veggie burgers, meat-free hot dogs and frozen chips that we'd bought en route. Sophie had taken an age to read each pack, presumably to ensure none of it contained the key ingredient that she, as a vegetarian, would not tolerate. A vegetable.

'I'll take my stuff upstairs,' Sophie said. 'Which is my room?'

Oh no. I'd been in such a rush to get to the station that I'd forgotten Rey had gone to get his airbed. I hadn't cleaned the spare room either. It was currently doubling as a morgue for insects. If Sophie saw it in that state, she'd never want to sleep in there.

'Have a biscuit while I check it's ready.' I hurled a packet of chocolate Hobnobs in her direction and hurried upstairs. The camp bed was gone from the landing, the loft hatch was back in place, the ladder was folded against the wall and the flakes of paint on the floor had vanished. Rey must have tidied and vacuumed. How unbelievably kind. Steve didn't seem to be aware that such things were within his capability. I eyed the door to the spare room, wondering how I was going to transform the musty, empty space and eradicate the scent of decaying woodlice in the two minutes it'd take Sophie to follow me upstairs. I peered in and gasped. Not only was the room spotless, but it also smelt amazing and was now dominated by the most luxurious bed I'd ever seen in my life. It was king size, with a headrest, and had been made with a sumptuous duvet and voluptuous pillows that wouldn't look out of place in Aphrodite's boudoir. Unable to resist, I lay down and instantly never wanted to get up again.

A quiet hum came from a wall socket and I realised the bed was motorised. Made sense. Rey had good arms, but he'd have to be a demigod of Dwayne Johnson's stature to inflate this bed with a bicycle pump. Also plugged into the socket was a diffuser releasing a subtle aroma of lavender, which was why the room smelt so nice. That was extremely thoughtful of Rey, especially after I'd disappeared when he went to get the airbed. I'd have to thank him. Ideally, while fully clothed. I cringed at the memory of standing in front of him in my bra. Perhaps I'd ask Josephine to pass on my thanks instead, and stick with my plan of avoiding him for the rest of my life.

'Hey!' Sophie said from the door. 'That's my bed.'

'I know.' I grinned up at her. 'It's like lying on a fluffy cloud.'

Sophie rolled her eyes. 'Clouds are made of minute water droplets. You can't lie on them.'

'All right, Einstein.' I patted the duvet beside me. 'You tell me what it's like.'

Sophie lay down. 'OK,' she admitted. 'It's like a cartoon cloud.'

We grinned at each other. It felt like mere weeks since she'd gazed up at me as a baby, her tiny fingers curled tightly around mine, clinging on as though determined never to let go. Time had gone by way, way too quickly. How I wished we could go back to when she wanted to cuddle up with me, and tell me everything, and hadn't learnt how to side-eye.

'Let's go and see your room,' Sophie said.

We slid off the enormous marshmallow of a bed and went into my room, with its tiny single bed, which was as cloud-like as a cactus. Sophie walked over to the mirror and pointed at the photo I'd found when I'd moved in. 'Who's that?'

'Me, when I was fifteen.'

'That's you?' Sophie leant closer. 'You were pretty.'

'Thank you.' My cheeks grew warm at this unexpected compliment.

'It looks nothing like you.'

My euphoria evaporated. 'It's called ageing.' I sighed.

Sophie shook her head. 'You look loads better with curly hair. That ponytail is well harsh. Stop covering your freckles too. Embrace your natural self.'

I smiled. 'Says the girl with pink hair.'

Sophie wound a long tendril around her finger. 'I'm expressing myself.'

'So am I.'

'No, you're *re*pressing yourself.'

Sophie sat down on my bed. 'Mum,' she said in a quiet voice. 'I need to tell you something.'

'You can tell me anything,' I said sitting next to her. 'That's what I'm here for.'

Sophie's eyes filled with tears and I put my arms around her. Sophie hugged me back, like she had when she was a little girl. My mind raced as she cried into my shoulder, each sob plucking at my heart. I willed her to tell me what was wrong, so I could comfort her and help in whatever way was needed. Possibilities hurtled through my mind: a break-up, pregnancy, revenge porn, addiction, self-harm . . . The longer I waited, the scarier the scenarios I envisaged.

Eventually, she stopped crying.

'It'll be OK,' I said, pulling back to look at her. 'Whatever's happened, no matter how bad it seems, it'll be OK.'

Sophie wiped her cheeks and extended her little finger. 'Pinky promise you won't get mad.'

'I promise.' I hooked my finger through hers.

'My loan's run out.' Sophie's face crumpled. 'I haven't got any money to live on.'

Relief flooded through me. Compared to what I'd been catastrophising, overspending wasn't that big a deal.

'It seemed like so much money,' she sniffed. 'I thought it'd easily last till January. I don't know how it's all gone.'

Guilt coursed through me. This was my fault. I should have taught her how to budget better.

Sophie rested her head on my shoulder. 'Everything's so expensive. Tickets to the club nights are £10 and then there's the rounds of shots. And it's always me who pays for the Uber.'

'Wouldn't the student union bar be cheaper than a club?' I said carefully, not wanting to criticise when she was at last opening up to me.

'We start there, but it gets boring. And all the restaurants have put their prices up because of the cost of living crisis.'

'Restaurants?' I gulped. 'You're a student. You shouldn't be—'

Sophie held up her little finger and gave me a pleading look. 'You promised not to get mad.'

I pressed my lips tightly together so as not to emit judgement, criticism or a blood-curdling scream. 'I'm not mad.' I tore a hangnail off with my teeth. 'Perhaps try walking,' I said. 'Rather than getting Ubers.'

'Walking?' Sophie couldn't have looked more horrified if I'd suggested she bungee jump into the open jaws of a great white. 'Do you want me to get kidnapped or attacked?'

'Of course not.' I somehow managed a smile. 'But you're not on your own, are you? You just said you're the one who always pays.'

Sophie shrugged. 'I'm a generous person. Everyone says so.'

I bet they did.

Sophie stood up. 'I've decided to get a job.'

Pride replaced my frustration. She had a plan in place to get herself through this predicament. Perhaps I hadn't been such a crap mum, after all. 'That's a brilliant idea,' I said. 'Have you started looking yet?'

'Give me a chance, bruh. I've only just got back.'

I frowned. 'Won't it be easier to look while you're in Manchester, rather than down here?'

Sophie's expression mirrored my confusion. 'No, I need to be near where the job is.'

This wasn't making any sense.

'Oh.' She rolled her eyes playfully. 'I forgot to say.'

'Say what?'

'I've dropped out.'

My stomach turned over. I must have misheard. 'Sorry, say that again.'

'I've dropped out of uni,' Sophie said with a grin. 'I'm moving back!'

# Chapter 17

'Really?' I gasped.

She nodded, a huge smile on her face.

Tears filled my eyes as I pulled her into a tight hug. The gaping hole that had appeared in my life instantly refilled. Sophie was coming back home!

'I can't believe it,' I said. 'I didn't want to say, but I've missed you so much.'

Sophie giggled into my shoulder. 'You told me in a message every day.'

I pulled back, my default setting of guilt kicking in. 'That's not why you're coming back, is it? Because of me?'

'No, I . . .' She shrugged. 'It's hard to explain. But you get it, don't you? Out of everyone, I knew you'd understand.'

I placed a hand on her cheek. How could I have ever doubted our relationship? This time apart had clearly strengthened our bond if she believed that, purely by virtue of being her mum, I understood how she felt, without her having to put it into words.

'You know what it's like, because you dropped out too,' Sophie added.

Oh. Not because of the unbreakable thread that wove us together, then.

Yes, I did know what it was like to drop out, but my situation had been completely different. I'd been so thrown by the discovery about my dad that I hadn't been able to concentrate. As well as grieving his death, I was consumed with looking for clues in my upbringing that signposted the truth. There weren't any, but it didn't stop me replaying every memory. In lectures, the words on the overhead projector swam in front of me and I couldn't absorb a single piece of information. I missed assignment deadlines and didn't have the mental capacity to study for exams. The end of term was approaching and I dreaded going home. Dropping out of a course I was probably going to fail anyway, and getting a job so I could rent a room, seemed the only option. It had been a knee-jerk reaction and one I'd regretted ever since.

I didn't want Sophie to have regrets. If she wasn't enjoying her course, then fair enough, but she'd seemed to be. She'd miss out on so much if she left, not to mention the opportunities that having a degree offered. And, much as I missed her and counted down the days till she was back, this wasn't about me. It was about her. Putting her needs ahead of my own was what being a mum was all about.

'Sit down a minute,' I said, gesturing to the bed and perching at my little desk. 'Your happiness is the most important thing, but dropping out is quite drastic. It would have been good to talk it through first and discuss your options before making such a monumental decision.'

Sophie stiffened. 'I can make my own decisions, Mum. I'm not a kid anymore. You don't have to tell me to eat my five-a-day and floss every night and "work hard to give myself lots of opportunities". I know all that stuff.'

True, she wasn't technically a kid, but eighteen was so young. She didn't yet have the maturity and life experience to see the bigger picture. She could barely see beyond the next weekend, let alone five, ten, twenty years into the future. It'd be irresponsible of me not to offer any guidance.

'Why not finish the term?' I said gently. 'Then we can see how you feel at Christmas.'

'Then *I* can see how I feel,' Sophie corrected. 'It's my life, not yours. You've got to stop taking over, and let me deal with my stuff.' She blew her fringe out of her eyes. 'Even if I wanted to go back, I haven't got any money to live on.'

'I can help a bit with money and you could get a bar job or something.' The HR manager couldn't be off much longer and then I'd get my redundancy package.

'Thanks, but it's not just that.' She exhaled loudly. 'Uni was fun at first, but since reading week, it's not been the same. It's got *really* cold.'

I nodded to convey my sympathy, although I wasn't sure how tropical she'd expected Manchester to be in the winter months.

'I like the course, but they've given us loads of extra work to do. It's too much.' She sighed heavily. 'And this one girl in my flat goes on about recycling *all* the time. It's doing my head in. I mean, come on, one bit of foil in the bin isn't going to make any difference, is it? It's not that big a deal.'

I was with the other girl on this. I'd tried to instil the importance of recycling, and it wasn't that Sophie didn't care about the environment, she just couldn't be bothered to bring her packaging and empty bottles downstairs. I should have enforced it but, as with most things, I'd got so fed up of nagging that I'd given up and sorted it out myself when I emptied the wastepaper basket in her room. Steve wasn't much better. He didn't put the empty bottles in the bin, but he placed them neatly beside it instead, presumably under the impression they'd find their own way downstairs. Which of course they did, courtesy of me. I'd once tried leaving them to see if he'd take the hint, but I'd had eventually given up when there were so many lined up that the bathroom resembled a bowling alley.

I decided to skip over Sophie's housemate's perfectly reasonable and justified objections. She needed to feel I was on her side. 'It's normal to feel like this,' I said. 'When a particularly hard assignment's due in, or the novelty of cooking has worn off, or when it's getting cold and dark. But you'll get through it and—'

'No,' Sophie said firmly. 'I've had enough of being told what to do and getting up early and meeting deadlines. I'd rather get a job.'

This seemed a little misguided, as she'd just outlined what was required in most jobs, unless you were a performer at Cirque du Soleil.

'Please don't decide yet,' I repeated, carefully keeping my tone neutral so as not to sound judgemental, disappointed or mildly hysterical. 'Especially when you're enjoying your course.'

Sophie pulled her knees into her chest. 'Thought you'd be happy to have me home. Don't you want me here?'

'Of course I do,' I said, another layer of guilt stacking on top of the mountain already there. 'But this is your future we're talking about. That's more important than me missing you when you're away.' The irony wasn't lost on me that after two months of wishing desperately she was still at home, I was now practically begging her to leave. But my role as her mum had to evolve: I should support her to move forward, not selfishly hold her back. 'The more qualifications you have, the more job opportunities you'll have,' I said softly.

'Dad wanted me to get a job straight from sixth form,' Sophie said into her knees. 'He said it was ridiculous to get into so much debt.'

Oh God, Steve. I'd temporarily forgotten about him.

'You'd better ring him,' I said.

'Me?' Sophie sat up straight. 'Can't you do it?'

I did a double take. 'You just told me to stop taking over and to let you deal with your stuff.'

'Yes, but not with Dad.'

In other words, I was to butt out when she was frittering her student loan on a lifestyle that a billionaire socialite would find excessive, but step in when the consequences of that life choice reared up.

Sophie pressed her hands together and said, 'Please, Mum. Dad might be glad that I'm leaving uni, but—'

'*Possibly* leaving uni,' I interrupted.

'*Possibly* leaving,' Sophie said, although I had a feeling she was saying it purely to keep me sweet. 'But he'll be mad about the tuition and maintenance loans.'

He would. I could already picture his monologue about the wasteful frittering of funds.

'Please.' Sophie looked at me pleadingly. 'You know he'll lecture me for hours. I don't have the energy for it.'

I nibbled on my thumbnail. I should tell her no, that this was her responsibility, and that I didn't have the energy for it either. But I didn't want to argue when she'd just opened up to me, and I should check in with Steve. We hadn't spoken about anything more substantial than what the symbols on the dishwasher represented since I'd left two weeks ago. Also, Sophie was right about Steve agreeing that leaving uni was the right thing to do. While I didn't want to undermine him, I wanted more time to convince Sophie to reconsider. So, actually, I did want to undermine him, but without him knowing I was.

'OK,' I said. 'I'll tell him, but you have to call him soon to talk it through.'

'I will. Thank you.' Sophie leant over and hugged me.

I squeezed her tightly, breathing in the scent of her shower gel and hair serum.

'I love you,' Sophie said.

My heart swelled.

'Can you get some stuff from my room while you're there?' she added.

My heart sunk. I'd planned on telling Steve on the phone, not in person. 'What do you need?' I asked.

Sophie shrugged. 'Just my salt lamp, winter clothes, free weights, dressing-table mirror with the lights and full-length mirror.'

'I can't carry all of that,' I spluttered. The full-length mirror was from IKEA and had been delivered by two very muscly men. On seeing my distress over how I was going to get the mirror up the stairs and into Sophie's room, they'd very kindly carried it for me. I hoped the veins that had popped out of their foreheads had gone back down now.

'OK, leave the big mirror,' Sophie said with a sigh at the huge sacrifice she was making.

We stood and I picked up my car keys. 'Sure you don't want to come?'

Sophie shook her head, then frowned. 'What's going on with your face?'

'Nothing,' I said, turning away. It wasn't worry about telling Steve that was causing my eye to twitch. It was that I didn't particularly want to see him – and that was far more worrying.

# Chapter 18

'You know that phrase: be careful what you wish for?' I wailed to Nikki on speakerphone, as I drove towards home. 'Well, it's just happened to me.'

'Ooh, which wish?' Nikki said. 'Has your Indiana Jones poster come to life?'

'No, not that one, unfortunately.' I gripped the steering wheel tightly. 'Sophie wants to drop out of uni.'

'Sweet Jesus.'

'I know!' I cranked the gears. 'After two months of going on about how much I miss her and how meaningless my life is without her in it, she's back and I wish she wasn't. I want her to stay and get her degree.' I pulled up at a traffic light and blinked hard. 'You don't think I've manifested this, do you?'

'No,' Nikki said flatly. 'That manifesting stuff is a load of bollocks.'

Good. That was one piece of guilt I could offload, then.

'I thought she loved uni,' Nikki said.

'She did, but she's spent all of this term's loan. She won't get any more money till January and it's panicked her.'

'That didn't last long. What has she spent it on?' Nikki asked.

'Well, she's not exactly living like a student. Her nearest supermarket is Waitrose and apparently there's a £30 minimum spend at her favourite takeaway to get free delivery.' I shook my head. 'I'm so annoyed and disappointed and f—' A car behind beeped and I realised I'd stopped at a green light.

'Fucked off?' Nikki suggested.

I'd been going to say frustrated, but fucked off worked.

'This is all my fault,' I sighed. 'I should have taught her how to budget properly.'

'Steve talks nonstop about budgeting,' said Nikki. 'It doesn't matter what anyone says. She's eighteen. People her age can't think beyond the next weekend. I know it was different for you, moving out young. You had to grow up fast, so you bypassed that self-centred, carefree, arsehole phase.'

I frowned. Did that mean I'd been old before my time? If so, why was I finding midlife so challenging? I should be an expert by now.

'Try not to worry,' Nikki continued. 'I'm sure she'll get over the shock quickly and go back to uni. She'll learn from this and manage her money better next term.'

'I hope so.' The way Sophie had automatically reached for the premium ranges in the supermarket didn't have me convinced. I pulled up outside my house and switched off the engine. Steve's car was on the drive, but I was in no rush to go in.

'Enough about me,' I said. 'How are you?'

'Knackered. Chiwetel's cousins want to do *everything*. We're off to Bath tomorrow, via Stonehenge. Then there's talk of Scotland the week after next.' I could hear her smile. 'It's fun, though, and I want to explore whenever we visit Nigeria, so I get it.'

'It sounds brilliant.' I loved doing touristy things, and learning more about the place we were in, but Steve viewed them as a waste of money. For years I'd wanted to do one of Norwich's famous ghost walks, but he'd thought it ridiculous to pay when we could walk around in the dark for free. Now that I was living with Josephine, paying £12 to get some tips on how to commit murder and cover up the crime seemed extremely good value for money.

'I'm around next Wednesday, if you want to get together?' Nikki said.

'Yes, please.' We hadn't seen each other for two weeks and I missed her. 'Josephine's getting her blood pressure checked and her cast off on Monday. I should be able to leave her for a few hours, especially if Sophie's here.' Although I hoped to have persuaded her to go back to uni by then.

'Great. Let's go out for lunch.' Laughter rang out in the background. What a contrast to Steve's inane chatter at home or the bubbling of a foot spa at Josephine's. 'I'd better go,' Nikki said. 'We're in the middle of a game of Monopoly.'

We said our goodbyes and I looked at my house through the car window. It was dark, but Steve was very vigilant about not having lights on unnecessarily. Many a time he'd automatically switched the light off as he left a room, forgetting I was still in there, and I'd been plunged into darkness. I gnawed on my thumbnail, alarmed at the realisation that I didn't want to go in. And not just because of the prospect of clearing Sophie's room, carting it all to the car and managing to forget something essential, such as a scrunchie she'd last worn when she was fifteen. No, it was because I didn't have the energy for a lengthy conversation with Steve.

My phone beeped and I picked it up, hoping it would be Steve replying to my earlier message announcing my imminent arrival. But it was a text from Sophie, asking me to get the air fryer, as Josephine didn't have one. Bracing myself, I got out of the car and walked to the front door. I briefly considered ringing the doorbell but decided to use my key. If Rey was comfortable letting himself in and out of Josephine's as freely as a looter in a blackout, then I could go into my own home.

'Hello?' I called out, shutting the front door behind me and feeling for the hall light switch. I heard Steve's voice from the kitchen and saw a sliver of light beneath the door. My stomach twisted with guilt at my earlier reluctance to see him. Poor bloke was so lonely, he'd taken to talking to himself. At least it guaranteed him an engaged audience. I opened the kitchen door. Steve was obscured by the open fridge door.

'Et voila,' he exclaimed. 'M&S's Best Ever beef lasagne.'

What?! On the rare occasion I bought anything from the M&S food hall, Steve reacted as though I'd come home with a Louis Vuitton handbag. So why the extravagance for himself? Unless that lasagne was well past its expiry date, I wanted an explanation.

Steve closed the fridge door and the explanation presented itself. A woman who looked in her mid-fifties stood facing me. She had dark grey feathered hair, a V-neck pink jumper and a beige pleated skirt. She was smiling at Steve and it didn't look forced. Then she clocked me and the smile vanished. Her horrified expression indicated she wished she could do the same.

'Hello,' I said.

Steve spun round. 'Becca?' He shoved the lasagne back in the fridge, as though hiding the evidence. He glanced at the woman as he shut the door, possibly weighing up if she'd fit in there too. 'I didn't realise you were coming over.'

'I need to pick some things up for Sophie. I did message.'

'Did you?' Steve looked around, presumably for his phone. 'Sorry, I missed it.'

I pointedly looked from him to the woman, waiting for an introduction and explanation. Steve appeared to be too busy looking for his phone to notice.

'Hello, Becca, I'm Collette.' The woman stepped forward and held out a hand. 'I work with Steve. In the claims department.'

'Hello.' I politely took her hand and shook it, wondering what department I fitted into in his life. Or was I redundant there too?

Formalities done, we both turned to face Steve.

'Bit of a funny story,' he started. I would be the judge of that. 'Collette and I are organising this year's Christmas quiz. Obviously, we can't meet in the office outside of working hours because of breaches to the insurance agreement.' Obviously. 'We were going to go to the pub, but then I remembered I had a coupon for Marks and Sparks that expires tomorrow. Made economic sense to use it and eat here while we formulate a plan of action.'

Collette nodded enthusiastically. 'I brought my *Dummies Guide to Risk Assessment* to get some inspo for the fun round.'

I eyed them both warily, then let my suspicions drop. I didn't have the emotional or mental capacity to take this further, and their explanation was so dull, it had to be true. Also, no one intent on seducing another woman's husband would take their chances in a beige pleated skirt.

'Sounds fun,' I lied, then turned to Steve. 'Can you give me a hand upstairs? It won't take long.' I took his arm and steered him out of the room.

'Why are we going upstairs?' he asked.

'We can talk while I get Sophie's things.' Inside her bedroom, I shook out a giant IKEA bag and began filling it with jumpers.

'About Collette . . .' Steve said. 'It's all above board, I assure you.'

'It's fine,' I said. 'If you were planning the quiz with a male colleague I wouldn't think anything of it. No reason why I should be suspicious just because your colleague is a woman.'

'No, no need at all.' Steve shook his head firmly.

I located Sophie's fleece hoodie and added it to the bag. 'There are a couple of things I need to talk to you about.'

Steve perched on the edge of Sophie's bed. 'Have you come up with a hobby for us to do together?'

'Sorry, I haven't had time. What with looking after Josephine and . . .' I took a deep breath and braced myself to tell him that I'd been made redundant, and finding a new job was taking priority over thinking up hobbies, before moving on to yet more good news – Sophie cannonballing her future.

'Why not give the pub quiz a go?' Steve said. 'The guys at work are a riot.'

The guys at work were not a riot. They were still laughing about the time an intern stapled a claim form to his tie back in the mid-1990s.

'We're commencing battle next Wednesday,' Steve said. 'Do you think Josephine could spare you for the evening?'

What luck I'd just arranged to see Nikki next Wednesday. I couldn't go out in both the day and the evening.

'Sorry, I can't,' I said, bending to unplug Sophie's light-up mirror. 'What I was going to say is that I've been made—'

'Are you taking all of this up to Manchester?' Steve interrupted. 'I'll come if you're visiting Sophie.'

'That's one of the things I need to talk to you about.' I turned to face him. 'Sophie's at Josephine's with me.'

Steve jumped up. 'Why? Is she ill? Has something happened?'

'No, she's OK.' I patted his shoulder. 'She's just taking a little breather from uni to recharge.'

'Recharge?' Steve looked confused. 'She only has nine hours of lectures a week.'

'Yes,' I said carefully. 'But it's a big adjustment, living on her own, being in a new place, learning to make decisions and, er, budget.'

'Don't need to worry about that.' Steve smiled. 'If there's one piece of wisdom I've passed down, it's look after the pennies, and the pounds will look after themselves.'

I winced. If looking after the pennies meant releasing them from the confines of a bank account out into the world, then Sophie had followed his wisdom to the letter. I decided not to mention that part just yet. No point spoiling his evening.

Steve watched me add Sophie's salt lamp to the enormous bag of clothes. 'How long is she recharging for? She won't get a refund on the lectures she misses.'

'I'm sure it won't be for long,' I said more optimistically than I felt.

Steve frowned. 'Did you know, statistically, students are—'

'You'd better get back to your quizzing,' I said, before he launched into a presentation to rival any statistician's, complete with flip chart and pointer. 'Don't want to stop the flow.' I hadn't told him about my redundancy, but that bombshell could wait for another time.

Steve carried the bags and mirror downstairs while I went into the kitchen to get the air fryer. Collette was still standing by the fridge, where we'd left her. We smiled politely at one another. I peeked in the air fryer. It was spotless, so Steve clearly hadn't mastered the art of using it. Although, I realised as I glanced around the kitchen, everywhere was spotless. So, he was capable of cleaning up after himself; he just chose not to.

'If Sophie's finding uni too much, she's better off leaving or she'll be in debt for nothing,' Steve said, as we loaded everything into my car.

'Let's not put any ideas into her head,' I said. 'This has to be her decision.'

'Tell her I'll call her tomorrow,' he said, giving me a goodbye peck on the cheek.

I jumped into my car and sped home. I had just twenty-four hours to put my own ideas into Sophie's head.

# Chapter 19

'Have you seen the state of the bathroom?' Josephine hurtled into the utility room where I was multi-tasking ironing and hiding. 'The floor's like a paddling pool and her clothes are all over the floor. She can't leave it in that state. It's appalling.'

When Sophie had arrived the previous day, Josephine had been twirling a pencil like a baton, in delight. The reality of sharing a space with a housework-shy student hadn't lasted long. I had to admit, I hadn't missed that side of Sophie's absence, particularly after a fake-tan session. Somehow, more product ended up smeared on the bath, toilet seat and towels than on Sophie's skin.

'The problem is she doesn't care if the place is a mess,' I said, taking one of Josephine's blouses out of the basket. 'When someone genuinely doesn't care, it's impossible to motivate them.'

'Well, I care, and it's my house.' Josephine pumped some cream into her palm from a pot that was on top of the washing machine. She began massaging it into her skin, with the fingertips that poked out from her splint. She was using her sling less, and her fingers were definitely regaining their strength. Decades of hand workouts and getting someone else to do all the menial tasks for her had paid off. 'You need to tell her to be more respectful,' Josephine added. 'And maintain my standards while she's living under my roof.'

Did she think I hadn't tried? If I had a pound for every time I'd asked Sophie to clear up after herself, I'd be living in New York and hanging out with Carrie and co from *Sex and the City*. Yes, I was aware that they were characters, not real people, but I could afford to pay the actors to pretend to be. That's how many times I'd asked Sophie.

'Just as well she's only staying for a few days, if this is how she behaves,' Josephine tutted.

'It might be a bit longer than a few days,' I said. My attempt to get Sophie to reconsider the night before had fallen on deaf ears. Literally – she'd put her headphones on to shut me out. I lowered my voice. 'She's run out of money and the honeymoon period of being away's worn off a bit. She says she wants to leave uni, but—'

'She's dropping out?' Josephine said, aghast. 'It's like history repeating itself.'

My heart pinched. 'Sophie hasn't just discovered that Steve isn't her dad. Not quite the same, is it?'

Josephine's cheeks reddened. 'I've told you how much I regret what happened. Please stop bringing it up. Geoff *was* your dad in every way that mattered.'

I stared down at the ironing board and blinked hard. I didn't keep bringing it up. On the contrary, it had barely been discussed in thirty years. I knew that a trained therapist wouldn't advocate this method of avoidance.

No doubt an untrained one wouldn't either, but I didn't see the point. It wouldn't change anything. She'd still have cheated on my dad and delivered the news like a gut punch, when I was at my most vulnerable.

Josephine took a deep breath. 'So, you and Sophie are here for the unforeseeable future, then?'

'No,' I said quickly. Unforeseeable was far too scary a concept. I needed our exit to be very seeable. 'Only till your wrist's healed.'

'Another month, then?'

Bloody hell, I hoped not. That was the average recovery time for a fracture, but the thought of four more weeks here was like staring into the abyss. Or into Josephine's cleaning cupboard, which was equally terrifying.

'I'm sure you won't need me here for that long,' I said briskly. 'You haven't had any more dizzy spells and you can do things by yourself when you want to.' I pointed to the hand cream that she'd just applied to prove my point.

'That's taken it out of me, actually. I'd better have a rest,' Josephine said weakly. 'Please tell Sophie to be tidier. The stress isn't good for my blood pressure.' She eased her wrist back into its sling and winced loudly. 'It's not fair on Rey either. He uses the facilities too.'

My cheeks burst into flames at his name. I should go and thank him for the airbed and his help tidying the spare room, but the memory of his shocked face when he saw me on the landing in my bra was too mortifying. I'd have to avoid him even more now.

'I'll ask Sophie to be more considerate,' I said, hanging the blouse I'd just ironed on the airer. 'But she's an adult and likes to do things her own way in her own time. I can't force her.'

'If you won't tell her, I will,' Josephine said, her delicate voice now back at full pelt as she started to leave the room. 'No wonder she wants to come back, when you do everything for her.' She silently clicked her fingers in the direction of the blouse I'd just hung up. 'Stop biting your nails and give that another once-over. I can see a crease.'

'Bloody double standards,' I muttered to myself, waving the iron in the vague direction of her blouse. Whenever I asked Sophie to hang up a wet towel, she said she'd do it in a sec. No wonder she was often bored. A second for her could last for up to three weeks. Each individual day must drag on for months.

Josephine had closed the door to the utility room behind her, leaving it so coated in hand cream that I had to use the hem of my top to open it, and then do the same again in the kitchen. It was easy to see where she was headed. I just had to follow the trail of slime. She'd gone into the living room, where Sophie was holed up watching TV. The door was ajar, making it easy for me to overhear their conversation.

'If we all do our bit, it's a nicer place to live,' Josephine was saying. I couldn't help but smirk at her attempt. I'd tried every strategy to get Sophie to tidy up – asking, coaxing, cajoling, guilt-tripping, bribery, blackmail, begging – nothing worked. 'I'm not asking you to do anything I wouldn't do,' Josephine continued. That was a blatant lie. She just about managed to hang her towel up, but she didn't clean her bathroom. I bloody well did. The door opened, and I sprung back and busied myself wiping hand cream off the banister. Sophie came out and headed straight upstairs.

Josephine followed and gave me a triumphant smile. 'All you have to do is exercise a little authority.'

'Just because she's gone upstairs doesn't mean she's tidying the bathroom,' I said. 'She's getting away from you.'

We heard the bathroom door open and eyed each other. Josephine was playing it cool, but her flared nostrils gave her away. I realised I was biting my nails and curled my hands into fists, willing Sophie to be using the facilities. I wasn't sure how I'd handle the hurt and disloyalty if she was cleaning up after one request from Josephine, after ignoring my millions of desperate pleas over the years. Or, even worse, how I'd handle Josephine's smugness.

The bathroom door slammed shut and Sophie hammered down the stairs, her arms full of clothes, her face flushed.

'There's a man in the shower,' she gasped.

Josephine's hand went to her mouth. 'I forgot Rey was in there.'

Sophie looked between the two of us, clearly unsure whether to be impressed or revolted. 'Who's Rey?'

'He's renting the coach house,' Josephine said. 'But the hot water's gone, so he's showering here.'

Sophie glanced back up the stairs and grinned. 'He's got a nice arse.'

'Sophie,' I said sharply.

She bit her lip. 'Yeah, sorry. I shouldn't objectify him.'

'No,' I said primly, although I was more annoyed about the image of Rey she'd managed to plant in my mind: his toned, athletic, naked body, with water cascading down him. It was enough to make my stomach plummet – all the way down between my legs. What was wrong with me? I was behaving as though I hadn't had sex for a decade, which was ridiculous. It had only been about three years. 'He's old enough to be your father,' I added. 'His son's in the first year of uni too.'

'Ew, gross.' Sophie visibly shuddered. 'I only saw him from behind. He looked younger.'

'He's always running,' Josephine said, staring eagerly up the stairs. 'Or at the gym.'

'Why doesn't he shower there, then?' I snapped. 'Instead of hogging our bathroom and scaring Sophie.'

'I wasn't scared,' Sophie said. 'I have seen a naked man before.' Her cheeks reddened, as she remembered she was talking to her mum and grandmother. 'In the film *Saltburn*,' she added. 'What's that?' She pointed to the small dent in the wall opposite the foot of the stairs. Since it had been there her entire lifetime, she was clearly desperate to change the subject.

'Your mother decided to sledge inside,' Josephine tutted. 'She came flying down those stairs . . .' She made a dramatic sweeping motion with her good arm. 'And straight into the wall. You'd think she'd know better at seventeen.'

Sophie's eyes widened. 'Sounds a bit wild for you, Mum. You won't leave the house without anti-slip grips on your shoes if there's even a bit of frost.'

'She was a different person back then,' Josephine said. 'Your mother used to have some spunk.' She jabbed the air to emphasise the word 'spunk', in case raising her voice tenfold wasn't emphasis enough.

And, of course, that was the exact moment Rey appeared at the top of the stairs. With just a towel around his waist. My cheeks instantly burst into flames and I looked away. Sophie and Josephine felt no such need to give him some privacy and were openly objectifying him with their gawping. The word 'spunk' was still reverberating around the hall.

'Sorry,' Rey said.

'Nothing to apologise for,' Josephine said, fluffing out her pale copper waves.

Rey cleared his throat. 'My clothes seem to have disappeared while I was in the shower.'

'Oh, shit.' Sophie looked at the clothes in her arms. 'Sorry, I thought they were mine. G told me to tidy the bathroom and I grabbed everything.' She giggled. 'I didn't see anything, honest.'

'Me neither,' said Josephine. Even someone deaf could have picked up on the disappointment in her voice.

'I expect Rey would like his clothes back,' I said sharply, glaring at them both. 'He's probably getting cold.'

Josephine reached for the clothes in Sophie's arms but struggled to grip them with just the one hand.

'I'll take them,' I said firmly. Since Josephine could undress him with her eyes from a few metres away, I dreaded to think what she'd achieve up close.

I carried them up the stairs to where Rey was patiently waiting, one hand gripping the towel around his waist. I focused on my feet till I reached him, then whipped my eyes up to his face, in no way registering his flat stomach, his chest covered by a smattering of dark hair or his toned arms.

'So sorry,' I said, handing him the clothes.

'My daily showers certainly aren't dull,' he chuckled, taking them.

My face grew hot, as I recalled swinging practically topless from the loft hatch the day before.

'Is the bed OK?' he asked.

My hand flew to my mouth as I acknowledged my rudeness. 'It's amazing,' I said. 'Sorry I wasn't here. Sophie got an earlier train. You really didn't have to make the bed or clean up or put the diffuser in her room. That was so thoughtful. I should have come straight round to say thank you, but got distracted by Sophie. Sorry.'

'No problem,' Rey said. 'The bed's a bit fiddly when you don't know what you're doing and I don't mind cleaning.'

A man who looked like this and didn't mind cleaning? It was a wonder David Attenborough hadn't dedicated an entire series to such a rare species.

'Well, thank you. It was really kind.' Our eyes met and my stomach contracted in a way usually reserved for Indiana Jones. 'Bye, then.' I turned and ran down the stairs almost as quickly as I'd descended them in the sledge all those years ago.

Sophie had retreated to the living room to continue lying down, watching TV. She'd been up for almost an hour, so no wonder she was exhausted, poor love. I went into the kitchen and frowned at my empty cafetière. Every time I filled it, it miraculously emptied itself. Josephine swore blind she didn't 'do' coffee, but what she really meant was that she didn't 'make' coffee. I joined Sophie in the living room. She was stretched out on the sofa, so I lifted her feet, sat at the end and rested them in my lap. I stroked her feet in their fluffy socks. This was what I'd missed. Little moments of intimacy that maintained our connection. It was hard to get that via a weekly FaceTime call. It was so tempting to encourage her impulse to leave uni, so she'd stay here with me, but I'd be doing it for my benefit, not hers. That wasn't the kind of mum I wanted to be. No, I needed to get her to see the bigger picture and then decide for sure what she wanted to do.

'Have you thought any more about going back till Christmas and then seeing how you feel?' I asked gently.

'No,' Sophie said.

Did that mean no, she hadn't given it any thought, or no, she wasn't going back? I opened my mouth to ask.

Sophie put a hand up. 'When I've made a decision, I'll tell you,' she said firmly. I closed my mouth. 'Dad rang. He thinks I should leave and get out into the workplace.'

I gnawed on a nail to supress a wail of frustration. After taking a back seat in parenting for almost two decades, he'd now decided to get involved? His excuse had always been that I was better at it all than he was. He seemed to believe I'd had a special chip inserted into my brain during labour that gave me instant knowledge and wisdom on magically making colic, teething pains and tantrums disappear; how to teach basic life skills such as using the toilet, crossing a road, and not sticking things into toasters, exhaust pipes or nostrils; and how to get poo, blood, vomit and pasta sauce stains out of clothing. If only. No, like all mums who hadn't been created by Hallmark, I'd made it up as I went along. But now he was jumping in and advising Sophie on what was best for his wallet rather than what was best for her.

'We're going for lunch on Saturday to talk about it,' Sophie said.

'I'll come too,' I said. I wasn't going to let Steve steamroll Sophie into going through with her decision to quit uni. She didn't need much encouragement and would possibly sign away her education to get him to stop talking.

'K. We're going to that café by the market.'

'Great.' I gave Sophie's feet another rub and got ready to stand up. I was aware I should get on with my feature for MAAM. Actually, it wasn't just a case that I should – I genuinely wanted to. I'd made a start and was getting more fulfilment than I had from *Norwich Now* for years. Which reminded me that I hadn't told Steve I wasn't working there anymore.

'Sophs,' I said casually. 'Do me a favour and don't mention my redundancy on Saturday.'

Sophie looked up from the TV. 'Why not?'

I hesitated, unwilling to admit, both to her and myself, that when I'd tried to tell Steve the night before, he'd interrupted me, as he always did when I spoke. That rather than missing him and realising how much he meant to me, this enforced time apart – and our differing opinion on what Sophie should do about uni – was actually highlighting what little connection we had.

'I haven't had a chance to tell Dad yet.' I cringed at how pathetic that sounded.

Sophie chewed her lip and I held my breath. Was she about to ask if something else was going on? Maybe her lack of interest was a mask, and in reality she was acutely aware that things between her parents weren't as solid as they should, or could, be. She looked directly at me and I swallowed hard.

'K. Can you get me some crisps before you go upstairs, please,' she said, turning her attention back to the TV.

I breathed a sigh of relief. Thank goodness for the self-absorbed nature of eighteen-year-olds. I could have sex on the coffee table with Rey and she wouldn't notice unless a limb obscured the TV screen.

My face flushed so hot, my eyes watered. Where the bloody hell had that image come from? And what was I going to do with it now?

# Chapter 20

The rest of the week sped by. I'd started work on my piece for MAAM, but every time I sat down to write, Josephine would summon me for something urgent, such as to replace the lemon in her water or take her for a pedicure. Or Sophie would need me to find a claw clip she'd mislaid, or wash her puffer coat without losing any of the puff, or help her dye her hair. While she'd been away, I'd remembered this activity with fondness, but it took just one session of Sophie shrieking that I was getting water down her back and shampoo in her eyes, followed by a crime scene-level clean-up operation to remove all traces of pink dye, to realise that my rose-tinted glasses needed a new prescription.

Before I knew it, it was Saturday, and Sophie and I were going up the city to meet Steve for lunch.

'Stop walking so fast,' Sophie grumbled. 'I'm tired.'

She was sulking because I'd refused to drive when it was a beautiful, crisp November day and it only took fifteen minutes to walk. I'd had to threaten to pull the plug on her airbed to get her out of it that morning. She'd got a job at the local pub and had worked till midnight, but I suspected her bad mood was less tiredness and more the anticipation of a lecture from Steve.

Eventually, we arrived at the café and sat at the table Steve had secured. Unfortunately, the table itself wasn't secured to the floor and tipped up every time one of us put any pressure on it. Steve's tea sloshed out of his cup when I put a hand on the table to lean down to kiss his cheek.

'How are you, Sophie?' he asked, as we both sat opposite him.

'OK, thanks,' Sophie said, holding her phone aloft while I mopped up spilt tea with a napkin. 'How are you?'

'Mustn't grumble,' Steve said, then launched into a ten-minute grumble about rising insurance claims costs, diminishing profits and the drop in share value. Thankfully, the waitress came and took our order before Sophie and I zoned out so completely, we wound up in a parallel universe.

We exchanged polite chit-chat till their meals of egg and chips, and my tap water arrived. My water was warmer than their meals looked, but they ate them anyway.

'Now, young lady,' Steve said once they'd finished. 'About uni.' He took his glasses off and shook out a handkerchief, then opened his mouth wide and breathed on each lens, before cleaning them. 'As you know, I'm not a fan, because of the excessive debt it creates.' Sophie squirmed and I felt my cheeks glow. 'But if you want to study,' he continued, 'my advice is to choose a vocation. Get a qualification that you can actually use.'

I looked at him with surprise. He'd actually given it some thought. This gave me hope. I could find my way back to this version of Steve. Although I'd encourage a different method of cleaning his glasses – one that didn't involve practically ramming them down his throat.

Steve put his sparklingly clean glasses back on and produced a ream of papers from somewhere. 'I've found the perfect course for you at the University of West England.' He placed a prospectus on the table in front of Sophie. 'Risk Management and Insurance.' Sophie made a strangled sound. 'You can do it part-time over two years, or an intensive one-year course, which makes much more sense,' Steve said. 'You'd have to wait till next September, but that gives you ten months to work and pay off the debts you've accrued.'

Sophie's face was ashen and she seemed to be having trouble breathing. I placed a hand over hers.

'Steve . . .' I started. 'It's really kind of you to have looked into all of this, but—'

Steve held up a finger. 'I know what you're going to say – where can Sophie find a decent job that'll earn enough to pay off all that money?'

'No, I—'

'No need to fret,' Steve said. 'I've got you a placement at my company. Starting next week.'

Sophie was hyperventilating now.

'Steve—'

'With that invaluable experience, and this qualification, you'll be set up for a job for life.' Steve rubbed his hands together.

I manoeuvred Sophie so that her head was between her knees and told her to take deep breaths. Steve didn't notice. He was too busy citing the joys of the industry and being proud of himself.

'Mum.' Sophie gripped my hands. 'Help.'

'Don't worry,' I said softly. 'You don't have to do this if you don't want to.'

'I'd rather die,' Sophie whimpered. That seemed fairly cut and dried to me.

I sat up straight. Steve was still talking, oblivious to the fact his daughter was slumped under the table, having a panic attack.

'Steve,' I said sharply.

He paused mid-sentence about his heady days as an insurance clerk. 'What?' He frowned as Sophie emerged from beneath the table.

'Can I go, please?' she whispered. I nodded. 'Bye, Dad.' Sophie scurried away, like an animal escaping from captivity.

'Where's she going?' Steve asked.

'To get some fresh air.' I placed a hand on the prospectus. 'Thank you for your hard work. It's really kind of you to have put so much thought and effort into it.'

Steve smiled. 'It's the perfect solution, isn't it?'

I chose my words carefully, not wanting to discourage his first attempt at parenting in, ooh, about eighteen years. 'For some people, this would indeed be perfect,' I said. 'But not for Sophie.' Steve's face fell. 'It doesn't take anything away from your efforts, but a career in insurance isn't for her.'

'Why not?'

The day wasn't long enough to list all the reasons. 'She's more suited to something creative,' I said diplomatically.

Steve took his glasses off and rubbed his eyes. 'I thought this was a good compromise,' he sighed.

Guilt gnawed at me for being so dismissive. His input was misguided, but it was well intended.

'I know,' I said. 'And I appreciate it. But we need to let her do what *she's* interested in, not what interests us.'

Steve nodded. 'If she's not at uni, she has to find employment. She can't sit around all day.'

'She's not,' I said truthfully. She was lying around all day, not sitting. 'She's got some shifts at The Vic.'

Steve sighed. 'If she leaves uni, she has to repay the first term's maintenance loan that she's already had, plus twenty-five per cent of the tuition fees for the year. A few shifts at The Vic aren't going to cut it.' He leant forward. 'Can you ask her to think about this job? She might find she enjoys it. It can get quite exciting in the claims department.'

I frowned. 'Doesn't Collette work in claims?'

Steve's ears went pink.

'Is that how you know about the job?'

'Um.'

I picked up the prospectus. 'Did she put all this together too?' He didn't reply, which meant she had. So much for Steve pulling his weight for once. He'd got someone else to do it for him. Not just someone – Collette.

'That's very kind of her,' I said. 'To research courses and job opportunities, especially on top of the Christmas quiz.' I watched him carefully. Was she on top of anything else? His cock, for example? I felt my cheeks flush at such a crude thought. What was wrong with me? I hadn't given that part of Steve's anatomy a second thought for years. Not even when it was inside me.

Steve shrugged. 'She has a lot of time on her hands. Both her children have flown the nest and her husband died a few years ago.'

'Oh. Sorry to hear that.' I was such a cow. Here was a lovely widow, helping out, and I was judging her for her career choice and beige pleated skirt. 'Please thank her for us.' I nibbled on a nail. 'Are you OK being on your own in the house?'

Steve shrugged again. 'It's a bit quiet. My sister's popping in to keep an eye on the place.' That explained why the house was spotless. Why wasn't he doing his own bloody cleaning? My right eye twitched. Steve didn't notice. 'How long till Josephine's recovered and you can come home?' he asked.

'Why? So you can get your usual cleaner back?' I said hotly. 'Isn't your sixty-three-year-old sister doing a good enough job for you?'

Steve's mouth fell open. 'Where's that outburst come from? I merely asked after the welfare of my mother-in-law.'

'You didn't ask how she was, actually?' I snapped. 'You asked how much longer I have to stay there for.'

Steve shook his head. 'I understand that the situation must be challenging for you – goodness knows, I couldn't live with the woman – but there's no need to take it out on me.' He stood up. 'I have to go. My free parking runs out soon.' He bent and gave me a chaste kiss on the cheek, then left.

I stared after him. Was he right? Was I taking my frustration with the situation out on him? Or was the increasingly dire state of our marriage the real situation?

# Chapter 21

'Much better,' Josephine said with satisfaction.

I stared at my reflection. Annoyingly, she was right. When I'd told her that Nikki was taking me to The Ivy for lunch, she'd insisted I borrow an outfit from her, rather than wear my usual skinny jeans and long-sleeved tee or my floral shirt dress. She'd picked out a chic navy, calf-length, sleeveless dress with a matching cropped cardigan that tied under the bust, and some navy ballet flats.

I hadn't dared apply my usual thick foundation, in case it marked the neckline. The dress was cashmere and would cost a fortune to replace. Almost as much as Sophie's outstanding fees. Or an average night on the tiles for her. I'd tried to cover my freckles with translucent powder but, being translucent, all it did was make me look slightly less shiny. Josephine had dabbed some brown shadow on my lids and talked me through how to apply mascara without it clogging. Her cast had come off two days before, but her right wrist was very weak and not yet up to the task of combing my eyebrows. Her blood pressure was also back to normal, which meant no more risk of dizzy spells and no more compression socks. The socks had been infinitely better news to her than the risk of falling again.

Nikki rang the doorbell before I'd had a chance to straighten my hair. I hurried down the stairs to let her in.

'Wow,' she said. 'You look amazing.'

'I'm so pasty, though.' I looked at myself in the hall mirror. 'If it wasn't for my stupid freckles, I'd be transparent.'

'Your freckles are pretty. It's a crime to cover them up.' Nikki opened her handbag and took out a red lipstick. 'Put this on to give yourself some colour.'

'Thank you. I'll straighten my hair first.'

'No,' Nikki said firmly. 'It suits you so much better wavy.'

I looked again at my reflection. All I could see was a big ball of frizz. I eyed Nikki's perfectly coiled hair enviously.

'OK,' Nikki conceded. 'It needs a bloody good cut. But please don't straighten and scrape it back. Have a gentle updo or something.'

As if I knew how to do that. I settled for a soft ponytail at the nape of my neck, fastened with a clip rather than a band, and then applied a coat of Nikki's lipstick.

'Perfect,' Nikki said. She put an arm around me and smiled at my reflection. 'How are you holding up?'

'I feel a bit unsettled,' I said quietly.

'Any particular reason?'

The front door opened and Rey walked in, dressed in running shorts and a vest, his sports bag over his shoulder. His dark hair was damp and a light sheen of sweat glistened on his defined arms.

Nikki's eyes widened to the size of dinner plates. 'Sweet Jesus,' she murmured. 'There's my answer.'

Thankfully, the sound of the door closing drowned out her words.

'Hi.' Rey smiled and held out a hand. 'I'm Rey, Josephine's lodger.'

'Nice to meet you. I'm Nikki.' She stepped forward and shook his hand, a huge smile on her face. 'So, you're in the coach house?' she said. 'Such a shame the hot water's out of action.'

Rey nodded. 'Hopefully, it'll be fixed soon and I can stop disturbing everyone.' His eyes slid to mine and my cheeks flushed at the memory of the time he'd disturbed me in the loft. And the time after that, when he'd appeared in his towel, which had resulted in some very disturbing thoughts. He smiled at me. 'You look nice.' He gestured to Nikki. 'Both of you. Going somewhere fancy?'

'The Ivy for lunch,' I said. 'Nikki's treating me.'

'Nice. Celebrating anything in particular?'

'We're celebrating life,' she said with a smile, then headed towards the living room. 'I'll just say hi to Sophie before we go.'

'I like her attitude,' Rey said.

I nodded and went to bite my thumbnail, before realising it'd smudge Nikki's red lipstick. I reached behind my head to tighten my ponytail instead, forgetting that it wasn't in its usual band. The hair clip fell to the floor.

Rey picked it up and handed it to me. Our hands brushed and I felt a jolt of something I hadn't felt for a very long time.

'Thank you.' I turned to the mirror to clip my hair back into place, then took a long, caramel coat from the cupboard under the stairs, which Josephine had told me to borrow. My usual khaki waterproof didn't work with the cashmere dress. As I put the coat on, the strap of my bag got caught in one of the sleeves and, within seconds, it was a tangled mess.

'Here, let me.' Rey dropped his bag onto the floor, took the coat and held it up. He was so close, I could feel his breath on my neck, as I slipped my arms into the sleeves. I forgot to hold on to the cuffs of the cardigan, so the sleeves slid up and bunched at the elbows, making it impossible for me to bend my arms. Rather than admit this, I stood with my arms poker straight, at forty-five-degree angles to my body, as though I were a 1980s action figure.

Nikki came out of the living room and smiled at Rey. 'Good to meet you.'

'You, too.' He picked up his bag and headed up the stairs. 'Have a nice lunch.'

I waited till he was gone, shrugged my coat off and adjusted my cardigan. 'I don't know what it is about that man, but he manages to make me all flustered, and I do something stupid every time I see him,' I whispered. I went into the living room to said goodbye to Sophie and Josephine and emerged twenty seconds later with an order of micellar water for the former and cod liver oil for the latter.

Nikki took my arm, as we walked across the drive. 'Flustered, eh?'

'Not like that,' I tutted. 'Just now, for example, he was helping me put my coat on and it got bunched up.'

'That doesn't sound that stupid.'

'No,' I admitted. 'The worst one was when I fell out of the loft and my top came off.'

'Whaaat?' Nikki spun round.

'It's not as bad as it sounds.' I thought back to the shock on Rey's face when he saw me in my bra. 'OK, maybe it was as bad.' Nikki stared at me, her mouth agape. A giggle escaped me, then another. Nikki joined in and within seconds we were both laughing hysterically. It felt so good. I hadn't laughed in ages.

'I've missed you,' I said when we eventually composed ourselves.

'You, too.' She slipped her arm through mine. 'Sorry I haven't been around.'

We stopped at a pelican crossing and I pushed the button. 'Don't apologise. You need to be there for your family. It's not as if I haven't been busy. Josephine comes up with a more elaborate task every day for me to do. She'll have me up on the roof polishing each tile individually before the week's out.'

'Can't you get Rey to help? Offer to fall off and lose your top again.'

We exchanged a giggle.

'Seriously, though.' Nikki fanned her face. 'He is hot. No wonder he makes you *flustered*.'

The green man beeped loudly. The unwanted image of Rey and I having sex on the breakfast bar flashed through my mind and my stomach flipped over. 'I don't think of him like that,' I said, hurrying across the road so that Nikki couldn't see my flushed face. 'And I'm married, remember?' I realised that I hadn't told her about Collette. 'Can't believe I forgot to tell you this – Steve's got a new female friend. She was round our house when I went to get Sophie's things last week.'

Nikki gasped. 'What was she doing at your house?'

'She's helping him with the work Christmas quiz. It's harmless.'

'I thought he wrote it in July,' Nikki said.

'He starts it then, but adds the topical questions at the end.' I said this without criticism. Steve's organisation was his key strength. A well-structured itinerary without the threat of spontaneity was as comforting as a security blanket.

'You're sure she's just a friend?' Nikki asked.

'Yes,' I said, with complete confidence. Steve wasn't the cheating type. I really couldn't imagine him in bed with anyone. Myself included, which, admittedly, was a huge part of the problem.

I filled Nikki in on what I knew about Collette and how she'd found a job and a potential insurance degree course for Sophie. 'Not that she wants to do that, of course,' I said. 'So he's dumped it all back on me.' I exhaled loudly. 'So much for this enforced break making him realise how much I do. He's got his sister cleaning for him and a colleague giving career advice for his daughter. He's carrying on as normal, responsibility-free, while I look after Josephine and her house, and try and coax Sophie back into education and not begrudge cleaning up her crap after weeks of missing her like crazy.'

Nikki tutted. 'This isn't fair. Especially when you're looking for another job too.'

I winced, and not purely because of the hangnail I'd just tugged at. 'I haven't told him about my redundancy yet.'

Nikki looked at me sideways. 'Why not?'

I'd been asking myself the same question. The conclusion I'd reached was that I didn't have the energy for his response, which would be so drawn out, it'd require popcorn, a detailed programme and several pre-agreed comfort breaks. It wasn't normal to keep something so momentous from one's partner, though, and this didn't bode well for bringing us closer together.

'I've been waiting to find out what package I'm getting,' I said instead. 'Ruby from HR's still off sick, so I've no idea yet.'

Nikki inhaled sharply. 'You need to take this higher. It's been more than three weeks now.'

I nodded. 'I will. I just want to get Sophie sorted first.'

We reached The Ivy and Nikki ordered a bottle of wine.

'Do you remember when we went out a few weeks ago and talked about this being your second act and opportunity for a comeback?' she asked.

I nodded. That was just before I'd been made redundant and moved in with Josephine. Back in the good old days.

'And how the whole point of this second act is to do things for yourself?' Nikki continued. 'Well, you can't do that if you're putting everyone else first.'

'I'm not going to turn my back on Sophie. She's come home because she needs help, even if she doesn't think she does.'

'Of course,' Nikki said. 'But she doesn't need help buying micellar water. Refusing to buy it won't make her love you less. It'll make her realise that she needs to do it herself. And Josephine's wrist's getting better. You don't need to prop them up the whole time. As for Steve . . .' She trailed off and I suspected that was because the waiter had arrived with our bottle and she didn't want to be thrown out for using abusive language.

She waited till he'd poured the wine, then raised her glass. 'This is *your* second act. Time to focus on things that excite *you*, remember?' She paused. 'Or that make you flustered,' she added with a wink.

My cheeks burst into flames.

# Chapter 22

The next day I woke with a renewed determination to sort my life out. This was my *second act* and I wasn't going to waste it. After helping Josephine get up, I went to the gym, then headed back to work on my feature for MAAM.

Josephine pounced on me the moment I got through the front door. 'Could you put some laundry on for me, please?' she asked in a delicate voice, clutching her wrist.

Giving a resigned nod, I ran upstairs to get the laundry basket, then made my way to the utility room. I opened the washing machine door, only to discover it was full of Sophie's wet clothes. I sighed heavily. This was one of her favourite tricks. Put a load on, then leave it, knowing I'd need to use the machine so would end up sorting it out. Well, no more. I loved her more than life itself, but she could blooming well do her own laundry. Before I could change my mind, I transferred it into an enormous bag for life, put mine and Josephine's washing on, and fled.

To my astonishment, Sophie was at the breakfast bar, eating a bowl of rice crispies, her phone propped up against the cereal box. I looked out of the window to make sure it was ten o'clock in the morning, not the evening.

'Are you OK?' I asked, filling the kettle and spooning coffee into my cafetière.

She blew her pink fringe out of her eyes. 'Why wouldn't I be?'

'No reason.' I wouldn't aggravate her by pointing out that usually this was classed as the middle of the night. I had other things to aggravate her about.

Sophie topped up her bowl with more cereal and poured milk to the brim of the bowl, which promptly sloshed over the side when she put her spoon in.

I fought the urge to tell her to clean up the mess. Pick your battles. 'Your washing's in the utility room,' I said. 'I had to take it out to put another load on, so you might want to put it in the tumble dryer or hang it on the airer.'

'I'll do it in a sec,' Sophie said, not looking up from her phone.

'Make sure you do, or it'll start to smell,' I said, pouring hot water into my cafetière.

'Don't put my cream sweater in the tumble dryer,' Josephine said. 'It needs to air-dry on a flat surface.'

'How come you do G's washing, but not mine?' Sophie asked.

'Hands.' Josephine made a fluid motion with her good arm, as though doing some form of interpretive dance. A very crap form. 'I can't risk the detergents damaging my skin.'

I raised my eyes to the ceiling. 'It's not exactly chemical warfare. You only have to put a tablet in the machine.'

Sophie slid off her stool and headed towards the door.

'Hang on.' I gestured to the bowl, milk carton, and coating of milk and rice crispies all over the breakfast bar. 'You need to tidy these away.'

'I will.' Sophie darted out of the room. The living-room door shut and moments later the TV blared out.

Sighing, I turned to pour out my coffee, but the cafetière was empty. I spun round. Josephine avoided my gaze as she sipped from a mug.

Gritting my teeth, I poured myself a glass of water. 'I'm going to my room to work on my MAAM feature.'

I turned around to leave and took in the carton of milk and mess that Sophie had left. She'd said she'd clear it up later. I had to hold my nerve and leave it for her, while I got on with my feature. My right eye twitched. But the milk would go off. I had to put that in the fridge. Rice crispies crunched beneath my feet as I crossed the kitchen. I couldn't leave them, I just couldn't.

Josephine eyed me over her mug – correction, *my* mug – as I swept them up. 'You're not helping her,' she said.

I tightened my grip on the dustpan and brush.

'Doing everything for her isn't teaching anything about responsibility or consequences. She won't have any life skills,' Josephine continued. 'Hashtag keeping it real.'

'What?' I said, standing up.

'Hashtag keeping it real,' she repeated.

'I heard you. I don't understand you.'

Josephine beamed as though she were privy to some superior knowledge. 'It's what the influencers say. Sophie showed me some on her phone.'

I rolled my eyes. 'You're not supposed to say the hashtag.'

'Nonsense. They use it constantly and I don't blame them. It's a wonderful word.' She wove her hands in and out while chanting: 'Haaaassssshtag.'

Turning my back on her in the hope she'd go away, I wiped down the breakfast bar.

Josephine tutted. 'Didn't you listen to what I just said? Sophie won't hashtag respect you if you do everything for her.' She put her mug down by the sink. 'I'm going to join Sophie in the living room. Bring some water with lemon through, would you.'

Like a pre-programmed puppet, I rinsed Josephine's mug and put it in the dishwasher, then poured her some water and added ice and lemon, before realising what I was doing. Did Josephine, Sophie and Steve have some power that enabled them to manipulate me into doing what they wanted without me having any say in the matter? If this was my second act, I'd happily fast-forward to the third one.

In the living room, Sophie was stretched out on the sofa, watching TV. Josephine sat in her velvet throne armchair, doing hand-strengthening exercises. God forbid she should strengthen them by actually picking something up.

I plonked the glass on the coffee table, pleased when some sloshed out. Until I remembered that I was the one who'd be wiping it up. 'Anything else, madam?'

Josephine didn't pick up on the sarcasm dripping from every word. 'No, thank you.' I turned to leave. 'Actually, yes,' she said. 'Pass me that little ball, would you.'

Was she having a laugh? Why was she sitting around finding jobs for me to do instead of focusing on her career?

'What happened to your Spotlight on Silver Supermodels campaign?' I asked sharply. 'Shouldn't you be working on that rather than watching TV?'

Josephine waved a hand. 'The problem is, much as we love my idea, we're not sure how to present it. It's all very well you telling me to launch a campaign, but some information on how to put it together would have been helpful. Surely, you don't expect me to go knocking on doors.'

'Of course not,' I said. 'Heaven forbid you bruise your knuckles.'

Josephine protectively cradled her weak hand.

I sighed inwardly. Expecting a ninety- and seventy-year-old to be adept at a modern marketing campaign was like expecting a horse-drawn carriage to have cruise control. 'Tell the advertisers that they're being ageist and should represent their target demographic with age-appropriate models,' I said.

'Write that down, would you,' Josephine said. 'With a list of suitable companies for us to contact.'

'Shall I put a proposal together too?' I said dryly. 'And a script?'

'Yes, please.'

My mouth dropped open. 'I wasn't being serious. I have a feature to write and I need to find my own job. I haven't got time to do Audrey's for her. She should be spearheading your campaign. That's what you pay her for.'

Josephine's nostrils flared. Why was she so touchy whenever I mentioned Audrey? Audrey was the perfect person for this, having been around when spearheads were in daily use.

Sophie's phone beeped and she stirred to read a message. Frustration coursed through me at the lack of care about her future.

'Had any thoughts about going back to uni?' I asked her.

Sophie sighed. 'Not this again.'

I tightened my ponytail. 'You can't keep putting it off. You need to make a decision.'

Sophie put a hand up and exhaled loudly. 'You do you. Let me do me.'

'Fine,' I said, turning sharply and heading out of the room. 'I'll go and do me, then.'

'Do me first,' Josephine called. 'The list and proposal.'

'I told you,' I snapped. 'Just think of the products you and Audrey rely on. Liver spot creams, colostomy bags, haemorrhoid cream, that kind of thing.'

Josephine's mouth puckered and I stomped up the stairs before guilt forced me into apologising.

I slammed my bedroom door, sat down at my little desk and opened my laptop. I would not let them spoil my second act. In fact, I would accept the lunch offer from Nina and Cath. Sod turning it down to stay here and look after Josephine. Sophie could keep an eye on her. She had a perfect vantage point from the sofa.

An alert popped up on my screen, notifying me that the online MAAM meet-up was starting in . . . two minutes!

Fear gripped me. I wasn't mentally prepared for this. I was still wound up from being treated like a servant by my mother and daughter, and I hadn't even had a coffee yet, as Josephine had pinched it. I stared at the Zoom invite code, my heart racing. It'd be so easy to pretend I'd had to take Josephine to a medical appointment and couldn't make it. But what message was that sending to Nina and Cath? Not one that was all in and committed to MAAM, which I wanted to be. Taking a deep breath, I clicked on the invite code and waited for the meeting to start, my heart pounding.

At exactly 10.30 the screen burst into life and Cath and Nina appeared, along with a handful of other women, all around my age, with their names displayed. Seeing Cath and Nina's smiling faces relaxed me and I was instantly glad I hadn't let my fear prevent me from attending, particularly as there weren't many of us.

'Hello to all you magnificent women,' Cath said. 'Thank you for joining us today at our first online get-together. It's great to have you here from the very start.'

I felt a flush of excitement, as though I was personally pioneering something great rather than meekly jumping on their coat-tails.

'We're here to chat about all things midlife,' Nina said. 'Health, careers, parenting, love lives, hairy chins.' She winked and we all laughed. 'This is your hour. Whatever you want to talk about, we're here for you. This is a safe space and we ask that you all respect that.'

'What happens in the MAAM community stays in the MAAM community,' Cath whooped.

If I attempted a whoop, I'd sound as though I was struggling to get out of a chair, but Cath's energy roused a cheer from us all. We were in this together. Thank goodness Sophie and Josephine had been so annoying that I'd come upstairs to get away from them, or I'd have missed this.

'We'll begin by introducing ourselves,' Nina said. 'Then, we'll invite you all to tell us a little about yourselves.'

My enthusiasm was instantly replaced with horror. I hated the pressure of going round a group and having to come up with something interesting or witty. I barely listened to Cath and Nina's warm, self-deprecating intros, as I was too preoccupied with what I could say when it was my turn.

'So that's us.' Nina smiled. 'Who wants to go next?'

No one moved. If it wasn't for Cath's head tilt, I'd have thought my screen had frozen. It seemed I wasn't alone in my reluctance to share.

'How about you, Becca?' Cath asked.

All previous regard I had for her evaporated. Why was she picking on me?

'Becca's writing a piece for us on the sandwich generation,' Cath explained to the rest of the group.

'Yes.' I cleared my throat and prayed for Josephine's alarm to go off so I had an excuse to leave. But, of course, the one time I wanted it to, it didn't. 'I'm staying at my mother's because she's fractured her wrist,' I said. 'And my daughter's back from uni.'

'That sounds tough,' a woman, Yolande, said. 'Looking after your mum and your daughter at the same time.'

'Not sure I could move back with my mother,' another woman, Wendy, said. 'You're a better person than me.'

'I'm really not,' I said. 'Believe me, I wasn't exactly jumping up and down with glee at the prospect, but there wasn't anyone else and . . .' I paused and looked at the group, buoyed up by their instant solidarity. 'And, as women, we do what needs doing, don't we?'

'Yes, we do,' Nina said, nodding with approval. 'Constantly putting ourselves on the subs bench while we look after everyone else.'

'That's why this community is so important,' Cath added. 'To support each other, share advice and know we're not alone.'

'Any advice on getting your family to realise that toilets aren't self-cleaning?' a woman called Rachel asked.

We all laughed and the apprehension I'd had disappeared. There was nothing to be afraid of. We were a group of women going through similar things at a similar time of life. I didn't want an excuse to leave. I was here to stay.

# Chapter 23

As the call progressed, and we were past the dreaded intros, we all became more comfortable and spoke freely about situations that wound us up – a never-ending laundry basket and unwittingly running a catering service were common themes. All of the others – well . . . apart from me – had successful careers, yet somehow still found themselves taking on the bulk of responsibility at home: the invisible mental load that most women dealt with, unseen and unappreciated.

Every frustration aired would make a relatable and interesting feature, and I jotted down ideas as we talked. I surprised myself by contributing as much as the others. They were like-minded and easy to talk to, and conversation flowed naturally. As the session ended, Rachel, who had her own law firm, invited me to contact her if I wanted anonymous, generic examples of 'the shit that can go down' between families, for future features. Wendy, a wellbeing coach, invited us to attend a free online class. And Yolande asked for our addresses so that she could send us all a gift from her Biscuits, Bubbles and Bants company. Everyone said how much they looked forward to reading my feature.

Rather than feeling pressured by this, though, their enthusiasm gave me confidence.

After the call, I was on a high, boosted by time spent with inspiring, motivating women, who were as warm and open as they were successful. I channelled my energy into the sandwich-generation feature and typed quickly, peppering the article with anecdotes from the conversations we'd had, along with the research I'd already done and, of course, my own experience. I could be honest about the challenges it brought, safe in the knowledge that Sophie would never be interested in reading an online article about middle-aged women, because they were old and boring. And Josephine wouldn't know how to access an online article – and also thought middle-aged women were old and boring.

When I'd finished, it was starting to get dark and I realised it was late afternoon. I went to use the bathroom, but the door was locked.

'Sorry, won't be long,' Rey said, over the sound of the running shower.

'It's fine. Don't rush,' I said, heading downstairs to use the loo off the hall and definitely not thinking about water cascading down his naked body. There was a leaflet on the doormat, advertising the city's ghost walks.

'Fancy doing a ghost walk with me tonight, Sophs?' I asked, going into the living room. 'I've wanted to go on one for ages.'

'Soz, I can't,' Sophie said. 'Hope Dowson's invited me to her birthday party tomorrow night and I need to fake-tan.'

I perched at the end of the sofa. 'Hope Dowson from primary school? That's nice.'

'Yeah. She came in The Vic the other day.' Sophie stretched her feet out and put them in my lap. 'Could you get me some voddie to take to the party, please?' she asked. 'And a bottle to give Hope, as a birthday present?'

I was aware of Josephine watching me. 'You should be getting that yourself,' I said firmly.

'I'm working all day tomorrow, so I won't have time,' Sophie said. 'I'll pay you back as soon as I get paid.' She pressed her hands together. 'Please. Nearly everyone's away at uni. I need to have some friends in Norwich.'

My resolve at being stricter crumpled like a cheap suit. I couldn't begrudge Sophie this friendship. 'OK. On the condition that you clear up after yourself in the bathroom and kitchen from now on.'

Sophie nodded eagerly. 'Thank you. I will.'

I could feel the breeze from Josephine's flaring nostrils.

'And have a proper think about uni,' I added quickly.

'I will,' Sophie said, less enthusiastically.

'I mean it, Soph.' I squeezed her feet. 'Your dad's right about having to get a full-time job to pay off the loan if you don't go back. It'd be a shame to have racked up all that debt and not have anything to show for it.'

Sophie held out her little finger. 'Pinky promise I won't have to take Dad's job.'

'What job?' Josephine asked, as I hooked my little finger around Sophie's.

'He wants me to work at his place,' Sophie said.

'Not in insurance?' Josephine twisted round, releasing an enormous fart. Sophie and I exchanged a shocked look. Josephine was far too sophisticated to pass wind.

''Scuse you, G!' Sophie giggled.

'It's these moisturising socks,' Josephine tutted, rubbing her feet against each other and creating an elongated, *pfffft* sound. 'Don't be so childish,' Josephine snapped, as Sophie clutched her stomach and I gripped her feet, laughing hysterically.

Josephine stared stonily at the TV, her nostrils flaring so much, it was like being in a wind tunnel. 'I thought you were going on a ghost walk,' she huffed.

I was about to say I wasn't going on my own, but stopped myself. There was no reason to miss out just because I didn't have anyone to go with. I wanted to be more assertive in my second act. Here was my chance. Sophie had already said she was spending the evening fake-tanning. This was a lengthy process, which involved washing, exfoliating, moisturising, applying the tan, leaving it to soak in overnight, then scrubbing it off the next morning. She would be in the bathroom for anywhere between an hour and the remainder of the winter solstice. Rather than lurk in my bedroom or pander to Josephine, I'd go by myself.

'I am going on the ghost walk,' I said. 'But I don't need to leave yet.'

Sophie's eyes widened. 'You're going on your own?'

I nodded. 'Why shouldn't I?'

'You defo should,' Sophie said, a look of something that could be admiration on her face. Or she might be wondering what else I could get her while I was up the city.

'Is a ghost walk the best thing to do by yourself?' Josephine asked. 'You know how dramatic you are.'

'I'm not dramatic,' I said indignantly.

A hand clamped my shoulder and I released a blood-curdling scream. See, not dramatic at all.

'Sorry.' Rey released his grip. 'Just wanted to let you know the bathroom's free.'

'Thank you,' I squeaked, glancing up at him from the sofa.

'Sorry,' Rey said again, although his eyes were twinkling, which did nothing to slow my accelerated heartbeat.

'What are you doing tonight, Rey?' Josephine asked.

Rey shrugged. 'No plans, really.'

'Becca's going on a ghost walk,' Josephine said. 'You should go too, Rey.'

I glared at her. 'I didn't say I was definitely going.'

'Yes, you did.' Josephine smiled.

'OK, I did, but I forgot that I have to, er . . .' My eyes fell on Sophie. 'I have to fake-tan.' My cheeks turned crimson. I needed to tone down my colour, not heighten it.

Sophie snorted and Josephine gave me a withering look. 'Don't be ridiculous. You're always covered from head to toe.'

I hadn't been when Rey found me on the landing. I sincerely hoped he wasn't thinking the same thing.

Josephine smiled up at Rey. 'You'd like to go, wouldn't you?'

Rey nudged up his glasses. 'I'm sure it'd be fun, but—'

'It's the perfect opportunity to see more of Norwich,' Josephine interrupted. She plucked the leaflet from the coffee table. 'It starts at seven at the Adam and Eve pub.'

'I'm not sure I can—' Rey started.

'But I have to—' I said at the same time.

'Becca has to do some shopping first, so she'll meet you there,' Josephine said firmly, putting the leaflet down and turning back to the TV.

Rey and I eyed each other warily, neither of us looking keen about the plans that had been made for us, but both unable to get out of them. Either out of extreme politeness, or, more likely, an inability to defy Josephine.

'I'll see you outside the pub at seven, then,' Rey said, with as much enthusiasm as a death-row inmate.

As soon as he'd left, I whipped round to face Josephine. 'Why did you do that? He clearly doesn't want to go and neither do I now.'

'Go on, Mum, it'll be fun,' Sophie said. I widened my eyes at her. She shouldn't be encouraging me to spend time with a man who wasn't her father. Not that I wanted her to encourage me to spend time with her father either.

'But your dad . . .' I trailed off, not sure where to go with that sentence. Steve had a female friend, so there was no reason why I shouldn't have a male one. But did I want to be friends with Rey?

'It's not like it's a date,' Sophie said.

'No,' I spluttered. 'It's definitely not a date.'

'Course not. You're too old for all that stuff.' Sophie stood up and stretched. 'I'm going to stick a pizza in the oven.' She left the room, then darted back. 'You won't forget my vodka, will you?' I shook my head and she gave me a grateful smile, before leaving again.

'Ah yes, Sophie's shopping,' Josephine said. I braced myself for a lecture on how weak I was, caving in to Sophie's demands. 'Pop into the pharmacy while you're out, would you.' Funny how she didn't think I was being a doormat when shopping for her. 'And get me some frankincense and myrrh.'

A laugh burst out of me. 'Did you get the baby Jesus in a Secret Santa?'

Josephine sighed theatrically. 'Don't be ridiculous. It's to make a cuticle oil. Much more nourishing than shop-bought ones.'

'Is that so?' I scoffed, then clamped a hand over my mouth, horrified that I'd used one of Josephine's put-downs. Thank goodness I was going out tonight. I was clearly spending way too much time with her. I scrambled up off the sofa.

Josephine looked me up and down. 'Is that what you're wearing?'

I glanced down at my skinny jeans and navy, long-sleeved tee. 'Yes.'

'You look as though you're doing the gardening rather than going out.'

'It's a ghost walk. It'll be dark.'

'Just as well,' she tutted.

'What does it matter what I look like?' I huffed. 'And why were you so keen for Rey to come? You do remember Steve, don't you?'

'Steve,' she said slowly. 'The name rings a vague bell. Are you sure you remember him, though? You've only seen him twice since you moved in, almost four weeks ago.'

My stomach tightened. 'Just because I haven't told you doesn't mean I haven't seen him. And we talk all the time.'

'Is that so?'

'Yes,' I snapped. 'It is so.'

I walked out and pulled the door shut firmly behind me, so she couldn't see my flushed cheeks. 'We talk all the time' was stretching the truth slightly. OK, massively. Steve and I exchanged the odd message about house maintenance or Sophie, but there was no talking. And, more worryingly, no inclination to talk either. Not on my part. Sighing, I looked at myself in the mirror. Perhaps it wouldn't hurt to freshen up a little. I ran upstairs to the bathroom, appreciating the dry floor, neatly hung bath mat, and spotless bath and sink. Rey was a lot cleaner and tidier than my mother and daughter.

I retied my ponytail, dabbed on some eye shadow and applied some mascara. I poked my head round the living-room door to say goodbye.

'Don't forget the voddie,' Sophie said.

'Or my bits from the pharmacy,' Josephine added.

'I won't,' I said, exiting before they could ask me to get them anything else, such as a new party outfit for Sophie and a little donkey for Josephine.

I pulled on my waterproof jacket and trainers, picked up my rucksack and left the house.

# Chapter 24

Rey waved as I approached the group standing outside the Adam and Eve pub. I swallowed hard. He really was a very handsome man. Objectively speaking. Without objectifying him. Unease swelled in my stomach. I shouldn't be meeting him. Even though it was perfectly innocent, it didn't feel right. I should make up an excuse and go home. I hoisted my rucksack up, weighed down by Sophie's two bottles of vodka and Josephine's gifts to bless the baby Jesus with, and willed a sore throat to manifest itself so that I could genuinely tell Rey I was ill and had to leave. Or a headache. Or tummy ache. Anything. I'd welcome a brief bout of dysentery if it got me out of this, although I'd prefer not to shit myself in front of everyone.

'Hi,' he said when I reached him.

I gave him a weak smile. 'Sorry,' I started, my mind racing with which illness to go with. Something that wasn't catching and would be gone tomorrow, in case he saw me and questioned my miraculous recovery. A migraine would be best, I decided. I put a hand to my temple to add gravitas to the lie I was about to tell.

'Welcome one and all,' a theatrical voice boomed behind me.

I jumped and spun round. A man in period costume was addressing the group. I wasn't sure what time period he was channelling but the look was a cross between a highwayman and a flamenco dancer.

'Tonight,' he said, spreading his arms wide, 'I will take you on a journey through the most haunted areas of the city, and regale you with tales of the many lost spirits and poltergeists who are still seen and heard to this very day.' He swung his arm theatrically. 'Follow me, good folk.'

Everyone shuffled after him and Rey looked at me expectantly. 'What are you sorry about?' he asked.

I couldn't leave now. It'd be so obvious I was making it up and then things would be even more uncomfortable when we ran into each other.

'Sorry Josephine ambushed you,' I improvised.

'That's OK,' he said. 'I like things like this. I'd have said no if I didn't want to come.'

Say no to Josephine? I admired his optimism.

The first stop was just a minute away and our flamboyantly dressed host detailed the grisly murder that was said to have taken place there, before leading us on to the next points of interest. He relished his role and told each tale with gusto, and was not at all intimidated by the hecklers passing by or cars beeping. Where did he get his confidence from? I felt self-conscious when the light flashed to summon an attendant at the self-serve checkout.

Most people chatted on the short walks between stops, but Rey and I walked together in companionable silence. If companionable silence meant a slightly awkward, non-verbal exchange.

We were about an hour into the walk, when we approached Elm Hill. It was a beautiful lane of Tudor buildings, but with cobbles so hard and round, it was difficult to walk on them, even in my robust trainers. The people around us automatically linked arms, as though in a formation. I clenched my buttocks to balance me and remembered Sophie's 'nice arse' comment when she'd accidentally walked in on Rey in the shower. Without instruction, and very much without my consent, an image of just how nice that arse might look in the shower popped into my head.

Rey cleared his throat beside me. Mortified, I stepped away, in case close proximity would enable him to see into my warped mind. My left foot slipped on a spitefully round cobble, closely followed by the right. Shrieking, I fell to the ground, landing with a loud clanking, as the vodka bottles bashed against each other in my rucksack.

'The ghost of the burnt man is making his presence known,' cried the tour guide. He and Rey bent down to help me up.

'Fear not, maid,' the guide boomed. 'We will protect you from the spirits.' All eyes turned to me and my face turned its usual crimson. 'Tell us, maid, what emotion did you just experience?' Humiliation was the overriding one, but I was too humiliated to admit that. 'Did you have the sensation of being pushed?' He strode back and forth, waving his arms and over-accentuating each syllable. 'Or of being possessed?'

'Not really,' I muttered.

'Come now,' bellowed the man. 'Surely you don't expect us to believe you simply fell.' He spun round on his Cuban heel. 'Not in as haunted a street as this.' His heel slipped in between the cobbles and he tumbled to the ground. 'Fuck, my ankle,' he screeched in a broad Norfolk accent. 'I'm in panto this weekend. I can't be injured.' He glared up at me, as though this were my fault.

'Shall we go?' Rey whispered.

I nodded and we backed away. Rey's arm was still hooked through mine from when he'd helped me up, which was just as well, as I slipped twice more before we reached the end of the lane and were back on firm ground.

'Thank you,' I said, disentangling myself.

'Do you think he was pushed or possessed?' Rey said.

I giggled. 'Funny how he wasn't so keen on making his own accident part of the story. So much for protecting me from the spirits.'

'Speaking of which . . .' Rey tapped my rucksack. 'It sounds like you've got a bottle bank in there.'

I cringed. 'Sophie asked me to get her and her friend some vodka for a party tomorrow.'

'No wonder you toppled over, with all that weight on your back. Is that the real reason Josephine fell over too?'

I giggled. 'Possibly. Although it'd be litres of hand cream instead of vodka.'

Rey grinned and put out a hand. 'Here, let me carry it home.'

I gripped the straps. 'No, it's fine.'

'I missed the gym today. You'd be doing me a favour.'

'OK, thank you. But let me know if it gets too much and you want to give it back.' I handed him the bag, hoping that if it did get too much for him, he'd be too proud to admit it.

'What did you think of the ghost walk?' Rey asked, as we turned towards Josephine's.

'It was fun. Apart from wanting to die when I fell over.'

'I think he wanted you to die too. It'd be great for his act.'

I laughed again. Rey was funnier than I'd realised. Probably because I hadn't given him a chance. It wasn't his fault Josephine had offered him the coach house, or that the shower had packed in, or that I was having a midlife crisis. I had to stop taking all of my frustration out on him. Josephine was a much worthier candidate.

I took a deep breath. 'I'm sorry I've been . . .' What was the right wording – rude? Moody? A bit of an arse?

Rey put his hands up. 'I understand.'

Did he? I wish he'd explain it to me, because I didn't have a clue.

'Sophie going to uni,' Rey said. 'Having to leave your home to look after your mother. Losing your job.'

I bristled. Just when I was starting to like him.

'It's a lot for anyone to deal with.' He gave a sheepish grin. 'And to make it worse, you have to put up with a stranger hogging the bathroom.'

My cheeks flushed. Was he joking or had he heard me complaining about him?

'I appreciate that me coming round every day isn't ideal,' he said. 'I have looked into other Airbnbs, but there's nothing available with a long-term let, until Christmas, within my budget. You know how it is, paying for student accommodation on top of everything else.'

Yes, I did know. It was particularly galling when the student wasn't living in the accommodation. Rey didn't know Sophie was considering dropping out, I realised. I'd thought she was just coming back for a short stay when I'd told him. Hopefully, she still was.

'Is Saif getting on any better?' I asked.

'Not sure. He doesn't say much.' Rey sighed. 'He's going to stay till the end of term and if he's still unhappy, then we'll have a rethink.'

This was exactly what I'd suggested to Sophie. How did Rey get Saif to listen, but I couldn't do the same with my child?

'The important thing is that they're happy and healthy, right?' Rey said. 'The rest will fall into place.'

It was true. You couldn't put a price on health. Well, Steve could, being a life-insurance underwriter, but figuratively speaking.

We stopped at a pelican crossing. 'How's the job-hunting going?' he asked.

'I'm writing a piece for an online magazine called MAAM,' I said. 'Middle-Aged and Magnificent.'

'That's brilliant – well done.'

My cheeks grew warm at his praise. 'Thanks. I'm really enjoying it, but it won't pay the bills. I need a guaranteed regular income, but women of my age aren't top of most employers' wish lists.'

Rey shook his head. 'Well, that's short-sighted of them. You have far more wisdom and knowledge, not to mention life experience.'

No need to admit that most of my life experience was sourced from Nikki and *Loose Women*.

'Which parts of your job did you enjoy the most?' he asked.

'I love talking to people who are passionate about something, and writing that up in a way that showcases what they do or represent, so that others are inspired by it.' I couldn't remember the last piece I'd written for *Norwich Now* that had made me feel this way. It certainly hadn't been the minutes from the council meeting about a proposed new dual carriageway.

'Presumably, you're used to working to a deadline?'

'Yes. I used to set up the schedules for the magazine and make sure everyone got their copy in on time.'

We rounded a corner and walked towards a group of youths; some of them were standing, others perched on a wall. Rey stiffened beside me.

'Let's cross,' he said, gripping my arm and steering me to the other side of the road. He quickened his pace, so I almost had to scamper to keep up.

'Everything OK?' I asked after we'd been speed-walking for a minute in silence.

'Yes, sorry.' He released my arm. 'It's getting late, so I thought we should hurry home.' Interesting that he called it home. It was more of a day release centre to me. 'And your mum's rebooting her career?' he said, changing the subject. 'You were never tempted to follow in her footsteps? Or hand-prints, I suppose.'

'Definitely not,' I said. 'Which is just as well. Apparently, my coarse weathered hands aren't suitable for hand jobs.'

Rey's eyes bulged behind his glasses.

'I mean hand-modelling jobs,' I spluttered. 'And yes, she's rebranding.' I ploughed on, pretending my previous comment hadn't happened. 'I suggested she and her agent challenge the agencies to employ age-appropriate models rather than much younger versions.'

'Good idea.' Rey smiled. 'Don't forget to apply that to your own career too. Challenge the employers to look past your age and focus on your skills and experience.'

Oh yes. No problem. I'd get them to throw in a company car, free healthcare and gym membership with one of the Gladiators as my personal trainer while I was there.

'All my clients have come from LinkedIn,' he continued. 'It takes a bit of time to build connections, but once you have, it pays off.'

'You're in IT, though. Would it work with creative jobs?'

'Designing websites is quite creative. Yes, I write the code to run them, but the satisfaction comes from listening to my client and designing a site that represents their brand and values. Not dissimilar to you with your writing.'

His job was more interesting than I'd realised.

'You should post about the work you're doing for MAAM too,' he said. 'That'll add credibility, show you're currently working and pinpoint your areas of expertise.'

We reached Josephine's and crunched across the gravel drive. Rey slid my rucksack off his back when we reached the front door and placed it at my feet.

I gave him a grateful smile. 'Thank you for carrying this back. I really appreciate it.'

'No problem.' Rey nudged his glasses up. 'Let me know if you want me to give you a hand with LinkedIn. I could sort out your mum's website too if she wants it updating.'

I snorted. 'She doesn't have a website.'

Rey couldn't have looked more bewildered if I'd revealed she identified as a basset hound. 'Well, that's stage one of her reboot.' He shook his head and exhaled loudly. 'I'll talk to her about it when I next see her. Although I should probably sort mine out first. The content is in dire need of a refresh. I wrote it when I set up the business a couple of years ago and it could definitely be better. If only I had your journalistic skills.' He smiled and turned, then swivelled back, his eyes bright. 'You could rewrite it!'

'What?' Panic surged through me. I couldn't write with authority about a topic I knew nothing about. I'd make a mess of it, which would be mortifying.

I shook my head. 'I don't know anything about websites.'

'You don't have to. It'll basically be a rewrite of what's already there, but done better.' He laughed at his clunky wording. 'See why it needs doing? I'll talk you through anything you don't understand. It'd be good for you to have this experience and additional skillset,' he added. 'I could write you a testimonial to add credibility.'

There wouldn't be much credibility if I was bloody awful. I nibbled on a nail, convinced I was the wrong person for the job. But one of my biggest regrets was turning opportunities down because I was scared of making a fool of myself. What was the worst that could happen? If I did a bad job, Rey would think I was an idiot and I'd have to avoid him, but that was daily practice already.

'OK,' I said, feigning confidence. 'I'll give it a go.'

'That's great.' Rey's face split into a smile. 'I reckon there's about three days' work. Would £1,000 be a fair price?'

Thank goodness I hadn't turned it down. For a thousand pounds I'd run the risk of looking as though I'd learnt to write from *Sesame Street*.

Rey slid his phone from his back pocket. 'Can I have your email address and phone number? I'll send over a link to the website and some notes on what I'm looking for.'

I rattled them off, my stomach twisting. Could I really blag this?

'Hopefully, this'll lead to more work for you,' he said, keying them into his phone. 'My clients often ask for recommendations of copywriters. I'll pass them to you in future.'

I gave what I hoped was a capable and reassuring nod. He might not be recommending me when he saw what I'd cobbled together for him.

'You're really helping me out,' he said putting his phone away. 'My website's not as good as it should be, which isn't great, given that it's a showcase for the service I provide.'

My stomach twisted. No pressure, then.

He said goodbye and headed off to the coach house. I took my key from my coat pocket and saw Josephine's face vanish behind the curtain in the living-room window.

'Why did Rey take your number?' she asked, before I'd even taken my coat off.

Sophie looked up from the sofa. She was in the same place she'd been in when I left, but there was a distinct smell of digestive biscuits emanating from her pores, so she had found the energy to fake-tan in my absence.

'Rey's offered me some work,' I said, more confidently than I felt. 'Writing content for his website.'

Sophie couldn't have looked more incredulous if I'd been invited to be an astronaut on NASA's next space mission. 'You don't know anything about websites,' she said. 'You still use www, even though that stopped before I was born.'

I couldn't be hurt by her lack of faith, when I'd had the same doubts. However, I wanted to instil in her a confidence that we could do anything we put our minds to. Apart from the astronaut mission perhaps. That was a bit too much of a reach, given my recent interaction with the loft hatch.

'I don't need to know about the tech side.' I looked down at the collection of plates and glasses that had amassed on the coffee table in the two hours I'd been out. 'I'm writing the words, not the code.'

Sophie grinned up at me. 'That's really cool.'

I flushed with pride. My phone beeped with a message and I flushed even more when I read it.

*Here's my number in case you need it. Looking forward to working with you. Rey*

Josephine mimed holding a phone to her ear. 'Hashtag call anytime.'

Not this again. I began gathering the abandoned crockery.

Sophie moved her arm to allow me access to an empty crisp packet by her elbow.

'Hashtag don't forget this,' Josephine shrilled, twirling a finger at a dirty side plate. 'Hashtag frankincense and myrrh?' she added, as I leant over to retrieve the plate.

Sophie sat upright. 'Hashtag vodka?'

I paused while reaching for a discarded tissue. Were they serious? I'd worked all afternoon while they sat around. Now they were barely giving me a chance to walk through the door before spouting their next lot of demands.

I straightened up. 'You two do know I'm not your servant, don't you?'

Josephine raised her eyebrows. 'Hashtag overreacting much.' She and Sophie exchanged a smirk.

I plonked the crockery down on the coffee table with a loud clatter. They were taking the piss and I'd had enough.

'I'm sick of you two leaving everything for me to do,' I snapped. 'It's not fair and it stops now.'

Josephine and Sophie stared at me, open-mouthed.

I strode to the door. 'You can bloody well clear this hashtag mess up yourselves.' I thumped up the stairs and into my bedroom. Flopping onto my bed, I waited for guilt at my behaviour to strike or for my eye to start twitching. But neither happened. Instead of feeling contrite, I felt emboldened. Hashtag I could do this.

# Chapter 25

'Hello, Becca, it's Ruby Carnegie, HR manager at *Norwich Now*.'

I almost fell off my chair. It had been four weeks since I'd been made redundant and my many, many emails and phone calls had gone unanswered up till this point.

'How are you?' Ruby asked.

'Good, thanks,' I said automatically, then corrected myself. Now was not the time to be my usual people-pleaser self and avoid confrontation. 'Actually, scrap that,' I said, trying to sound professional and authoritative, and not at all as though I was speaking from a tiny desk in my childhood bedroom with a poster of Indiana Jones on the wall. 'I'm not good. I've been emailing you for the past four weeks.'

'I'm sorry,' Ruby said. 'I've only just come back to work. I've not been well.'

That was a long time to be off sick. My maternal instinct went to red alert, and I hoped she was OK, but I didn't feel it was my place to pry.

'What can I help you with?' Ruby asked. 'I'm working through my phone messages, but haven't got to my emails yet.'

My face grew hot. Was my employment so insignificant that no one had thought to tell the HR manager it had ended? I cleared my throat. 'Declan made me redundant four weeks ago.'

'What?' Ruby inhaled sharply. 'There's been no discussion or notification. What did he say?'

I outlined our meeting. Saying it out loud made me realise how brief and unprofessional the whole thing had been.

'Was anyone else in the room?' Ruby asked.

'No.'

'Did he give a specific reason as to why you couldn't be part of the reshuffle?'

'No,' I said again, my voice quieter. My cheeks burnt with embarrassment. How could I have been such a fool to accept what he was saying without question?

'Don't feel bad,' Ruby said, intuitively picking up on my discomfort. 'You were probably in shock and the onus was on Declan to follow protocol, not on you to ensure he implemented it.'

Her words didn't bring me the comfort she no doubt intended. I felt like such a fool.

'Do you want to dispute it and try to get your job back?' she asked.

'No.' The word came out without permission and my hand flew to my mouth. What was I saying? I was desperate to be in full-time regular employment, with stability and a full-time regular salary. 'I don't mean no,' I said. 'I mean . . .' I trailed off. The thought of going back to work for Declan, being undermined and undervalued, filled me with more dread than the uncertainty of being out of work. Especially now I'd done one piece for MAAM, which would hopefully lead to more. Writing it had reminded me why I'd become a journalist in the first place and I was proud of the feature I'd emailed to Cath and Nina. Plus, there was the work to do for Rey now. He said he'd pass my details to other potential clients too.

'Actually, I do mean no,' I said.

'Are you sure?' Ruby asked. 'You have the right to contest it, especially given the circumstances in which you were told.'

'No,' I said firmly. 'I'd like my redundancy package.'

'Don't blame you,' Ruby said. There was a clicking of calculator buttons down the phone. 'You've been with the company for thirty years. Which means you're entitled to approximately £14,000 tax-free redundancy pay, plus three months' pay.'

Fourteen thousand pounds? These words brought considerably more comfort than her earlier ones.

'You might be entitled to more, though,' Ruby continued. 'What was his exact reason for your redundancy? Reshuffle is too loose a term.'

I recalled the way Declan had looked at me as though my age was some sort of disease that he was in danger of catching if I spent any longer in his office. 'I got the impression he wanted me out of the way because I was too old.'

Ruby gasped audibly. 'That's unacceptable. I can only apologise for his behaviour. He hasn't followed fair process, so we'll push for a larger payout.'

I crossed my fingers. 'That would be fantastic if you're able to. Either way, I appreciate having you on my side.'

'Between you and me, the way this place is run is getting me down,' Ruby said. 'That's why I've been off – with stress.'

'I'm sorry,' I said. 'I hope the break helped.'

'Getting another job would help more,' Ruby said. 'Don't tell anyone, but I'm looking.'

'Of course I won't.' I paused. 'If you could put my redundancy package through first, though, I'd really appreciate it.'

'I will,' Ruby said. 'Can you send me another email detailing everything, so that I can put your claim forward?'

'I'll do it now. Thanks, Ruby. And good luck.'

'Good luck to you too. Speak soon.'

We said goodbye and I grinned up at Indiana, feeling pleased with myself. Rather than just accepting the situation, I'd pushed back and got a result. A £14,000 result! That should soften the blow when I told Steve. Which I *really* needed to do. But first I should email Ruby, while our conversation was fresh in her mind. Just in case she got lucky in her job hunt and left before she'd actioned my redundancy package. After all, she was only in her thirties, so there wasn't more probability of her being struck by lightning than getting a job, like us nearly fifty-year-olds.

There were two emails in my inbox after I'd written to Ruby. One from Rey, about his website, and the other from Nina and Cath. I opened that one first and squealed with delight when I read how much they enjoyed my feature. *Warm, entertaining and relatable. Exactly what we aim to give our readership*. My cheeks glowed with pride. They went on to say that they'd like to commission me to do another couple of pieces and also talk about growing the community's profile. They were meeting for a late lunch that day, which was such short notice, they didn't expect me to be free, but they'd love to see me if I was.

I nibbled on a nail. It wasn't even ten o'clock. A train to London took less than two hours. If I got my act together, I could make that lunch. Josephine didn't have any medical appointments today and Sophie was working from midday onwards. If I was home, I'd end up doing things for them that they were perfectly capable of doing themselves, such as making coffee in my cafetière and cleaning fake tan off the bathroom tiles. I'd decided last night that I wasn't going to pander to them anymore but would instead do things for myself. This meeting with Nina and Cath was the perfect place to start.

Invigorated, I replied to say that I'd see them there and changed out of my skinny jeans and long-sleeved navy tee into my floral shirt dress. Nikki was right. I really needed to get some decent clothes, but for now this would have to do.

Downstairs, Josephine was in her armchair, deep-heat mitts on both hands.

'Did you manage to get those on yourself?' I asked.

'Of course,' Josephine said sharply. 'I'm not an invalid.'

'Good. The physio's working, then.' I tightened my ponytail. 'As you're so much better, I'm going out for the day.' I looked at my phone to check that the train to London was running on time. My stomach tightened when I saw that it was. A very small part of me had been hoping for a cancellation, so I could say I'd tried, but circumstances beyond my control had prevented me from going. The rest of me gave that very small part a bollocking for being such a wimp. I didn't want to be that timid person anymore, too scared to do anything for fear of failure. From now on, I was going to view challenges as opportunities, step outside my comfort zone and overcome my fears. I wasn't sure many people would consider a nice lunch with two very nice women much of a challenge, not compared to skydiving or climbing Kilimanjaro, but it was a big deal to me. And less likely to end in death or injury.

Josephine was abnormally quiet. Several minutes had passed without her demanding something, which was unheard of.

'Are you all right?' I asked.

'Think I overdid it putting these heat mitts on by myself,' she said in a weak voice. 'Must remember not to overdo it. Help me take them off, would you.'

I knelt and eased the mitts off, then gently massaged moisturiser into her hands.

'Do you have to go out today?' she asked when I'd finished. She cradled her wrist. 'Just because I'm not an invalid doesn't mean I'm at full strength yet.'

I reverted to my default setting of guilt. The whole point of me staying was to look after her. But, I reminded myself, she was perfectly capable when she wanted to be. Just the day before I'd caught her performing Chappell Roan's 'HOT TO GO!' cheerleading routine. She'd had plenty of strength in her for that.

'I'll be back long before bedtime,' I assured her.

'What if I need you before then?' Josephine asked quietly. 'Sophie's working all afternoon, then going to Hope's party.'

'You'll be OK,' I said firmly, refusing to back down. 'You can always call Rey if it's an emergency.'

Josephine's eyes lit up. 'That's true. Where are you going?' she asked, her previously weak status miraculously cured at the prospect of a visit from Rey. I hoped I hadn't dropped him in it. The last thing he needed was to be summoned to help Josephine into a cheerleading outfit.

'To London. I'm meeting Cath and Nina from MAAM.'

'I used to love going into London for photo shoots.' Her smile wavered and she clutched her wrist.

I felt a rush of sympathy. Was it possible she felt the same loss of purpose as I did without a job?

Josephine fanned her fingers in the direction of my dress. 'You're not wearing that, are you? Borrow my navy cashmere dress again.' She looked at my face and grimaced. 'And take off that horrendous foundation. Only Claudia Winkleman can carry off that shade of satsuma.'

My sympathy disappeared.

Half an hour later, I was ready to go. I wouldn't admit it, but Josephine's dress was a big improvement. I'd also removed my foundation, more in an effort to avoid criticism than for fear of getting it on the dress.

'I'll message when I'm on my way back,' I said. 'My phone will be on silent during the lunch, but I'll check as soon as I'm out.'

'No need,' Josephine said. 'As you said, Rey can help if I need anything.' Before I could remind her that she was only to contact him if it was an emergency, she disappeared into the living room, lest any UV rays shot through the front door as I opened it and zapped her.

'Bye, then.' Tightening my ponytail, and ignoring the butterflies in my stomach, I set off for the train station, on my way to the meeting with Cath and Nina.

# Chapter 26

On the train I checked my email. Ruby had written, confirming my £14,000 redundancy pay, which she'd told the accounts department to pay immediately; she also reiterated that she'd be taking my case further.

I'd never had control over money like this before and it was empowering. I could afford to treat myself to a mini-break. Just a little one. I had to be careful I didn't fall into the same trap as Sophie had and spend frivolously, believing it would last forever. I'd give Sophie some money to see her through till the next loan instalment arrived, or pay off her loan if she didn't go back to uni.

'You're not helping her.' Josephine's words sprung to mind. I brushed them away. She had no right to preach about raising a daughter when she'd hardly been mother of the year herself. But Nikki had said something similar and I did value her opinion. Steaming in and fixing Sophie's problems, often before they'd even happened, hadn't worked out well so far. By taking charge and doing everything for her, I hadn't taught her the importance of sticking at something, even when the going gets tough. Or the importance of sticking to a budget. If I bailed her out whenever she got into financial trouble, where would it lead? A few years down the line, would I find myself paying off credit cards and car loans and her electricity bill, because she hadn't put money aside for the essentials? I bit my lip. Where was the line between being a parent your child could rely on and turn to in times of crisis, and a parent who didn't give their child the tools necessary to grow into a responsible adult? I honestly didn't know. Would the internet?

An online search didn't give me the exact answer I was hoping for, but I did learn which actor was rumoured to be the next Bond and, slightly more relevantly, I came across the details of a compassionate coach, Marenee, who specialised in helping women struggling with midlife anxieties. What could be more anxiety-inducing than feeling you were failing your child, and pretty much every other area of your life? Marenee's website revealed that she helped women overcome their challenges, find a new life purpose, and value themselves and recognise their qualities. I almost bit my thumb off. She could be describing me. And, presumably, there were a lot of women like me, if Marenee was making a living out of helping us.

I read on. Marenee had originally been in banking but, realising she was more interested in getting people to add up than numbers, retrained. Stepping away from a secure, financially rewarding career was a bold move and an inspiring story. I'd be interested in learning more about Marenee. And if I was, perhaps other women would too.

* * *

'Definitely!' Cath said. Her blonde curls bounced as she gesticulated with her hands. 'Motivational women, who are real and support other women, are exactly who our members want to read about.'

Nina nodded. 'Retraining later in life shows that we don't have to stick with the career we started out with.' She popped an olive into her mouth without smudging her red lipstick. 'With the right support, we can reinvent ourselves. She'd be a great person for you to interview.'

I grinned, relieved that they didn't think it was a crap suggestion and thrilled that they wanted me to write it. I forced myself to be brave and put another idea on the table. 'If you like that suggestion, I thought perhaps it'd work as the start of a good series. Regular interviews with women who have changed direction and stepped into something new in midlife. Proving that, as you said, we can reinvent ourselves.'

Cath and Nina smiled at each other and nodded.

'One of the things that's most impressed us is that you put ideas forward.' Cath smiled.

'And we love them all,' Nina added, smoothing her dark bob behind her ears. 'You really understand what our members are looking for.'

'As people say nowadays, they'll make them feel seen,' Cath said. 'The problem we have is getting MAAM seen.'

Our meals arrived, and she paused while our plates were being set down and we all complimented each other's choices.

Cath bit into a chip. 'Feedback shows that our members value what we're providing. We'd like to give them more, expand the community with a podcast and, eventually, in-person events.'

'But all of this needs funding,' Nina said. 'Our income comes from memberships, which is growing, but slowly. Until we have more members, we can't afford to advertise or provide more content – such as your brilliant features.' She winked and I felt a glow of pride.

'But we're not going to get more members quickly if we don't advertise.' Cath picked up her burger. 'It's the old chicken-and-egg situation.'

Nina speared a broccoli floret with her fork. 'Any suggestions you have would be greatly appreciated.'

I hesitated. Coming up with and writing features was one thing, advising them how to grow their membership was entirely different. If I turned in an article they didn't like, they could ask me to rewrite it. If a promo proposal I suggested tanked, they'd have lost time, money and their members' confidence in them. I would no longer be the capable, resourceful person they thought I was.

'Don't worry, we're not expecting you to have all the answers,' Cath said. 'We just thought we'd ask on the off chance. You mentioned that you helped promote the magazine and events you used to work on.'

It was true. I *had* worked on the marketing and PR. I swallowed and sat up taller, recalling Marenee's words about encouraging women to value themselves and recognise their qualities. I mustn't let fear of failure hold me back. I *was* capable and resourceful. I *could* help.

I put my knife and fork down. 'I might not have all the answers,' I said with a smile. 'But I definitely have some of them.'

* * *

'Thank you so much.' Cath hugged me, as we said goodbye outside the restaurant. 'Collaborating with like-minded companies is such a great idea.'

'We'll definitely look into your other suggestions too,' Nina said, air-kissing both cheeks. As her bold red lipstick was still intact, despite having eaten an entire meal, I was grateful for the non-contact.

'Thank you for lunch,' I said. 'It was great to meet you both in person. I'm so glad I could help.'

'You really have.' Cath squeezed my arm. 'Let us know how you get on with Marenee and of any other women you think would be good to profile in the series.'

'I will.' I didn't know yet who else I could get for the interviews, but rather than be daunted by this, I was excited about finding them.

'Looking forward to your next feature too,' Nina said. 'The sandwich-generation piece generated a lot of traction. How's it going, living with your mum?'

'So-so,' I said. 'We've fallen into a routine. Similarly, I assume, to the way people adjust to life in prison.'

Cath and Nina laughed, wrongly presuming I was joking.

They waved me off and I headed to the Tube, excited to email Marenee when I was on the train and, hopefully, set up an interview. She lived in Bath, a city I'd always wanted to visit. Perhaps this could be where I took my mini-break.

I reminded myself that my redundancy package wasn't a windfall; it was in lieu of a regular salary that I now wouldn't be receiving. Thanks to Steve's job, we didn't have to rely on my salary to get by and, although we didn't live extravagantly, we never had to worry about paying bills or how to put food on the table. I had to start appreciating what I had – a comfortable life, a healthy child, a nice house and a steady, reliable marriage. What right did I have to expect passion and excitement, in addition to all that stability? Very few people had a relationship like Nikki and Chiwetel's. Soap operas would soon run out of plot lines if they did. Steve and I would be in a better place once we found a joint hobby and I stopped trying to force a fervour that just wasn't there. I would get stimulation and satisfaction from my career instead. For some reason, the email from Rey popped into my head.

# Chapter 27

*Fantastic work. The website's so much better now than it was originally. You've got my message across perfectly. Thank you very much.*

I felt a flush of pride at Rey's email. Rewriting his web content hadn't been as difficult as I'd feared when he'd asked me the week before, and the work had been more interesting than I'd expected it to be. Instead of a load of computer jargon, Rey was quite poetic in detailing how he worked with each client to create bespoke websites that showcased their values, as well as products or services. He was clearly passionate about what he did and, judging by the case studies on his website, very talented at it.

I read on.

*I have a couple of clients I can put your way if you're interested.*

Yes, I was interested. Those projects would fit in perfectly around the pieces I was doing for MAAM. Rey's email continued:

*I also have a business proposition for you. Writing a blog post for my site on a weekly basis.*

A regular income sounded promising.

*Can I tell you all about it over dinner?*

My eye twitched. Dinner? Why dinner?

*I created a website for the new Asian fusion restaurant in town and they're giving me a freebie meal tonight as a thank you. I can bring a guest, but my sister's out, my parents are babysitting, and Saif refuses to be seen in public with me.*

And there was me, thinking they were inseparable. Sophie actually didn't mind being seen in public with me. Provided I was buying something for her, obviously.

*You'd be doing me a favour, so I don't look like a loser dining alone and I could talk you through the business of blogs – with menus instead of flip charts. No pressure, but if you'd like to, the table booking's at 7 p.m. Alternatively, we can chat here or at Josephine's if you think you might be interested.*

I moved on to another nail. Dinner at the new restaurant was tempting. It was unlikely they took Tesco vouchers, so going with Steve wouldn't be possible, and Nikki was busy most of the time, although we were meeting for a coffee that afternoon.

Rey had made it very clear that this was a business meeting, so I didn't need to feel I was being disloyal to Steve. It was dinner with a colleague, not dissimilar to Steve's meeting with Collette. Except that ours would be at a restaurant, and insurance and quizzes would not be discussed. I hoped. I still hadn't contacted Steve, but I'd been busy with Rey's web content and my work for MAAM, and, well, hiding the fact I'd been made redundant. What was Steve's excuse for not ringing to see how Sophie and I were?

I replied to Rey's email, saying that I'd meet him at the restaurant at 7 p.m., then realised that I hadn't thought to check if Sophie needed me for anything. I picked up my phone to ask, but stopped myself. She was eighteen. The advantage of her being this age was that I didn't have to check in with her before making plans. This was compensation for all the years of chasing my tail, making sure Sophie was where she needed to be, wearing whatever outfit was required for school, that night's activity club or themed party (funny how quickly you could go off some parents, when they gleefully announced their plans for a do to rival the Met Gala). Then there was the conveyor belt of cleaning, laundry, cooking, feeding, homework, bathing and hostage-level negotiations to get Sophie to bed. Once she was asleep, my leisure time had consisted of life admin, present sourcing, buying and wrapping, online-supermarket shop orders, untangling hair accessories from the vacuum cleaner or washing machine filter, excavating cereal from the car seat, DVD player and the depths of my handbag, and, depending on what stage Sophie was at, removing glitter, slime or foundation from every visible surface – and many that weren't.

The consolation prize for her no longer being my little girl was that I no longer had to deal with all that crap. If I wanted an evening out, I could bloody well have one.

# Chapter 28

'I'm going up the city,' I told Josephine and Sophie, after we'd had lunch. Well, lunch for me and Josephine, and breakfast for Sophie.

'Whereabouts?' Sophie asked.

'I'm meeting Nikki for a coffee at four but thought I'd do a bit of Christmas shopping beforehand.' Usually, by early December, I'd have had everything ready, but I hadn't even thought about it. I'd been too busy with work, Sophie and Josephine.

'Shopping?' Sophie slid off her breakfast stool. 'I'll come with you. I need some new trainers.'

Happiness bubbled up inside of me. Sophie wanted to spend time with me! Yes, she was probably hoping I'd buy her the new trainers, but it was better than her finding some online and asking for the money. In exchange for the shoes, I'd insist she talked to me about uni. She was still avoiding the subject whenever I brought it up.

'That'll be lovely.' I beamed. I went to tidy away her breakfast things, then stopped myself. 'But,' I said firmly, gesturing to the bowl and milk, 'you need to clear that up first.'

'I'll do it later,' she said, heading to the door.

My stomach twisted. Insisting she did it now could cause an argument and lead to Sophie deciding not to come up the city with me. But, disappointing as that would be, I had to take the risk if things were going to change.

'No,' I said firmly. Sophie paused and Josephine looked up from applying a nail serum. 'Please do it now.'

'It's not that big a deal,' Sophie huffed. 'I said I'll do it later.'

I tightened my ponytail. 'The milk will go off if it's left out, and it's not fair to leave your things for me to put away.'

Sophie groaned, slouched across the kitchen, snatched up the milk and bowl, and deposited them in the fridge and sink.

I fought every instinct to accept that she'd made some effort and finish the job myself. 'In the dishwasher, please,' I said.

'Seriously?' Sophie blew her pink fringe out of her eyes. 'We could be up the city by now if you weren't making me do all this stuff.'

'The sooner you do it, the sooner we can leave,' I said lightly, but inwardly bracing for a backlash.

'Fine.' Sophie all but hurled the bowl into the dishwasher, and stomped out of the kitchen and up the stairs.

I released a breath I hadn't been aware I'd been holding in. I'd done it: I'd told Sophie to do something and, although without the joy of a forest creature aiding one of the Disney princesses, she had done it. This was a breakthrough for me. I fully appreciated that this shouldn't be a big deal and that most parents would probably view me as pathetic for having let Sophie get away with so much for so long. I'd thought it demonstrated how much I cared. But instead of being appreciated, it was just expected that I'd do everything, quietly in the background, without fuss, like a Victorian chambermaid. Not only by Sophie, who had never known any different, but also by Steve and Josephine, who should have known better and not taken advantage. I wasn't naïve – Sophie wouldn't automatically clear up after herself from now on, and I'd have to constantly remind her, but now that I'd done it once, I knew I could do it again. And she wasn't the only person.

'That applies to you too,' I said to Josephine's retreating back.

She stuck her head back around the kitchen door. 'Did you say something?'

'Yes.' I nodded to her plate and cutlery. Josephine cradled her weak wrist with her other hand. 'You're not an invalid,' I reminded her. Ignoring her flaring nostrils, I walked past her and up the stairs.

* * *

'I'm going now,' I called up the stairs ten minutes later. I held my breath as I zipped up my khaki waterproof jacket, fully expecting Sophie to have taken such umbrage that she'd refuse to come. But, to my delight, she came out of her room.

'Just need to pee,' she called down the stairs, before heading into the bathroom.

Strange how on many occasions a casual 'how are you?' was considered a cross-examination, but she happily shared her toilet habits.

Josephine came out of the living room, deftly took her caramel coat from the hall cupboard with one hand and swung it over her shoulders. When she realised I was watching, she clutched her weak wrist and winced. 'Think I—'

'Overdid it?' I suggested.

She nodded. 'Loading the dishwasher was more arduous than you realise. You're supposed to be looking after me.' My mouth fell open and she patted the air. 'I'm not saying you haven't been, but I'm not out of the woods yet. I still need to be careful.'

I crossed my arms. 'I saw you juggling earlier. You don't think maybe that was more arduous than putting a plate and fork away?'

'That was a hand-strengthening exercise,' Josephine snapped, her cheeks turning pink.

'Is that so?' I said and immediately cringed. Thank goodness I only had another two weeks here before I picked up any more of Josephine's mannerisms. If I started using flamboyant hand gestures and believing that ironing socks was the norm, then I'd have to ask Nikki to shoot me. 'Where are you going?' I asked.

'Up the city.'

I frowned. 'But I'm going up the city, with Sophie.'

'Are you?' Josephine said innocently. 'What a lovely coincidence.' She added a Burberry scarf and tossed one end over her shoulder with a flourish. 'Don't worry, I won't get in your way. Hashtag I'll do you.'

'I'll do you in, if you keep saying hashtag,' I muttered.

'It's you do you, I'll do me,' Sophie said, forcing her feet into her trainers, without undoing the laces and standing on the backs. No wonder she needed new ones.

Josephine nodded. 'Yes, hashtag that.'

'You don't need a hashtag,' I said through gritted teeth.

'Nonsense. Everything deserves a hashtag, doesn't it, Sophie?'

But Sophie didn't hear. She'd put her earbuds in to avoid having to communicate. Usually I found this infuriating. Today I wished I'd thought of it first.

I'd planned to walk, but a bus pulled up at the stop as we were passing, and Sophie and Josephine had already boarded before the driver had put the handbrake on. It took us on such a convoluted route that I could have walked up the city and back several times before we arrived, but Sophie took the opportunity to have a power nap. Either to catch up after a late shift at the pub the night before or to avoid Josephine's incessant chatter about her hand-modelling career, spoken loud enough to ensure everyone around heard. Whenever I fell asleep in the car, which was often, given Steve's monotone narration of the entire journey from, I stumbled out disorientated and crumpled, with creases all over my face. When Sophie disembarked from the bus, she looked as fresh as if she'd emerged from a cryotherapy chamber.

'There's Hope,' she said, running over to a young woman.

While Josephine and I waited for her, I pushed my hands into my pockets and rounded my shoulders to try and keep warm.

'Stand up straight. You look as though you've got a hunch.' Josephine placed a hand in front of her stomach and raised it slowly to the top of her head, demonstrating how to elongate one's spine. 'It's important to keep everything upright and flexible.' She went on to perform a series of side stretches, oblivious to the shoppers stepping around her as they passed.

I pressed my chin into my chest, in an attempt to shrink myself as much as possible, and moved a few metres away. How was it possible that at the age of almost fifty, my mother was still embarrassing me?

Sophie came over. 'This is Hope and her mum, Lindsay.'

'Hi.' I smiled.

Lindsay put a hand to her chest. 'I have to say, I hope I look as good as you do when I'm seventy.'

I made a strangled noise.

Sophie snorted with laughter. 'No, this is my mum. It's my grandma who's seventy.'

'I'm so sorry,' Lindsay stammered. 'I misunderstood what Sophie said.'

I should have said: 'Don't worry, it's all right.' But being mistaken for someone twenty years older was not all right, and no amount of British politeness could force me to pretend it was.

'Hope and I are going to hang out,' Sophie said. My eye twitched. There went my chance to talk to her about uni.

The two girls walked away, and Lindsay and I looked at each other awkwardly.

Lindsay touched her cheek. 'Do you have something in your eye?'

I sighed heavily. 'No. It spasms sometimes.'

'Oh.' Judging by her expression, if Lindsay were able to manipulate the ground into opening up and swallowing her, she'd be en route to the Earth's core right now. 'I'd better get on.' There was a note of panic in her voice, no doubt caused by fear that she'd say something else kind or helpful, such as how small breasts really suited some women. 'Nice to meet you,' she added. I didn't return the sentiment. Lindsay scuttled off and I wandered over to Josephine.

'I told you scraping your hair back like that is ageing,' Josephine said, giving me a triumphant look.

I tightened my ponytail. 'It was a mistake. She thought I was you.'

'But she believed you could be seventy.'

'Which makes you ninety, don't forget.'

'Hardly, darling. Could a ninety-year-old do this?' She reached down and touched her toes.

'Can you please get up?' I hissed. 'People are looking.'

Josephine straightened up. 'Which people?' she asked, looking around eagerly. Her smile dropped and she spun back to me. 'Let's go,' she said, slipping her arm through mine.

'Hello, there,' came a voice behind us.

It was geriatric Audrey's sparkly-haired son.

'Oh, hello,' Josephine tugged at my arm. 'Can't stop, I'm afraid.'

'That's a shame,' he said. 'I was going to get a pot of tea. Can I tempt you ladies to join me?'

'Another time perhaps,' Josephine said. 'We're going Christmas shopping.'

I grabbed the opportunity to escape, quicker than a bargain hunter at a sample sale. 'You go and have tea,' I said brightly. 'I can't get your Christmas present while you're with me.'

'But I—'

'I'll see you back at the house.' I unhooked Josephine's arm from mine and proffered her hand, like a father passing a bride to her groom. Or a police officer handing over a criminal. 'I'm meeting Nikki at four, so I'll be home about six.'

Before she could object, I turned and speed-walked to the Lanes. Once I was sure I was far enough away that two septuagenarians couldn't catch me up, I slowed down. Despite the festively decorated displays, my earlier enthusiasm for Christmas shopping had gone completely, thanks to Lindsay's belief that I was seventy. I slowed when I reached a hair salon and stared at my reflection in the window. Did straightening my hair and scraping it back really make me look so old? I didn't mind being mumsy, but I wasn't ready to be grand-mumsy. The hair salon, FoundLove, had its logo etched on the window – *Taking care of you*. My throat tightened and, inexplicably and slightly embarrassingly, tears pricked my eyes. I was so tired of taking care of everyone else. I yearned for someone to take care of me, even if it was just for an hour. Taking a deep breath, I went in.

# Chapter 29

'Look at you!' Nikki clapped her hands with delight and circled me.

I'd messaged and arranged to meet in the womenswear department of Jarrolds rather than the café. The time had come to get her fashion advice.

I grinned and ran a hand through my new, graduated bob. It fell in soft waves to my chin, but was shorter at the back, to get rid of the damaged hair and create a healthy, stylish look. The experience had been wonderful. I'd left the salon energised and hungry for more. My next stop had been the MAC counter, where I'd had a full makeover. My MUA had advised against using foundation. He said my skin didn't need it and it'd be a crime to cover up my freckles. So, after years of trying to erase them with the equivalent of creosote, I was embracing them.

'I love it.' Nikki grinned. 'The hair, the makeup. Talk about glow-up.'

I gestured to my waterproof jacket, skinny jeans and navy jumper. 'Not in this outfit. Which is where you come in.'

Nikki shimmied her shoulders. 'I've waited years for this. Follow me.'

Two hours later we were sitting in Mr Postles' Apothecary, surrounded by bags, toasting each other with a cocktail.

Nikki chinked her margarita glass against mine. 'Here's to the new you.'

There was a mirror on the wall behind her and I couldn't resist taking a peek. Was that really me? My green eyes stood out thanks to the shimmery brown eyeshadow, and a rose-coloured lip plumper made my mouth fuller, especially as it wasn't drawn into a thin, resentful line – as was often the case when around my family. My original clothes were now in a carrier bag. Nikki had wanted to throw them away, but I persuaded her to let me keep them, on the condition I only wore them when gardening. I was now wearing a teal, wide-legged jumpsuit with a thin black belt to accentuate my waist, and black boots. The other bags contained wide-legged jeans in blue and dark denim, black cigarette pants, a sleeveless emerald green top, a powder blue silk shirt, an assortment of thin knits, a chunky, long cardigan, some white and gold trainers, and some Mary Janes with a chunky heel that hopefully I could stay upright in. I'd blown all of the money I'd earned from Rey in one afternoon – as much as the holiday home in Spain cost for a week. I should be racked with guilt, but I wasn't. I was on a high.

My phone beeped and I got it out of my new shoulder bag. My rucksack didn't have the right vibe, as Sophie would say, for my new image. It was a message from Sophie. She'd gone back to Hope's and was asking if I could pick her up at seven and take her straight to the pub for her shift. Not so long ago, possibly even the day before, I'd have abandoned my margarita and run home to get my car so that I could collect her. But what would that be teaching Sophie? That she didn't need to plan or figure out the logistics of a situation because her mum would make sure she was where she needed to be at the allocated time. No, it would not help her develop essential life skills. I was doing her a favour by saying no. And I could work on my own essential life skills at the same time – drinking cocktails with Nikki.

'Everything OK?' Nikki asked when my phone beeped for a third time after I'd replied to Sophie.

'Yes. I've just told Sophie I can't pick her up from her friend's and take her to work.' The phone beeped again. 'I think she's trying to put her case forward as to why I should.'

'There is no case. You're busy. End of,' Nikki said. 'I love Sophie, you know I do, but she's eighteen. She can figure this out. If she was at uni, she wouldn't be ringing and asking for a lift, would she?'

I shook my head.

'Speaking of uni . . .' Nikki said. 'What's she decided to do?'

'I don't know.' I nibbled on a nail. 'She says she's still thinking about it. I'm not convinced she is, but I feel guilty pressuring her.'

Nikki held a hand up. 'Stop with the guilt. You have got to make her talk about this. It isn't a game.'

'I know. I don't want it to seem as though I actively want her to go back. Although . . .' My face grew hot and I held the glass against my cheek to cool it.

'Although?' Nikki prompted.

'I'm starting to agree with you about not being able to fully embrace my second act. It's not that I don't want her around,' I said hurriedly. 'You know how much I missed her when she was away, and I absolutely love having her here, but . . .' I glanced around, fearful of voicing out loud how I was feeling, in case somehow Sophie heard or another mother did and judged me. 'I was just starting to appreciate the benefits of not having to be a mum all the time. Of not having to think about someone else before agreeing to the lunch date with Cath and Nina, for example. I'm having to take Josephine into account at the moment, but that's only for another two weeks. After that, if Sophie's back at uni, I'll have the freedom to do what I like when I like. I can go to Bath without worrying if there's enough food in the fridge and tampons in the bathroom and a spare key hidden somewhere for when she inevitably forgets hers.'

Shame flooded through me as I confessed what I didn't want to admit to myself. 'I feel like a hypocrite, because this goes against everything I felt when she first went to uni. I didn't know what to do with myself initially. Now, I want to focus on MAAM and pursue other opportunities. But I feel selfish if I prioritise these when Sophie's at home.' I looked miserably at Nikki. 'I'm so torn between being excited about what's ahead and feeling like a selfish mum who puts her own needs before her child's. That's how Josephine made me feel a lot of the time when I was growing up. Her modelling career always came first and I swore I wouldn't be like that.'

Nikki shook her head vigorously. 'You're nothing like Josephine. You've given everything you had to Sophie, physically, mentally and emotionally. It's not selfish to do something for yourself now. You've more than earned it. And it's not like you're going to ignore her and not be there when she needs you. Regardless of whether she goes back to uni or not, you're entitled to a fulfilling life.'

'Thank you.' I released a shaky breath. 'Any advice on how to get Sophie to talk to me about uni? She could get a degree in avoidance techniques.'

Nikki raised her eyebrows. 'Wonder where she gets that from.'

I looked at her in surprise. 'What do you mean?'

'You don't think maybe you're avoiding talking about Steve?'

'No.' I reached round to tighten my ponytail, but of course it wasn't there anymore.

Nikki put her head to one side. 'We've been together for over two hours and you haven't mentioned Steve once. I know all about MAAM and Marenee and your trip to Bath, and Sophie's job and her friend's rude mum, and Josephine's silver supermodels campaign, and the unfair dismissal claim.' She ticked them off her fingers. 'But Steve's name hasn't come up once. That's not a criticism,' she added gently. 'It's an observation.'

I stared at my hands, searching for a hangnail. 'It's not that I'm avoiding talking about him. There isn't anything to say, because we haven't seen each other. I wouldn't have anything to say about Josephine either if I hadn't seen her. If only,' I added with a small laugh.

'Have you come up with any common interests?' Nikki asked, kindly sidestepping the more obvious question – *why* hadn't I seen my husband?

'Not yet,' I said. 'But all my time and energy are being channelled into work and worrying about Sophie and managing Josephine. I've still got two weeks till I go home. I'll make some time to focus on it properly.'

Nikki wound a coil of hair around her finger. 'You don't *have* to go back in two weeks.'

'What?' I spluttered. 'I'm not staying on once Josephine's fully recovered. That'd be masochistic.'

'I'm not suggesting you do,' Nikki said gently. 'There is another option.'

My stomach lurched. 'What? You don't mean move somewhere else? Leave Steve?' I shook my head vigorously. 'No. That's ridiculous. Why would I do that?'

'This comeback I keep banging on about doesn't just have to be about your career.' Nikki reached across and took my hand. 'Have you missed Steve while you've been apart?'

I took a large mouthful of my drink. 'No, but there's been a lot going on.' I'd found time to miss Nikki, but that was different. I wasn't sure why, but it was.

'Are you looking forward to being back together?'

The tequila swirled around my throat and I swallowed hard. No, I wasn't. Not in any way. In fact, I'd go as far as to say I was dreading it. My eye twitched.

'What else can I do?' I whispered. 'My redundancy pay won't last long if I have to rent somewhere.'

'You own half that house,' Nikki said gently. 'You wouldn't be destitute.'

I shook my head. 'I can't do that to Sophie.'

'Sophie would handle it. She might even understand. She's not a kid anymore.' Nikki clocked the dubious look on my face. 'Yes, she's got a lot of growing up to do, but that's not a reason for you to stay if you're not happy.' She took my hand away from my mouth, where I was chewing on a nail. 'If you go back, go because you want to, not out of duty or guilt. If you're not ready in two weeks, pretend Josephine's had another turn to give yourself more thinking time. Life is long. Make sure you do what's right for you.'

'I thought life was short.'

Nikki gave a small smile. 'Not if you're in an unhappy marriage, it isn't.'

Tears pricked my eyes. What the hell was I going to do?

My phone beeped on the table. Nikki picked it up. 'Sophie can't still be asking for a lift, can she? She looked at the screen and her eyes widened. Smiling broadly, she turned the phone to face me. Instead of a message from Sophie, it was a calendar alert. For dinner with Rey in ten minutes.

I gasped. 'Oh no. I forgot about dinner. It's a business thing,' I added, seeing Nikki ready herself for a shoulder shimmy. 'The restaurant owners are giving him a freebie because he did their website. He wants to talk to me about writing a regular blog post for his website, so suggested I go with him.' My stomach swirled at the prospect of it just being me and Rey. I wasn't sure about this, especially after the conversation I'd just had about Steve.

I clutched Nikki's hand. 'Can you come too?'

'No! He invited you, not me. Besides, Chiwetel's cousins are cooking, as a thank you for having them.'

I looked around desperately for an excuse. 'I can't take all these bags to the restaurant.'

'I'll take them home and drop them round tomorrow.' She winked. 'What time does Rey have his shower?'

I gave her a disapproving look. 'It varies. And no, I'm not giving you a tip-off.'

Nikki smirked. 'Are you still getting flustered around him?'

'No.' My cheeks grew warm. 'Although, I did fall over when we were on the ghost walk.'

'Did you manage to keep your top on this time?'

My cheeks exploded.

Nikki laughed and scooped up my bags. 'You'd better get going, so you're not late for your *business meeting*.' Her voice dropped an octave.

'I don't want to go,' I said, my own voice rising a few octaves.

'You have to. It'd be rude to cancel now. And you look too good to stay in.'

I caught sight of myself in the mirror. She had a point. Without the help of trained professionals, I'd never look like this again, so I should make the most of it.

She hugged me tightly. 'Have a nice evening. I'll see you in the morning.'

'Thanks for everything.' I drained my glass and slipped on the calf-length, moss-green coat that Nikki had also insisted I needed. She'd known instinctively what clothes were right for me. Did that mean she knew instinctively what was right for me in my marriage? I pulled the belt tight and took a deep breath. I'd think about that later. I had to get through dinner with Rey first.

# Chapter 30

My stomach somersaulted during the whole of the short walk to the restaurant. I blamed Nikki for saying 'business meeting' in such a sensual way that implied it was taking place in a boudoir, when it was all very professional and above board.

Rey was waiting outside the restaurant. His eyes lingered on me for a few seconds as I approached, then he looked past me.

I stopped in front of him. 'Hi.'

He looked at me questioningly, then his eyes widened. 'Becca?'

I nodded, blushing.

'You look . . .' He nudged his glasses up. 'Great. Really great.'

I swallowed a smile. 'It's just makeup and a new haircut. It'll have worn off by tomorrow.' I tightened the coat belt. 'Shall we go in?'

'Yes, yes, of course.' Rey opened the door. 'After you.'

The manager, Soraya, greeted Rey and welcomed me as warmly as a potential bride for her brother. Or a restaurant inspector. We were given a table in the window and some prawn crackers arrived instantly, along with two glasses of fizz.

'*Chon*,' Rey said. 'That's the Thai equivalent of cheers.'

'*Chon*,' I repeated, raising my glass.

We took a sip, put our glasses down and smiled at each other awkwardly. My stomach fluttered. Meeting Nikki beforehand had been a mistake. Putting doubts in my mind about going back to Steve. Making silly excited 'oohs' and 'ahs' about my dinner with Rey. Making me come to the dinner, full stop. I could still leave, I reasoned. Pretend I'd had a call from Sophie, saying she was sick, or that something serious had happened to Josephine. Rey didn't need to know that breaking a nail constituted an emergency. I reached for my bag, ready to excuse myself to go to the ladies, where I'd receive my fictitious call.

'I . . .' I started but was interrupted by Soraya.

'I hope you don't mind, but I've put together a tasting menu, so you can experience as many flavours as possible.' She placed a platter of incredible-looking delicacies on the table. I inhaled the scent of lemongrass, ginger and coriander, and dropped my bag with the speed of the BBC cancelling a disgraced TV presenter.

Rey and I thanked her profusely and tucked in, filling the silence with appreciative noises. Soraya brought over a bottle of white wine that she felt would complement the meal and smiled at our enthusiasm over the food.

'You can't beat authentic Thai food,' Rey said. 'If I lived there, I'd be obese.'

'It's amazing,' I agreed. 'Though your mum's food is incredible too. I always eat enough for four people when she drops some round to Josephine.' Josephine never ate any herself, as the spices might cause an imbalance in her skin tone, but I didn't mention this, in case the food parcels stopped.

'Can I ask something?' Rey leant forward. 'I don't want to sound rude, but why are her door handles slippery? I didn't think I was going to get out once.'

I giggled. 'Hand cream. She thinks her hands will shrivel like a vampire in the sun if she isn't coated in it at all times.' I put my head to one side. 'Don't know if she's told you, but she's a hand model.'

'She may have mentioned it in passing.'

We grinned at each other and my stomach flipped over. I cleared my throat. 'You were going to tell me about the blog posts.'

'Ah, yes.' Rey blotted his mouth with his napkin. 'What I like about your writing is the warmth behind it. You can tell it's been written by a person. So much content is churned out by AI now. That's not what I'm about. I want clients to see that we have personality and that we care.'

Rey refilled my wine glass and I nodded my thanks.

'I'd like to offer my clients something extra, and hopefully attract potential customers,' he continued. 'A weekly blog post providing them with something new or interesting or fun would keep them coming back, hopefully.'

I nodded. 'If you get people to sign up to a newsletter, you can email them each week with a brief outline of the blog post, so they don't have to remember to seek it out. You'd be directing them to it, and you'd have their email address for future marketing campaigns.'

'That's a brilliant idea.' Rey thrust his hands in his hair. 'My concern had been getting people to know the blog posts are there. A newsletter's the perfect solution. Thank you.'

I sipped my wine to hide a smile.

A server cleared away the empty platter and replaced it with a selection of bowls containing a variety of delicious dishes and side portions of rice.

Rey and I chatted easily about music, films and TV, as well as his childhood – I changed the subject when he asked me about mine; this was a business dinner, not an episode of *Jeremy Kyle* – and my time at *Norwich Now* and the varying roles I'd had before Nikki trained me to be a journalist. Rey reinforced what he'd told me before about how running his own business was so much more fulfilling than working for someone else. When he spoke about what he did, his passion for helping people shone through. I knew then that I'd enjoy writing the blog posts. If I could capture and put down in words the messages he wanted to get across, they'd be compelling and interesting, to write as well as read.

Somehow, despite the vast quantity of food we'd been given, we worked our way through most of it, as well as being halfway down another bottle of wine that had appeared as soon as the first was finished.

Soraya came over after our plates had been cleared away. 'How was everything?' she asked.

'It's official,' Rey said, sitting back in his chair. 'Thai is my favourite food.'

Soraya clasped her hands together and I tried to think what Steve's favourite food was, but then realised he didn't have one. His palate tended to favour whatever was on offer.

'It really was incredible,' I said. 'Such a fantastic fusion of flavours.'

'A fantastic fusion of flavours,' Soraya repeated. 'I like that.'

'I'll add it to the website,' Rey said. 'If Becca doesn't mind me quoting her.'

I shook my head. 'It's the least I can do to say thank you for such an incredible meal.'

Rey excused himself to go to the gents and Soraya smiled at me warmly. 'You really enjoyed it? You're not just saying that to be nice?'

'Definitely not. It was amazing.' I placed my hands on my stomach. 'Wish I could keep going, but I'm full to the brim.'

'You'll have to come back another time and try something else then.' Soraya grinned. 'Bring your family, friends, colleagues . . . random strangers off the street.'

I returned her smile. 'I will.' And I would. But with friends, not family. I wanted Soraya to like me. Steve would grumble that there were no sachets to pocket; Sophie would be put out that they didn't serve ketchup; and Josephine would use her chopsticks so flamboyantly that she'd end up knitting a scarf with the noodles.

'Not sounding too desperate, am I?' Soraya asked. 'We need all the customers we can get. Rey's done a fantastic job with the website and charged half what he should have. We could only afford a basic page, but he added visuals and a booking system and a feedback form. All for free.' No wonder tonight's meal was on the house. 'But we need to get people in regularly if we're going to make a success of it,' she added.

'You certainly deserve to be a success. Have you thought of running a giveaway with the local press and radio?' I asked. 'They're happy to promote companies if the reader or listener's getting something out of it, and it's a good way to create awareness.'

'That's a great idea,' Soraya said. 'I used to be an accountant, so while I'm good at balancing the books, I have no idea how to promote this place.'

'You haven't always worked in hospitality?'

'No.' Soraya laughed. 'It probably sounds crazy, because I was pretty successful, but when I turned forty, I realised that I didn't want to be part of the rat race any longer. I always thought I'd reassess when I had children, but unfortunately that never happened, so I kept going.' A flicker of sadness crossed her face, and I had a yearning to ring Sophie and tell her how much I loved her and that she could live with me forever. Actually, if anything was going to encourage her to go back to uni, that was probably it.

'I took a sabbatical and stayed with family in Thailand for a couple of months while I figured out what to do,' Soraya continued. 'I really connected with the food and the cooking, and the way meals bring everyone together. It ignited a spark, so I left my job, enrolled on a cookery course, then opened this place.'

'That's so impressive,' I said, genuinely in awe.

'The chefs are the impressive ones.' She smiled. 'My cooking is very basic compared to theirs, but I wanted to learn enough to understand the process and use my previous experience to run the business side of things.' She stepped to one side to let Rey sit back down. 'It's hard work, but I love it and really hope we can make a success of it.'

She was truly inspirational and exactly the kind of woman worthy of a profile in MAAM's new series. 'I'm interviewing women who have changed career for an online magazine,' I said. 'Do you think you might be interested? The restaurant would get some exposure, as well as you.'

'Definitely.' Soraya nodded eagerly. 'I'll do anything to get the name out.'

'Great. I'll get your details before we go.'

'Perfect. I'll leave you to enjoy the rest of your wine. No rush to leave.' Soraya pressed her hands together and bowed her head, first to me, then to Rey. '*Khob Khun Ka*.'

Rey stood and returned the gesture. '*Khob Khun Khrab*,' he said.

I quickly pressed my hands together and lowered my head, feeling ignorant for not being able to join in.

'Do you speak Thai?' I asked when Soraya had left.

'*Mai ka*,' Rey said.

'That's impressive.'

He shook his head and smiled. '*Mai ka* means no. I learnt a few basics when Saif and I went to Thailand last summer. Have you been?'

I shook my head, embarrassed to admit that Steve and I went to the same Spanish villa every year. It wouldn't have been my first choice of destination. Rather than experiencing the culture and beauty of the country, we were stuck in an expats' haven. The only remotely Spanish heritage we saw were the fans and flamenco outfits in the souvenir shop at the airport. But we knew what we were getting and there were no surprises. That had been its key appeal for me. Now, though, the thought of going back to the same, insular, parochial community filled me with dread. Especially as Sophie had already said she wouldn't be coming anymore. I drained my glass. How would I cope with Steve on my own for a whole week?

'It's an incredible country,' Rey said. 'The beaches are breathtaking, and of course the food's incredible. Bangkok is something else. The Grand Palace with the Temple of the Emerald Buddha and the Reclining Buddha is out of this world. Has to be seen to be believed.'

I smiled. 'Thailand was on my list of places to visit when I planned to go travelling.'

'Was?' Rey cocked his head. 'Why the past tense? You could still go.'

Something inside me flickered, but then I remembered Steve's reluctance to travel. It wasn't purely financial – he saw hazards everywhere. Every time a tourist was killed overseas, it bolstered his argument that staying in an expat community was the safest option.

I fiddled with my napkin. 'I guess I'm a bit risk-averse.' Heat flooded my cheeks as I realised how pathetic I must sound.

'Thailand's no more dangerous than anywhere else,' Rey said gently. 'You have to keep your wits about you wherever you are.' He indicated out of the window with his thumb. 'You could get your drink spiked, or be mugged or beaten, in any city centre.' His eyes flitted to mine, then down to the table. 'I should know. It happened to me in Brighton.'

I gasped. 'I'm so sorry.'

He nodded grimly. 'It's why I don't run at night anymore.' His grip tightened on his wine glass. 'I used to love running along the seafront when it was quiet, but one night a gang of lads attacked me.'

My hands flew to my mouth. 'A gang?'

Rey shrugged. 'There were four of them. The police referred to them as a gang. Makes it slightly less shameful that I was outnumbered.'

I shook my head. 'It wouldn't be shameful if it was just one person. That there were four is horrific.'

Rey gave a grim smile. 'It wasn't pleasant, that's for sure.'

'Were you badly hurt?'

'Could have been a lot worse. They got a few kicks in, but luckily some people saw from a pub across the road and shouted that they were calling the police, and the lads ran off.'

'Did they get caught?'

'No. The police didn't have anything to go on. They didn't steal anything. It was just a mindless racist attack. They saw a "paki" coming and jumped me.'

I flinched at the use of the word. How horrific for Rey to be the victim of something so bigoted and sadistic, and how disgusting that those men had got away with it.

His hand shook as he smoothed the tablecloth, and I instinctively placed my own over his. 'I'm so sorry you went through that.'

'Thank you.' He took a deep breath and released it slowly. 'I'm OK now, but it really screwed me up at the time. Nightmares, being afraid to go out.'

'That's understandable,' I said softly. 'It'd be strange if you weren't affected.'

He nodded. 'I'm sure it's why I was made redundant. I'd worked all hours before then. My parents drummed it into me that being a person of colour in a predominantly white country, I'd have to work harder than everyone else to succeed. I thought that putting in long days, working my way up the career ladder and earning a good salary made me a good son, husband and father. Then the attack happened.

'I went from accepting everything my manager offloaded on me, to questioning why I was the one who had to stay late every night, on my own.' He ran a hand across his jaw. 'It was partly because I didn't feel safe, but mainly because I realised that time's precious and I shouldn't spend it all at work. Don't get me wrong, I didn't come close to dying and see my life flash before my eyes. But I reassessed my priorities. I got lucky with the redundancy, really. It was a decent package and allowed me to have some time to sort myself out, work out what I really wanted, what was important, and set my business up.'

I nodded. I needed to view my own redundancy in the same way and be thankful it hadn't come about as the result of a brutal attack prompted by nothing more senseless and cruel than the colour of my skin.

'It led to the breakdown of my marriage too,' he added.

I inhaled sharply and Rey gave me an apologetic look. 'Sorry. You don't need to hear about this. TMI, as the kids say.'

I shook my head. 'No, it's not that. I just, well, feel terrible that all of this has happened to you.'

'It's OK. The marriage was over already, really. My wife had met someone else.' My mouth dropped open and Rey gave me a reassuring smile. 'It wasn't her fault. I was always at work, remember? She was lonely. She told me and ended it, and we tried to put it aside. But after the attack, I knew there was no point carrying on, when we were just going through the motions. It wasn't fair on any of us. We waited till Saif had done his GCSEs, then told him. She's married to the guy now and is happy, and I no longer have to feel guilty for not being the person she wanted me to be.'

He nudged his glasses up. 'I wasted too much of Saif's childhood working. That's why I moved to Norwich for his first term, while he's struggling. I need him to know I'll always be there for him. I regret those early years. I don't want to regret any more.'

I nodded, my own guilt at having done so much for Sophie lifting slightly. I'd done it to give Sophie security and the knowledge that she'd been loved and looked after. Now I was having to navigate between being a nice mum and a pushover. It was a fine line. In the same way there was a fine line between a light breeze and a gale-force wind.

Rey misread my frown. 'Sorry. Didn't mean to bring the mood down. My point was that bad things can happen anywhere, so don't let that put you off going to Thailand.'

I had a sudden yearning to go to Thailand. To experience all the wonderful things Rey and Soraya had. But Steve would never consider it. Not when the Spanish villa was as cheap as chips. Which were also served with every meal, as indicated in the laminated photos on sandwich boards outside each restaurant.

'Or anywhere,' Rey added. 'Just go. We only get one life. Don't waste it not daring to do things that could bring you joy and happiness.' I nodded and he smiled and squeezed my hand. I hadn't even realised it was still in his. 'Thank you for listening,' he said softly.

Our eyes locked. He had beautiful deep brown eyes. And a beautiful face. And, as I was discovering, a beautiful heart. And that was before I even started thinking about those toned arms and calves. My stomach fluttered alarmingly. The most alarming aspect being that it wasn't actually my stomach that was fluttering. It was somewhere significantly lower.

# Chapter 31

I swallowed hard and snatched my hand back. 'The blogs sound as though they'll be a great asset to your website, moving forward,' I said. 'Email me over the information when you're ready to proceed and I'll action them.'

If Rey was surprised by the sudden change in conversation, from compassionate confidante to someone playing corporate bingo, he didn't show it. 'Thank you. I will.' He took a twenty-pound note from his wallet and placed it under his glass. Steve never left any money for the servers. Not even when we'd had a free meal, courtesy of our Tesco vouchers. I always left some myself, then had to suffer a monologue about how he wasn't paid anything extra on top of his salary, so why should they be? It was one of the reasons we no longer went out. One of the many, many, *many* reasons. Including his loud nasal breathing while eating, which sounded like a vacuum cleaner trying to hoover up a sock.

'I'll call a cab,' Rey said.

I was about to say that I didn't mind the walk, then realised he'd probably prefer not to, after what he'd been through. It had been much earlier when we'd walked back from the ghost walk. I remembered him steering me across the road when we approached a group of youths. How sad that he was always on red alert like that. Although, women had to be all the time. I was constantly reminding Sophie to never walk home alone.

Before we left, I took Soraya's email address so I could contact her about the interview for MAAM. She asked if she could buy me a coffee in exchange for advice on how to put a press release together, which I happily agreed to. Soraya was so warm, inspirational and capable, I'd have agreed to meet her for advice on defrosting a freezer if that's what she wanted.

'Thank you for coming tonight,' Rey said as we walked up Josephine's drive and reached the point where I went straight ahead and he took the more enviable route to the coach house. 'It was much more fun with you there.'

'Thank you for inviting me.' Should I shake his hand? Reinforce the work aspect of the evening?

Rey nudged his glasses up. 'Sorry I got a bit heavy. I hadn't planned to say any of that. It just came out.'

I smiled. 'I'm glad you felt you could talk to me about it.'

'You're a very good listener.'

He wasn't to know I'd had years of training. But, in contrast to Steve, Rey had interesting things to say, and he asked me questions, making it a conversation rather than an onslaught of information or vacuous white noise.

'You've got so many good ideas too,' he said. 'Your editor was a fool to let you go. Your suggestions about my newsletter and the giveaway for Soraya were great.'

'Soraya's lovely,' I said, embarrassed at having the focus on me.

Rey nodded. 'She is.' Something twisted in my stomach. Indigestion probably. 'Her husband's a really nice guy too,' Rey added. Whatever had lodged itself in my gut loosened.

'She said you did lots of extra bits on her website for free,' I said. 'That was nice of you.'

'No point having your own business if you can't help people who deserve it.' He rubbed his jaw and regarded me thoughtfully. A warm tingle spread through me, despite the chill of the air. His deep brown eyes shone behind his glasses. His lips were full and slightly parted. My pulse quickened and I dug my nails into my palm to prevent a small moan escaping from me.

He took a deep breath. 'Becca—'

'What time do you call this, young lady?' The front door swung open to reveal Josephine in a long dressing gown, her cotton-gloved hands on her hips. 'You said you'd be home at six and it's gone eleven.'

Rey and I jumped and blinked into the light.

'Sorry, my fault,' Rey said. 'I invited Becca to join me for dinner.'

'Oh, how kind.' Josephine's tone switched from drill sergeant to Doris Day. 'Well, don't mind me.'

I snapped back to reality. What was I doing? I was married. I shouldn't be out here gawping at Rey's mouth and wondering what it might be like to feel it on mine.

'Thanks for dinner,' I blurted, not daring to look at him. 'Night.' I shot inside, yanking Josephine in with me and shutting the door.

She looked at me slyly. 'Dinner?'

'A *business* dinner,' I corrected. 'We discussed some blog posts I can write for his website and he introduced me to the restaurant manager, who's looking to attract new customers.'

Josephine raised her eyebrows. 'Is that so?'

'Yes,' I snapped. 'It's very much so.' I hung my new coat up and sat on the stairs to ease off my boots.

'You look nice,' Josephine said. My irritation eased slightly. 'I didn't realise it was you at first.' And then it shot back up again.

'Good night,' I said tightly and huffed my way up the stairs.

Once in my room, I sank onto the bed. My hands trembled as I gripped my knees. A strange sensation coursed through me and I struggled to identify it. Annoyed? No, nothing unfamiliar about that emotion. Upset? No, that wasn't it. Anxious? Not particularly. I searched my mind till I landed on the word that perfectly described how I was feeling.

*Flustered*.

My right eye twitched manically. Oh no.

# Chapter 32

'OK, you were right,' I whispered to Nikki, ushering her into the kitchen and closing the door. Josephine was doing her physio exercises in the living room and Sophie was in bed.

'Right about what?' she whispered back, putting my bags down.

I covered my eyes with my hands. 'I do feel a bit flustered at times around Rey.'

'Sweet Jesus,' she squealed. 'Did something happen last night?'

'Of course not,' I said, but my cheeks grew warm under her penetrating gaze. 'Not really.'

She inhaled sharply. '*Not really* isn't a no.'

I sat at the breakfast bar. 'At the end of the night, I felt that maybe, just maybe, we shared a moment.' My stomach flip-flopped at the memory of his eyes on my face.

'What happened?' Nikki asked breathlessly.

'We were looking at each other and he said my name, then Josephine opened the door and asked why I was back so late.'

'What do you think he was going to say?' Nikki asked.

I clutched the front of my dressing gown. In the fantasy I'd had once in bed, he'd invited me back to his for a nightcap. A nightcap being very much a euphemism.

'Something to do with his website probably.' I rolled my eyes. 'I'm making more of it than there was. I'd had quite a bit to drink.'

'How did you leave it?'

'Just a normal goodbye.' If shooting through the door as though I'd been zapped with a cattle prod could be classed as normal. 'And then a telling-off from Josephine for being late home, like I was a teenager.'

'She was probably worried.'

'More likely she wanted me to turn back her covers or squeeze some toothpaste onto her toothbrush.'

Nikki chuckled. 'I take it the evening went well if it led to you *having a moment*.'

The way she said it made it sound as though we'd had full-on sex on the bonnet of my car. My eye spasmed. 'Yes, the evening went well. I'm going to write those blog posts for him. I really like the way he works, his values and passion for his work.'

'His passion, eh?' Nikki murmured.

I ignored her. 'The owner of the restaurant, Soraya, is perfect for an interview for MAAM, and she asked if I'd give her some advice on putting together a press release. Just as a friend, not a paid job, but it'll be a nice thing to do. We'll have to go there some time. The food was amazing and Soraya's lovely.'

'I'd love to, but stop changing the subject,' Nikki said. 'What are you going to do about Rey?'

'What do you mean?'

'You like him,' she said simply. 'And he obviously likes you.' I opened my mouth, but she carried on before I could speak. 'Before you say, "But I'm married," remember what we talked about yesterday. You don't *have* to go back to Steve. I'm not saying that breaking up and starting again would be easy, but staying together if it's not right would be a lot harder.'

'I can't leave Steve for Rey,' I spluttered. 'He's just a friend.' I hoped my overactive imagination was listening and stopped putting the two of us in compromising positions, particularly ones that threatened to put my back out.

'Of course not,' Nikki said. 'If you leave Steve, it has to be for you – no one else. I just think that this flustered feeling you get around Rey is worth examining. I've known you a long time and it's good to see a sparkle in your eye.'

'It's not a sparkle, it's a twitch,' I said.

We both giggled.

'OK, have it your way,' Nikki said. 'But I'm glad you and Rey are friends. He's obviously a decent bloke.'

I nibbled on a nail. Yes, Rey was a decent bloke. But so was Steve, in his own way.

She looked at her watch. 'I've got to go. Having a last brunch with Chiwetel's cousins before they leave for the airport.' She raised her hands to heaven. 'Then I'll get my house back and can have sex with my husband again.'

We couldn't be at more opposite ends in the relationship spectrum. Having sex with my husband was the thing putting me *off* getting my house back.

'Thanks for bringing my bags round.' I hugged her. 'Enjoy yourself.' I hooked the sleeve of my dressing gown over my hand to open the front door.

'Before I go, can I leave you with one thought?' Nikki whispered. 'Would you and Steve be friends if you weren't married?' She gave my arm a squeeze. 'I'm playing devil's advocate here, but it's worth taking into consideration when you're deciding what to do.'

We said goodbye and arranged to meet for lunch the next day. After she'd gone, I paced the kitchen, my heart thumping. I didn't need to give her question any thought. The answer was no. Steve and I were husband and wife, not friends. We never sat chatting, or laughed together, or sent each other funny messages or memes, the way Nikki and I did. I didn't miss him when he went away with work or look forward to him getting back. We'd barely seen each other or spoken for the past few weeks, and I hadn't once wondered what he was doing or been tempted to ring just to hear his voice. The overwhelming feeling had been one of relief that I didn't have to listen to his constant droning on, or cook, clean and wash for him. Admittedly, I was doing all of that for Josephine, but at least she paused for breath occasionally, asked me the odd question and didn't expect me to reuse coffee granules. I blinked with horror. Things with Steve were worse than I'd feared if Josephine was outranking him as a housemate.

Sophie wandered into the kitchen and went straight to the cupboard to get some cereal. Determined not to let her know I was maybe, possibly, probably not, but hypothetically, considering leaving her dad and turning life as she knew it upside down, I filled the kettle, hoping she wouldn't notice my trembling hands.

'Up to anything today?' I shrilled.

'Dunno yet.' Sophie sat at the breakfast bar and propped her phone up against the milk carton. She hadn't so much as glanced in my direction, so I needn't have worried that she'd clock my anxious demeanour. Thank goodness for the self-absorbed nature of teenagers. I could burst into flames and she'd only notice if the glare reflected off her screen.

My own phone beeped and Rey's name flashed up on the screen. My stomach performed its now familiar loop-the-loop.

> *Thanks again for last night. Really glad you're able to write the blog posts. I'm around today or tomorrow if you want to come over and talk through some ideas?*

My stomach skidded to a halt, then plummeted at the thought of going to the coach house and being alone with Rey. No, that definitely wasn't an option. Not until I'd got this silly flustered feeling under control. Much better to deal with him via email. Keep it professional, I reminded myself as I typed.

> *Thank you for your reply. I'm busy today, but please email the information and I'll have a look tomorrow. Yours respectfully.*

I pressed send, then instantly regretted every word I'd chosen. *Yours respectfully* was too formal. And why had I thanked him for his reply? He wasn't replying to my message, I was replying to his. Tutting to myself, I reread the message.

*Thanks for the role play.*

A shriek escaped me. Bloody predictive text! I scanned the rest of the message and groaned when I got to the last two words – *Yours resentfully*. What must he think of me?

'What's happened?' Sophie asked.

I stared at my phone. 'Autocorrect changed the wording in a message and I didn't realise till I sent it.'

'No biggie. You can edit it if it hasn't been read.'

Hope flared within me, then was instantly extinguished as two blue ticks appeared by the message. Too late.

# Chapter 33

*Reply!* I typed as quickly as I could, making sure I pre-empted the autocorrect this time. *Not role play! And I meant yours respectfully! Predictive text took over. Sorry!!!*

I pressed send. Was that too many exclamation marks? I stared at the screen, but, typically, this message – the one I wanted him to see instantly – was left unread. After five minutes of nervously chewing my nails while I waited, I gave up. He must be on a call. Or on a run. I gulped. A run meant he'd be coming round to use the bathroom shortly. I gathered up my bags and hurried upstairs to get dressed. Greeting him in my dressing gown wasn't the level of professionalism I was determined to maintain.

I'd showered earlier and my hairstyle had miraculously stayed in place overnight. I put on my new wide-leg jeans and blue silk shirt. The white and gold Veja trainers would go perfectly with them, but I didn't put them on yet, in case Josephine came back and told me off for wearing shoes indoors. The make-up I'd bought was quick and easy to apply, and I smiled at my reflection. It had taken half the time to get ready than it usually took to layer on foundation and electrocute my hair. And, without wanting to appear vain, I looked infinitely better.

Downstairs, Sophie was still at the breakfast bar. She looked up as I came through the door. 'You've had your hair cut.' She looked me up and down. 'Wide-legged jeans – at last! Don't ever wear those horrible skinny ones again.' She grinned. 'Good glow-up.'

'Thank you.' I said it casually but couldn't have been more delighted if I'd won a million pounds and Harrison Ford himself was presenting me with the cheque.

Christmas music wafted from Sophie's phone. 'Can we put some decorations up?' she asked.

'I don't think G has any.' I hadn't seen any in the loft when I'd been up there. The memory of Rey manfully getting the camp bed down, his muscular thighs at eye level, sprang to mind. I stuck my face in the fridge to cool it down.

'Can't we get some from home to put up here?' Sophie said.

I thought of our decorations. Being of a frugal nature, Steve refused to update them. Our Christmas tree was older than Sophie and the glitter had worn off most of the baubles, leaving them so bald, I had to give them comb-overs with the tinsel. Perhaps it was time to invest in some new ones. And a shopping trip would give me an opportunity to talk to Sophie about uni. Nikki was right – I *had* to get her to take this seriously.

'How about going to the garden centre and buying some?'

'To the grotto?' Sophie's face lit up. 'I love it there.'

I grinned. I'd taken her every year when she was younger, and it warmed my heart to know that she had fond memories too.

'Can we get a real tree?' Sophie asked.

Steve was anti real trees – why fork out year after year when you could buy one that'd last for decades? – but I couldn't envisage Josephine coping with pine needles on her pristine carpet. Or me coping with being summoned to do a clean-up operation every time one fell to the floor.

'I think an artificial one would be better,' I said. 'Let's wean G in gradually.'

'OK.' Sophie stood up and went to leave the kitchen. I cleared my throat and looked pointedly at the bowl she'd left. She exhaled loudly, but emptied the excess milk into the sink and placed it in the dishwasher before heading upstairs. Christmas really was a time for miracles.

'We'll go as soon as you're ready,' I called after her.

'Go where?' Josephine asked, coming into the kitchen.

I hesitated. A trip to the garden centre was the equivalent of a night with Antonio Banderas to most senior citizens. But Josephine wasn't like most people, so I took a risk that she wouldn't want to come, when I told her the truth. My gamble paid off and she pulled a face.

'What do you want to go there for? It'll be full of old people.'

'Christmas decorations. Do you mind if we put some up?'

Josephine shuddered. 'I'm not having tinsel in this house.'

'I won't get tinsel,' I promised. 'Just a little tree and—'

'No tree,' Josephine said sharply. 'It might scratch my hands as I walk past.'

'A couple of garlands?'

Josephine recoiled, as though I'd suggested we slaughter a reindeer on the living-room floor and hang its dismembered head above the fireplace. 'Make the place look like a cheap office party? I don't think so.'

I sighed. 'Didn't realise I was living with the Grinch.'

There was a knock at the front door.

'Get that, would you,' Josephine said, cradling her practically fully recovered wrist, as though that gave her immunity.

My new shirt was buttoned at the cuffs, so I couldn't pull it over my hands as I usually did when wrestling with cream-coated handles. 'Just a sec,' I called through the door after a few failed attempts. I wiped my hands on my jeans and was about to have another go, when the door swung open and Rey let himself in. His face was obscured by a huge poinsettia. My face instantly turned the same shade as the red leaves.

'Morning,' he said, handing Josephine the plant.

'For me? Rey – you're a ray of sunshine!' She gave a tinkly, girlish laugh as she took it. I cringed.

'Hope it was OK to use my key,' Rey said. 'Sounded as though you were struggling to open the door.' He grinned at me and winked. A tinkly, girlish laugh escaped me. Oh no.

'I'll email you later with the information about the blogs,' Rey said.

I blushed. How could I have forgotten about the mortifying message I'd accidentally sent?

He gave a low laugh. 'Don't worry. I've been caught out by autocorrect loads of times.'

'Yes, sorry about that. Obviously, I am not resentful in any way or up for any, er . . .' I cleared my throat, unwilling to say role play out loud.

Rey rescued me. 'Got any exciting plans? You said you were busy.'

'Sophie and I were going to get some Christmas decorations from the garden centre, but we're not allowed any.' I side-eyed Josephine.

Rey grimaced. 'Sorry, didn't realise you weren't a fan, or I wouldn't have bought you a poinsettia.'

'Nonsense.' Josephine pulled the plant protectively to her bosom. 'I love decorations. Don't know what Becca's talking about. Put up as many as you like.'

Rey rubbed his beard, but I could see the corners of his mouth twitching. I swallowed a smile.

'Have a nice time,' he said. 'My parents love it there.'

Josephine gave me a 'told you so' look, which made no sense, as Pervinder was the same age as her.

Rey gestured to the stairs. 'Is it OK to use the bathroom, please?'

'Of course.' Josephine swept one arm out. 'Be our guest.' She started humming the tune from *Beauty and the Beast* and waved her arm as though choreographing the dance sequence where all the crockery and cutlery perform. And she thought she was too cool for the garden centre?

Josephine stopped humming as soon as the bathroom door closed. 'Make sure you get tasteful baubles,' she whispered. 'In cream, to match the rugs.'

'Not white? As in snow-coloured.'

'No, it'll clash with my colour scheme.'

'I'll see what I can do,' I lied, heading upstairs to get my bag. The shower was running, as I went into my room. I did not give this any thought whatsoever as I got my things together.

# Chapter 34

Sophie came downstairs with a spring in her step. The spring may well have been caused by my new trainers.

'Thank you for lending me these,' she chirped. 'Just till I get some new ones. Mine are falling apart and these are vegan.'

'Yes, but don't eat them, please,' I said, chuffed that I had something cool enough to borrow. I pulled on the boots I'd worn the night before.

'Make sure you go to the toilet before you leave,' Josephine called from the living room. 'You don't want to have to go at the garden centre, with all those old people and their UTIs.'

Sophie and I exchanged a smirk.

'Hashtag no tinsel, remember,' she said, coming out into the hall.

I groaned. 'You don't need to say "hashtag".'

'Yes, I do.' She waved her arm with a theatrical flourish. 'Haaaashtag.'

Sophie swept her hair up into a topknot and fastened it with a bobble. 'G – Mum's right. You're not supposed to say "hashtag". I was messing about the other day.'

Josephine's nostrils flared.

'Thank you,' I said, unable to hide my delight. Sophie hadn't publicly agreed with me about anything since we'd watched *SpongeBob SquarePants* in 2008 and declared it the worst film of all time.

She rolled her eyes. 'It's not that deep.'

It was deep to me, though.

* * *

'Have you spoken to Dad recently?' I asked, when we were in the car.

'He sends me a link to Wordle every morning,' Sophie said. 'It's quite sweet.'

It was sweet, but not exactly deep and meaningful conversation.

'Why not call him now?' I suggested. 'Put him on speakerphone and we'll both talk to him.' Nikki's observation that I never mentioned Steve had been a bit of a jolt. If we were going to get our marriage back on track, which would be the ideal outcome for everyone involved, then speaking now and again was a good place to start.

'Won't he be at work?' Sophie asked.

I tapped the clock on the dashboard. 'It's eleven o'clock. He'll be on his tea break.' Steve was a stickler for routine. Even during an official minute's silence, the only concession he made was sucking on his digestive biscuit rather than crunching it.

Sophie blew her fringe out of her eyes. 'But he'll go on about the insurance job.'

'If he does, I'll remind him you're not taking it.'

She held up her pinky finger. 'Promise?'

I took one hand off the steering wheel and hooked mine through hers. 'Promise.'

Sophie dialled Steve's number. 'Hi, Dad.'

'Hello, Sophie.' He swallowed loudly. That'd be the digestive biscuit. 'To what do I owe this unexpected pleasure? Ringing to tell me you want to apply for the claims job after all?'

Sophie's little finger shot up.

'Hi, Steve,' I said. 'I'm in the car with Sophie.'

'Oh, hello. Why aren't you at work?'

Ah. I'd forgotten he didn't know. Out of the corner of my eye, I could see Sophie staring at me. 'Long story,' I said. 'I'll explain later.'

'Okey-dokey.' Steve accepted this without question. 'What have you been doing with your time, Sophie?' he asked.

'I've been doing lots of shifts at The Vic.'

'That's good.' Steve bit into another biscuit. 'But working behind a bar's not a long-term prospect, is it? If you're not going back to uni, you have to get a proper job, and you're not going to find a better one than in insurance.'

Sophie waved her pinky finger manically at me.

'Nothing's definite yet,' I said, gripping the steering wheel tightly. '*If* Sophie decides not to go back to uni, she'll get a job that *she* wants to do.'

'Yes,' Sophie muttered. 'Something cool.'

A crackling noise came through the speaker, which may well have been Steve choking on his biscuit.

'Is having your car stolen and not having the money to replace it cool?' he spluttered. 'Is being in an accident and unable to claim for damages to the car cool?' He paused. 'No, it is not. Ergo, insurance is cool.'

I could practically hear Sophie's eyes rolling in her head and I suppressed a giggle.

'How's the Christmas quiz coming along?' I asked, knowing that was one topic he'd allow himself to be distracted by.

'All done, ready for the party,' Steve said. 'Bets are already taking place for which team's going to win. My money's on The Indemni Team. They've won the last three years, but even they can't get all the answers.' Pride shone through in his voice and I felt a glimmer of affection for him. This quiz meant a lot to him and it was good that his hard work was appreciated. There was a loud gulping noise, as he consumed another biscuit, which made it difficult to sustain the glimmer of affection.

'We'd better let you go,' I said before he shoved another one in. 'Take care and speak soon.'

'Bye, Dad, love you,' Sophie said. 'Why haven't you told Dad about being made redundant?' she asked as soon as she'd ended the call.

It was a good question. The truthful answer was that it would require a lengthy conversation, which I didn't have the stamina for. But I couldn't admit to Sophie that I was finding her father rather irritating at the moment. I'd probably have her sympathy – she had just witnessed the biscuit consumption and use of the word 'ergo' – but she had her own issues to deal with. I wouldn't distract her with mine. Plus, if I was very careful, I could use this as a segue into a conversation about uni.

'I don't want to worry him,' I said. 'I'd hoped to find another job quickly, so I could present him with a solution rather than a problem.'

'You've got a job,' Sophie said. 'Two jobs – the stuff you're doing for Rey and the old-lady website.'

My stomach contracted and I chose to believe it was because I'd been referred to as an old lady. Again.

'They're not permanent positions with a steady, regular income.' I indicated to turn into the garden centre carpark. 'All the jobs I've come across require a degree or a formal qualification, which I don't have. I trained on thc job rather than at college.'

'But you worked at *Norwich Now* my whole life,' Sophie said. 'You must be able to get a job somewhere else.'

I pulled into a space. 'My experience doesn't count for anything on paper. If I could talk to someone, they might appreciate all that I've learnt and done, but it's impossible to get an interview. All CVs and applications are filtered out by bots looking for keywords. Such as *degree*,' I added meaningfully.

Switching the engine off, I turned to face her. 'This is why you need to think seriously about what you're going to do next. I'm not saying you have to go back to uni, but you need to do something that will give you some credibility and value, so you don't end up like me.'

'Like you?' Sophie chewed her lip. 'Having to do all the housework because you don't earn as much, you mean?'

I inhaled sharply. Was that the impression Sophie had of our marriage?

'It doesn't matter who earns what, when you're in a partnership,' I said. 'You're equals, regardless of that.'

'Why do you do everything at home, then?'

'I don't. Your dad . . .' I looked around wildly in the hope of seeing something that I could give Steve credit for. 'Your dad insures the cars,' I said.

Sophie rolled her eyes. 'He works for an insurance company. That doesn't count.'

My cheeks grew hot at the realisation that mine and Steve's dynamic was what Sophie had grown up with and was the model she had of how a typical marriage operated. I didn't want that for her. I didn't want it for myself either, but that was on me to rectify. I'd allowed it to happen, but that didn't mean Sophie had to.

'You're right,' I said. 'I have somehow ended up doing the lion's share around the house. But that doesn't mean it's how it should be. When you live with someone, make sure you split the jobs fifty-fifty from the start, so that it's fair.'

'I will,' Sophie said. 'No way am I doing more just because I'm a girl. You don't need to tell me – it's Dad you should be telling.'

It was good to know that Sophie wasn't using our marriage as a benchmark for her own future relationships, but we had somewhat drifted off course.

'What I actually meant when I said you don't want to end up like me,' I clarified, 'was not being qualified to do anything. I'm in a really vulnerable position because

I have nothing academic to show. The better qualified you are, the more opportunities you'll have.'

Sophie slouched down in her seat. 'Can we not talk about this now?'

I gnawed my thumbnail. I didn't want to spoil the lovely trip we had planned, and I understood why she didn't want to discuss it. Not knowing what you were going to do next was a scary situation to be in. I should know. But we might not get another opportunity to talk for a while. The combination of Josephine's FOMO, and Sophie's job at the pub and need for extensive naps meant that days could go by without us spending any real time together. But Sophie *had* to grasp the seriousness of the situation. The longer she buried her head in the sand, the worse it'd get – she'd either be massively behind with her course or massively in debt for a course she wasn't going to get a degree out of. What sort of parent would I be if I shied away from helping her face up to the problem? It'd be cowardly and irresponsible. I'd be batting the problem away to make my life easier in this moment, just as I did with almost everything else. That needed to stop.

'Can I ask what changed for you at uni?' I asked gently. 'I'm not going to force you to go back if you're unhappy. If you really want to leave, then of course I'll support that decision. But you seemed to be enjoying it so much.'

Sophie stared out of the window for so long, I thought she must be ignoring me, but eventually she spoke. 'I did enjoy it at the start. Till the lecturers dumped loads of essays on us, with hardly any time to do them.' Her lower lip trembled. 'They don't help us – we have to figure everything out by ourselves.' Guilt coursed through me. She wasn't used to having to deal with things by herself because I'd always done everything for her. 'And I've no money,' she continued, her voice cracking. 'I couldn't afford to go out. All I had to eat was the pasta and tuna you got me when I moved in. If it wasn't for that, I'd have starved.' Tears rolled down her cheeks and my own throat burnt. 'Being at uni is harder than I thought it'd be. We have to find a house to rent for next year and I don't know whether to stick with my flatmates or go with people on my course. I don't know who my real friends are yet and who I want to live with for a whole year.' She blinked at me, her eyelashes clumped together with tears. 'I don't have to think about all that stuff here,' she sniffed. 'It's easy and . . .' She paused while searching for the right word. 'Safe.'

Safe. That had been my mantra. Play it safe. Don't take risks. And look where it had got me. Sophie was confident enough not to be lumbered with running a joint household single-handedly, but her lack of confidence in herself was heartbreaking. There was no shame in being scared or anxious about her situation, but I didn't want that fear to define her and restrict her future, the way it had mine. She deserved more.

It struck me that my second act wasn't just about my new phase of life – it was also about my new phase of motherhood. It was time to redefine my role and support Sophie in a new way. Instead of shielding her, the best way to show my love was by getting her to see that she was strong and capable and could handle this. And that included not shying away from painful truths, my own included.

I twisted round to face her. 'What I said earlier about not wanting you to end up like me – I wasn't just talking about housework and qualifications. There's more to it.'

Sophie wiped her cheeks. 'Like what?'

I swallowed hard. 'When I was your age, I was always out, doing new things, wanted to go travelling after uni.'

'Travelling?' Sophie couldn't have looked more surprised if I'd revealed I sang backing vocals for Katy Perry. 'Why didn't you?'

'I dropped out of uni, got a job at *Norwich Now* and moved into a shared house. Couldn't afford it after that.' My heart pinched at how different my life might have been.

'Why did you drop out? You've never said.'

I hesitated. There was no need to detail Josephine's revelation. This was about Sophie, not about what happened between her mum and grandmother years before she was born.

'It all felt too much,' I said, which was true. 'I lost my focus, got behind, failed some assignments. Getting back on track and revising for the end-of-year exams seemed too overwhelming. It was easier to leave. I got scared, so I ran away. And I've been running away from anything scary ever since. I went from being outgoing and adventurous to never daring to take a chance.' I swallowed hard. 'If you leave uni, make sure it's for the right reasons.' I reached over and took her hand. 'Don't end up like me – so afraid of failing that you daren't try.'

Sophie's shoulders shuddered. I put my arm around her and pulled her tightly to me, rocking her as I had through colic, vaccinations, grazed knees, first days, last days, friendship dramas, hormone surges, One Direction disbanding, exam nerves.

Eventually, her tears subsided and we sat in silence, cocooned from the rest of the world, the windows of the car steamed up, the only sound the distant squeak of shopping trolleys. Or possibly walking frames.

'What kind of scary things did you run away from?' Sophie asked eventually.

I sighed. 'Anything that threatened to push me out of my comfort zone. I kept my head down and tried to pretend I wasn't there most of the time.'

'But you're a journalist. You ended up with a cool job without a degree.'

I nodded. 'I was extremely lucky. Nikki took me under her wing and taught me. I doubt that would happen now. She wanted me to go for the job of editor when she left, but, as always, I was too scared.' I grimaced. 'That was a *really* stupid decision – I wouldn't have made myself redundant.'

'Sorry that happened to you,' Sophie said.

'Me too.' I paused. 'Actually, I'm not.' I smiled at her. 'I was bored. The redundancy forced me to overcome my fear of change and not shy away from anything remotely challenging. I wouldn't have had the courage to contact the team behind MAAM. Now I'm writing for them and helping with their marketing.'

Sophie nodded. 'You do seem different. Not just the hair and clothes – which are way better – but the way you're acting. Not letting G get away with so much.' She gave a sheepish smile. 'Or me. You never made me tidy up before. I guess I didn't ever think about it.' She chewed her lip. 'Probs why my flatmates got annoyed sometimes.'

I kissed the top of her head but refrained from commenting.

'I sent the group a Snapchat last night. They liked it, but no one wrote back.'

'What did you say?' I asked.

'Hi.'

I waited for the rest of the message, but that seemed to be the extent of it. 'You might want to say a bit more than that,' I said.

Sophie thought for a moment. 'What, like tell them I'm sorry for being so messy and not doing the stupid recycling?'

'Sounds like a good idea.' I paused. 'Maybe don't include the word "stupid".'

Sophie sat up and checked her reflection in the mirror. After wiping mascara from her cheeks, she turned to face me. 'I don't know what to do,' she said quietly. 'But I know I need to decide. Is it OK to think about it a bit more and tell you tomorrow?'

I smiled. 'Yes. You'll feel better once you've made a decision and can work out where to go from there.'

Sophie nodded solemnly. I needed to get her to the grotto. It was impossible to stay solemn when surrounded by gonks.

I opened the car door. 'Let's go and have a look at these decorations. No hashtag tinsel, remember.'

Sophie rolled her eyes, but with a smile. 'Shall I get a trolley?'

I was about to tell her not to worry, I'd get one, but stopped myself. Why would anyone ever offer to help if I automatically said no when they did? Was the pattern we'd fallen into, where I did everything around the house, partly down to me? Had I, if not brought it upon myself, then not resisted it either? And, if so, how had I allowed it to happen? That girl who had sledged down the hall stairs wouldn't have done. And I wasn't going to either.

# Chapter 35

'Morning,' Sophie said brightly, as I walked into the kitchen.

I blinked in surprise. She hadn't been up before me since becoming a teenager.

'Everything all right?' I asked, perching on a bar stool.

'Yes.' She smiled. 'I've made a decision. I'm going back to uni.'

These were the words I'd been hoping to hear since she'd turned up three weeks ago, but my heart pinched. The previous day had been perfect. Sophie and I bought up half the grotto, joined the OAPs for a hot chocolate and gingerbread Santa, and watched *Elf* while putting up the decorations. Even Josephine got in the spirit, although I would go to my grave content if I never had to see her candy-cane twirling routine again.

I felt closer to Sophie than I had since her hormones had taken over, and now she was leaving. But it was right for her and that's what mattered. The thought of being with Josephine on my own again was grim, but I was a grown-up (not as grown-up as seventy, but a grown-up nonetheless) and would manage.

'That's great.' I forced a smile. 'What was the deciding factor?'

'I chatted to one of the girls on my course last night.'

'On the phone?'

Sophie pulled a face. 'No, that's just weird. On Snapchat.'

Of course. Telephone conversations were for old codgers like me.

'She's really nice and said she'd go through what I've missed,' Sophie said. 'Everyone got an extension on the last assignment because the lecturer's been off ill, so I'll have time to catch up.'

'That's handy.'

'I know. I'll try not to get behind again.' She blew her fringe out of her eyes. 'Oh, this is for you.' She placed a coffee in front of me on the breakfast bar. I almost toppled off my stool in shock. I couldn't remember the last time I'd been made a coffee without having to pay the person making it. She clocked my expression and laughed. 'Thought I'd get some practice in. I'm going to have to be on my best behaviour in Manchester.' She rolled her eyes, but I could see she was excited.

'Thank you.' I picked up the mug. 'What about the house situation? Do you really have to find somewhere for next year already?'

'Yes. All the decent places go really quickly.' She sat opposite me. 'I might stick with my flatmates for now. They're OK and if they get on my nerves, I can go and visit my course friends. If I live with my course friends and they annoy me, I've nowhere else to go.'

Wow. She'd really thought this through. It was a logical decision. When Steve annoyed me, I went and visited

Nikki. I nibbled on a nail. Josephine had driven me up the wall while I'd been living with her, but I hadn't once contemplated visiting Steve to escape.

'Can you give me a lift to the station please?' Sophie asked. 'My train leaves at eleven.'

My breath caught. 'Today?' This was all happening very fast.

Sophie nodded. 'I don't want to miss any more lectures. There's a Christmas party this weekend too.'

I braced myself for a request for money.

'I sold a load of clothes on Depop and I've got my money from the pub, so I've enough for food and going out,' Sophie said. 'The pub says I can work there when I'm home in the holidays, and I'll look for a job in Manchester too. If I'm not worrying about money, I don't think the other stuff will seem so scary.'

I couldn't have been prouder. She seemed to have matured from self-centred teenager to self-aware young woman in just twenty-four hours.

Sophie came over and put her arms around me. 'Thanks, Mum, for all the stuff you said yesterday. It really helped.'

I hugged her tightly. We were at a new stage of our lives now, but I was still her mum. Nothing would ever change that.

'Has anyone seen the candy canes?' Josephine asked, coming into the kitchen. She paused when she saw us. 'What's going on?'

'Sophie's going back to uni today,' I said, releasing Sophie and standing in front of the drawer where I'd hidden the candy canes.

'But you've just put all the decorations up,' Josephine said, rotating her hands towards a sparkly reindeer on the windowsill.

'They'll still be up when I get back in two weeks,' Sophie said, then glanced at me. 'Will I be coming back here, though?'

'Why wouldn't she be coming back here?' Josephine asked, glaring at me.

'Because your six-week recovery period will be up,' I said.

Josephine threw her arms in the air and splayed her fingers theatrically, as though about to launch into a flamenco routine. 'I might not be recovered by then,' she said indignantly. 'My wrist is still fragile.'

All three of us looked up at her hands, which were more than ably supported by her wrists. Josephine's cheeks flushed pink and she lowered her arms slowly, cradling her left hand.

'It's your right wrist that was fractured,' I said.

Josephine's nostrils flared.

Sophie giggled. 'Don't worry, G. I'll come and visit you and the decs as soon as I get back.' She went over and hugged her. 'Thank you for having me.'

'Any time, darling.' Josephine patted her back lightly. 'It's been lovely having you. Especially now you've learnt how to hang towels up.'

'I'll go and finish packing.' Sophie left the room, and Josephine and I looked at each other.

'Stop biting your nails,' Josephine said sharply. 'Shame you haven't learnt that in your time here.'

I removed my thumb from my mouth. The rest of my stay was going to be challenging – Sophie had been a good distraction from the underlying tension between us. Thank goodness I was seeing Nikki later. Coming straight back after dropping Sophie at the station was too depressing to contemplate.

'I'm meeting Nikki for lunch,' I told Josephine. 'I'll go there after I've dropped Sophie off.'

'How long will you be?' Josephine asked.

'A few hours.' I certainly wouldn't be rushing back.

'Before you go, pass me . . .' Josephine started, then stopped herself. 'Never mind.' She took a wedge of lemon from the fridge, cut it into slices and put them into two glasses of water. 'Drink that, would you,' she said, handing one to me on her way out of the room. 'Your skin's looking dry.'

It was the second time that day I'd been made a drink by people who usually expected me to provide a silver service for them. For the second time that day I felt a sense of pride. But it wasn't for Sophie this time. It was for myself.

* * *

At the train station, instead of slouching, Sophie was standing taller. There was a new air of determination and purpose about her, and a quiet confidence. She was no longer the girl who ran away from tricky assignments or money concerns or issues with her housemates, and who resisted anything more testing than an ice bucket challenge.

There was also a shift in her perception of me. A new-found respect that I'd previously worried had been lacking. When we said goodbye, instead of ducking away from my outstretched arms and running to the platform with such speed she could overtake the train, she hugged me back and didn't dry-heave when I kissed her forehead repeatedly.

'I'll miss you so much,' I said, my voice breaking. 'But I'm really proud of you.'

'I'll miss you too.' She prised herself out of my arms with a smile. 'I'll be back in two weeks.' She let me kiss her one last time, then walked through the barrier and was gone.

I walked to my car, chewing furiously on a nail to stop myself from curling up into a ball on the tarmac and wailing. There was no need to cry. Sophie was back on track, and I'd helped with that. Now all I needed to do was work out how to get my marriage back on track too. I slid into the driver's seat and gripped the steering wheel. Or did I? Nikki's question kept going round my head. Sophie had been wondering which friends to live with in her second year. Did I really want to live with someone I wasn't friends with, for the rest of my life?

My phone beeped with a message. It was from Nikki. She'd woken with a stinking cold, so would need to rearrange lunch. I replied wishing her a speedy recovery, careful not to reveal how disappointed I was. It wasn't that I didn't have anything to do – there were plenty of interview prospects to investigate for MAAM and I had some questions for Rey about the blog posts – but I was in no rush to go back to Josephine's without Sophie there. Sighing, I started the engine. Best to get it over with, like ripping off a plaster. I just hoped she hadn't found the candy canes.

Back at Josephine's I had to park on the road, as a dark grey Mercedes was taking up my usual space. I recognised it as being Audrey's son's car. Perhaps he'd brought his mother over for a visit. I sighed. I wasn't in the mood for making small talk with that wizened old crone. I'd say a polite hello and go straight to my room.

Inside the front door, a pair of men's shoes sat by the mat. Both the living room and kitchen were empty. I was about to shout out hello, when I heard a rhythmic thumping noise coming from upstairs. I froze. Was that what I thought it was? With Audrey's son? Eugh. Disgusting. I backed out of the front door, then paused. Should I check Josephine was all right? Make sure she wasn't being held against her will. A moan of pleasure came down the stairs. I grimaced, wishing I'd had a less acoustic answer to the question. I had no desire to know how she was being held, but it seemed to be with her consent. I briefly wondered if I should be concerned for Anthony, but reasoned that it had to be a willing act. Josephine's hands were so slippery, it would take real grit and determination to stay within their grasp.

I closed the front door quietly. What was I going to do now? Pace the streets all afternoon? Sit in my car with the engine running to keep warm? I began to walk across the drive and came to the fork leading to the coach house. Rey had said he was free if I wanted to come round and discuss the blog posts. I tugged at a nail with my teeth. But what about my vow to stay away from him after our dinner together? I glanced back at Josephine's, then towards the entrance to the coach house. I was being silly. Whatever *moment* I'd thought had happened was solely in my imagination. Rey and I were business associates and I was going round purely to talk about business. Where was the harm in that? Pulling my coat tightly around me, I headed towards the coach house.

# Chapter 36

'Oh, hello.' Rey couldn't have looked more surprised if Jeff Bezos had knocked on his door, hand-delivering an Amazon parcel.

I immediately regretted coming. 'Sorry, I should have messaged,' I said. 'I'll come back another time.'

'No, come in.' Rey stood back. 'I didn't mean to sound as though you weren't welcome. Let me take your coat.'

'Thank you.' I registered his outfit as I stepped inside. Grey joggers and a blue fitted shirt. 'Zoom call?' I guessed.

He looked down and laughed. 'Yes. Give me a minute to get changed. Make myself look more respectful. Or should that be resentful?'

My cheeks grew hot. 'I'm so sorry about that message.'

'I'm teasing,' he called from the other room. 'Autocorrect acts up all the time. I messaged your mum the other day, asking if I could come over at one and it changed to "nun".'

I grimaced. She certainly wasn't acting like a nun right now.

He returned, wearing a fitted, navy T-shirt instead of the formal shirt. 'I was about to make myself an omelette. Would you like one?'

'No, I'm all right, thanks,' I said automatically. My stomach growled loudly at the mention of food. It was clearly missing the lunch I was supposed to be having with Nikki.

Rey smiled. 'I'll make enough for two, so if you change your mind, you can have some.'

'OK, thank you.'

Rey whisked some eggs.

'Shall I chop these?' I asked, gesturing to the salad vegetables on the chopping board.

'Please.'

The galley kitchen was small, but it didn't feel claustrophobic in the way that Josephine's did, despite hers being five times bigger. Possibly because Josephine wasn't waving her arm around, pointing out smears I'd missed when cleaning the hob or wiping the sink.

'How was the garden centre?' Rey asked. 'The decorations look good.'

'We had a lovely time,' I said. 'Sophie and I talked about uni, too, which was great.'

Rey poured the eggs into a pan. 'How did that go?'

'She's on a train back to Manchester, so pretty good.'

'Well done.' Rey turned and grinned at me.

My stomach tightened and I focused on slicing a tomato into segments. 'What about Saif? Is he any more settled?'

'Seems to be. I'm seeing a lot less of him because he's out with friends and he's stopped asking my advice.' Rey tutted good-humouredly. 'Not that he took much notice anyway. He only really pays attention when it comes from someone with a blue tick.' He ran a fish slice around the edge of the omelette. 'What about your husband?' he asked. 'Does Sophie talk to him?'

'Yes, but not about the big stuff. She tells me and I pass it on. I'm her spokesperson, kind of.' I glanced up to see Rey studying me. My cheeks grew warm. 'I'm not sure if that's how it should be, but . . .' I tailed off.

'There's no right or wrong way for a family to operate,' Rey said. He rubbed his jaw. 'Although, I was wrong in thinking that providing for my family financially was more important than physically being there. Wish it hadn't taken me so long to realise.'

'Don't be hard on yourself,' I said. 'You were doing it for the right reasons.' Was I saying that to make Rey feel better or to justify allowing Steve to put work first?

In Steve's eyes, he did more than his fair share for the family by paying for the mortgage, bills and food, so running the house and raising our child was down to me. And I'd just accepted it, which Sophie had noticed and, thankfully, had no intention of replicating. But why had I accepted it? I didn't believe it was right and fair that the person who earned less should do significantly more, not if they were working full-time too. Had Steve's obsession with money resulted in me feeling I had less worth as a person than him because I didn't bring as much in? Subconsciously, did I try and make up for my financial deficit by doing everything and going along with everything? Or had we somehow conformed to the gender stereotypes, where everything to do with the home was down to 'the girl'? How the hell had I allowed this to happen? And how could I reverse it?

'It must be difficult living away from home,' Rey said.

Right now, it was difficult contemplating living back home, but Rey didn't need to know that.

'It's certainly challenging living with Josephine,' I said instead.

'I hear you.' Rey put his hands up. 'With parents in general, I mean, not Josephine. Those few nights staying with mine were testing. They're lovely, of course, but they wanted to know what I was doing, where I was going, every moment.'

'Josephine's the same,' I said tipping the chopped veg into a bowl. 'You saw her come to the door and demand to know where I'd been.' My stomach somersaulted at the memory of his eyes on my face and the frisson I'd felt. It must have been my imagination. Frissons belonged in romance novels, not in my underwear. 'She's like one of those pop-up ads that you can't close,' I sighed.

Rey laughed and looked across at me. Our eyes met, just as they had the other night.

I swallowed hard. 'The omelette smells nice.' I looked pointedly at the pan. 'Really eggy.'

Rey turned back to the hob. 'Eggy, yes. It's my secret ingredient. Don't tell anyone.'

I giggled. 'Shall I get us some water?'

'Yes, please,' Rey said. 'To wash the omelette down. In case it's too eggy.'

He cut the omelette in half and transferred it to two plates. I picked up the bowl of salad and we carried everything through to the living room, where we sat at the tiny table in the corner.

'Josephine said that this was your dad's studio,' Rey observed.

I nodded and looked around the well-lit room, remembering the white sheet pinned up in one corner and my dad's tripod and camera set up. My heart gave a little tug.

'A photographer and model are pretty cool careers,' Rey continued. 'I know you weren't interested in modelling, but what about photography?' Rey asked.

I shook my head. 'I like it, but I prefer writing. How about you? Have you always been into computers?'

'Yep. Always been a nerd, I'm afraid.' He smiled. He waggled his glasses to prove the point. 'So much of a nerd,' he continued, 'that I've been thinking about you even when you're not around.' My stomach contracted and I gripped my fork tightly. Rey leant forward. 'I think you should set up your own business.'

Oh, right . . . Wait, what?

Rey laughed at the confusion on my face. 'Having had so many different roles at *Norwich Now* means you've got a really strong toolkit of skills. The other night, for example, you instantly came up with an idea for Soraya to promote the restaurant. That was off the cuff. I bet you could come up with another ten if you devoted some time to it.'

I shook my head. 'That was a really easy, obvious thing to do.'

'To you, yes. Not to me or to most people.' Rey nudged up his glasses. 'Your years in the business have given you an instinct and understanding of what works for different organisations. You've got the skills to put together PR campaigns, and write marketing literature, press releases, web content, blog posts, even award applications. You could offer to do the whole lot as a package, or they could pick which elements they want you to do.'

I blinked at him. 'Who's "they"?'

'Anyone.' Rey splayed his hands. 'Everyone! Up to you if you want to specialise in a particular sector.'

'But I haven't a clue how to set up and run a company.'

'You're already doing it, to a certain extent. The features for MAAM, writing web content for me and the clients I passed on to you, as well as my blog posts. This would be an extension of that.'

My heart rate sped up. Being self-employed was risky, but the thought of being my own boss – of never having to work for a turd like Declan again, and picking and choosing the jobs I took on – was too exciting to dismiss without consideration. Finding a reliable nine-to-five job was proving impossible, and if I did manage to get one, I wouldn't have time to do the work with MAAM, which I desperately wanted to do. I felt a thrill at the prospect of my own business. What better way to fully embrace my second act and achieve the comeback Nikki envisaged for me? I could be someone who seized opportunities rather than the kind of person who spent a whole day deliberating over whether a banana was ripe enough to peel yet.

'How would it work?' I asked. 'How would I get started?'

Rey grinned. 'I could design your website, if you'd like me to, and I'll keep passing your details on to my clients.'

'Thank you.' I sat up straight. With Rey's blog posts, his clients and MAAM, I'd have a small, steady income. I could ask them for testimonials to kick-start a marketing campaign. Perhaps Soraya would give me one, too, in exchange for some free advice. It'd take time to get the word out there, but I'd have my redundancy pay to fall back on if I needed it. What better way to invest it than in my career?

'You're already mapping out your marketing campaign, aren't you?' Rey's eyes shone behind his glasses.

I laughed. 'Let's not get carried away.' I smiled at him over my glass. 'Maybe, a little.'

'Good.' Rey ran a hand over his jaw. 'I did have another idea. It's a bit left-field, but hear me out. Josephine's Spotlight on Silver Supermodels campaign.' He gave me an encouraging smile. 'You're the perfect person to run it.'

I almost sprayed water all over the table. 'That is so left-field that you've actually left the field,' I spluttered.

I could never, ever work for Josephine. She was fastidious enough about the shine on the inside of her cupboards, which no one ever saw. Imagining how nitpicky she'd be over web content or press releases that'd be in the public domain gave me palpitations. Kim Kardashian's PR officer probably came under less scrutiny. As for the campaign itself, I wouldn't be doing my unpaid job properly if I didn't secure endorsements from Helen Mirren, Michelle Obama and the Princess of Wales, plus a cover shoot for all three of them with Josephine for *Vogue*.

'It'd be another case study for you,' Rey said.

'Mmm.'

Rey's smile wavered. 'That's the response you give when you don't agree with something, but don't want to be rude and say so.'

'Do I?' I wasn't aware I'd made a noise. How often did I do that, just go along with whatever was being said? When had the habit started and why did I feel I had to agree rather than say what I really felt? Did my feelings and opinions count for so little that there was no point voicing them, even to myself? And if I didn't think they were worth validating, why would anyone else?

Rey eyed me thoughtfully. I squirmed in my seat. I wasn't used to silence. At home, Steve filled the air with his monologues, and at Josephine's there was the constant sound of her inane chatter, the bubbling of her foot spa or the squelching of hand cream.

'I couldn't work with Josephine,' I said, reaching round to tug my ponytail and getting a handful of cropped curls instead. 'It's flattering how capable you think I am, but I couldn't do it.'

'You're more than capable.' He looked directly into my eyes. 'I wish you had some self-belief.' The sensation I'd had the other night returned, but this time stronger. It swirled through me, causing my nipples to harden beneath my silk shirt. Rey's pupils were dilated, his lips full. I'd never kissed someone with a beard before. Hell, I hadn't kissed anyone apart from Steve for twenty-five years, and no more amorously than a chaste peck on the cheek for the past decade. Not that I would be kissing

Rey, I firmly reminded myself. No, those lips would not be pressing against mine, before making their way down my neck and inside my shirt.

'We've got two weeks to do it,' Rey said.

I gasped. 'Do what?'

'Set up your website.'

Ah, of course, that's what he was talking about. What else would it have been?

'What's happening in two weeks?' I asked, hoping my racing heart didn't cause my voice to quiver.

'Saif finishes uni then, and we'll be going back to Brighton.'

My stomach plummeted. Of course. I'd forgotten Sophie's timetable applied to Saif too.

'Do you think you'll come back in the new year?' I asked, as casually as I could.

He shook his head. 'Saif's settled now. I can't afford to keep renting when he doesn't need me around. You and I can still work together, though. We're only a Zoom call or a train ride away.'

'Mmm.' No doubt his intentions were sincere, but he'd soon get absorbed back into his normal life when he was back home, and forget about me. Which was for the best, I told myself firmly before I had any more ridiculous fantasies about the two of us.

'There you go again, pretending to agree.' Rey nudged his glasses up. 'Tell me what you're really thinking.' His eyes were on mine. My heart pounded so hard, it was possibly visible through my shirt. I had to get out of there before I ripped it open to show him. 'I'm thinking that I need to get back.' I stood up. 'Thank you for lunch and for your suggestions. Apart from the one about working with Josephine.'

Rey chuckled and followed me to the front door. 'Let me know when you're free to talk about your website. I can send you some template ideas if that'd help.'

I nodded, but I wouldn't be taking him up on his offer. I couldn't work with Rey when I couldn't even look at him without wondering what his beard would feel like between my thighs.

'Thanks, bye,' I said, grabbing my coat and hurtling down the stairs in case he could somehow see into my dirty mind.

'Bye, Becca,' he called after me. 'Take care of yourself.'

I hurried along the side of the coach house. Thank goodness he was leaving in two weeks. My flustered feelings had escalated into a full-blown crush, and I was ashamed of myself. What was going on with me and Steve was no justification to fantasise about Rey. An uncomfortable thought struck me. This was what had happened to Josephine. She and my dad had been on a break, and she'd developed feelings for someone else. I pressed a hand to my mouth. I hadn't acted on it, as she had, but I'd wanted to. Did that mean I was no better than her?

All this time, I'd been worried that Sophie would end up like me. Should I also have been worrying that I'd end up like Josephine?

# Chapter 37

I turned the corner from the coach house and walked across the gravel to Josephine's. Anthony's Mercedes was still there. I briefly considered going somewhere else, but decided to sneak up to my room and hide instead. They were in their seventies. They couldn't still be at it. I grimaced at the thought and opened the front door as quietly as I could.

Josephine was in the kitchen, her back to me. I tiptoed across the hall towards the stairs. Sod taking my boots off or using shoe covers. The rustling would attract too much attention. I had one foot on the bottom step, when the door to the downstairs cloakroom opened and Anthony emerged. He wore chinos, with a beige diamond-knit golf jumper, and his silver hair had more sheen than a freshly waxed show car. He did an exaggerated leap back when he saw me and clutched his heart. I had a moment of panic that my appearance had brought on a cardiac arrest, but then he chuckled.

'You made me jump there, young lady,' he said with a smile.

'Again?' Josephine trilled from the kitchen. 'You said I'd worn you out earlier.' She came into the hall, her face flushed with excitement. Then she saw me and all the colour drained away. 'Becca. I didn't expect you back yet.' She ran a hand down the front of her blouse, as though making sure all the buttons were done up. If she checked the fly on her trousers I'd heave.

'I was gone quite a while,' I said. Long enough to realise that I fancied Rey, which meant that I could no longer work with him, that my marriage was in a critical state and that I was more similar to my adulterous mother than I'd thought possible.

Josephine seemed to be rooted to the spot.

Anthony cleared his throat. 'Hello, Becca.' He stepped forward and extended a hand. 'I'm—'

'Just going,' Josephine said, springing back to life. 'Thank you so much for dropping by.' She extended an arm towards the front door and, even in her most flustered state, couldn't resist adding an elaborate hand flourish to the movement.

'Oh, right you are.' He bent to slip on his shoes. The sun streaming through the glass in the door reflected off his hair and I put a hand up to shield my eyes. It should be his civic duty to provide blue light glasses for everyone within a ten-kilometre radius, for their own protection. He straightened up and went to kiss Josephine, who was fetching his coat from under the stairs. She sidestepped him and he almost toppled into the cupboard.

'I'll call you,' he said, once he'd composed himself.

Josephine thrust his coat at him and practically pushed him out, before shutting the door in his bewildered face.

I crossed my arms. 'So, you and Anthony, then?'

Josephine's cheeks flushed.

'How long has this been going on?'

Josephine studied her nails. 'A few months.'

'Why didn't you tell me?' I asked.

'It's none of your concern.'

'Does Audrey know?'

Josephine stared at her nails so intensely that it was a wonder the polish didn't peel off.

'Or don't you think it's any of her concern either?' I said.

Josephine's nostrils flared. 'Shows how much attention you pay to what I tell you.'

'What do you mean?'

'Audrey's in a care home, recovering from a stroke,' Josephine snapped. 'She'd be dead if it wasn't for the genius police officer who gave her CPR while waiting for the ambulance. I did tell you.'

Guilt coursed through me. I blocked out most of what she said, but I should have registered that. 'Sorry,' I mumbled. 'But you said Anthony was taking you to see Audrey.'

'He does – at the care home.'

'What about your Silver Supermodels campaign? I thought Audrey was helping you with it.'

'She's beyond that, sadly.' Josephine sighed. 'Anthony thinks it's a great idea, but he doesn't have the contacts anymore.'

'Anthony's an agent as well?'

'Used to be,' Josephine said. 'He did a couple of bookings for me back in the day, but he's retired now. We met up when we were both visiting Audrey. Hadn't seen each other for fifty years.' A smile crept across her face. 'He said I hadn't changed a bit.'

'You must have been a rough-looking twenty-year-old, then,' I muttered. 'Joke,' I added when her nostrils flared. 'So, you met at the care home, got chatting and, what . . . he asked to stay in touch?'

'Yes.' Josephine pumped some hand cream into her palm. 'Enough about me. Put the kettle on, would you.'

I looked at her quizzically. She never changed the subject when she was the subject. It was her favourite topic. There was something she wasn't telling me. 'He hasn't asked you for money, has he?' I said. 'Invited you to invest in a new business venture that's guaranteed to make millions? Or loan him the airfare to courier his destitute daughter and her thirteen children out of a poverty-stricken country?'

'Don't be ridiculous,' Josephine tutted. 'He was a very successful agent in his time, much more so than Audrey. He doesn't need my money.'

'Mmm.' Something was niggling at the back of my mind and I couldn't work out what it was.

Josephine's head was bowed as she gently massaged her hand cream in, but a flush was creeping up her neck.

'So, Anthony is an agent you worked with, briefly, fifty years ago?' Something about this was ringing a vague bell.

'Very briefly.' Josephine glanced at me, then at the door. 'Think I'll go for a walk.'

The sun was shining brightly. Josephine would never venture out in such harshly ageing weather conditions.

She was trying to get away from me. Under normal circumstances this would have been encouraged, celebrated even, but today it made me suspicious. I forced myself to focus. Why did this story sound familiar to me? What happened fifty years ago that Josephine was trying to avoid talking about? I caught sight of my reflection in the hall mirror. My almost fifty-year-old self looked back at me. The vague ringing escalated to the sound of an almighty alarm.

'Oh my God,' I shrieked.

Josephine bolted across the hall and wrestled with the lock on the front door, but her fully working hand was too coated in cream to get any purchase.

'Anthony?' I said shakily.

Josephine released a long sigh and rested her forehead against the door.

'Anthony,' I whispered. 'He's the man, isn't he? The man who . . .' I couldn't bring myself to say it.

'Yes,' Josephine said quietly. 'The man who may be your biological father.'

# Chapter 38

'What do you mean *may* be my biological father?' My legs gave way and I sank down onto the stairs. 'How many contenders are there?'

Josephine turned around to face me. 'Only Anthony. It was a one-off with him – just him.'

'Why the *may be*, then?'

'Because . . .' Josephine's already flushed cheeks darkened. 'Because it could also be your dad, Geoff.'

I blinked up at her. 'What could be?'

'You could be,' Josephine whispered. 'Either of them could be your father.'

'What?' I stood up so fast, my head spun. 'All these years I've been distraught that my life was a lie, that my dad wasn't my dad . . . And now you're saying he might be?'

Josephine nodded, clutching her wrist to her chest. 'I regretted it immediately. It was a terrible thing to say, and you have no idea how much I wish I hadn't.' She leant against the door. 'It ruined everything between us. I wanted to take it back, but it was too late. You wouldn't have believed me.'

'Why bloody say it in the first place?' I snapped. 'You must have known it'd screw me up.'

'You were petrified you'd inherited SCAD, remember?' Josephine said, blinking up at me. 'I told you over and over that you didn't have it, but you wouldn't believe me. Telling you Geoff wasn't your biological dad was a stupid, stupid thing to say, but I was desperate for you to calm down. You were hysterical. I wanted to make that go away for you. It was the only thing I could think of.'

'The only thing you could think of? Seriously?' I turned and strode into the living room to get away from her.

'I tried over and over to reassure you, but you wouldn't listen,' she said, following me. 'I'm sorry, I truly am. It was a terrible thing to do but, at that moment, when you were convinced you were going to drop dead any instant, it seemed the only way to convince you that you wouldn't.'

I spun around. 'I still might have inherited it, then.' My head felt as though it was going to explode. The sadness I'd lived with all these years may have been unfounded. But how could I get any comfort from that, when there was no certainty? And now there was the fear that I'd inherited SCAD after all. 'You telling me I couldn't possibly get it was another lie, if he really is my dad.' An even greater fear gripped me. 'What about Sophie? Could I have passed it on to her?' A sob escaped me. Sophie mustn't have it. She needed to have a long life ahead of her.

Josephine put a hand on my arm. 'The likelihood of you having it is so minute, it's negligible. I've read every piece of research available. It's not caused by one single gene. I even looked into paying to get you tested, but the doctors say there's no point, as passing it down the line is so rare. Both you and Sophie are safe.'

She smiled and for a moment I almost returned it, but then the enormity of the situation returned and my stomach twisted. Did she really think that a bit of research made up for all the hurt she'd caused me? I shook her hand off and paced the room. She sank into her armchair, still holding her wrist to her chest. Funny how it only played up around me. It hadn't caused her any trouble earlier, when she'd been upstairs with Anthony. The man who may or may not be my father.

I glared at her. 'How can you not know which one of them it is?' Something else she'd said came back to me and I stopped in my tracks. 'You told me you were on a break from Dad. How did you have sex with him while you were on a break? Or had he just popped out to get a paper, and you thought that counted as one?'

'We *were* on a break.' Josephine's cheeks went even pinker. 'We weren't very good at it, though. Whenever he came round to pick something up, we couldn't keep our hands off each other. You understand how it is.'

I opened my mouth to disagree, then closed it again. She didn't need to know that, actually, I didn't understand how it was, as Steve and I had never had that problem.

'If you were so into each other,' I said instead, 'why were you on a break and why did you cheat on him?'

'Emotionally, we needed some time apart to think things through. We kept arguing and I couldn't handle . . .' She trailed off.

'Couldn't handle what?'

She shook her head. 'Nothing.'

'You can't start that sentence and not finish it. Don't keep any more secrets from me. Nothing you say can make me feel any crappier.'

She clutched her wrist tighter. 'You've got your dad on a pedestal, but he wasn't a saint, you know.'

Anger bubbled away within me. 'Don't try and blame this on him. You're the one who cheated, not him.'

'Yes, he did,' Josephine wailed. 'He cheated constantly in the first few years of our marriage.' Her hands coiled into fists. 'It was never his fault, of course, all these beautiful models throwing themselves at him. How could he resist?'

I froze. She was lying. Trying to justify her own adultery. I shook my head vigorously. 'He wouldn't do that. He was a lovely, kind man. A people pleaser. That's where I get it from.'

'Oh, he was a people pleaser, all right,' Josephine snapped. 'Pleased plenty of women in his time. And I did it once, just once, and it's me who's been punished for thirty years.' Her bottom lip quivered. 'Me. Not him. Me.'

'I don't believe you,' I said coldly. 'You're saying that because you've been caught out in your lie.'

'Why would I do that?' Josephine wailed. 'What would it achieve?'

'I have no idea why you do anything.' I swiped away angry tears. 'First you tell me my dad's not my dad, then you say he might be. Then you tried to hide who Anthony really is. And to round it off, my dad was a philanderer who couldn't keep it in his pants, which drove you to cheat on him, and we're back where we started.'

Josephine bowed her head.

I sank down onto the sofa. 'I dropped out of uni because I was so thrown by my dad not being my real dad. I took a job I didn't want. I lived in a shitty shared house with people I didn't like. I married a man I didn't . . .' I pressed my fingertips into my eye sockets, trying to force my tears back in. 'Does *he* know? Anthony.'

'No,' Josephine said quietly.

'More lies, then.'

'I couldn't tell him.' Josephine glanced up, mascara streaks down her cheeks. 'He might have asked to meet you, opening it all up for you again.'

'It never closed.' My voice cracked and I took a deep breath, willing myself to stop crying. 'Why have you just started a relationship with him? You must have known that eventually we'd meet and this would come out.'

Josephine dabbed at her eyes with a tissue. 'I was lonely, especially after Audrey went into the care home. And Anthony and I . . . We have something.'

'Oh my God,' I shrieked, as another fact presented itself. 'Audrey might be my grandmother.' I stood up again, unable to keep still. I didn't know what to do with myself. I didn't know what to think. All I knew was that Josephine had yet again distorted my sense of reality. I shook my head, trying to make some sense of it all. 'You're my mum. You're supposed to look after me, not repeatedly pull the rug out from under me.'

'I didn't mean to,' Josephine whispered. 'I was trying to protect you. I went about it the wrong way, but I thought I was doing the right thing. Just like you don't always get it right with Sophie.'

'What do you mean?' I snapped. Was she seriously comparing my parenting style to hers?

'It's no wonder she's terrible with money, when you always bail her out,' Josephine sniffed. 'Or that her housemates got cross that she never tidied up after herself. It wouldn't have occurred to her, because she's not used to having to do it. You did everything for her.'

An anger I didn't know I was capable of coursed through me. 'Are you seriously criticising my parenting after lying to me in the cruellest way possible?' I shouted. 'After tearing apart everything I thought I knew when I was only nineteen, and doing it again now, you still feel you have the right to judge me?'

Josephine's cheeks flushed scarlet.

My heart was pounding so violently, it was a wonder it didn't leap out of my chest. I took a deep, steadying breath. 'Perhaps I have pandered to her,' I said in a low voice. 'But she knows she can rely on me, she knows I wouldn't lie to her, and . . .' I paused and glared at Josephine. 'And,' I repeated. 'She knows who her dad is.'

Steve. Steady, dependable, consistent, reliable, safe Steve. That was why I'd married him. I could see that now.

I ran out of the room and up the stairs. Tears blurred my vision, as I shoved my clothes into a case, leaving hangers on the floor and the chest of drawers open. When I'd packed, I picked up my phone.

My call was answered immediately.

'Steve,' I said, relief flooding through me. 'I'm coming home.'

# Chapter 39

My throat burnt as I drove home. When I'd come downstairs with my case, Josephine had sat silently in the living room, cradling her wrist. I'd had a momentary pang of guilt that I was leaving before she'd been officially signed off by the doctor. But she was perfectly capable of looking after herself. If she needed anything, bloody Anthony could do it for her. He'd clearly been doing it for her that afternoon.

I'd left without saying goodbye. A little dramatic perhaps, but she was always accusing me of being dramatic, so for once I was. My exit hadn't been quite as smooth as I'd have liked, due to the bloody hand-cream-coated door handle, but I'd got there in the end and stormed off down the drive. As much as one can storm when dragging a wheelie case through gravel.

I'd left the new clothes that I hadn't unpacked yet. What had possessed me to blow all that money? Steve would have a fit if he knew how much I'd spent, and it wasn't as if I'd be needing any of them now. I'd collect the bags when I went back for Sophie's things. I'd have to let Sophie know I was back home and things could go back to normal.

I gripped the steering wheel. Yes, normal. That's what we all needed. No more silly worrying that Steve and I didn't have enough in common, or wondering if there was more to life and what true happiness was, and all that nonsense. What I wanted was a calm, harmonious, chaos-free existence. To get up in the morning and know what the day ahead held, without such elaborate hand gesticulations that made each conversation feel like a game of charades, or Ofsted-level reports on housework, or hashtags, or my coffee being pinched, or unexpected bombshells about parentage. Who needed hobbies when you had sanity and stability?

I pulled up outside our house. Thank goodness I hadn't done anything extreme and talked to Steve about possibly breaking up. I couldn't wait to be in his reassuring presence. It had taken a while to fully appreciate what I had, but now I did. And, just as he'd been exactly what I'd needed when I met him, he was exactly what I needed now.

My stomach fizzed with nerves as I walked up the garden path. It was over a month since I'd left. The plants in the window box had died, and the lawn and flower beds were covered in dead leaves. I'd sort those out tomorrow. I went to put my key in the door, but it swung open and Steve stood there. His hair was cut shorter than usual, and he was wearing brown corduroys and a rust-coloured jumper that I didn't recognise. It seemed I wasn't the only one who'd had a bit of a makeover. His well-worn, sheepskin slippers were on his feet, though, so the fundamentals hadn't changed.

I gave a nervous smile. 'Hi.'

'Hello there.' His smile was familiar and my nerves evaporated. 'Come on in.' He stood by to let me in. I bumped my case up the doorstep and into the hall. Steve frowned at the trail of sodden leaves the wheels deposited on the carpet.

'I'll clear that up in a minute,' I said.

Steve patted my shoulder. 'No rush.'

What a pleasant change to be able to vacuum when I chose to, rather than before the dirt had even hit the floor, as was the case at Josephine's.

'Cup of tea?' Steve said.

I was about to say I'd have a coffee, then realised my cafetière was at Josephine's. Another thing I'd have to collect. If she hadn't already nabbed it. She seemed to think it was hers. 'Tea would be lovely.'

I hung my coat up and followed Steve through to the kitchen.

'Great news about Sophie,' Steve said, leaning against the work surface, as I filled the kettle. 'I'd have preferred to see her in a secure job, but at least she's doing something constructive.' He stepped aside so I could get to the cutlery drawer behind him. 'Josephine's fully recovered, then?'

My face grew hot. 'Pretty much.'

'Good.' Steve smiled. 'I've got something for you.' He opened the junk drawer and took out a charity collection bag. 'Came through the door this morning. When you were cleaning Sophie's room, you were always over the moon when these bags came, so you didn't have to go to the charity shop.' He handed it me. 'Saved yourself another trip now.'

'Thank you.' I laid the bag on the work surface with the care and respect it clearly warranted. A charity bag didn't exactly fulfil the 'over the moon' brief, but it was nice that he'd thought of me.

Steve listed the other items of post he'd encountered that week, both at home and work, while I made the tea. His chatter was reassuring. It signified that nothing had changed, that we could slot straight back to where we'd been before, as though my unsettled, lost feelings had never existed.

'What have you been up to?' I asked.

'Had a couple of trips with work. Finished the quiz.' Steve pointed to his head. 'Got my hair cut.'

'It looks nice. So did I.' I twisted round, so he could see the back.

'Oh yes. I thought you had it tied up but, no, I see it now. Very nice.'

'Your new clothes look good too,' I said.

Steve nodded. 'Got them in the Black Friday sale – fifty per cent off. I'm going to do all my shopping on Black Friday from now on. I'll never have to pay full price for anything ever again.'

My stomach twisted with guilt. My new clothes had not been discounted. My bra probably cost more than Steve's entire outfit. Luckily, he didn't seem to have noticed, but I put an apron on to hide my new silk shirt and jeans, just in case.

I put our mugs onto a tray with a packet of own-brand digestives. They wouldn't be my first choice of biscuit – and I suspected if they weren't the cheapest, they wouldn't be Steve's either – but they were a comforting staple, which was perfect. We went through to the living room and took our usual places: Steve in the imitation La-Z-Boy armchair, me on the sofa. The snooker was on, and Steve filled me in on who was playing, what previous matches had been on and the ranking of each player. I drank my tea, ate some biscuits and made a 'mmm' noise every now and then. My eyes grew heavy and Steve's voice began to fade into the background. I leant my head back against the sofa and, feeling more content and secure than I had for the past few weeks, I drifted off to sleep.

The room was in darkness when I woke up. The snooker must have finished, because the TV was off and Steve had gone. Groggily, I felt my way along the sofa to the door. The hall light was off too, so I fumbled for the switch and blinked furiously when the light came on. I turned to check what my hair was doing in the hall mirror, before remembering that it was Josephine who had mirrors everywhere, not us.

I checked my phone. There was a message from Sophie, saying she was back in Manchester. That was a first. Usually, I had to rely on the Find My Friends app to make sure she'd arrived. I replied, telling her I was back home, then checked the time. It was six o'clock. I should think about making dinner. My case was still in the hall, along with the trail of shrubbery I'd dragged in. I'd take that up, vacuum, then find Steve and ask what he wanted to eat.

Steve's voice grew in volume as I climbed the stairs, carrying my case. It sounded as though he was on the phone in my room. I swallowed hard, as that sank in.

It wasn't *my* room anymore. He'd moved back into the master bedroom. Of course he had. Silly to stay in the spare room when the bigger room was empty. A sense of unease formed in the pit of my stomach. Did this mean we had to go back to sharing a bed, after several years of sleeping apart? And did that mean we had to go back to having sex occasionally? I picked at a nail. In my haste to get home and back to normality, I'd neglected to consider that aspect of the marriage. It had come to a natural end and I'd hoped it would stay that way, in the same way I'd hoped to never be afflicted with nits again once Sophie started secondary school.

Rather than tackle the issue, I did what I did best – ignored it for now and hoped it resolved itself. I left my case on the landing, then went downstairs and ran the hoover round. Steve came down when I was checking the contents of the fridge.

'Not much in there, I'm afraid,' he said. 'I was going to eat out.'

New clothes *and* eating out? Next he'd be laying claim to a charity donation.

Steve rocked back and forth on his heels. 'Quiz night at The Highlander with the work team I told you about. Free entry if you buy a meal.' He took his glasses off and shook out a handkerchief. 'It's a decent-size meal, so I only need a light lunch. Makes it quite cost-effective, with the free quiz entry.'

My heart went out to him. My sudden departure, leaving him to fend for himself, must have been hard. At the age of fifty-nine, of course he should be able to cook for himself, but when he'd never had to before, it would have been a hell of an adjustment. Even though his sister had done the cleaning and I'd stocked the freezer before I'd left, I was proud of him for coping so admirably.

'I'll come to the quiz with you, if you like?' I said. 'We said we'd try and do more things together.' Hopefully, by doing this, he wouldn't expect us to do anything else together this evening.

Steve rubbed his glasses studiously on his handkerchief. 'That would have been nice, but I already told Collette I wouldn't be going and she could give my place to someone else.'

So that's who he'd been on the phone to. 'Collette's on the team too, then?'

'She's excellent at quizzes,' Steve said. 'She won *The Weakest Link* once, when Anne Robinson was the host. The Queen of Mean didn't break her.'

'That's impressive,' I said truthfully. Anne Robinson's icy insults would have me breaking everything, including wind, live on national television. Collette was clearly made of sterner stuff than her beige pleated skirt implied. Should I be worried? 'You two seem to have become good friends,' I said as nonchalantly as I could.

'She's my quiz partner.' Steve glanced up from the complicated business of folding his handkerchief back into a neat square. 'Nothing untoward happened between us, if that's what you're getting at. I am married, you know. To you,' he added, in case I'd forgotten. Although, as I hadn't been around for a while, perhaps he felt I needed reminding.

'Yes,' I said firmly. 'I am your wife and I am going to get you, my husband, some dinner. What would you like?'

Steve slipped his perfectly squared handkerchief into his pocket. 'We could go to one of the restaurants that accepts Tesco vouchers. I've been saving my points.'

I'd been at a restaurant just two nights ago – with Rey. Guilt coursed through me as I recalled how my heart had pounded when he'd smiled at me, and how I'd fantasised about kissing him, and then again today at lunchtime. Steve had been right to remind me that we were married. I wasn't doing a very good job of remembering it by myself.

'No, let's stay in.' I opened the fridge again.

'We could have omelettes,' Steve said.

My cheeks flushed at the memory of my lunch with Rey. 'Not really in the mood for that,' I said, as lightly as I could manage. I tried the freezer. 'Pizza?'

Steve pulled a face. 'I had one last night.'

I opened my mouth to say sod the expense, I'd pay for a takeaway. But I needed to reel my spending in. I'd got a bit gung ho with money lately, which I couldn't afford to do without a job. My stomach contracted. Oh no. Steve didn't know I'd been made redundant.

'Omelettes it is,' I said. 'You sit down. I've got something to tell you.'

# Chapter 40

'Redundant?' Steve spluttered. 'They can't do that, can they?'

I sighed. 'It seems they can.'

Steve put his arms around me. 'Are you all right?'

I leant my head against his chest, enjoying the familiarity and comfort it brought. 'Yes, but it did knock my confidence.'

'Why didn't you tell me when it happened?'

'I'm sorry, I should have done.' It was ridiculous that I hadn't. How had I expected to get our marriage back on track if I was keeping something so significant from him? 'I was in denial at first and then I was waiting to hear about my redundancy package. The HR manager is pursuing an unfair dismissal claim, and I've got three months' salary and £14,000 for now.'

Steve released me and smiled. 'If you get another job quickly, that'll be a nice bonus to add to the pot.'

He sat down at the table and I carried our plates over. Unable to face an exact replica of lunch, I'd substituted the salad for new potatoes and frozen veg. 'I tried looking for a job,' I said. 'There weren't any in journalism that I could do. Or jobs in general for women my age.'

'That doesn't seem right.' Steve speared a potato with his fork.

'It's not, but . . .' I smiled proudly. 'I'm writing some pieces for an online magazine called MAAM – Middle-Aged and Magnificent. They've commissioned me to do a series of interviews with inspirational women and I'm going to help with their marketing and future events.'

Steve swallowed his potato noisily. How could I subtly introduce the concept of chewing? 'So, you have got a job, then? Well done you.'

'Kind of. It's freelance.' I tugged the back of my hair. 'It doesn't pay much, but I'm writing some web content too, which is decent money.'

'I assume you're looking for a permanent job while you're doing this,' Steve said, slicing into his omelette. 'Freelancing is too unpredictable. You might have one good month, then get nothing for another six.'

'I know, but—'

'Goodness knows why some people choose such recklessness over a regular salary.' Steve shovelled another mouthful in. 'I don't know how they sleep at night.'

An unbidden thought of how Rey slept at night leapt into my mind and I thrust it away. It was of no interest to me if he slept on his back, on his side or hanging from the ceiling. The memory of me hanging from the ceiling and his shocked, flushed face replaced the image of him shirtless, tangled in a sheet. I booted that thought away too. What was wrong with me? I shouldn't be thinking about Rey. I should be focusing on my husband, who was sitting opposite me, detailing statistics about how being self-employed significantly affected insurance premiums.

Steve was right, of course. Freelancing was unreliable and the MAAM work didn't pay much. Focusing my efforts on finding a permanent job, with a decent regular salary, was the safe thing to do. My eye twitched. Going back to the demoralising task of job-hunting and being knocked back constantly before even reaching the interview stage filled me with dread. And I didn't want to end my friendship with Cath and Nina just as it was starting, or tell them I could no longer interview Mareenee and Soraya. I was excited about the work I could do with them and there was the potential for much more if the community grew. The web-content projects had been interesting too and although I wouldn't be working with Rey anymore – my eye twitched again – hopefully what I'd already done would lead to more. I fiddled with my cutlery. My second act didn't have to end just because I was back home. I didn't have to choose between my marriage and my career. I could have both. Steve would understand once I'd explained it to him.

I waited for his analysis to draw to a close. Once I was sure he'd finished and there weren't going to be any postscripts, I reached across the table and placed one hand over his.

'Do you remember how sad I was before I went to Josephine's?' I asked. 'With Sophie at uni, I was lost. This freelance work has filled that void. It's got me through my empty nest syndrome.'

'But Sophie's been living with you during that time,' Steve said. 'You're hardly going to have empty nest syndrome without an empty nest.'

'True,' I said. 'But I was feeling unfulfilled in general. I didn't feel as though I had a purpose or had done anything of any worth. My dream of travelling had never happened. I was bored at work. Sophie didn't need me. That's changed now. I'm proud of what I'm achieving and excited about what's ahead.'

'But you don't know what's ahead,' Steve said. 'Without wishing to sound negative, who's to say where the next job will come from.'

'I know.' I gripped his hand, willing him to understand. 'But we only get one life. I regret the things I didn't do, like travelling, I don't want to regret not giving this a go.'

Steve nodded thoughtfully. He turned his hand over and laced his fingers through mine. 'That's twice you've mentioned travelling,' he said. 'I hadn't realised it was so important.'

I hadn't realised myself. I'd written off my adventurous, spirited plans as reckless, frivolous notions and stuck to a safe, steady path. It wasn't until I'd begun to find myself again that I remembered how keen I'd been to experience everything life had to offer and grasp every opportunity I could. I'd fully intended to go backpacking around Asia by myself. Then Josephine had dropped her revelation, and overnight I went from mapping out my route along the Silk Road to considering an Indian takeaway on a Saturday night decadent.

It was pointless dwelling on this loss, though. It wouldn't change anything and would just eat away at me. What I *could* change was what I did next. I'd wasted too many years playing it safe. It was time to take a chance.

'I'd like to give the freelance work a shot,' I said. Steve opened his mouth, but I carried on. 'I don't expect you to fund me. I have my redundancy pay as backup if I don't earn very much, which I probably won't while I get established.'

'Or . . .' he said. 'You could get a permanent job and spend your redundancy package on something else entirely.' He beamed at me. 'Something much more exciting.'

'Such as?' I asked cautiously. High-interest savings accounts and ISAs were the equivalent of porn to Steve, so I didn't have high hopes.

Steve squeezed my hand. 'Travel.' I gasped and he looked delighted. 'We could set sail on the seven seas and delight in all the wonders of the world.'

My heart pounded. Was he serious? I'd been thinking we had nothing in common, when all along we had this shared passion. If only we'd had this conversation twenty-five years ago. 'You'd like to travel?' I asked breathlessly.

He nodded enthusiastically. 'Collette told me about the cruises she and her husband used to go on. They sound wonderful, but astronomical. However, with your redundancy pay, we could afford it.'

My heartbeat thumped in my ears. A cruise? I didn't want to go on a cruise. I knew many people loved them, but I wanted to immerse myself in the culture of the country I was visiting, not spend a designated few hours in a tourist spot before being ushered back on board to dress for dinner and pray food poisoning wasn't on the menu. Disappointment coursed through me. I'd thought for a moment there that we wanted the same thing, but of course Steve didn't want to travel in the same way I did. We wouldn't have spent every summer in that bloody awful expat villa in Spain if he had.

I looked at Steve's eager grin and my disappointment turned to guilt. For once, he'd actually listened to what I'd told him. He was trying to please me and make things good for us. Suggesting we spend the money on a holiday rather than squirreling it away was an enormous gesture and I mustn't dismiss it ungratefully. I would have to be much more subtle in the way I dismissed it.

'That's a lovely idea,' I said carefully. 'But I don't think we should blow the whole lot when I don't have a guaranteed income.' Steve's face fell. I felt wretched but was determined not to revert to my default setting of agreeing to something I wasn't on board with to make life easier. And I definitely did not want to be on board a cruise liner.

'I'm not saying we can't do something special in the future,' I continued. 'But I have several freelance projects lined up and some contacts to find more. It makes sense to follow those up, especially when I've enjoyed what I've done so far.' I gave what I hoped was a reassuring smile. 'I really want to give this a go. If nothing comes of it after six months, I'll look again for a permanent job. But I'd like to try first.' Steve didn't look reassured, and I squeezed his hand. 'I understand your concerns about being self-employed, but I've just been made redundant from what I thought was a secure position. Even if I did somehow get another job, it could happen again. Being employed by a company doesn't automatically mean your job's safe.'

'It does if you work for a reputable company.' He sighed. 'Such a shame Sophie was so short-sighted about the claims clerk job. Excellent prospects, pension, health insurance, no risk of redundancy.' He glanced at me, then did a double take. His face lit up like the Christmas tree now in residency at Josephine's. 'You could do it.'

I shook my head. 'I couldn't make Sophie take a job she doesn't want. But it's irrelevant now anyway – she's back at uni.'

Steve's fine, sandy hair was practically standing up on end with excitement. 'No. I mean you could do the claims job.'

My stomach hit the floor. I could do what?

He was looking at me so eagerly, like a dog who's just retrieved a ball for his owner. 'It's perfect,' he said. 'This way you can go back to a regular, reliable income, so you won't feel bad about spending your redundancy on the holiday of a lifetime.'

And there was me thinking he'd listened. I withdrew my hand from his and stacked our plates. 'I just told you how much I enjoy what I'm doing and that I have more work lined up, which I'm hoping to grow.'

Steve puffed out his cheeks and exhaled loudly. 'You said yourself there aren't any jobs out there. Well, here's one staring you in the face, but it won't be here in six months. Why risk waiting, only to discover there are still no jobs?'

I stood to put the plates in the dishwasher, turning away from him so he couldn't see the frustration on my face. 'I don't know anything about insurance.' That wasn't strictly true. After twenty-five years of Steve banging on about it at length, some information had been absorbed. But telling Steve I wasn't interested in insurance would be like Joseph telling Mary that religion wasn't really his thing.

'No need to worry, this is an entry-level position and you'd receive training.' Steve gave me a reassuring smile, as I sat back down.

I was not reassured. He wasn't listening to me, so I tried a different tack. 'I can't do the freelance work as well as a full-time job,' I said evenly. 'It would be unprofessional to let the people down that I've already made commitments to.'

Steve nodded solemnly. 'Of course you must honour those obligations. You have a moral duty.'

I breathed a sigh of relief.

He closed his eyes and we sat in silence, which I hadn't been aware Steve was capable of. I chewed on a nail as I watched him, unsure whether to enjoy the peace or administer CPR.

After a minute, his eyes snapped open. 'Yes, you can,' he boomed.

I jumped. 'Can what?'

'Do both.' He rubbed his hands together. 'You can do the claims job nine-to-five and work on your freelance projects in the evenings and weekends. That'll take your mind off Sophie being away and give you a sense of purpose. Two purposes, in fact,' he added with a chortle.

I extracted a sliver of nail from my mouth. There was some sense in what he was saying. The freelance work wasn't taking up much time at the moment, and without Josephine to pander to, there was the possibility I'd find myself at a loss with nothing to do. But insurance? I fully appreciated its importance, and I was very grateful that there were people like Steve who made it happen, but I did not want to be one of those people. I'd feel like I'd made a bargain with the devil, but instead of exchanging my soul for wealth or eternal youth, I'd exchanged it for a mediocre salary and eternal boredom.

Steve smiled eagerly. 'You'll still be giving the freelance work a six-month chance, but will have a decent wage coming in alongside it.'

I sat back in my chair, unable to think of a counterargument. Everything he'd said was rational. It would be useful to have an income while I launched my business and maybe the claims job wouldn't be as bad as I feared. One of the things I loved about being a journalist was learning about people and their skills, products and trades. I'd be learning every day with this job, and while I wasn't sure I'd ever share Steve's passion for insurance, it'd give us something to talk about – after all, a lack of common interests had been one of the initial problems.

'OK,' I said. 'There's no harm in applying.'

'Super.' Steve beamed at me. 'I'll talk to Collette first thing Monday morning about arranging an interview.'

Well, that alleviated any suspicion I might have had of them being more than just quiz partners. He'd hardly want his mistress and wife working together.

His face fell. 'Oh dear.' Or there *was* something going on and he now realised he'd monumentally screwed up. 'All the places for the Christmas party have gone, so I'm afraid you won't be able to come.'

That was even better news than confirmation they weren't having an affair. 'Never mind,' I said. 'There's always next year.' Plenty of time to think up an excuse to get out of that one.

Steve smiled. 'It's good to have you home. Don't think I'm cut out to live alone. I like having someone to talk to.' He stroked his earlobe. 'Things were, er, a bit tense before you went. Are you sure it wasn't anything to do with me?'

'No,' I said firmly. It had been me, not him. Josephine's latest bombshell had been the grenade I needed to make me see sense.

'I worried I wasn't exciting enough for you,' Steve said quietly and I felt a surge of guilt. 'But when you get to our age, you don't expect much excitement, do you?' he continued. 'Routine, stability and companionship is the best we can hope for, which I thought we had.'

There was that magic word – stability. I nodded enthusiastically. 'We did. We do.'

'You're definitely feeling better in yourself?' he asked.

I nodded again.

'In that case . . .' Steve's cheeks coloured slightly. 'It would be nice to, um, stay in our bedroom, not go back to the spare room.'

My stomach lurched with guilt. Partly due to this poor man being forced to beg to come back into his own marital bed. But mainly because I didn't feel the same way. What was wrong with me? This was my husband, whom I loved and was happy to be back with. I couldn't select which parts of the marriage I wanted to enjoy and which I'd avoid, as though our relationship was a pick 'n' mix. Either I was in or I wasn't.

I swallowed hard. 'Of course.'

'Super.' Steve smiled at me. 'There are some yoghurts in the fridge if you'd like a dessert.'

'Yoghurts? Brilliant!' I jumped up and dashed to the fridge, overwhelmingly relieved that he hadn't suggested we go straight upstairs and have a dessert of another nature. 'Have we got any wine?' I asked, depositing yoghurts and spoons on the table and transferring our plates to the dishwasher.

'Only a bottle of Merlot,' Steve said.

'Perfect.' I took two glasses from the cupboard.

'But you don't drink red wine.'

I didn't drink red wine because it made me very drunk very quickly. 'I don't mind the occasional glass,' I said, handing him a corkscrew.

Being very drunk very quickly was exactly what I needed to get through tonight.

# Chapter 41

The next morning, I woke early to the sound of Steve's heavy breathing. The operation to cure his sleep apnoea had stopped his snoring, but not his breathing. Which was good, of course – breathing was rather essential – but it'd be nice if I didn't feel as though I was sharing the bed with a coffee percolator.

I eased myself out of bed and went downstairs, having to make do with tea rather than coffee, as my cafetière was still at Josephine's. If that was all I'd left there, I'd buy another, but I needed to get Sophie's things at some point. I couldn't face it today, so threw myself into gardening, raking up leaves and weeding as though my life depended on it. I stopped briefly to make sandwiches for lunch and listen attentively to Steve's survey of local electricity providers' quotes. Then I did a supermarket shop just before the store closed to ensure I got as many discounted items as possible.

I was about to drive home when Nikki rang.

'Run that by me again,' Nikki said after I'd filled her in on the last twenty-four hours.

'Which part?'

'All of it.'

'There's no point. It'll sound exactly the same.'

I could practically hear Nikki's eyebrows arching. 'When I saw you three days ago – *three* days – you'd had this amazing makeover. You were excited about doing the blog posts for Rey and writing web content for his clients. You'd realised you had feelings for Rey, which wouldn't have happened if things were right with Steve—'

'I never said I was leaving Steve,' I said defensively.

'No,' Nikki said. 'But I got the impression you'd realised it was an option. Now, you're back with him, you're returning the clothes that made you look and feel fabulous, and you're applying for a job in . . . insurance?' She said the word questioningly, as though not sure she'd pronounced it correctly. 'It's great news about Sophie, but the rest of it . . .' She exhaled slowly. 'What happened, Becca?'

'Josephine happened.' I regaled the story.

'Sweet Jesus.' Nikki released another long breath. 'I'm sorry. That must have been hard to hear.'

'It was.' I blinked back tears. I hadn't let myself think about it since it happened. 'But it made me appreciate what I have with Steve. An honest, secure, grounded marriage. The complete opposite to my parents'.'

'Are you being honest with yourself, though?' Nikki asked gently. 'What Josephine threw at you is a lot to process. Are you sure you haven't gone home because it's safe and familiar, and you don't have to make difficult choices?'

'No,' I said firmly. 'It was the jolt I needed to see how out of proportion I'd blown things. Every parent goes through a period of adjustment when their child leaves home. They don't all end their marriages.'

Nikki wasn't giving up. 'What about the lack of common interests?'

'We've found one, actually.' Not the nocturnal one, but we couldn't all be like her and Chiwetel. 'Steve's keen to take more adventurous holidays too.' OK, currently our interpretation of an adventurous holiday differed somewhat – mine involved fewer all-you-can-eat buffets and show tunes – but I'd work on that.

'Well, that's a definite breakthrough.' Nikki paused. 'OK, I'm going to play devil's advocate again. Holidays aside, which will only happen once, maybe twice a year, what about the rest of the time? Can you handle him talking at you constantly?'

'It's nice that he likes talking to me,' I said. 'He said it was one of the things he'd missed when I was away.'

'It's not actual conversation, though, is it?' I could hear the frustration in Nikki's voice. 'He's on transmit – it's all one-sided. He releases a stream of consciousness without any expectation that you'll join in. You've told me countless times how it drives you mad.'

'It used to,' I conceded. 'But he actually listened to me yesterday, when I told him how I regretted not travelling. We talked about it and he came up with the idea of an exotic holiday.' Again, I omitted mentioning the cruise element. 'And he made a point of asking how I was and if I'm feeling better.'

'Does he think you were ill?' Nikki sounded taken aback. 'Is that how he's interpreting this?'

'No. He meant better emotionally.' Why was she seeing problems when there weren't any?

'And are you better emotionally? Even though you've now got to deal with the dad drama Josephine dropped on you?'

I sighed. 'I'm not going to waste any energy thinking about that. She's taken up enough of my headspace, and my time.'

Nikki was silent for a moment. I could tell she was choosing her words carefully. 'I hear what you're saying, but maybe talking to Josephine, getting to the root of why she said and did this, would help you more than ignoring it.'

'What, so she can spin me another load of lies?' I drummed my fingers on the steering wheel. 'No, I've done my duty and looked after her when she was recovering. We can go back to being polite and distant now. It's worked for the last thirty years.'

'What about your freelancing, then? You're a creative person – a brilliant writer. You can't give that up.'

'I'm not giving it up. I'll do it at weekends and evenings, around the day job.'

'But insurance?' Nikki wailed. 'This isn't a comeback – it's a setback, and such a waste of your talent.'

'Maybe I have a hidden talent for insurance,' I said indignantly.

Nikki snorted. I snorted back. A giggle came down the phone and I couldn't help but return it.

'OK,' I laughed. 'That's stretching it, but it's not a setback. The insurance job will be a means to an end – I'm doing it purely to pay for travel. I'd never be able to afford to on what I earn freelance.'

'How many blog posts does Rey want you to write?'

My cheeks grew warm, which reinforced my decision not to work with Rey anymore. I didn't trust myself around those beautiful eyes. Or smile. Or arms. Or . . . I cleared my throat. 'I don't think that's happening now. He's going back to Brighton.'

'That's a shame.' Nikki sounded genuinely disappointed. 'Will you keep in touch?'

'No,' I said firmly. 'Which is for the best.'

Nikki was silent for a moment but didn't push it. 'Sorry if I sound negative. This is all so unexpected. I was envisaging cocktails in New York to celebrate your successful business and fiftieth birthday.'

'We can still do that,' I said.

'In that case, you *have* to keep the clothes. I'm not taking you to the Rainbow Room in that khaki hiking jacket.'

'OK.' I smiled. I'd burn the receipts so Steve could never find out how much I'd spent. 'Lunch soon?'

'Definitely.'

We said goodbye and I pulled out of the carpark. Nikki would soon see that things were good between Steve and I now, and put any silly notions of me and Rey out of her mind. I headed towards home. Home, where the heart is. I frowned, as something struck me. When Steve and I had talked the night before, matters of the heart hadn't come up. He'd said it was good to have me home, but neither of us had mentioned love. I nibbled on a nail as I waited for the traffic lights to turn green. For the first time since coming back, I had a flicker of doubt but immediately dismissed it. I was almost fifty and Steve was almost sixty. We were too old for all that romantic nonsense. There was no need to shower each other with declarations of love. It was a given. As Steve had said, stability and companionship were the cornerstone of our relationship, and who could want for more than that?

Rey's smile flashed through my mind. I ignored it.

# Chapter 42

Collette phoned at ten o'clock the next morning. Steve had been true to his word and spoken to her first thing. Of course he had been. It was one of his most admirable qualities. He said a hell of a lot of words, but he was true to all of them.

Collette was polite and professional. There was no reference to our unexpected meeting in my kitchen or the M&S Best Ever lasagne. We went through my CV and I elaborated on the work I'd done for *Norwich Now*. Collette detailed what my role as a claims clerk would involve, but my brain refused to absorb the information. I had this problem with everything I wasn't particularly interested in, such as the rules of cricket, the difference between baking powder and bicarbonate of soda, and Justin Bieber lyrics. I must have concealed this adequately, as Collette said I'd be an asset to the team and it wasn't necessary to have a formal interview. I would, however, need to do an online aptitude test, which filled me with dread. Not only would it be humiliating for me if I failed, but it'd also be embarrassing for Steve to have such an incompetent wife. Although it would guarantee with absolute certainty that I'd never be asked to join his quiz team.

I did the test there and then to get it out of the way, then faced up the other thing I needed to get out of the way. Collecting Sophie's things from Josephine's.

* * *

Relief flooded through me when I let myself into Josephine's and was met with silence. But I still needed to move fast – there was no knowing how long she'd be out for or where she was. She could be at the gym, the shops, or conducting a seance.

I ran up the stairs to Sophie's room. The advantage to her laziness was that she'd never actually unpacked, so most of her belongings were still in the giant IKEA bags I'd brought from home. I unplugged her salt lamp and light-up mirror. A high-pitched whistle filled the room and I froze, thinking it was Josephine's alarm, but then realised with relief that I'd accidentally unplugged the airbed. Never mind, it wouldn't be needed now, and Rey could hardly take it back to Brighton inflated. Not unless he had an enormous roof rack and didn't mind getting some odd looks on the motorway. In my room, I collected my shopping and double-checked I hadn't left anything behind. Indy grinned down at me and I blew him a kiss. I would take him with me, but he'd been up there so long, the Blu-Tack would probably peel half the wall off with it – and I wasn't taking any reminders of this place home.

I dragged the bags and mirror down the stairs and put them by the front door, then went into the kitchen and took my cafetière from the cupboard.

'You're taking the cafetière?'

Josephine stood by the breakfast bar, as still as a statue. I screamed so loudly, it was a wonder the walls didn't cave in.

'What are you doing here?' I asked shakily.

'Waiting to talk to you,' Josephine said.

I opened my mouth to tell her that she wasn't supposed to stand, but I didn't need to tell her that anymore. Her blood pressure was back to normal and my period of looking after her was over, thankfully. 'I'm not stopping,' I said instead.

'I've done a lot of thinking the past couple of days,' Josephine said, ignoring me completely, as usual. 'And I feel I owe you an explanation.'

I clenched my jaw. I didn't want to hear her excuses, but some ingrained sense of duty kept me there.

'What I did was wrong,' Josephine said. 'As I've told you many times, I regretted it as soon as I'd said it. But you were so worked up, in such a panic. I was desperate to make you feel better.' She released a shaky breath. 'You were in a fragile state, which was natural – your dad had just died.' She blinked hard. 'But I think you forget that he was also my husband. I was in shock, grieving, not acting rationally.'

I crossed my arms. Was I supposed to feel sorry for her now, after everything she'd put me through?

'I was devastated when you moved out,' Josephine said softly. 'I lost my daughter as well as my husband. You even stopped calling me Mum. You're the only person in the whole world who can, and you refuse to do it.'

I blinked hard.

'It's why I never changed your bedroom. I always hoped you'd come back.' She looked at me, but I refused to meet her eye. 'It felt as though I'd been given a second chance when you came to look after me.' She ran a fingertip along the scar on her wrist. 'I hoped that by living together, we'd be able to rebuild our relationship.'

'Well, that backfired,' I snapped. 'I'm angrier with you now than I was before.'

'I know.' Josephine sighed heavily. 'I told Anthony everything. In case you want to get a paternity test, so you know one way or the other.'

'No,' I said instinctively. 'No, I don't.' I gripped the work surface. 'I want to forget any of this happened.'

'Anthony must feel the same.' Josephine looked down. 'He hasn't answered my calls since.'

'Nice guy.' I thrust my hands in my hair. 'How could you have cheated on Dad with him?'

'I was hurt and lonely and I'd been betrayed.' Josephine sniffed. 'I felt lost.'

Lost. I could relate to that feeling. Not that I'd be admitting it to Josephine.

'I was looking for someone to see me, I suppose,' Josephine continued.

Rey had made me feel seen. He'd been interested and attentive and funny and charming. But I hadn't done anything about it, unlike Josephine. I could face Steve without guilt or remorse or a questionable pregnancy.

'I suppose I wanted to get back at your father, too, for cheating on me,' Josephine said in a small voice. 'Although, of course, he never knew.'

I tutted. 'If he was cheating on you, as you claim, why did you stay with him?'

Josephine blinked hard. 'Because I loved him and desperately wanted to believe him each time he swore it would be the last time. When I had you, he promised he'd never do it again, that our family was too precious to risk losing. As far as I know, he never did. You were the glue that brought us together.'

Inexplicably, tears sprang to my eyes. I turned around quickly and unplugged the air fryer, ready to take home.

'You made us both so happy,' Josephine continued. 'Our beautiful, funny, spirited little girl.' Her voice caught, but I kept my back to her. 'I'm truly sorry, Becca. I wish I hadn't done it.'

A tear trickled down my cheek and I swiped it away. 'You wish you hadn't told me or you wish you hadn't cheated on my dad?'

'The former,' Josephine said. 'As I have no idea if Geoff or Anthony is your biological father, I can't have any regrets about that.'

I gasped and spun round. 'You cheated on my dad and don't know which one got you pregnant. How can you not regret that?'

'Because if it hadn't happened, you might not be here.' Josephine gave me a watery smile. 'How could I possibly regret that?'

# Chapter 43

I had no idea what she expected me to say, and I had no idea what I could say, so I said nothing. Instead, I turned and walked away. Josephine followed me into the hallway and watched me from the safety of the living-room doorway, well away from any ageing beams of autumnal light, kneading her palms together – wringing them would have been far too damaging – as I hauled everything out onto the doorstep before slamming the door behind me.

My hands shook as I drove home and I gripped the steering wheel tightly to steady them. The trembling had eased enough for me to make myself a coffee in my reclaimed cafetière once I got home. I waited for the caffeine to relax me as I sipped from my mug, but it tasted bitter and I tipped most of it into the sink.

Josephine had poleaxed me yet again. It seemed to be her specialist skill. Just when I thought I'd got to a good place, where I was comfortable with who I was and regaining my confidence, she knocked me off balance. The feeling of loss and worthlessness that had taken hold when Sophie had left hit me again and I suddenly, desperately, missed her. Taking my phone from my bag, I FaceTimed her on the off chance she was free.

'Hi, Mum.'

It took all my self-control not to burst into hysterical sobs at the sight of her beautiful face.

'How are you?' she asked.

'Good, thanks,' I lied. 'How about you? Settled back in OK?'

Sophie nodded. 'I spent all afternoon at the library yesterday, working on one of my assignments. I've got a lecture at two, then I'm going to the library again.'

I felt a flush of pride. She was actually doing it. 'Well done. You'll have caught up in no time.'

'That's the plan,' Sophie said with a smile. 'What did Dad say?'

'He's pleased you're doing something constructive.'

Sophie smirked. 'At least he'll stop going on about that claims job now.'

My heart sank. 'Yes, about that . . .' I picked at my cuticle. 'He suggested I do it. Supplement my income while I build up my freelance work.'

Her mouth dropped open. 'Seriously?'

I nodded, pushing away the sense of trepidation that threatened to overwhelm me each time I thought of it. Was this how fundraisers felt on day one of back-to-back marathons? Or fire walkers before embarking on their dash across hot coals? Or celebs in the jungle when told they were getting a kangaroo's bollock for lunch?

'What happened to the web writing you were doing with Rey?' Sophie asked.

My face grew hot. 'All done.' I rested my chin in my hands. 'I'm doing some web content for a couple of other clients and my MAAM features and interviews, but I can do that in my free time. Your dad and I thought we might go on a more exciting holiday than the usual one, with the money I earn.'

'Really?' Sophie looked even more taken aback by this news. 'I might come with you if you go somewhere decent.'

Choruses of heralding angels couldn't have spread more joy than those words did. Here was definitive proof that my relationship with Sophie was nothing like mine and Josephine's. The only holiday I'd consider with her was a trip to the Bermuda Triangle – on the condition she went on ahead.

Sophie peered into the screen. 'It's funny seeing you back at home. I'm used to you being at G's now.' I stiffened and Sophie's eyes widened. 'Has something happened to G?'

I shook my head. 'She's the same as ever.' I smiled, but it couldn't have looked more forced if I'd been told to 'say cheese' by a masked gunman.

'What's going on?' Sophie asked.

'Nothing,' I said. 'Everything's fine.' Sophie didn't need to know the history.

'Have you and G had a barney?'

I didn't want to lie. That was the root of my problems with Josephine. I chewed thoughtfully on a nail. Sophie didn't *need* to know the history. But maybe she'd *like* to know.

'Yes,' I said. 'I suppose you could say we've had a barney.'

'When?'

I cleared my throat. 'About thirty years ago.'

# Chapter 44

'Wow,' Sophie said, when I'd told her the whole story. 'It's like *Mamma Mia!*, but with two dads, instead of three.'

'Two's enough, believe me,' I said.

'Does Dad know?'

I shook my head. 'Only you. And Nikki. Oh, and Anthony now. G told him in case I wanted to get a paternity test, but I don't.'

Sophie grimaced. 'That's going to be a bit awks on Christmas Day.'

Oh God, Christmas Day. I'd have to invite Josephine, even though it would be awks times a hundred. It'd be too mean to leave her on her own. I'd drink myself into oblivion to get through it. That seemed to be my go-to strategy for dealing with unpleasant situations. It flitted through my mind that intercourse with my husband shouldn't be categorised as an 'unpleasant situation', but I pushed it away.

'Do you think she'll bring him?' Sophie asked.

'Who?'

'Anthony. If he's G's boyfriend, or whatever old people call it, won't he start coming to family stuff now?'

'No, I think that's over now.' Thank goodness. Having to see him would be awks with a capital A. 'She hasn't heard from him since telling him.'

Sophie pouted. 'Poor G.'

I felt a spark of irritation. She didn't deserve Sophie's sympathy. 'She's brought it on herself, lying about who my biological dad is. It really messed me up when she told me. Imagine how you'd feel if I told you that Dad isn't your real dad?'

Sophie nodded. 'Yeah, it would be crap.' She paused. 'Unless Indiana Jones is my dad? That'd be pretty cool.'

'That'd be *very* cool.' I quivered slightly at the thought. 'But he's not, sorry to disappoint you.'

Sophie shrugged. 'That's OK. I mean, he's old and a bit boring, but he's a dad. He's supposed to be like that.' She blew her fringe out of her eyes. 'G and Grandpa weren't boring, though. Was everyone wild and exciting like them in the olden days?'

I gave her a stern look. 'Cheating isn't exciting. It's deceitful and wrong and hurts the people you're supposed to love. What G did is still hurting people now.'

'Sorry,' Sophie said quietly.

I shook my head. 'You're not the one who needs to be sorry.'

'Has G said sorry to you?'

'Yes, but she can't just apologise and expect me to forget about it. It's too "deep", as you'd say.' I swallowed hard. 'I felt as though my life had been a lie. And I was so angry with her for cheating on Grandpa.'

'But he cheated on her first,' Sophie said.

'I didn't know that then.' I tugged the back of my hair. 'Although that might have screwed me up even more. This is the real reason I was too upset to focus on uni and left. The loss of everything I thought was set in stone threw me so completely, I lost all my confidence. It's why I never dared to try working anywhere other than *Norwich Now*.' I sighed. 'If I'd finished my journalism degree, and not been too scared to put myself forward for new things, who knows where I'd have ended up.'

'No, but you became a journalist in the end,' Sophie said. 'You love writing about people and telling their stories, and that's what you do.'

'Yes, but if I hadn't felt the need to play it safe all the time, I'd have had so many more opportunities.' I sighed wistfully. 'I might have travelled with work.'

'But if you were away travelling, I'd never have seen you,' Sophie said. 'I like that you picked me up from school. You used to bring a pot of chopped-up apple for me to eat on the way home.' I smiled, delighted that she remembered. 'I always wanted crisps.' Oh, OK, not so great that she recalled every precise detail. 'You watched all my netball games and helped out at Brownies. I got serious aura points when you came into school and helped us make a class magazine.' Sophie smiled. 'I'm glad you worked at *Norwich Now*.'

She made a valid point. It might not have been exciting, but it had meant I was around for her. The fact she remembered and appreciated it made it all worthwhile.

'I wouldn't have met your dad if I hadn't worked there,' I said. 'His company entered an industry award that I helped organise.'

Sophie grinned. 'So, if it wasn't for *Norwich Now*, I wouldn't be here.'

'No,' I said. 'And you are, without doubt, the best thing that ever happened to me.'

'Cringe,' Sophie said, but her smile stayed in place.

I smiled back at the beautiful, self-assured, strong woman she was becoming.

'I'm glad you told me about G and your dad,' Sophie said. 'Dads,' she corrected.

I shook my head. 'You were right the first time. I only ever had one dad.'

Sophie gasped. 'I've just thought of something – if we don't know for sure who your real dad was, we don't know who my real grandpa was.'

'That's true,' I said. 'But I don't think that matters. You're you, wherever you came from.'

'And you're you,' Sophie said. 'I don't think it matters where you came from either.'

After we'd said goodbye, I went straight to Sophie's room, curled up in a ball on her bed, and sobbed and sobbed. Her words had truly touched my heart. But they also scared me. Because if it didn't matter where I came from, then what had the past thirty years' worth of resentment and hurt and self-doubt been for? And what did I do with it all now?

# Chapter 45

The rest of the week passed quickly. Steve and I slipped straight back into our routine, as though we'd never been apart. Surely that proved how right we were together? Each evening I cooked, then we ate our dinners while watching various quiz shows or documentaries, accompanied by Steve's running commentary. The only input required from me was the occasional 'mmm' – presumably to prove I was still in both the room and the land of the living.

As the days passed without me hearing anything about the claims job, I began to hope that either I'd failed the aptitude test or I'd imagined the whole thing. I'd take humiliation or temporary insanity over the job any day.

'Perhaps they've given the position to someone else,' I said to Steve, hopefully.

Steve shook his head. 'Collette said that unless you left your aptitude test blank, the job's yours.'

If only I'd had that piece of information earlier. I'd foolishly completed the bloody thing.

Aware that once I started the claims job, my time would become restricted, I did as much work as I could. I wrote another feature for MAAM and got two more agreed by Cath and Nina. Soraya invited me for lunch at her restaurant, where she served me an incredible meal. She elaborated on her time in Thailand and we chatted so naturally, I almost forgot I was interviewing her about changing career midlife. In the evenings, against the low hum of Steve's monologues, I researched more potential candidates for the series and was delighted when several came straight back to say they'd love to be profiled.

Rey had sent me an email with the subject heading 'Blog posts', but I hadn't opened it. My stomach fluttered whenever I saw his name in my inbox. And everything else fluttered if his face popped into my mind, which confirmed that I was right to stay away. I had, however, followed up with the leads he'd given me and secured three more clients who wanted me to rewrite their web content. One was for a photographer, which inevitably led to me thinking about my dad.

Josephine had been right – I'd put him on a pedestal. In my rose-tinted memory, he'd been full of smiles and hugs and completely devoted to me. In reality, I'd hardly seen him. He was either in his studio or away on shoots. He was lovely when he was around, but he was rarely around. Josephine could have told me what he'd been up to, to justify her own affair, but she hadn't. She'd protected my memory of him.

It cut to the core that he'd regularly cheated on Josephine. How horrendous for her every time he went on a fashion shoot. I certainly never worried about Steve getting up to anything when he went away on his risk-assessment assignments. Thankfully, I hadn't had to worry about it at home either. Although we were sharing a bed, he seemed content to go straight to sleep, and I was more than content for this to continue.

As for Anthony, part of me felt bad for Josephine that he'd buggered off when she told him about me, but the greater part was massively relieved. I didn't want to see him. He'd be a constant reminder that my dad wasn't my actual dad. Although, of course, he might be. That was going to take some getting my head round.

One particular thought that didn't sit comfortably, but refused to go away, was the parallels of my feelings for Rey, with Josephine's for Anthony all those years ago. I'd been appalled by her infidelity, but if Steve and I had been on a break and I'd thought something was going on with him and Collette, would I have been tempted to sleep with Rey? I'd certainly fantasised about it. I'd never condone Josephine's actions, but I was beginning to understand how it could happen.

Maybe, for my sanity as much as anything, I should let it all go. Geoff was the man I'd grown up with. He was the man I thought of as my dad. As Sophie had so beautifully said, I was who I was – it didn't matter who I came from. Or, as Josephine less tactfully put it, why did it matter whose sperm it was? I grimaced. No one should ever have to hear their mother use the word 'sperm'.

* * *

On the Friday, I received a request for a video call from Cath and Nina. I eagerly dialled in, keen to tell them about the women I'd found for the series I was writing.

'Becca – thank you for joining us at such short notice,' Cath said, pulling her blonde curls back into a messy ponytail. 'We've got good news.'

Nina nodded, her signature red lipstick framing her broad smile. 'We have not one, not two, not three . . .' She counted on her fingers. 'Four new sponsors! They all want to place advertisements by your features.' She extended her hands towards the screen. 'You're a hit, Becca.'

I gasped. 'That's fantastic. I'm so pleased.'

'So are we.' Cath flexed her muscles. 'With you!'

'Even better,' Nina continued. 'They're all interested in collaborating on any events we do. That's the green light we've been waiting for, and it's thanks to your suggestion.'

'Your event experience will be invaluable,' Cath said. 'If you'd still like to be involved.'

Excitement coursed through me. 'I'd love to. Tell me what you're thinking and I'll start putting together ideas of how to go about it.'

'Any chance you could come to London next week?' Nina asked. 'We'll get some lunch in and spend a few hours going over it.'

'Definitely,' I said enthusiastically, then paused. I wouldn't be able to if I was doing the bloody claims job. But I hadn't even been offered it yet. I'd tell them I couldn't start till the week after.

'There's more,' Cath said. She leant into the screen. 'How would you feel about editing the magazine?'

My mouth dropped open. 'That would be amazing, but don't you currently do that?'

'We're going to start a podcast,' Nina said. 'With that, the event planning and growing members and sponsors, we won't have time to run the magazine too. You're the perfect person – if you'd like to, that is. We appreciate that it'll take more of your time, which we'd pay you for, of course.'

I sat on my hands to stop myself from biting my nails. It'd be hard to fit the extra work in alongside the claims job, but I'd worry about that later. This was an amazing opportunity and there was no way I was going to turn it down.

'Yes, please,' I said. 'I'd be honoured to.'

Cath put a hand to her chest. 'What a relief. We don't know what we'd have done if you'd said no.'

Nina laughed. 'No, there is no plan B. We want you and only you.'

'You're an integral part of our team now,' Cath added.

I blinked several times, blown away by their enthusiasm. Only a few weeks ago, Declan had dismissed me for being old and useless. Now I was being told by two women I respected and admired that I was an integral part of their team.

'Is that OK with you?' Cath asked.

I nodded so enthusiastically, my neck hurt. It was more than OK with me.

We made arrangements for our team – team! – lunch the following week, then said goodbye. I went into my email and tensed when I saw there was one from Ruby Carnegie. What if she was writing to tell me that she'd made a mistake and I needed to return the £14,000?

I chewed on a nail as I opened the message and read the contents. I almost bit the top of my finger off when I got to the bottom. My unfair dismissal appeal had been approved and I would be receiving a settlement of £40,000 on top of the £14,000 I'd already received. Forty thousand pounds! That was more than a year's salary. My head spun at the realisation that this was the safety net I needed to go freelance full-time. I wouldn't have to take the claims job. I could go to team meetings with Cath and Nina whenever they were held and throw myself into this new career that I was loving. Maybe it wouldn't work out, but I'd give it a bloody good go.

I tapped out a reply, thanking Ruby, then phoned a local florist and ordered a bouquet to be delivered to her, and another for Nikki with the message: *Start saving for NYC. The first drink's on me!*

I rang Sophie and excitedly told her the news.

'You're slaying, Mum!' she squealed. 'Can I come to New York with you and Nikki?'

'I was thinking of something else for us.' I smiled. 'Let me talk to Dad first.'

# Chapter 46

I spent the next hour online, looking at beautiful destinations in Thailand and growing increasingly excited with each vista. When Steve got home, I beamed up at him from the kitchen table. He looked equally animated.

'I've got some good news,' he said, placing his briefcase carefully on the table.

'So have I.' I smiled at the scene on my laptop. 'You go first.'

He rubbed his hands together. 'Someone's had to drop out of the Christmas party, so you can come after all.'

Ah. In my excitement about MAAM and the redundancy package, and thoughts of New York and Thailand, and not having to do the claims job, I'd forgotten that I had to tell Steve I wasn't going to take it.

I stood up and took his hands. 'I'm sorry, but I'm not going to take the job.'

The remains of Steve's fine, sandy hair stood up on end. 'The claims job?'

I nodded. 'I've been offered an amazing opportunity by Cath and Nina at MAAM. They want me to be part of the team, edit the magazine and help organise an event.

It's not a full-time position, but alongside the writing I'm doing for them, it's definitely part-time.'

Steve took his hands out of mine and stepped back. 'Can't you still do that in the evenings and at weekends?'

I shook my head. 'I'll need to have regular meetings with them in London, and speak to suppliers and speakers for the event during working hours. I can't do that if I'm in a full-time job.'

Steve removed his glasses and whipped a handkerchief from his pocket in one fluid motion. 'Without a full-time salary.'

'Yes, but you know I'm hoping to build my other freelance work too. I can do that properly now.'

Steve removed the lens he'd just inserted into his mouth and polished it furiously. 'Have you any idea how humiliating it'd be for me to tell the company that my wife has refused the job they've offered her?'

I pressed my hands together. 'I'm sorry, I really am. But it's not as though I'd be integral to the success of the company. The wheels will keep turning without me.'

'That's not the point.' Steve breathed onto the other lens. 'You'll have wasted their time and it'll reflect badly on me.'

'I'm sorry,' I said again, though my initial guilt at letting him down was being replaced by frustration. 'But I wouldn't have enjoyed it, whereas I love what I'm doing now.'

He was polishing his glasses with such vigour, it was a wonder they didn't shatter. 'You'll be getting the official offer next week and you're morally obliged to accept it.'

'Aren't you morally obliged to listen to your wife?' I snapped. 'Aren't my feelings more important than your colleagues?'

Steve opened and closed his mouth a few times. He looked down at the handkerchief in his hand. 'Of course they are,' he sighed. 'What I don't understand is why you've changed. Turning down stability in favour of the unknown. It's not like you.'

He was right. Until very recently, the thought of rejecting a reliable, regular income in favour of a fluid one would have petrified me. I hadn't changed completely – I'd always be the person who listened intently to the safety demonstration on a plane and never left home without a tissue up my sleeve – but now I felt strong enough to take a chance. I needed Steve to understand that.

'I need a little more in my life,' I said. 'Things had become staid and this new work has given me something to look forward to.'

Steve shoved the handkerchief into his pocket without folding it. He was more upset than I'd realised. 'I thought travel was the thing you were going to look forward to. Don't you want to do that anymore?'

'Yes, more than ever,' I said. 'That's the other part of the good news I was going to tell you. My unfair dismissal claim has gone through. They're giving me another £40,000.'

Steve's eyes widened behind his freshly cleaned glasses. 'Did you just say £40,000?' he choked.

I laughed. 'Yes! So, you see, I'm not being reckless. I have enough to support me while I build up my freelance work, and for us to go away.' I turned and opened my laptop to show Steve the destinations in Thailand I'd been looking at.

'Well, that changes things considerably.' Steve snapped open his briefcase and took a brochure out. He handed it to me with a broad smile. 'Good job I picked this up from the travel agent's.'

The glossy cover profiled a sleek cruise ship and a multigenerational, white family gleefully smiling, showcasing what an amazing time they were having, as well as their dentistry. I cringed. How could I break it to Steve that I didn't want to go on a cruise? By turning down the job in insurance, I'd crushed one dream of his – crushing another in the same evening would be cruel. I stared at the cookie-cutter family on the brochure. It might be cruel to destroy another of Steve's goals, but it was necessary.

'I'm not sure I'm a cruise sort of person. I haven't had my veneers done, for one thing.' I attempted a laugh, but it petered out when I saw Steve's face.

'But you said you wanted to travel,' he said miserably.

'I do. Look.' I flicked through photos on my laptop, of beaches and temples and steps cut deep into cliffs. 'Thailand is beautiful and there's so much to see. We'd get much more out of it than a cruise, where you're on the ship more than on land.'

'Thailand?' Steve sank down into a chair. 'I'm too old to go backpacking.'

'I'm not suggesting we backpack.' I giggled. 'We could do it in style.' I opened up a photo of a hotel with bungalows on stilts in the sea.

Steve clutched his chest. 'That would never pass a safety assessment in this country. You can't possibly expect me to stay somewhere like that.'

'I'm pretty sure they do risk assessments in Thailand.' I said it lightly, but his negativity was starting to grate.

Steve shook his head. 'Places like Thailand are for people in their twenties. I know you regret not going when you were younger, but that ship has sailed.' He held up the brochure. 'This one hasn't.' He smiled, pleased with himself for his wit. 'We'll be fifty and sixty next year. A cruise is the appropriate holiday for our age.'

I'd been so worried about turning fifty. It seemed to signify the end of opportunities – of nowhere to go except slowly downhill, listening to Steve wittering on until one of us was blessed with the sweet release of death. Now, thanks to Nikki, Cath and Nina and all the amazing women I was interviewing, I was inspired to reframe my age. Instead of, 'Oh no, I'm fifty!' it was, 'I'm *only* fifty.'

I pulled myself up tall. 'Age is a state of mind. I'm about to interview a sixty-five-year-old woman who's taken up abseiling.'

Steve turned pale. 'You're not suggesting we do that, are you?'

'No,' I admitted. I wanted to be more adventurous, but not if it required a harness.

Steve frowned. 'Why mention it, then?'

'Because age shouldn't be a barrier to what we do.'

'What's got into you?' He took his glasses off and rubbed his eyes. 'For twenty-five years everything's run smoothly. Then all of a sudden, you're off to Josephine's without a backward glance, pandering to Sophie's indecision, going freelance and talking about wild holidays that we're far too old for.' He pinched the bridge of his nose. 'All I want is to go back to our normal, stable, secure life, without any more unexpected turns of events.'

A normal, stable, secure life without any unexpected turns of events. Those words had been everything I'd wanted for more than half my life. Now they brought a sour taste to my mouth. My stomach churned with guilt and fear. We didn't want the same things anymore. We hadn't for some time, years in fact, but it had taken Sophie leaving to highlight the void in our marriage. Deep down I must have known this, but I'd put it down to empty nest syndrome, and then I had the distraction of looking after Josephine. If Steve and I had had a good, healthy relationship, we'd have seen each other regularly while I'd been staying there. As it was, we'd barely spoken.

I swallowed hard. I had two choices here. I could pretend everything was fine and we could drift along as we had been, living alongside each other rather than with each other. It would be easy enough and it wasn't as though I disliked him – although the fact I had to get drunk to sleep with him was a slight red flag. Or I could stop running away and face up to my problems, the way Sophie had. I could tell Steve our marriage was over. It'd be scary starting again, especially without a secure job. But staying would be far scarier. I was *only* fifty, I reminded myself. Far too young to give up and stagnate when there was so much life to be lived.

I took a deep breath, desperately searching for what to say, when I felt a hand on my shoulder. I turned and met Steve's gaze. He looked as wretched as I felt.

'That's not quite true,' he said. 'I don't want things to go back exactly the way they were.' His Adam's apple bobbed up and down as he swallowed. 'You never join in when I talk,' he said. 'Collette, on the other hand . . .' My eyes widened and he shook his head. 'No, no, she's just a friend. Nothing untoward has happened, I give you my word.' I nodded and he carried on.

'In fairness, you've always been quiet, so I'd got used to my conversations being one-sided,' he continued. 'But Collette . . . Well, she can talk for England.' He chuckled. 'Hard to get a word in edgeways sometimes, but I like that two-way element. It was never there with us, was it?'

Wow, someone who could rival Steve in the talking department. If Collette had found a way to break through Steve's wall of words, then she was a better woman than me. Or perhaps a woman who was better suited to Steve than me. Maybe if I'd tried harder, I could have got through. Maybe I'd never cared enough, which was unfair on Steve. He deserved to be with someone who was interested in him enough to want to engage in conversation.

'I'm sorry.' My heart pinched, as I realised this was actually happening. We were breaking up. Our twenty-five-year marriage was ending. A noisy sob escaped me. 'You're right, I have changed. It'd be easier if I hadn't, but I can't pretend. That wouldn't be fair on either of us.'

Steve took my hand. 'And I can't pretend to be someone else either.' He gave me a watery smile. 'Sorry, but Thailand's not for me. I'll stick with the cruise.'

I wiped a tear away. 'Perhaps you should go with Collette?'

'Oh, I don't know about that.' Was it my imagination or did the tips of his ears go pink? 'There's probably nothing more to our friendship than our common interest in insurance. That's one of the reasons I had hoped you'd take the job. Give us something to talk about.'

I squeezed his hand. He'd tried in his own way to make our marriage work. It wasn't his fault it hadn't.

Steve took his handkerchief from his pocket and blew his nose loudly. 'I'll move back into the spare room. Stay as long as you need to. I missed having someone to talk to when you weren't here.'

That's what he'd said when I'd moved back. He missed having someone to talk to. Not *me* – someone. Further proof that this was the right thing to do.

'Unless you want to move back with Josephine?' he added.

'No!' The claims job was a more attractive prospect. 'I'll stay, please. While I look for somewhere for me and Sophie.' A picturesque little two-bedroom cottage flitted through my mind.

'You could always buy Josephine's coach house.' He smiled to show he was joking, but my stomach lurched.

The coach house. Rey still had a few days left there. I thought of his email. I'd reply and tell him that I'd do the blog posts. I'd take all the work I could get. But I'd do it next week, so he couldn't suggest we meet up before he left. I didn't trust myself around him, especially now that my marriage was over. If I threw myself at him, he'd never want to work with me, and I needed as much income as I could get to pay for that two-bed cottage. I'd never bumped into him around the city before – should be easy to avoid him for the next few days.

# Chapter 47

'Were you briefly abducted by aliens and now they've returned you?' Nikki put her coffee cup down. 'Because this is the complete opposite to what you said you wanted last week. Which was the opposite to what you said the week before.'

I grimaced. 'I know. Talk about midlife crisis.'

'This is the opposite of a crisis. It's bloody marvellous.' Nikki smiled broadly. 'I'm so pleased for you. You can live the life you were meant to now.'

I nodded but couldn't respond quite as enthusiastically. I felt slightly numb and a little sad, even though I knew that breaking up with Steve was the right thing to do, for both of us.

'How's Sophie?' Nikki asked.

'She doesn't know yet. Not the sort of thing I want to tell her on the phone. She'll be back from uni soon, so we'll tell her then.' I started to pull at a hangnail, then stopped and picked up my cup instead. Why did I do this to myself? My fingertips were constantly sore, which made opening cans and peeling off labels so painful, it could qualify as an event in *Squid Game*. 'I think she'll be OK once she's got her head around it,' I said. 'At home she spends most of her time in her room, because she doesn't want to watch what Steve has on the TV. At Josephine's she was downstairs more and we watched things together. It was nice. We can do that all the time when we're in our own place.' *Our own place.* The thought filled me with joy. No more dark-wood furnishings chosen because they were in the Boxing Day sale, or a rickety filing cabinet that had been about to go in the work skip instead of a chest of drawers.

Steve and I had talked late into the night. Well, I'd mainly listened, obviously. For someone so frugal – OK, mean – he'd been remarkably comfortable discussing how the money from the house and our savings would be divided in two. He seemed to view the situation the same way he'd view a life insurance claim. There were procedures to follow and appropriate sums to be designated, and he would follow those rules. He'd gathered his box files and gone through everything, tapping into his calculator and making lists. He seemed to be in his element, only one step away from breaking into a merry whistle.

When he'd showed me the final figure, my mouth had dropped open.

'Half of that's mine?' I'd gasped.

He'd shaken his head. 'No, all of that's yours.'

'How have we been able to save that much money?'

'Look after the pennies and the pounds look after themselves.'

Sadness had washed over me. All those years of discounted food, crap holidays, secretly squirreling money away so Sophie could get something in the cake bake sale or have a replacement school jumper when the elbow went, rather than putting a patch over it. All those fun family experiences we'd missed out on because they were 'a waste of money'. And all along that money had been sitting there doing nothing. Well, not nothing – it had been accruing interest, which was now benefitting me massively, and doing a fantastic job of curing my momentary sadness.

I smiled at Nikki. 'Thanks to Steve's scrimping and saving, I can afford to buy outright. Sophie and I can go house-hunting when she's here at Christmas.'

'You scrimped and saved too, remember?' Nikki said. 'Your salary went straight into the joint account and he gave you a pathetic allowance.'

'I might be living on an even more pathetic allowance, depending on how much freelance work I get.'

Nikki put a hand on my arm. 'You'll be OK, won't you?'

'Yes, as long as I'm careful. I'll be getting a regular income from MAAM and will work hard to build the freelance side. Plus, there's the money from *Norwich Now*, although I'd rather not use it on bills.'

Nikki tightened her grip. 'Have you heard? Declan's been sacked. He'd already had a warning for the way he treated you, and Ruby filed a complaint about him. Then he changed the magazine title and instructed the typesetters to take out the vowels and add an exclamation mark, so it reads *NWCH NW!*' She tried to pronounce the new title and made a sound not dissimilar to a farmyard animal.

I snorted with laughter, a sound which unfortunately also belonged on a farm. 'How are they going to introduce themselves or answer the phone?'

'Who knows?' Nikki giggled. 'The shareholders are furious. They'd told Declan they didn't like it when he suggested it, but he went ahead anyway. Said they didn't know what they were talking about and they needed to stop with the outdated vibe if they wanted to slay.'

We laughed till my stomach hurt and my cheeks ached. It felt good.

Nikki dabbed at her mascara with a napkin. 'So, there's an editor's position going if you fancy applying?'

I shook my head. 'I want to move forward, not backwards.'

'Good. Your freelance career sounds much more exciting.' She coiled a curl around her finger. 'Had a rethink about doing something with Rey?'

My face grew hot. I'd spent far too much time thinking about doing something with Rey, none of it professional or appropriate. I cleared my throat. 'I'll do his blog posts and he's going to give my details to his clients in the hope they want me to write their content.' I stared into my mug to avoid meeting Nikki's eyes. 'He said he'd set up a website for me, but I think that'd be too much.'

'Why? Because he makes you so *flustered*?'

'No,' I said indignantly. Nikki raised her eyebrows. 'OK, yes,' I admitted. 'We'd need to talk a lot about the design and maybe meet up.' I fought the urge to bite my nails. 'I can't trust myself not to want more.'

'He might want more too.' Nikki grinned. 'I was definitely picking up an *interested* vibe.'

'All in your imagination.' I shrugged nonchalantly. 'He's going back to Brighton in a couple of days anyway.'

Nikki winked. 'Nothing like sex by the seaside.'

I crossed my legs and refused to indulge in a brief fantasy of just what that sex by the seaside might entail. 'No,' I said firmly. 'Even if he is interested, which he isn't, I don't want a relationship. For twenty-five years I've been dependent on a man. From now on, I'm going to be an independent woman.' I sat up straight. 'I emailed UEA earlier and asked if any of their tech students did web design to grow their portfolios. I've got lots of work to do for MAAM while I'm waiting to hear back.'

'I'm so proud of you.' Nikki smiled. 'When I said you should make your second act your comeback era, I never expected you to achieve this much.' She raised her mug. 'Here's to your successful career and the mother of all comebacks.'

My hand shook slightly as I lifted my own cup. I'd be lying if I said I wasn't nervous about launching myself into the unknown. But I'd spent thirty years playing it safe and avoiding anything remotely daring or interesting. Even boarding an escalator with a takeaway coffee would make me break out in a sweat. But not anymore. This was my chance to go for it, even the scary things. And to start me off, I was going to do the scariest thing of all. I was going to go and see Josephine. But first I needed to buy something.

# Chapter 48

My heart pounded as I knocked on Josephine's door. There was no answer. She was probably at the gym, walking on the treadmill with her cap pulled down low to protect her from the fluorescent lighting, or having a treatment at the salon. But what if she'd had another fall? She could be lying on the floor injured, in pain, waiting to be found.

I didn't have my key with me, so walked round the side of the house, looking in the windows, but there was no sign of her. I went back to the front door and peered through the glass pane. A face peered back.

Shrieking, I leapt back, toppled off the doorstep and landed with a wallop on my bottom.

The door flew open. 'Becca, I'm so sorry.' Rey strode over to help me up. 'Are you all right?'

'Yes, thank you.' Mortified, I ignored his outstretched hand and scrambled up, refusing to acknowledge the pulsing sting in my palms, coccyx and bum. 'Is Josephine home?'

'No.'

'Are you sure? Could she have fallen and you haven't come across her?'

Rey nudged his glasses up. 'I haven't done a recce of the house, but her car's not on the drive.'

'Oh. Yes.' Should she be driving? Was it safe?

'You're bleeding.' Rey placed his hands beneath mine and lifted them to reveal grit and gravel embedded in my bloody palms.

I gasped. No wonder it bloody hurt. I dreaded to think what state my arse was in.

'Would you like me to help you clean your hands?' Rey asked.

That would involve us being alone in the house together, which didn't align with my plan to avoid him. 'No. I'll be OK, thanks.'

'Are you sure? You need to make sure all the dirt's out, so it doesn't get infected.'

Infected? I studied the grit and mud that was probably full of bacteria eagerly waiting to multiply and infiltrate my blood supply. People died from sepsis. Rey was right; I needed to get this dirt out, immediately, and his help in this matter would be very much appreciated. I just wouldn't look at him. It'd be safer that way for both of us.

'Actually, if you've got time, that'd be great.' I kept my head bowed. 'Thank you.'

'No problem.'

I followed him into the house and through to the kitchen, my hands outstretched. He pulled a bar stool over to the sink and helped me onto it. So much for avoiding him. We were practically recreating a scene from a medical romance.

'Does Josephine have any disinfectant and cotton wool?' he asked, putting the plug in the sink and running the tap.

'In the bathroom cupboard,' I said, watching beads of blood congeal on my hands. Was it my imagination or could I actually see the bacteria breeding?

Rey belted up the stairs and back. Those daily runs of his had not been in vain. He poured some disinfectant into the water and took one of my hands.

'Are you scared of blood?' he asked, clocking my concerned face.

'Only when it's my own and it's pouring out of me.'

He gave a low laugh. 'That's probably the most sensible time to be scared of it.'

He dunked some cotton wool into the water. 'Sorry, this is probably going to hurt.' He gently dabbed my palm, easing the grit and gravel out of the crevices in my flesh where they'd wedged themselves. I pressed my lips together and willed myself not to scream with the intensity of the woman in the shower scene in *Psycho*. Then I had to intensely will myself not to think about Rey in the shower. It took so much concentration, my head started hurting, which did at least distract from the agonising pain in my hands.

'You're doing really well.' Rey smiled. 'Sometimes it's mind over matter, isn't it?' He wouldn't be smiling if he knew what was going through my mind. 'Almost done,' he said, tenderly wiping the last of the dirt away. His bowed head was so close to mine that his hair was tickling my cheek and I could feel the warmth of his skin.

A whimper escaped me that had nothing to do with the pain in my hands.

'Sorry.' He tilted his head to give me a sympathetic look. I could melt in those dark brown eyes. He blinked and looked away. Oh God, I hadn't been drooling, had I?

'I think I've got it all out,' he said. 'Do you want to check?'

I studied my hands with the intensity of a VAR analysing a disputed foul. 'I can't see any dirt. Thank you.'

'Anywhere else hurt?'

'No.' He didn't need to know that my arse was throbbing.

'It's best to let them air-dry,' Rey said. 'Can I get you a drink while you're waiting?'

A shot of whisky would have gone down a treat, but it was hard enough keeping my composure around him when I was sober.

'Some water, please,' I said instead.

Rey filled two glasses and sat at a bar stool across from me. My hands were outstretched and we both watched them drying.

'You don't have to stay with me,' I said, after a few minutes. 'It's very kind, but you've probably got things to get on with.'

'I don't mind.' Rey ran a hand across his jaw. 'Did you get my email about the blog posts?'

'Yes, sorry. I've been so busy, I haven't had a chance to read it yet,' I lied.

'That's OK, I know how it is.'

Could he please stop being so nice. He smiled at me. That wasn't helping.

'I included some suggestions for your website too.' Rey nudged his glasses up. 'Let me know what you think when you've had a chance to look.'

'Thank you, but you've got enough going on with your own business and Saif and moving back to Brighton.'

Rey grinned. 'I'm a nerd, remember? Web design is my hobby as well as my day job.'

I smiled back, but I wouldn't take him up on the offer. The blog posts could be discussed by email. Designing my website would involve lengthy conversations and possible meet-ups, which were best avoided if I was going to get over this pathetic crush of mine.

His phone beeped and a calendar notification flashed up onto the screen.

'I'm afraid I've got a client call coming up,' he said. 'Will I get to see you before I go?'

Not if I could help it. There was too great a risk I'd accidentally reveal how much I liked him. Possibly by throwing myself at his feet and begging him not to leave. 'Probably not,' I said. 'But I'll email you about the blogs.'

He stepped towards me and my heart skipped a beat. Then I realised he was putting his glass by the sink. The sooner he left, the better. Then I could stop fantasising that something was going to happen, when it clearly wasn't – and shouldn't.

'Thanks for your help.' I lifted my palms and winced at the throbbing pain.

'You're welcome. Be careful with them.' He put a hand up and walked out of the kitchen. And out of my life. Well, not completely out of my life, as we'd be in touch via email for work. But I wasn't tech-savvy enough to proposition him online. I stared at my hands and sighed.

'Becca.'

My head jerked up. Rey stood at the kitchen door. Was the front-door handle so coated in hand cream he couldn't escape?

He nudged his glasses up. 'I just wanted to say that I've really enjoyed getting to know you.' He cringed. 'That sounded much better in my head. I hope it didn't sound like a weird come-on.'

'No,' I stammered. 'I know you'd never come on to me.'

'No,' Rey agreed.

All right, no need to hammer it home.

He raised his arms then let them fall back to his sides. 'You're married,' he said. 'Having been cheated on, I would never do that to someone else.'

Of course he wouldn't. He was far too decent a person. I wouldn't be attracted to him if he didn't have any morals. Well, OK, I might be a bit – those eyes and arms would turn a nun's head – but I wouldn't have wanted to be involved with him. Which I did, I suddenly realised. I would very much like to be involved with him and the thought of him leaving and never seeing him again was crap. Heat rushed to my face as I replayed his words. Was he intimating that he *would* like me if I wasn't married? I swallowed hard. There was only one way to find out.

‘Steve and I broke up,’ I blurted out.

‘Oh.’ Rey rubbed his jaw.

Disappointment flooded through me. He wasn’t interested. Of course he wasn’t. I’d got carried away by Nikki’s excitement and projected my own feelings onto him.

Rey moved his hand so I could see his mouth. He was smiling. ‘Oh,’ he said again, his eyes twinkling.

I gasped. Had I contracted sepsis and was now hallucinating? He stepped towards me and the jolt that shot through my body and settled between my legs was not, I suspected, a typical side effect of sepsis.

An ear-splitting siren came from the hall. I shrieked and Rey sprang away from me.

Josephine came into the kitchen, her arm extended, holding out her personal alarm. ‘Switch this off for me, would you,’ she shouted. ‘I knocked it when I was putting my keys away.’

Rey took it from her and pressed the button to deactivate it. ‘I’d better go,’ he said. ‘I’ve got a call in . . .’ He looked at his watch. ‘Two minutes. Sorry to run, Josephine.’ He hurried past her, then paused and grinned at me over his shoulder. ‘I’ll message you later,’ he said, before yanking the front door open with the cuff of his sleeve and disappearing.

Josephine raised her eyebrows at me.

‘I fell over on the drive.’ I held out my grazed hands to show her.

She went paler than her ecru cashmere sweater. Scarred hands were practically on par with being told she’d never walk again.

'Rey cleaned them for me,' I said. My cheeks were on fire. So was the rest of me, but fortunately she couldn't see those bits. 'Made sure all the dirt was out so I didn't get sepsis.'

Josephine raised her eyebrows. 'Is that so?'

# Chapter 49

'Yes,' I said defensively. 'It is so.'

Josephine picked up a pot of Bio-Oil from the breakfast bar and dabbed a small amount onto her wrist. She gently massaged it into her scar, avoiding my gaze. I instantly regretted snapping at her. It had been a reflex response and wasn't justified. If Nikki had walked in and made it clear she didn't buy my story, I'd have giggled and told her the truth, not bitten her head off. I was so on edge around Josephine that whatever came out of her mouth wound me up.

I needed to stop being so frustrated with her. Yes, her revelation had sent me spiralling in a different direction to the one I'd planned, but it was me who'd chosen that direction. And it wasn't as though my life had gone badly. I hadn't ended up homeless and alone. I might not have had the exciting career I'd imagined, or the spontaneous, glamorous adventures, but who's to say I would have done anyway? And, as Sophie had pointed out, if I hadn't worked at *Norwich Now*, I wouldn't have met Steve and she wouldn't be here. And I wouldn't change that for anything.

Also, the exciting career and spontaneous adventures could still happen. In fact, they *were* happening. I was embarking on a completely new stage of my life and, yes, I was nervous, but I was also loving it.

I watched Josephine methodically rub oil into her skin. Had she always been quite so obsessed or was this her crutch, in the way that yanking my ponytail tight and biting my nails had been mine?

'How's your wrist?' I asked.

'Much better, thank you.' She rotated it and added a finger flourish to prove how well it worked.

'Any more dizzy spells?'

'No. I've been checking my blood pressure every day and it's excellent.'

'That'll be the compression socks,' I said.

Josephine shuddered. 'I am never wearing those hideous items again.' She ruffled her pale copper curls. 'The doctor says I'm in better health than someone half my age.'

I swallowed a smile. Course she was. 'Are you sure you're OK to drive?'

'Yes. I've been signed off. All back to normal now.' She ran a finger along the scar on her wrist. 'Apart from this. But I can get laser treatment to speed up the healing process, and the cosmetic makeup available now is superb.' She rolled her fingers inward from pinky to thumb, like a delicately closing flower. 'I'll be modelling again in no time.'

I watched her conduct her synchronised finger routine. Did she really believe she could reignite her career at the age of seventy? Her bright smile indicated that she did. A long-forgotten feeling of admiration unfurled within me. Why the hell shouldn't she make a comeback? I'd initially come up with the concept of challenging companies to use age-appropriate models as a way to occupy her time and stop her finding jobs for me to do, but it was actually a good idea. If anyone deserved to be the poster girl for it, it was Josephine. I thought back to what Rey had said, momentarily got distracted with other thoughts of him that didn't involve my mother, and then refocused.

'Your Spotlight on Silver Supermodels campaign,' I said. 'Would you like me to help with the promotion? I can't guarantee it'd work, but I can give it a go.'

Josephine clasped her hands together. 'Would you? Anthony and I have no idea where to start.'

My throat tightened. 'Anthony?'

Two spots of colour appeared in Josephine's cheeks. 'He called me and apologised for his disappearing act. Said discovering he might have another child had momentarily given him the willies.'

It was an unfortunate turn of phrase, but I chose not to comment.

'He's accepted the situation now,' Josephine continued. 'At our age, surprises are to be welcomed, not feared.' She cleared her throat. 'He said he'd do a DNA test if you wanted him to.'

I shook my head. 'That's nice of him, but no. Like you said, Geoff was my dad. Let's leave it at that.'

'Well, the offer's there if you change your mind. He's got four children himself and goodness knows how many grandchildren.'

Strange to think that I could potentially have a huge family, when so far it had just been me, Steve, Sophie and Josephine. And now it wouldn't even include Steve. I didn't want to go down that road, though. I didn't need to be part of Anthony's family. Far too many Christmas cards to write.

'I'm really sorry about Audrey,' I said. She'd been in Josephine's life for longer than I – and most other people on the planet – had been alive, and seeing her decline must be a terrible wrench. I was deeply ashamed that I'd been too preoccupied with my own life to listen, let alone sympathise. 'How's she doing?' I asked.

Josephine sighed. 'Not too well, unfortunately. Some days she can barely speak. Although she managed to croak "fifteen per cent" when I told her about the Silver Supermodels campaign, so she's still got her business head screwed on.'

I suspected only death would prevent Audrey from claiming her cut, but it seemed rather callous to mention this.

'There's something else I need to say,' I said quietly. A lump formed in my throat and I had to swallow several times before I could continue. 'I shouldn't have judged you the way I did.' I stared down at my grazed palms splayed on the breakfast bar. 'I had no idea what Dad had done. That must have been horrible for you. I'm sorry I reacted the way I did.' I released a long, shaky breath. 'Really sorry.'

Josephine placed a hand on my forearm. 'Thank you,' she whispered. 'I'm sorry too.'

We stayed like that for some time, neither of us speaking or looking at the other, but her hand on my arm was a comforting presence.

'Steve and I have broken up,' I said eventually. 'Sophie leaving was the catalyst for me questioning our relationship. Then while I was here, I realised I didn't miss him and wasn't particularly in a rush to get back. He feels the same.' I straightened up. 'It's amicable. There are no hard feelings. No one else is involved . . . It's just come to an end.'

Josephine's eyes darted in the direction of the coach house. 'Is that so?'

My cheeks grew hot. I should accept defeat and just paint my face red. It'd save my blood vessels a lot of work.

Josephine smirked but didn't comment. Instead, she smoothed her trousers down. 'Would you like a drink?' she asked.

I almost fell off my stool in shock. She hadn't offered to make me a drink since the 1980s.

She gestured to my grazed palms. 'You can't do it. You'll get blood all over my china.' She filled the kettle. 'I would offer you a coffee, but you took your cafetière back. Not that we'd have got two cups out of it anyway.'

That reminded me. I slid off the stool, hooked a gift bag onto my finger and passed it to her. 'This is for you.'

Josephine reached in and took out a tissue-paper-wrapped box. It took her forever to tear the paper because of the bloody hand cream, but she got there in the end. It was a medium-sized cafetière. Perfect for making two cups of coffee.

She blinked hard. 'Thank you,' she said, her voice wobbling.

I blinked back my own tears. 'You're welcome. Mum.'

* * *

I ended up staying for a while. We sat at the breakfast bar, chatting over our coffees, as any mum and daughter in a normal relationship would. It felt natural and nice, and when I left, I voluntarily offered to come round again in a couple of days – and genuinely wanted to.

I started walking home, but stopped, turned around and headed back up the city, my steps quickening as I got closer. I wove through the Lanes, until I reached The Book Hive, then went straight to my favourite section. How many times had I stood and stared at the array of travel books, wishing I could go to one of the amazing countries? I'd been convinced that my desire to go somewhere – *anywhere* – other than that crappy villa meant I was ungrateful. That it was selfish to want fulfilment in addition to having a functional home, an annual holiday and a steady, reliable marriage. What was it Steve had said? When you get to our age you don't expect excitement – routine, stability and companionship was the best we could hope for. Well, I *did* want excitement and fulfilment at my age. And I was going to have it.

'Can I help you with anything?' the bookseller asked.

'Yes, please.' I took *Your Guide to Thailand* from the shelf and handed it to him. 'I'll take this.'

# Epilogue

## Eight months later

'Close your eyes and surrender to the experience.' The reiki healer's voice travelled across the water. 'Feel your tensions melting away, replaced by a profound sense of peace and relaxation. With each exhalation, sink deeper into a state of meditation. Allow the gentle movements of the water to carry you into a state of blissful serenity.'

I released a long breath and focused on the rhythmic lapping of water around me and the gentle sway of my floating lounger. This was it – the start of my journey into inner harmony.

'Let go of all distractions,' the healer said softly. 'Foster a deeper sense of mindful awareness by being fully present in the moment.'

'Is that a plaster?' my mum screeched.

So much for letting go of distractions. I pulled up my eye mask and glared across at her. Instead of lying back on her lounger and surrendering herself to the experience, like everyone else in the pool, she was frowning into the water.

'There,' she said, delicately unfurling a finger and pointing. 'How am I supposed to relax knowing there's a germ-infested plaster bobbing about next to me?'

'I can't see anything,' I whispered. Well, apart from the latex gloves my mum wore for protection against the chlorine. Even with the lights turned down low, she was determined to make sure her hands were on display.

'Right there.' She pointed again and looked expectantly at me.

'I'm not diving into the water to retrieve it,' I hissed. 'Stop talking and lie back down.'

I pulled my eye mask back into position and tried to focus on the healer's voice, but it was hard to immerse myself in the experience with my mum wriggling around on her lounger next to me and sighing loudly. Sophie and I had done a floating sound bath in Thailand and it had been a wonderfully tranquil hour. Naïve of me to think I could recreate that at the local swimming pool with my mum.

Sophie and I had gone to Thailand in her Easter break and spent three weeks exploring. We'd visited the Grand Palace, Old City, temples, street markets, an elephant sanctuary and breathtaking beaches; we'd also swum in clear blue water, gone on a river cruise, celebrated my fiftieth at a wellbeing wilderness retreat and eaten so much incredible food that I was almost the size of an elephant by the end of the holiday. Thankfully, a weekend with Rey when I'd got back helped burn some of that off. I wiggled my toes with excitement at the memory. I had no intention of throwing myself straight into a serious relationship the moment my marriage ended. After twenty-five years, I needed some time for myself and was enjoying being independent and having my own space while Sophie was at uni. I had no problem with throwing myself into Rey's bed, though. Or my bed. Or any surface in his flat or my cottage. The libido I'd begun to think was missing from my DNA turned out to have been lying dormant and was now intent on making up for the past two decades. If Rey felt objectified by my constant desire for sex, he was doing a sterling job of hiding it – without wanting to sound too Jilly Cooper about it, he always rose to the occasion.

'Have you given my marketing idea any more thought?' my mum asked, her voice reverberating around the otherwise quiet pool.

I jumped and almost rolled off my lounger into the plaster-infested pool.

'Stop talking,' I whispered.

'But there's nothing else to do.' She sighed heavily. 'I thought it'd be livelier than this.'

'Please can I remind you to be quiet throughout the session,' the healer instructed.

My cheeks burst into flames at the obvious telling-off. The gentle sound of a gong rang out, which I hoped was part of the ritual and not to mask my mother's voice.

'Why aren't we allowed to talk?' My mother's attempt at whispering was on par with the average person hollering across the street to get someone's attention.

The ringing of the gong grew louder, as the healer marched towards our end of the pool. 'I really do need you to be quiet, please,' she said. 'Silence is crucial to allow your system to benefit from the sound of the gong and reach a meditative state.'

My mum's lilo squeaked next to me.

'Please remain lying down,' the healer said firmly. 'It's hard for me to create the necessary ambience if you sit up. Here, let me help you back down.'

I lifted my eye mask to see the healer leaning over the edge of the pool and reaching towards my mum.

'No need for that,' my mum said tartly. 'I'm not an invalid.' To demonstrate this, she thrust a hand in the air, inadvertently catching the side of the healer's gong. There was a splash as the gong fell into the pool, followed by some very unspiritual muttering.

* * *

'That was fun,' my mum said fifteen minutes later, as I drove her home.

'It was *not* fun.' I winced, recalling the healer's distress at the possibility of her gong getting damaged by the chemicals in the pool. 'The poor woman was distraught.'

'She was overreacting.' My mum batted the air, knocking my rear-view mirror in the process. 'It's not as though she has to go on another pilgrimage to South-East Asia to get a new gong. They're probably ten a penny on Amazon.'

I adjusted my mirror and put my foot down. Just because our relationship was in a much healthier, happier place now, it didn't mean that she wasn't still massively annoying a lot of the time.

'About my marketing idea,' she said.

'No,' I said firmly, pulling up at a red light.

'Why not?' My mum threw her hands up, paused momentarily to admire them, then glared at me. 'It would be very impactful.'

'Yes – for all the wrong reasons.'

'But it did wonders for Miley Cyrus when she relaunched her career.'

I tugged the back of my hair. 'She was twenty. You're seventy-one.'

Her nostrils flared. 'How hypocritical. You've just had an article published in the *Guardian* about the irrelevance of age.'

I felt a brief flicker of pride but pushed this aside and stayed focused. 'In most situations age is irrelevant,' I said. 'However, not this one.'

'But—'

'Mum, listen to me.' I gripped the steering wheel. 'For the final time, you are *not* posing naked on a wrecking ball.'

The traffic light turned green and I ignored her muttering beside me about ageism and lack of opportunities, and focused instead on getting her home as quickly as I could before she came up with another suggestion. So far I'd secured her a job modelling splints for carpal tunnel syndrome and another for a wrist-operated fall alarm. Although pleased to be working, she was yearning for a more glamorous contract, and she and Anthony kept coming up with increasingly ludicrous marketing proposals to garner attention. I didn't want to dampen their enthusiasm, but it seemed unlikely their 'You can keep your hard hat on' approach would persuade De Beers or Cartier that she was the perfect model for their platinum ranges.

'Thank you,' she said, when I dropped her home. 'How long's Rey staying with you?'

'Just till Friday,' I said casually, although my stomach somersaulted at the thought of him waiting for me at home. 'The MAAM event's next week, so I need to prep over the weekend and travel first thing Monday morning.' My stomach contracted again. For the past six months, I'd been working with Cath and Nina on creating MAAM's first event. We had a line-up of motivating, inspiring speakers, interactive sessions, 'getting to know you' opportunities (networking sounded too formal and dry), and a marketplace crammed with independent retailers, creatives and F&B suppliers. The event had sold out and had been widely covered by the media. I'd even persuaded BBC *Breakfast* to do a business piece on the rise of midlife female entrepreneurs. And, after a meeting with the *Guardian*'s lifestyle editor, I had had a piece published, with the opportunity to write more. My career couldn't look more different than it had a year ago. Back then, I'd been stuck in a thankless job, counting down the days till I could retire. Instead, every day I was excited to get up and go to work. Well, unless I'd spent the night with Rey. Not getting up was exciting on those occasions.

'Are you sure you don't want me to speak at the event?' my mum asked. 'Rey scanned all my photos and they'd make a striking backdrop to my presentation.'

'That's very kind, but we've got a full schedule.' I'd briefly considered putting her forward as a potential speaker. She had a strong work ethic, and I greatly admired her refusal to let her age stop her. In the right arena, she'd be a great speaker. But that arena would need to be full of people who wanted extensive information on hand care and a desire to be talked through, at length, all 180 photos in her portfolio. In the end I decided it was probably best not to have her on the line-up. 'I'll tell you all about it over lunch next week. Say hi to Anthony for me.'

Anthony had moved in a couple of months ago. Audrey had apparently given her blessing to the union. That's how they'd chosen to interpret her request for a large brandy, anyway.

I still felt a little awkward around Anthony, although I was getting to know him better. We seemed to have formed an unspoken agreement to never talk about the possibility that I might be his daughter. No good could really be gained from that discovery. I had a dad, and Anthony had his own family. Neither of us was missing anything or had a void that needed to be filled, so it seemed better to leave it be. From what I could tell, he was a nice man, and he clearly adored my mum and made her happy, which was the main thing. He didn't even seem to mind being summoned by an alarm whenever she wanted a hot water and lemon or collagen capsule. Either he was much more patient than me or had turned the batteries down on his hearing aid.

Ten minutes later, I pulled up behind my own cottage and gazed at it with a mixture of pride and joy. I couldn't believe that this lovely little terraced house on the outskirts of the city was mine. Both bedrooms had en suites, which meant Sophie and Rey never had any awkward bathroom encounters on the occasions they were both there, and I never had to encounter any fake tan. There was a log burner in the living room and an AGA in the kitchen, although it was mainly decorative. The air fryer had been one of the first things I'd unpacked.

The garden gate squeaked as I went through and walked up the back garden. Rey had offered to oil it, but I'd said no. I was determined to be completely self-sufficient, plus I liked the advance warning it gave when my mum 'popped in'. Not that I actually minded. It had got a bit much when I'd lived at the coach house for a few months, after Rey had moved out and before the sale on the cottage had gone through. My mum hadn't fully grasped the concept of boundaries, and several times I'd come out of my bedroom in the morning to find her at the table doing hand exercises with my kitchen utensils.

I opened the back door and inhaled the scent of fresh spices. Being cooked for on a regular basis was one of the benefits of being with Rey. One of the *many* benefits. The others being his warmth, wit, support, ability to ask questions – and to stop talking so I could answer – weird enjoyment of cleaning, and some other things that brought me a great deal of enjoyment.

Rey had his back to me in the little galley kitchen and was chopping coriander. The outline of his biceps was visible through the sleeve of his green T-shirt. I shivered with anticipation at the thought of those arms wrapping themselves around me and holding me tight, as he lowered me onto the bed.

Rey must have sensed I was there – the low moan I'd emitted might have had something to do with it – and he turned with a broad smile.

My stomach scissor-kicked as he stepped forward to kiss me. The brush of his cropped beard against my face and the firmness of his lips were as intoxicating now as they had been when he'd first kissed me six months earlier. We'd met for lunch in London, half-way between Brighton and Norwich, after a few weeks of teenage-like, back-and-forth messaging, long conversations and Zoom calls. After lunch, we'd walked around Spitalfields Market and Exchange Square, so wrapped up in conversation and the excitement of being together that we'd barely registered what was going on around us. At the end of the day, when we'd both had to leave to catch our last trains, Rey had walked me to Liverpool Street station, taken my face in his hands and kissed me with such intensity, it was a wonder we didn't get arrested.

Since then, we'd seen each other every other week, either in Brighton or Norwich, although we didn't see much of either city when we were together. I finally understood why Nikki had been keen for Chiwetel's cousins to leave. I couldn't think of anything crueller than having Rey lying next to me but being unable to have sex for fear of making a noise and disturbing our house guests. Thankfully, that wasn't an issue for us. When Sophie or Saif were home from uni, their sleep patterns were so out of synch with ours that there were very few hours when we were all in our beds at the same time.

'Smells amazing, thank you,' I said, helping myself to a cube of mango that hadn't been added to the chutney yet.

'Dinner won't be ready for half an hour,' Rey said. 'I didn't expect you back so soon.'

'The class ended early. My mum accidentally knocked the reiki healer's ancient gong into the pool.'

Rey laughed as he nudged his glasses up. 'Well, her loss is my gain.' He slipped his hands around my waist and pulled me to him.

'Is that so?' I cringed and hoped Rey hadn't noticed me using one of my mum's favourite sayings. He responded by kissing me, which I took to mean he hadn't. Then he pulled his T-shirt up and over his head, and I stopped thinking about my mum. And everything else.

'I got you a present,' Rey said a couple of hours later, after we'd eventually got around to eating.

'Another one?' I said, playfully peeking under the blanket. We were snuggled on the sofa, where we'd eaten the delicious curry he'd made.

Rey grinned and stood up to get something from his bag. I tried not to ogle him as he walked across the room naked. Admittedly, I didn't try very hard. He was so at ease with his body, and so complimentary about mine, that I felt comfortable too. I was never going to perform the cancan topless or go to a nudist colony, but I certainly wasn't shy about Rey seeing me without my clothes on. How different to the way Steve and I had averted our eyes to give the other privacy as we'd slid in and out of bed, and backed away spluttering the most sincere of apologies if we ever caught each other in the shower, as though we'd walked into a stranger's hotel room.

Rey took three small parcels from his bag and handed them to me. They were rectangular, identical in size and wrapped the same.

'You can only open one,' he said, sitting back down beside me. 'For now, anyway.'

'How do I know which one to open?' I asked, turning them in my hands.

'You don't.' Rey smiled. 'That's the whole point.'

I smiled back. I had no idea what was going on, but that was OK. More than OK – it was perfect. After decades of knowing exactly what was going on, at every given moment, I craved spontaneity and surprise now. I shuffled the packages, put two down and opened the third. It was a travel guide . . . to Venice. I gasped and looked up at Rey, who was grinning.

'Venice?' I breathed. 'Does this mean we're going to Venice?'

'Yes.' Rey wrapped his hands around mine. 'You wouldn't let me get you a birthday present, so here's a belated one.'

I felt my cheeks grow hot. 'It's too generous.'

'There's an ulterior motive.' Rey leant over and kissed me. 'I'm coming too.' He pulled back. 'Unless you wanted to take Sophie, of course?'

I shook my head. 'No, we had our big trip to Thailand at Easter. She's joining Hope on her travels for a month in the summer, and she's got a week in Ibiza with her uni friends. She'll be working at the pub the rest of her summer break to pay for it all.'

'I thought maybe we could go in September,' Rey said. 'It'll be quieter, as it's after the school holidays, and it will be warm, but not too hot.'

An excited giggle burst out of me. We were going to Venice! Thailand at Easter and now Venice in the autumn. And I still had cocktails in New York with Nikki to come. I never imagined I'd be having such amazing holidays. And not a Union Jack flag or laminated menu in sight.

I slipped my arms around Rey's neck and kissed him. 'Thank you. It's the best present ever.' As I shifted my weight to climb into his lap, the corner of one of the other parcels dug into me. 'What are these?' I asked. 'Did I get lucky and open the right one first time?'

Rey shook his head. 'They're for another time. Maybe one for Christmas, or to mark the anniversary of our first date . . . or just because.'

'Because what?' I asked innocently, totally fishing for a compliment.

Rey laughed as he pulled me onto his lap. 'Because, without wanting to sound like a cheesy hair commercial, you're worth it.'

Because I was worth it. I swallowed a smile. It was crazy to think that just eight months ago my life had seemed so devoid of any worth or purpose. I'd been so caught up with approaching fifty and losing my identity as a mum that I didn't appreciate all the benefits and freedom that midlife and an empty nest offer. It petrified me that I'd been prepared to settle and limp on.

Now, not only was I in a bloody brilliant career that I loved, championing magnificent women and running my own business, but my relationships were bloody brilliant too. Sophie and I were so much closer. I felt valued and appreciated by her and proud of the independent, self-assured young woman she'd become. Being a Gen Z meant she couldn't bring herself to talk on the phone very often, but we frequently exchanged messages and funny memes, which filled me with joy. As for my mum, she still drove me mad sometimes but I viewed her quirks with affection now and enjoyed our time together. Although, I fervently hoped we never had to live together again. I thought I'd be sadder about my marriage ending, but Steve seemed to feel the same relief I did, and our interactions about the divorce and Sophie were amicable. And I didn't have to witness him cleaning his glasses in a phone call.

I was relaxed, in control and excited about what came next, even – no, *especially* – the unknown. For someone who had avoided change with the same fervour that teenagers avoided running out of data, I was totally slaying my second act.

And yes, that is so.

# Acknowledgements

As always, there are a zillion people I'd like to thank, but first up is Emily Glenister, who further cemented her status as Best Agent Ever during the writing of this book by being on hand to advise, support and brainstorm, despite the fact she was on mat leave. I can't imagine anybody else doing that and I appreciate it so much. Thank you for meeting up with me and bringing baby Cora. Please can she be an essential part of our meetings from now on? (I'm not joking.)

A huge thank you to David Headley for looking after me while Emily was off. I know how incredibly busy you are so it really means a lot. Although I think the only time Emily was actually unavailable was during the birth itself and one Tuesday in July when it was too physically hot to work!

Thank you to the amazing team at Embla, particularly Bea Grabowska and Laura Gerrard. Your understanding, compassion and care when I was struggling to meet my deadline means so much and I will always be grateful. Thank you for sticking with me to make this book the best version it can be. Thank you also to Charlotte Brown, Emma Wilson, Vishani Perera, Tia Ungar and

Daniela Nava. Daniela – your comments in the copy edit were the boost I needed when juggling a house renovation, temporary move, family life and a deadline. Apologies for causing you to laugh so much you spat tea onto your keyboard. (Sorry, not sorry!) Thank you, Jane Dixon-Smith, for the gorgeous cover that radiates positivity and vibrancy. Thank you, Bea, for humouring my colour request, so that I can wear my new orange dress in the promo shots!

Thank you, Helen Lederer and Comedy Women in Print, for your continued support. Helen set CWIP up to recognise, encourage and celebrate witty women writers. As well as offering a prize that changes careers (my book *Has Anyone Seen My Husband?* was shortlisted, which didn't exactly hurt when submitting to Emily Glenister), CWIP has grown into a wonderful community of women who champion and support each other. A special thank you to my CWIPster friends, particularly Faye Brann and Nancy Peach, who I owe a Dishoom and Aperol Spritz to. I'm so touched and grateful for your generosity and kindness. Let's lock in that Bletchley Park field trip!

Continuing the kind and generous theme, a huge thank you to Jill Dawson for your advice and encouragement with my author mentoring, editing, teaching, interviewing and panel hosting. I'm not sure I'd have had the courage to do it without you. And my debut novel, *Wife Support System*, definitely wouldn't have happened without your tutelage through Gold Dust. I'm so happy we've become friends. If you could roll a six at our next Dishoom meet up I'd be even happier! Emma Dowson, thank you for also for your friendship, festival expertise and for keeping me company in the queue to meet the legend that is Jeff Goldblum!

Fran Boast – thank you for yet more HR advice. At this rate I'll be able to get a job in HR myself! Jack and Gill – thank you for the loan of your gorgeous Airbnb in Norwich, the setting of this book. Thank you, Rodney, Collette, James and Rachael Fisher, for keeping me company on the Norwich ghost walk. In case you're wondering, unlike Becca, I didn't have two bottles of vodka in my rucksack!

Emma Croxon – thank you for your decorating help. Everything needed doing at the exact moment my deadlines hit, and I'd have curled up on the floor and wept if it wasn't for your motivating positivity – and for going over all the bits I'd done badly. (Which was all of them!)

Two other people who always pep me up are Nicola Washington of *Too Much Social* and Isabelle Knight of *Build Your Author Brand*. Not only are they lovely people who radiate positivity, they offer practical, achievable advice for authors on how to promote our books to people who will genuinely be interested in them. Thank you both for all your help and advice. If you're also an author – check them out now!

Finding somewhere quiet to write where I can't be distracted by builders, deliveries, laundry and family members is essential when I'm on deadline (and trying to retain some sense of sanity!). Thank you Jo Carnegie and Celene Yon for the loan of your desks, and Sarah Peace (best surname ever), Bekah and Alex Nicolas and co at Hitchin library, and Ruth Nye, Phil Ryan and the team at Hermitage Café for letting me practically move in. This book wouldn't have got written without those much-needed boltholes.

In *The Mother of All Comebacks*, Becca's friendships are hugely important to her, as are mine. I honestly don't know what I'd do without my amazing friends. Thank you Strictly Sistas, Fishy Business, Strawberry Daiquiris, Freudian Slop, Writers' Room, CWIPesses, Socially Isolated, Flapping Flaps, Ladies of Leisure, Readers Wives, Blows Like a Man and RNA Buddies. And no, I'm not expanding on any of those WhatsApp group names!

A special shout-out to Anna, Becky, Brigid, Cath, Jo, Kate, Marie, Sarah, Sinéad, Tonya, Vicky and Zoë – thank you for your unwavering friendship, support, care, love, LOLs – and for putting up with me for so long!

A huge thank you to Rawaa, for suggesting Rey's gift of multiple guide books – it made it the perfect ending! Rawaa is part of a writing group I run, made up of the most talented, wonderful, inspirational, grounded, kick-ass women you could meet. The only downside to us all getting on so well, is that writing is often secondary to talking, but I wouldn't have it any other way!

This book is also about family, particularly the relationships between Becca and her mum and daughter. Happily, my mum is nothing like Josephine. No hand gestures, summoning with a personal alarm or dubious parentage. Thank you for that, Mum – and for everything else. You're a truly wonderful person and I am so lucky to have you. I'm also incredibly lucky to have two amazing daughters – Eve and Elena. Don't worry, Sophie isn't based on either of you. For one thing, I know you'd never want to borrow my shoes! Thank you for allowing me the honour of being your mum. I love you so much I can't even begin to put it into words. Just as well I don't rely on that skill in my day job!

Linda and Jed – you are the most incredible in-laws ever created. You do so much for us and we are so, so grateful. Thank you for everything. Christmas dinner is on us next year. Possibly literally.

Thank you also to my brother Adam, sisters-in-law Deryn and Laura (on different sides of the family – Adam isn't a bigamist), bro-in-law Andy and gorgeous nieces and nephews Brady, Charlie, Holly and Isla. And to all my extended family for always being so interested and enthusiastic about my writing. (You've got those game faces nailed!)

I have such an incredible support network of women in life, which I am so thankful for. Happily, there are some pretty incredible men in my life too. Harrison Ford being one. Well, in photo form anyway. His picture has adorned my wall since I fell in love with him aged seven watching *Star Wars, A New Hope*. I've accepted that there's no hope I'll meet him now, but luckily I met someone else, who doesn't say 'I know' when hearing declarations of love or bugger off around the galaxy whenever the dishwasher needs unloading. James – thank you for your reassurance, strength and love when I've had a wobble. And for not judging my poster choices.

Last, but definitely not least, thank you, dear reader, for buying/borrowing this book. You're the reason I'm able to do this and I am eternally grateful.

# A Note from Kathleen Whyman

Thank you so much for reading *The Mother of All Comebacks*. I really hope you enjoyed it and perhaps it resonated and made you feel seen. Or it made you laugh and provided some escapism for a few hours. I'll take either!

This book is probably the closest to my own circumstances of all the books I've written. (I'd have loved to move in with my friends when the children were little, as they do in *Wife Support System*, but that was pure fantasy!) I wasn't looking forward to turning fifty initially, but, as Becca eventually does, I've come to embrace it. Growing older is a privilege and not everyone gets to experience it. Also, being older comes with so many advantages. I'm quietly self-assured now, whereas I used to hold back for fear of failure. Now I go for every opportunity, talk to everyone, and don't care if I make a fool of myself. Much to my teenagers' mortification! I'm also trying to stop overthinking everything and feeling guilty all the time. My memory has become shockingly bad which helps, as the ability to dwell on things is massively reduced!

I'm not an empty-nester yet, but my eldest is now at uni. Saying goodbye and leaving her behind was one of the most heart-wrenching moments of my life. Luckily I still have my youngest at home, but she, understandably, doesn't want to spend every waking moment with me. Not that our waking moments coincide very often! Knowing that my hero Michelle Obama felt bereft when her children left home helped me appreciate that empty nester syndrome is a real phenomenon which affects many of us.

It's easy to lose our identity when this happens. We're not needed in the same day-to-day way as a mum. But, as Becca discovers, there are many advantages – the freedom and time to do things for ourselves, and a hell of a lot less laundry. (I'm blocking out the amount that comes home at the end of each term.) So, seize this opportunity to put yourself first and don't feel guilty about it. It doesn't mean you love your child any less. You'll still be there when they need you. But your car will always be where you left it with the same amount of petrol in it, and your air fryer won't need cleaning as much!

And if you're not fifty or an empty nester yet, take heart in the fact that you will be one day! Neither are things to be afraid of. Quite the reverse in fact.

I'd love to know your thoughts on the book and if you've had any similar experiences or staged a comeback yourself. Please DM me on Instagram or Facebook @kathleenwhymanauthor. I'm always up for a chat – not procrastinating from writing the next book or cleaning the air fryer at all!

I know I've already said thank you for reading this book, but I'd like to expand on that. At a time when books are being pirated and AI is threatening to take over all creative pursuits, to know that people like you are buying books written by good old-fashioned humans is pure joy – and a relief if I'm honest! So, on behalf of all authors out there, THANK YOU! It means so much and we are so grateful.

Now I'm going to be really cheeky and ask another request. If you're able to share a review on Goodreads, Amazon, social media and/or wherever you bought (or borrowed) this book please, that would be incredible. This applies to all books you read, not just mine. Although mainly mine, obviously. 😉 Getting our books noticed amongst the sea of celebrity authors, and competing for people's attention when they have so many other demands on their time, is challenging (aka f'ing hard!), so all help is massively appreciated and will guarantee you a fast track to Heaven. (Other destinations are available.)

As well as writing, I regularly interview authors at bookshops and events. I've done a few online too with some amazing authors, including Milly Johnson and Paige Toon, plus publishing power house Sara-Jade Virtue. To have a look, please go to YouTube and search for AuthorEventsUK: https://www.youtube.com/@authoreventsuk

I also offer mentoring for writers, particularly female authors over forty. I've nothing against men (see my reference to Harrison Ford in the acknowledgements), but championing women is very important to me and I love to help at all stages of your career, be it starting your first draft, wanting advice on your current MS, navigating the path to publication, brainstorming ideas, or having someone to motivate you and be accountable to for achieving your writing goals.

If you'd like more info, please email me at kathleenfwhyman@gmail.com. (The F isn't for Ford, but it's a natural assumption to make.)

Thank you again for reading *The Mother of All Comebacks*. I can't wait to hear what you thought and hope you 'come back' for more. Until then, take care, happy reading and enjoy life whatever age you are!

Kathleen x

# Book Club Discussion Questions

### Character & Relationships

What did you think of Becca's marriage to 'Steady Steve'? Do you feel their relationship was salvageable, or had they simply grown apart? Have you seen similar dynamics in long-term relationships around you?

How did you feel about Josephine's choice to lie to Becca at 18? What alternative approaches could she have taken? Do you think Becca's response to the revelation was understandable?

Sophie's decision to move back home creates tension in Becca's journey toward independence. How well do you think Becca handled this? Is it ever fair to tell your adult children 'no' when they need help?

### Themes & Personal Growth

The book explores the idea of losing your identity when your roles change. Which of Becca's 'labels' (mum, wife, employee) do you think defined her most? Have you ever experienced a similar loss of identity?

What does the tagline *Could it be time for a rebrand?* mean to you in the context of the story? Do you think we can truly 'rebrand' ourselves in midlife, or are we limited by our past choices?

Becca struggles with putting herself first versus meeting others' expectations. Where do you think the line should be drawn between selfishness and self-care?

**Broader Questions**

How did the book portray the 'empty nest' experience? Did it feel realistic to you? What surprised you most about Becca's reaction to Sophie leaving?

The novel touches on ageism in the workplace. How did this aspect of the story resonate with you? Do you think things are changing in this regard?

If you were Becca's friend, what advice would you have given her at the beginning of the book? Would your advice have changed by the end?

What do you imagine happens to Becca five years after the book ends?

# About Kathleen Whyman

Kathleen Whyman is a bestselling humorous women's fiction author. She writes for all the multi-tasking, mentally overloaded women, who put themselves on the subs bench for the sake of their family, and are beginning to realise that they don't have it all – they do it all!

Kathleen's books, one of which was shortlisted for the Comedy Women in Print prize, are inspired by her own struggle to juggle a career with children, housework, life admin and never-ending laundry. The laundry's winning.

As well as writing, Kathleen teaches and mentors writers. She also interviews authors at events, as a host of the online Author Talks series (https://www.youtube.com/@authoreventsuk) and for publications, including *Writers' Forum* magazine. She's regularly a panellist and hosts panels at writing festivals, and teaches writing workshops with an emphasis on writing humour.

Kathleen lives in Hertfordshire with her husband and two teenage daughters. There's a lot of door slamming.

Website: https://www.kathleenwhyman.com/
Instagram: https://www.instagram.com/kathleenwhymanauthor/
Facebook: https://www.facebook.com/kathleenwhymanauthor/

# About Embla Books

Embla Books is a digital-first publisher of standout commercial adult fiction. Passionate about storytelling, the team at Embla believe our lives are built on stories – and publish books that will make you 'laugh, love, look over your shoulder and lose sleep'. Launched by Bonnier Books UK in 2021, the imprint is named after the first woman from the creation myth in Norse mythology. Embla was carved by the gods from a tree trunk found on the seashore; an image of the kind of creative work and crafting that writers do, and a symbol of how stories shape our lives.

Find out about some of our other books and stay in touch:

X, Facebook, Instagram: @emblabooks
Newsletter: https://bit.ly/emblanewsletter

